THE PILLERTON SECRET

THE PILLERTON SECRET

GAYLE SIEBERT

THE PILLERTON SECRET

PROLOGUE

This was a bad idea. Maybe the worst idea he's ever had.

Despite the chill, Brother Weaver feels sweat running down his back. He fights off the case of nerves that's been causing his gut to churn ever since he followed the queue of black-robed supplicants into the tunnel. When the tunnel opens out into a large cavern, they push him to the rough table in the center where the three red-robed figures wait and form a circle around them.

They assured him he knows these people, but he's the only one without a hooded robe, and in the small pond of light given off by three stubby candles in the middle of the altar, he can't see anyone's face.

The silence is as complete as the darkness outside the feeble candlelight. It's as quiet as a grave. That thought unnerves him further.

Is it too late to back out?

Then the silence is broken as the black-robed people begin chanting. They take small steps—forward, back, forward, back—with voices so quiet they're barely more than whispers, and the tallest of the red-robed figures says, "Are you, Brother Weaver, present of your own free will and volition?"

"I ... I am ... Im-Imperial Leader." It's true. He agreed to this. But maybe he shouldn't have. Maybe he should tell them he's changed his mind. Then he remembers the money. He needs the money. How much can it hurt, anyway? A sharp pain and then an ache for a few days? Like the time he stubbed his big toe and nearly ripped the toenail out?

Now there's sweat on his forehead threatening to run into his eye. He wishes he could mop his face but doesn't want to appear anxious, so with force of will, he ignores it.

"Are you, Brother Weaver, committed to the Lord?"

"Y-yes, Imperial Leader."

"And are you, Brother Weaver, committed to the Lord through this, his holy church, the one true church, until death?"

The candles gutter as if from a breeze and then blaze more brightly for an instant.

"I am, Imperial Leader."

"And do you truly desire purification?"

"I do, Imperial Leader."

"Do you truly desire the highest level of purification?"

"I do."

"Place your hand upon the altar."

A shudder wracks his body. Then he summons all his courage and lays his hand on the block.

The outer ring of shrouded figures begins chanting louder and starts moving around the circle in a kind of bridal march step in time with their chanting. Two of the red-shrouded figures come forward with silken ropes. One puts a loop around Brother Weaver's thumb, pulls it away from the index finger, and holds it. The second figure loops the middle, ring, and little fingers, pulls them away from the index finger, and holds them there.

The chanting and shuffling of the black-robed figures stop when Imperial Leader raises his hands and holds them out, a foot-long blade in one. Light from the candles dances along its edge. He sings in a powerful baritone voice that reverberates through the cavernous space:

> Respice, quaesumas, Domine
> Famulam Ivami selectorum renati Weaver
> In infirmate et animam refove quam creastes.
> Uti castigation ibus emenidata.
> Se tua sentiat medicina salvatam
> Per Christum Dominium
> Qui iwute et renati Weaver
> Per omnia sascula secular seculorum
> Awww mennnn!

The others respond in a chorus of "Awww-mennnn!"

Imperial Leader puts both hands on the knife handle and raises his hands above his head, and the blade flashes down in a swift arc, nearly severing the index finger.

Brother Weaver screams and falls forward over the altar, knocking over one of the candles.

He's pulled back upright, his white shirt now streaked with red, by one of the red-shrouded men, who holds him up while Imperial Leader makes another swift cut to complete the amputation of the finger. Then the cords are pulled off his hand, and he's released.

Brother Weaver collapses partway over the altar, almost knocking over a second candle, singeing his hair. Pain unlike anything he's ever experienced shoots through his entire body. He struggles to maintain consciousness, to remain standing. He puts his left hand on the altar and straightens, steadying himself.

Imperial Leader says in his clear, strong voice, "And the Lord sayeth, 'Notwithstanding no devoted thing, that a man shall devote unto the Lord of all that he hath, both of man and beast, and of the field of his possession, shall be sold or redeemed: every devoted thing is most holy unto the Lord.'"

A red-shrouded figure picks up the severed finger and places it on a silver platter. He hands it to Imperial Leader, who lays the knife next to the finger, holding the plate reverently in both hands and then raising it over his head.

"Behold, this man hath set apart to the Lord this part of himself, his own precious flesh, of his own person. It is therefore most holy to the Lord! Hallelujah!"

The shrouded figures shout, "Hallelujah!" and resume chanting and circling the block. One of the red-shrouded figures lights the fallen candle by touching it to another and then hands it to Imperial Leader, taking the offering plate from him as he does so. He turns and hands the plate to one of the black-shrouded figures, who steps aside. The three from the inner circle, now each holding a candle, file out.

The black-shrouded figures, led by the one carrying the offering plate, follow single file. Still chanting, they move on silent feet into the darkness.

Brother Weaver slips bonelessly to the ground. He becomes vaguely aware that the last supplicant is bending over him, wrapping his damaged hand in something. Then everything goes black.

Brother Weaver regains consciousness. He finds he's lying on cold, wet earth, and he smells urine. He's wet himself. And there's a tangy, metallic smell. Blood.

He sits up, leaning against what must be the altar. The darkness is impenetrable. He can't see his hand to get a look at what they've done to it. By feel, he knows it's wrapped in something, likely to stop the bleeding, but it does nothing for the pain.

The pain! It's all-consuming, crowding to the forefront of his brain, and for some moments he's unable to think about anything else. Then he feels a sharp needle of cold stabbing into his very center. *Blood loss*, he thinks. *I need help! Someone, help me! I have to get out of here!*

He gets to his feet and runs into the dark, not knowing which way he's going; then he shrieks with pain when he bumps up against a solid dirt wall, smashing his right hand. He slips into unconsciousness and collapses again.

When he next comes to, he sits up. He thinks with longing of the bunk he's been sleeping in while purifying himself for this ritual. He remembers running like an idiot and hitting a wall. *You're not an idiot*, he tells himself. *It was a bad idea but not your fault, just the mental confusion that comes with being in shock. Before you do anything else, think it through!*

Everyone's heard the urban legends of people getting into these tunnels and never being seen again. He tries to push those thoughts away, but they keep niggling at the corners of his mind. He knows fantasizing about that nice warm bed does no good. He knows there's no one coming to help him. He knows he must get out on his own.

He gets to his feet, and after standing a moment until his light-headedness clears, he begins to follow the wall back to the tunnel access. At least he thinks he's heading back toward the tunnel access. *Why didn't I put a lighter in my pocket?* he thinks. *Wouldn't have mattered. They'd have taken it away from me anyway. I wasn't thinking. I could have put it in my ass. They didn't do a cavity search, just had me turn out my pockets. But I never would have believed it could be this dark.*

Holding his right hand with his left, in what he gauges to be about ten feet, he comes up against another wall. He doesn't know which way to turn and mutters, "Left? Right?"

He wishes he'd paid more attention on the way in, but he thought it was almost a lark and just kept visualizing the three and a half million dollars—in cash! How big a pile would it make? How heavy would it be? Would it be in nice tidy bundles of beautiful new bills?

He remembers shock at seeing the altar in the center of the ceremonial crypt. Altar? More like a chopping block. His gut reaction was to turn and run. The pain is excruciating, and he curses himself for not listening to his gut.

Keep thinking of the money, he tells himself, *the money!* Lots of people are missing digits. Farmers especially. Not that he's a farmer. He can hardly have a work-related accident that severs a finger. He'll have to think up a good, believable cover story. He thought of a few possible scenarios in the purification days. Maybe an accident with the paper cutter? But no. There'd be witnesses; an ambulance would be called. When he gets back, he'll write a list of possible explanations, spend time on it. Make sure what he comes up with has a ring of truth to it.

How could I have been so wrong about the pain? he wonders. His hand is throbbing. Every time he moves, it's as if the missing digit tries to move too, setting off more needles of pain.

It dawns on him he's going to have to climb back up that ladder one-handed. If he ever finds the ladder.

He manages to open some shirt buttons with his left hand and gingerly slides his damaged hand inside, making a kind of sling. The throbbing abates somewhat. He takes a few deep breaths, leans against the wall, and pushes back against the befuddling in his brain. *I'm going into shock*, he realizes. *I can't keep passing out, or I'll never make it out of here.* He decides to follow the wall left.

He congratulates himself on thinking to put his hand inside his shirt. That keeps it secure, so now he can just slide his right shoulder along the wall. His progress is slow, but he's sure he's on the right track.

Then he bumps into another wall. He shrieks with pain and reflexively jerks his damaged hand from his shirt. The light-headedness returns with a rush. He leans back against the wall, fighting it off, and then realizes he's not leaning against dirt. Is it brickwork?

And is that music? Singing? Very faint.

It's not real, he tells himself. *You're delusional. Another indication you're in shock.*

He wipes his face on his sleeve, and with sheer force of willpower, he uses his left hand to tuck his right back into his shirt. He stands still for a moment until the worst of the throbbing and light-headedness settles, and then he starts back along the same wall.

Now the wall is on his left, and he doesn't have to keep his shoulder on it if he keeps contact with his hand. He begins to hurry despite the pain and cold.

The walls are featureless dirt and rock. He can't judge how far he's gone. Is he past the ceremonial crypt?

A few feet farther, there's a bump, and the wall is now hard and even. Concrete? This is promising.

Then his foot strikes something on the floor.

What?

He feels along the floor with his good hand until it closes around something smooth and round. It almost feels silky ... It's attached to something ... There's a rattle like dry sticks when he pulls on it. It comes loose. Holding it between his knees, he runs his left hand over it. Kind of a notched lump on one end. It's not very long, not long enough to be a cane. Heavier at one end. Is there a chunk of cloth on it? Maybe it's a torch. Not that a torch would help. He has nothing to light it with. He slides his hand down to find the reason for the thing being heavier at the end. Much wider there ...

He drops it, screaming, and scrambles back against the opposite wall.

Then he leans over and vomits.

It's not a stick but a leg bone and a shoe with a foot in it.

Never mind, he tells himself. *Keep focused, or you'll end up like this guy.* He tries to go around the skeleton but hits another wall.

Dirt and rocks rattle down and pile up around his feet.

He once again leans back against the wall and closes his eyes. *Be smart,* he thinks. *Calm yourself.* He takes several deep breaths and manages to think of a sunny day, how rich he'll be, what he can do once he has all the money. Not just the up-front cash but also a constant flow of money, for doing nothing. He sees himself in the voluminous red robe being idolized and fussed over. These are soothing thoughts.

When he opens his eyes again, he realizes he can see a little bit. His eyes finally must have adjusted to the dark. Is that a slightly lighter patch in the wall just a few feet back, almost directly across from the skeleton? The entrance to the cross tunnel maybe? With light in it somewhere? Or is it his imagination like when he thought he could hear piano music and singing?

He scurries toward it and discovers it is another branch of the tunnel as he'd hoped, and there's a faint light somewhere ahead. There's a bare light bulb hanging down, not that much farther.

He's almost jogging now.

There's the ladder! And the opening in the ceiling of the tunnel!

He struggles to climb up, using both hands, the pain now pushed to the back of his mind. He pulls himself into the basement and lies face down on the concrete floor to catch his breath. Then he summons every scrap of fortitude, stands, and climbs the stairs.

He pushes the door open and takes a few uneven steps into the house.

The shrouded figures have pushed their hoods back and are now milling about the kitchen, living room, and dining room. He recognizes many, even if he doesn't know them by name. There's the pharmacist. The woman who works at the Gas-N-Go. The kindergarten teacher he met just a few weeks ago while enrolling his eldest son. The older but still attractive piano teacher his wife took lessons from and still invites for dinner occasionally. An obese man he's never met but recognizes as his across-the-cul-de-sac neighbor, who annoyingly mows his lawn at seven o'clock every Sunday morning. One or two he knows from the prayer meetings. Others are strangers. The chatter stops as he's noticed, and they all turn toward him, smiling.

He stands taller. Straighter.

They gather around him. Imperial Leader comes forward out of the crowd and says, "Brother Weaver! You took your time. We were beginning to think you might not make it. We've started the rest of the ceremony without you." He indicates the stemmed glasses of red wine they all have. "But we've saved the most important part."

They drape a black robe around him, covering his badly soiled clothes, and then sit him on one of the kitchen chairs with his right arm on the table. Someone carefully unwraps his damaged hand while someone else gently wipes his face with a warm, wet cloth.

The warm kitchen and the warmth of the robe finally stop his chattering teeth.

He recognizes the rotund figure of his family doctor coming into the kitchen. Dr. Benzi gives his shoulder a squeeze before taking the chair next to his and examining the amputation. "How'd you get this so dirty? Never mind, we'll clean it up, and I'll put in a couple of stitches after the ceremony," he says. "For now, I'll give you something for the pain." He nods to the pharmacist, who passes him a syringe. Dr. Benzi rolls Brother Weaver's sleeve up, examines his forearm, taps it a couple of times, and then deftly slips the needle into a vein.

In moments, a sense of profound calm floods over him. He's never felt anything so wonderful.

Voices around him now seem hushed, as if they're off in the distance. Someone says, "You should have done all this before we came up," and he thinks it's Dr. Benzi, who says, "If you want me down there, you're going to have to find a better entrance. That ladder is impossible." But he's floating and doesn't pay much attention.

Then they're bothering him, nagging him to stand. They insist and are now hauling him to his feet. Then they help him to the narrow table at the front of the living room. He's given a chair at one side while the three Illustrious Ones stand around him. Behind him!

On the table is a shining pot on a little stand. A flaming can of Sterno beneath it keeps its contents warm. At a signal from Imperial Leader, one of the women begins ladling liquid from the pot into a small cup.

Each black-robed figure comes forward to drink from the demitasse. Imperial Leader offers his hand, and they kiss his ring. Then he touches their foreheads with his three-fingered right hand and says, "Gustate et videte."

Finally it's Brother Weaver's turn, but he doesn't have to rise. Instead a young woman kneels before him. Her robe is black like the others, but unlike the others it has a wide red stripe along the edges of the hood and sleeves. Her hair is long and blond, and although dyed (he can see dark roots), it suits her Nordic bone structure and skin tone. With a jolt, he realizes it's his brother-in-law's ex-wife. He wonders how he missed seeing her until now and thinks how much he's going to enjoy porking her. He can't suppress a giggle. She bows her head and holds up an engraved silver goblet.

No demitasse for him! *As befits my status*, he thinks. He nods graciously, gives her a benevolent smile, and then takes the goblet with his left hand. The liquid is brownish, pungent. Odd. He was expecting an alcoholic beverage. Maybe it's a hot toddy? But there's something floating in it. Meat? Some kind of sausage? Not a hot toddy then.

Then the little piece of sausage rolls, and he sees the fingernail.

Kathy's eyes snap open. She wonders why she's awake.

Then it comes again, the loud banging and tinny clanking. It seems to be coming from the heat duct. Someone or something's crashing around in the basement! Her heart speeds. *My phone! Where's my phone?* She remembers it's in her purse, hanging on the hallstand downstairs.

But then it's quiet again.

She lies staring at the ceiling, barely breathing, but now the only sound is the swishing of cars on the highway across the open field, just near enough that their headlights play across the ceiling as the wind sighs around the bay window.

I should go see what made that noise, she thinks. But it seems to have stopped. She lets her breath out and closes her eyes. *Maybe I was wrong. Maybe there's no one ...* Then there's a bang! bang! bang! as if someone has come in and let the screen door slam.

I have to go look, she tells herself. *But if someone has come in, I need something to protect myself with! What can I use?*

She mentally reviews what she'd seen when looking through the house earlier that day but can't think of anything. Then she notices the brass lamp on the vanity. She quickly gets out of bed, picks up the lamp, and unplugs it with a sharp tug on the cord. She unscrews the shade and then, more carefully, the bulb. Holding the lamp by the light bulb end like a bat, she creeps out into the hall.

The house is quiet again.

She starts down the stairs, holding the lamp in both hands,

1

supporting herself by leaning slightly back against the wall, and picking her way carefully from step to step. The house is dark, and the only light is from the streetlight half a block away, shining weakly through stained glass windows.

She's nearly down to the landing when the tread creaks under her weight, alarmingly loud in the quiet. She holds up, heart pounding, listening. A rattle in the kitchen startles her. She recognizes it as the sound the ancient refrigerator makes when its compressor starts up. And there are no more sounds.

Then there's the banging again, coming from the front door.

She takes a deep breath, exhales through her mouth, and straightens. It's the screen door, all right, just rattling in the wind. She puts the lamp down, tells herself she was silly, and takes the last few steps down to the foyer. She goes to the front door and turns on the light.

The thumb turn on the antique deadbolt is vertical. Unlocked! *Didn't I lock that?*

She opens the door and finds the screen isn't latched. But how odd! The wind isn't strong, especially here on the sheltered veranda. How could it rattle the door? But what else could it be? Kathy pokes her head out but can't see anything unusual. She latches the screen door and pushes the inside door shut, this time making sure it's locked. Still puzzled, she goes into the kitchen for a drink of water. When she returns to the foyer, she turns off the light and picks up the lamp on the stairs as she goes back up into the bedroom. She sets the lamp down and considers putting it back together, but she decides against it. It seems too finicky. *I don't need the lamp now anyway. I'll deal with it in the morning,* she tells herself and gets back into bed.

But she can't keep her eyes shut. Even though she knows the sounds that woke her were nothing to be concerned about, her heart rate is still up. Adrenaline. She realizes she'll be awake for a while.

She wonders again why she came back to Pillerton.

Her mother died weeks before, and she didn't even know about it. Maybe she'd never have known if Penny hadn't called to say she'd seen the obituary. But there was no reason to come back, not really. Settling her mother's estate could've been handled from her home in Vancouver. The church elders assured her they would take care of everything.

But she felt a pull, a need, to come back to the house where she'd lived for nearly the first eighteen years of her life. Why now? It doesn't make sense. In fact, she can't fight off the thought that nothing in her life makes sense anymore. It's an unsettling feeling and one she doesn't like.

She tears up, tells herself not to feel sorry for herself. She turns over, fluffs her pillow, and squeezes her eyes shut. But it's a long time before she's able to sleep.

Droplets splatter the mirror and snake to its bottom edge. Hunkering over the sink, Rick stops throwing water on his face and stares at his reflection beneath the streaks for a long moment. *Why do I still expect to see a young man*, he wonders, *and when did my laugh lines become crow's feet?*

He towels his face and arms, pulls a clean shirt over his head, and ponders last night. He and his buddies went to Regina for the Riders game and to a sports bar afterward. That woman ... Her face was slightly too long and her nose slightly too large, but she had beautiful gray-green eyes and a pretty smile. How old was she? Definitely no spring chicken. Maybe thirty-seven? Thirty-eight? About his age. And they were able to talk. She didn't seem to notice his love handles, the deepening lines on his face, or his receding hairline. If she did, it didn't turn her off.

He can't remember whose idea it was, but they got a room. He feels a stirring deep in his groin as he remembers all they did. He'd fallen asleep thinking it might be the start of something, that they might do something together the next day. But when he awoke, she was gone. No second go at it in the morning. No breakfast. She said she was single but leaving like that? No exchange of phone numbers? Isn't that what guys get criticized for doing?

My God, he thinks, *am I feeling* used?

"Rick!" His mother's bark on the other side of the door startles him. He'd gone from the motel to the auction and then to the feed store, and of course swung by Al's Place for a couple of hours before coming back to the farm. She hadn't seen him since the previous afternoon, and he didn't come into the house until he'd unloaded the feed. He avoided the kitchen and the questions and disapproving looks he knew she'd give him, by coming in from the front. Yet somehow, she knew he was there.

"Rick! Supper's on!"

"Okay."

"And don't leave a mess!"

Frowning, he flings his dirty shirt into the hamper. "Nuthin' ever changes," he mutters. He wipes the mirror, sink, and taps before carefully folding the towel and poking it through the top ring of the towel pole. The door, as usual, sticks. He wrenches it open and strides down the hall and around the corner into the kitchen.

Having the oven on for hours, coupled with the fact that it's thirty degrees in the shade, has made the kitchen unbearably hot. The window's open, but there's little breeze stirring the curtains. He can already feel sweat soaking the underarms of his clean shirt. The guys from just across the border in North Dakota who farm in the area—and frequent Al's Place—are always baffled at how hot thirty degrees is. They constantly ask what the "real" temperature is. This afternoon, the bartender wrote on the sandwich board: 30 Degrees C = 86 Degrees F. We're Air-Conditioned! He stood it on the sidewalk outside, not only so they'd quit asking him about it but also to lure customers inside.

His mother's old enough to remember when Canada used the Fahrenheit scale, but she never cares about the temperature, Celsius or Fahrenheit, when she wants to use the oven. Her only concession to the heat is a sleeveless housedress, now with large, underarm sweat circles. She's happy to sweat. *Part of her self-imposed martyrdom*, Rick thinks. He's given up trying to convince her to use the barbecue or to let them have their meals on the veranda. It's as if she enjoys discomfort.

Already at the table are his daughter, Sarah; his sister, Jeanie; Gramps; and two hired hands. Jeanie is flushed with the heat and the advancement of her fifth pregnancy. She gives him a smile. Rick takes the chair beside her.

The hired hands, Ryan and Shane, are boys from town chosen for their size. They'll be off to university in the fall and are working summer jobs to make money for tuition. Both are tucking into their food with enthusiasm. Ryan looks up and nods at Rick. Gravy runs down his chin.

He wipes it on the back of his hand and then glances across the table at Sarah and reddens.

At nineteen, Sarah is the image of her mother at that age. She's well aware of the effect her white-blond hair, big blue eyes, and long, slim legs have on the opposite sex, and she enjoys it. Big, good-looking Ryan, though, seems to be having an effect on her too, judging by the flush that colors her cheeks and the look on her face when she watches him.

"Didn't wait supper for you," Rick's mother grumbles. "You're always late." Standing over the table, she slams a mound of mashed potatoes onto his plate.

"Not so much, Mutti!"

She clucks. "You need a decent supper. You're gettin' thin." While she's standing, she serves everyone another helping of potatoes.

"Thin? I'm finally losing my winter belly."

"A man needs some girth to him." Meat fork in hand, she spears a thick slice of beef, and with a quick jerk of her arm, it's on his plate next to the mountain of potatoes.

One day, Rick vows, *I'll get her to quit putting food on my plate*. But today he just shakes his head. Turning to Jeanie, he ruffles her hair. "Where's the rest of your tribe, muffin?"

"Megan took the boys to the lake. They're gonna have a fire on the beach. S'mores and hot dogs."

"Megan?"

"My new friend. Clarence introduced us."

"Oh? How's he know her?"

"She goes to his church. He thought I'd like her, and I do. She's nice, and pretty too. She's the one I've been wanting you to meet."

"Oh yeah, the new friend from that wing-nut church."

"Yes. Megan."

"Thanks, but no thanks," he says. He scoops potatoes and gravy into his mouth, gives a perfunctory chew, and swallows.

"Mom goes to that church too, you know, Dad," Sarah says.

"How could I forget?" He turns back to Jeanie. "Speaking of Clarence, where is he?"

"He's in Toronto at the head office for some special training, since last week. He says they're grooming him for a promotion."

"They better not transfer him!" Mutti says. She loads creamed peas into her mouth and talks around them. "Take the kids to a new school? Upset everyone?"

"If he gets the promotion, Mutti, it'll just be to the new branch in Regina. He can easily commute. It'll mean a big pay raise, which we can sure use." Jeanie sighs. Apart from flushed cheeks, she's pale. Her dark blond curls are tied back but are limp and droopy, her bangs sweat-wet. "And you do know our kids aren't in school yet."

"Hmmpff!" Mutti snorts.

"I didn't see your van," Rick says. "How'd you get here?"

"Megan's car's too small for my kids and hers, so I loaned it to her. I didn't think I'd need her car, so I didn't get the keys. Mutti came and got me."

"What for? Why not stay in your nice, cool, air-conditioned house and enjoy some time to yourself?"

"The last of the strawberries needed picking. Raspberries too." Mutti slides the gravy boat toward Jeanie. "Eat! You're eating for two you know!"

"In her condition? In this heat?" Rick shakes his head. "I'm gonna plough those goddamned berries under!"

"No, don't do that, Rick," Jeanie says, patting his thigh. "We love the berries. On ice cream? Better than any you can buy. Well worth the effort."

"Do we have ice cream?" Gramps pipes up. "I hope we have ice cream. I like strawberries."

"I like 'em too, Gramps." Rick gives him a warm smile as he pours more gravy over his meat and potatoes. He cuts a piece of beef, loads it with potatoes, gravy, and creamed peas, and stuffs the lot in his mouth.

Everyone's quiet, busy eating, for a few minutes.

Then Rick looks sideways at his sister. "I'm gonna take a run into town. I'll give you a lift. You can spend some quiet time in your nice cool house before the kids get home."

"It's a deal."

"To the pub again?" Mutti asks. "Don't you have hay to turn?"

"It's been turned."

"Are we having strawberries?" Gramps asks, looking up expectantly.

Mutti ignores him. "Only once. Your father always turned it twice."

"Pops didn't make good hay."

"Hmmpff!" Mutti snorts. "It was good enough to keep us on easy street. We weren't scraping to make mortgage payments then." She scowls, her lips pressed into a thin line. Her eyes narrow and her nostrils flare.

Not this again, Rick thinks. "Mutti, you know this. Back then, we made hay for our own cattle. Now most of it's to sell, and it's horse hay. Cattle will eat hay horses won't even look at, and at the prices we get, it has to be green and leafy—especially second cut, which this is. If I turn it again, it won't be. Besides, I've checked it. It's dry right through. We'll bale tomorrow." Then, for the benefit of the non–family members, he adds, "We aren't scraping. We're managing just fine." He runs a hand through sandy-brown hair and wonders how he's been drawn into this again. In front of others, to top it off. Appetite suddenly gone, he pushes his plate away.

"And whose idea was it to grow alfalfa so we'd need all the new equipment? Those new wells that we've got payments on? At least your father's hay didn't burn the barn down."

"Without the irrigation, we'd be damn lucky to get a second cut, and during the drought we'd've had to sell our cattle for a song, like our neighbors did, because we wouldn't've had enough hay to get them through the winter. Or we'd've had to buy hay at sky-high prices, instead of having hay to sell. And we *damn* sure wouldn't've had *any* hay to sell."

Her bright eyes darting, his mother turns her attention to the hired hands and continues as if uninterrupted. "Remember when our barn burned? People said they could see the flames from town!"

The young men squirm and look at each other, then at Rick. Sarah studies her plate.

Rick throws up his hands. Once his mother warms up to this story, there's no shutting it down. He visualizes a piece of duct tape over her mouth.

"What're you grinnin' about?" Mutti asks him. But she doesn't wait for an answer and turns instead to the boys. "You two were just kids then, I guess." She waves her fork back and forth. A red flush floods her cheeks. "Caused by hay not properly cured. Just cooked away until—*poof*!"

"The hay was fine when it went into the barn. But it was a rainy fall and the roof was bad. We tarped it, but part of it got wet anyway." Rick looks at the young men and continues, "You know how hot it gets when it starts to rot. Spontaneous combustion." He turns back to his mother and asks, "Do we have pie today?"

"Strawberry pie?" Gramps asks. He's the only one who doesn't seem affected by the heat, even though he always wears long-sleeved shirts. "I hope we have ice cream!"

Rick's mother ignores his attempt to change the subject and speaks louder. "My husband was trying to save Jeanie's horses."

Rick rises abruptly, scraping his chair back. "You want a ride into town, Sarah?"

"Um, no thanks. I'll just stay home tonight." She's looking under her lashes at Ryan. And Ryan is blushing but meeting her gaze.

"Okay. Tell you what. I bought some heifers at the auction today. You can go pick 'em up tomorrow 'n' put 'em in the small pasture on the other side of the ravine. Why don't you and the boys take a run out there tonight 'n' make sure the trough's topped up? Don't want them runnin' short of water in this heat. You could check the trough in the big pasture too." He gives her a wink and sees her blush deepen.

"Whenever you're ready, muffin," he says to Jeanie. "Maybe you could take a look in the freezer to see if there's ice cream. If there isn't, I'll pick some up in town. I've got a few things to do at the barn. I'll see you down there." He strides out the door, letting the screen door bang shut behind him.

His mother's words follow him. Even his abrupt departure hasn't caused a break. "My husband had two of the horses out, and when he went back for the other one, the whole barn collapsed with Rick standing there with the garden hose. Oh, you should've heard that horse scream and no insurance!"

I wanted to stop him, Rick wants to shout. *I tried to!*

"Do we have ice cream?" Gramps asks. "I hope we have ice cream."

Maybe if Pops hadn't refused to take on just that little bit more debt and they'd reroofed the barn. They'd talked about it. Rick thought he was going ahead. Then Pops changed his mind. He wouldn't explain. The most he would say was maybe when the line of credit was paid down. Maybe next year. Instead they spent hundreds of dollars on tarps that were ripped off in the plough wind that came with the rainstorm. But new shingles might have been ripped off too.

The shady veranda feels cool after the heat of the kitchen, and the view is usually soothing. Scattered outbuildings are repaired, gleaming white with green trim. The yard is mowed. Farm implements are parked in neat rows.

The sun mellows the distant fields, making them pastel. The sprawling Caledonia Chemicals potash mine infrastructure, far off across the farthest canola field, is miniature and hazy in the distance. The low Blue Hills to the southwest are a pale indigo. But the serene beauty of the southern Saskatchewan landscape that usually fills him with contentment isn't soothing tonight. The horror of that night is playing through his memory.

He jumps off the step, landing with a puff of dust, and hurries to the equipment shed that was converted to a horse barn after the fire.

By now his mother would have reached the part in the story where she says the horses were for Jeanie. Impractical. Expensive. But he always did spoil his little girl. And then what does she do but drop out of college just a few months before she would've gotten her degree and come home pregnant!

Rick thinks, *This is where Jeanie makes her exit.*

In fact, Pops loved horses. Claiming they were for Jeanie was just an excuse to stave off Mutti's complaints about them. Cattle were business; horses, pleasure. Smell them, he'd say. Don't have to ride them to enjoy them. Even their smell is beautiful.

The two horses have come up from their pasture and are milling around the paddock, raising dust, nickering, anticipating their dinner. The chestnut mare blows softly and nuzzles Rick's shoulder. As he scratches her forehead, the stiffness in his neck eases. He makes a silent promise: *Pops, the horses stay. No matter what Mutti thinks about whether it's sensible to keep feeding them or whether they're old and lame, they'll never be shipped. They will die here.*

He opens the barn door and lets them in. They obediently head for their stalls, and Rick slides the doors closed behind them. He goes into the feed room and readies their feed. Dodi has only a few teeth so her dinner is soaked soft.

"If Mutti knew about the alfalfa cubes I buy to keep you alive!" he says to the mare as he hangs her bucket. "Our little secret, eh?"

Jeanie comes into the barn, reaches into the stalls, and gives both horses scratches on their withers while they finish eating.

"Dodi's so thin," she says.

"Can't seem to fatten her up," Rick says. "I could feed her more, but she doesn't eat everything as it is. You'd think with all the pasture …" He gives his head a quick shake. "I just don't know." He gets a scoop of kibble for the barn cats beginning to congregate in the alleyway and puts it in their dish by the feed room door.

"I know you're doing all you can." Jeanie's quiet, watching the old mare chew. Then she says, "And you know … nobody thinks that barn fire was your fault."

"Hmmpff!" Rick snorts. "Nobody but Mutti, you mean."

"I know. I doubt she'll ever quit harping about it. I'm sorry."

"She's pretty hard on you too."

"Well," Jeanie sighs, "she's right though. About me, anyway."

"No, Jeanie, you don't deserve it, and even if you did, it's old news and nobody's business. Neither are our finances anyone's business. It's embarrassing. I wonder if she was always like this or if she's getting worse as she gets older."

"I wonder."

They turn the horses back out and go to his pickup truck.

"Mmm," Jeanie says as she hoists herself into the passenger seat. "Still has that new car smell!"

"You mean the 'new to me' car smell. Dunno how you can smell anything but dust. Fuckin' gravel roads."

He starts the engine, drives out to the road, and turns toward Pillerton. He reaches across and gives his sister's shoulder a squeeze. "You look done in, muffin."

"Yeah," she sighs, "it's been a long day."

"You know … it's not my business … but I hope you won't have any more babies. After little Winnie …" There's a sudden lump in his throat; he turns his head to look out the side window while he swallows a couple of times to get rid of it. A family of mallard ducks bobs in the slough next to the road. Soon the little ones will be getting their fledgling feathers. *They'd better get them soon. That slough will soon be dried up,* he thinks. *It'll be a long walk on those little legs to the next one.* Then he continues, "That was just such a short time ago …"

"I know, Rick. I wouldn't have believed it myself. To get pregnant again so soon." She's quiet and wipes at her eyes before continuing. "She was so tiny. But it's his religion. 'It is necessary that each and every marriage act remain ordered to the procreation of human life.' See? I've even memorized it."

"No sex for fun, eh?" he teases, "and you wonder why I'm not interested in meeting your new friend." He stops at the intersection in a cloud of dust, waits for a car speeding along the highway from the south, and then pulls out onto the pavement behind it. "Some seriously crazy church he was raised in, wasn't it?"

"Um, yeah, and he was homeschooled. I think there was a lot of religion in that … not mainstream ideas either. But it's what he grew up with, so I think that's why he joined the Children of Noah when we moved here. He's been after me to join too."

"Will you?"

"Well, I already know Megan. Tina too, of course. And they seem to have made Clarence welcome. But you know, growing up we were never much for church. I guess we went once in a while."

"Yeah, I remember."

"Mutti wanted to. Pops was against it. If I was going to join a church, the Children of Noah wouldn't be my choice, though. I wouldn't even consider it if it wasn't that it might be good for my marriage. It would be a struggle for me, even though we weren't brought up in any religion. They don't even believe in the New Testament. Everything they preach is from the Old Testament."

"Ah, well, doesn't make a difference to me, and I think Jews are still waiting for the Messiah too."

"True. And I guess Catholics don't believe in birth control either. But this baby's it for me, no matter what Clarence says. I don't care if it's another boy. I'm going to get my tubes tied."

11

"He'll go along with that?"

"Oh, he's against it, big time. Blows a gasket when I bring it up."
She has a sharp intake of breath and winces.

"Something wrong?" Rick asks.

"Just a little tightening. Braxton Hicks contractions, my doc says.
It's nothing. It's passed now. Anyways, I don't care what he thinks.
He's not the one who has to live like this." She points at her distended
stomach. "I've gained so much this time. I'm so uncomfortable."

"Maybe I should have a talk with him."

"Like you 'talked' to Benny Zimmerman?"

"Yeah, well, he didn't bother you or your little hillbilly friend again,
did he?"

"No." She shakes her head. "But we're not in school, and Pops isn't
around to buy you out of trouble."

"I can fight my own battles," he says, his face grim.

"I know," Jeanie says softly. She reaches across the console and rubs
his forearm.

Rick nods and turns onto the Pillerton exit. They ride along the
tree-lined street in silence for a block or two as forties- and fifties-era
houses with wide lawns and picket fences roll by. "Tell you what," he
says, "when my house is done, you 'n' the kids come 'n' live with me."

"And how will you get a wife, with five extra bodies in the place?"

"Wife!" he exclaims. "Not that again. I'm happy as I am."

"Oh yeah? The one-night stands still doin' it for you?" Jeanie tugs
the hem of her shorts.

"Steady diet of the same thing didn't do it for me either."

"That was years ago … talk about old news! And you know I don't
mean another wife like Tina," Jeanie chides. "No offense, but your
choice in wives was lousy."

"You should talk! 'N' at least I divorced my mistake."

"I'm not sure marrying Clarence was a mistake. Remember how
he was when we were first married? Sure, he can be grouchy, but down
deep he's a good person."

"Grouchy? That's the understatement of the year."

Now the houses they pass are newer, eighties and nineties. He turns
up Elm Street into the newest, most prestigious subdivision in Pillerton.

No starter homes here; these houses fill up their lots, and the trees are just saplings.

"He wasn't always so grouchy, though," Jeanie insists. "He's changed."

"Sure, he's changed. He used to think his shit didn't stink. Now he thinks it's good to eat."

"That's not funny, Rick!" She frowns, shaking her head. "You don't know him like I do. He's changed since we bought the new house. Stress, I think. Maybe we shouldn't've taken on such a big mortgage."

"Hmm."

They've reached her house. Rick pulls into the driveway and nudges the gearshift lever into park.

"By the way, there's a couple buckets of ice cream, vanilla and Neapolitan. So you can go ahead and spend the rest of your evening at Al's Place," Jeanie says with a grin as she opens the door and slides out. "Thanks, Bro. See you soon!" As tired as she is, she manages another of her sweet smiles. She shuts the door and waddles away, her canvas running shoes flapping. She's given up closing them on her swollen feet, plus she can barely reach them to tie them, so she pulled out the laces and now just slips them on and lets them flap.

Rick feels a burn as he watches her struggle up the front steps and curses the selfishness of her asshole husband for the thousandth time. *Clarence has always been all about Clarence*, he thinks, clenching his teeth and shaking his head. *He is not a good person, deep down or otherwise. Why can't she see it?*

He's a scab on our family.

But you don't choose your relatives.

Unfortunately.

Kathy smiles to herself as she aims the jet of water from the garden hose at the flower bed. The sun is hot on the back of her neck, promising another scorcher of a day. Already water sprayed on the concrete is evaporating, raising steam clouds, and spawning tiny rainbows.

She's wearing shorts and a halter top she last wore two decades ago. Odd, of all the things she left behind, her mother kept this one pair of shorts and one halter top. She wouldn't be able to get the shorts on if they weren't stretchy, or the halter top if it was fitted instead of elastic at the waist and tied at the back of the neck, but still she's pleased she can get into clothes from her high school days.

Turning the nozzle off, she lays down the hose, squats, and begins pulling some of the weeds threatening to choke out the perennials. It's much easier now that the ground's softened with water, and the heap on the sidewalk beside her grows quickly. The scent of newly mowed grass, the dirt, and even the bruised weeds is primal and comforting.

I'm going to have to seriously prune that rosebush in the corner back there, she thinks. *Need to get loppers next trip to RONA. I'll need help with that crazy caragana hedge and the immense cottonwoods hanging over the house, though. Between the hedge and the tall trees, the house can barely be seen from the street.*

At her apartment condo in North Vancouver, she has one small planter on the tiny deck, filled with a few petunias and a trailing strawberry. It produces a strawberry or two each week. That's been the limit of her gardening. She buys berries for shortcake at the Chinese produce market in Lonsdale Quay. The simple pleasure of taking care of the land, even on this small scale, was forgotten as if unknown.

In fact, she'd forgotten many things about Pillerton, about the prairies. Wide open skies. Spectacular sunsets. Shimmering seas of waving crops. Away from city lights, night skies ablaze with stars.

If it wasn't for my mother's death, she wonders, *would I ever have come back?* Originally planning to spend a few days at most, now she's settling in for several months at least. She wipes sweat off her forehead with the back of her hand, leaving a dirty smudge.

Brent didn't argue. For some months, they'd been wondering if time apart would kick-start their flagging relationship. Well, now they'll find out.

She looks up at the aging two-story house and notices how the gingerbread trim is deteriorating. Flakes of paint are ready to fall off. The address, 10 Front Street, has lost a letter and now reads 1_0 Fro t Street. Even the zero is drooping drunkenly. *The old girl is really starting to show her age*, she thinks. And the yard, the huge yard. Elder Reeves was so quick to point out they did such a good job of cleaning. Why couldn't they have done something with the yard to make it look a little less forbidding? Intimidating? The shrubberies are badly overgrown. The grass is tall and going to seed—what a job it was to get just the small section of lawn right in front of the house mowed with the ancient gas mower that quit running every five minutes! And weeds obscure the basement wall.

But it's not really different from when she was a kid.

The porch swing reminds her of her father. For a moment, she can almost feel the peaceful comfort of snuggling next to him while he stroked her hair and called her his baby. His sweet girl. She liked it best when he'd just shaved, with his face so smooth, and she remembers standing on a stool next to the bathroom sink, watching him lather his face. He still used soap and the mug with that round brush. He'd put a dab of lather on her nose, and then he'd lift her up so she could see herself in the mirror. The pleasant Daddy smell!

She visualizes herself rocking in that porch swing when she's eighty. *I won't be able to manage this huge yard then*, she thinks. *I'll have to hire someone to do the gardening.*

With a jolt that's almost physical, she realizes she's letting her imagination run away with her. She doesn't own the house. Her mother gave it to her church, the Children of Noah, in exchange for a life estate.

When she learned of her mother's death, Kathy called Elder Reeves. He told her there was no reason for her to come to Pillerton because the Children of Noah had taken care of everything. If there was anything in the house she wanted, they'd be happy to pack it up and ship it to her. In fact, they'd ship everything to her if that's what she wanted, but Elder Reeves cautioned she would need quite a bit of space to put it all, since it's a big house! Two stories, an attic, and a basement, all full, did she remember?

She thanked him for the offer and said she'd think about it, then asked him to e-mail the will. He said he would see if the executor could legally do that—privacy issues, of course—and he'd get back to her in a few days.

After more than a week passed and there was no word from Elder Reeves, and no will, she called Penny Meier. She'd known Penny for as long as she could remember. Like Kathy, Penny moved to Vancouver after university. She'd articled for a big law firm and made partner. Penny thought something sounded fishy (that's a complex legal conundrum, she'd explained with a chuckle). She said she'd do a will search. When she called back to say there was no will registered, she cautioned there may have been an unregistered will, but it was suspicious they hadn't produced it. She advised Kathy to return to Pillerton immediately. She had a few files she couldn't leave, but she would get them organized so her assistant could handle anything that might come up and fly out to join her. It would be a vacation of sorts! They could strategize, gather documents, and make whatever legal filings necessary to assert her claim on the property.

"But can't a person leave their property to anyone they choose?" Kathy asked. "You hear of old ladies leaving their house to their cat. And often, to their church."

"I didn't say it would be easy," Penny replied. "It could take a long time. If they knew your mother was terminally ill, maybe we can argue coercion. Or that she wasn't of sound mind and didn't have the mental capacity to make such decision … I don't know exactly. Meanwhile, the property will be tied up in legal finagling. Goddamned Children of Noah won't like that! I would love to *Scheiße in ihren Hut!* But seriously, your interests are best served by living there. And you and Brent have been talking about a trial separation, so it's serendipitous. I'll join you in a few days."

"I don't know. Maybe I should just forget it."

"Why, if it's rightfully yours?"

"But I don't know that."

"There's a reason they're withholding that will."

"But if it means a fight with the Children of Noah …"

"You can do it, Kathy. *We* can do it."

Yes, Kathy remembers with a grin, *she actually said* scheiße in ihren Hut. *Shit in their hat.* Penny's grandfather had taught her a bit of German. Mostly swearing, as it turns out.

Once the decision was made to go, Kathy realized she needed to, even if she didn't challenge the transfer of the property to the church. *I get such feelings of angst every time I think about that house*, she thought. *It's like I'm afraid of it. Why, when I remember so little? Maybe I do need to go there. Look at it with adult eyes. I should at least pack up my mother's things. Maybe there's something of hers I should keep.*

She flew to Regina, rented a car, and drove to Pillerton. She called Elder Reeves from the veranda and waited for him on the porch swing. His expression as he came up the front walk caused her to take a step back, but he was cordial and somehow managed to keep his tone of voice mild despite his clenched jaw and frown. "This is a surprise," he'd said as he unlocked the front door and stepped aside to let her enter ahead of him. She managed to summon a smile.

The place had that old house smell overlaid with lemony furniture polish, Comet, and other cleaners, strong enough to cancel out the cloud of cologne enveloping Elder Reeves. He told her the church ladies came in every week to clean. Don't they do a fine job? And he asked how long she planned to stay. In deference to her bereavement, they could temporarily move their meetings to the community center, but that costs money, didn't she know, and theirs is a small congregation. He hoped she wouldn't stay long, so meetings at 10 Front Street could continue as usual.

Elder Reeves. Still a good-looking man despite obviously dyed hair and being well into his sixties. He spoke in such a soothing voice and with such a sympathetic smile. Were his eyes really that cold?

"I don't know how long I'll need," she'd told him.

And she didn't. Depending on how things went, her tenure in the old house might turn out to be even longer than two or three months. Could she really live here? Maybe for the rest of her life?

For the hundredth time, she thinks, *Maybe I should walk away from the house. Can I really weather a drawn-out legal fight? Besides, I had no contact with my mother for the last twenty years. Maybe I don't deserve it, whatever Penny's views are.*

Maybe I should walk away from my dead-end, minimum-wage job too. That idea is really appealing to her. No more first-of-the-month stacks of files coming up for renewal to be worked through, struggling to get them all done before the next stack hits. No more staying hours after the office closes to balance the Insurance Corporation of British Columbia car insurance documents for the day, no more panic when there's a decal not recorded. *I'll consider leaving that job even if I don't stay in Pillerton,* she decides. *I'll be a brand-new Kathy Klein. No job, no husband, no fight with the Children of Noah. Maybe move to a new city. Start over from scratch.*

But the house. It was her father's, and his father's, and his grandfather's. *I'm the last of the line. That's one reason I didn't change my name when I married. I thought it was the last thing I had from my father. I hadn't even thought of the house. His house. My father would want me to have it!*

She's realizes her knees are sore, and she's reminded of the hundreds of Children of Noah meetings she attended growing up. Weekly torture! She and Penny were the only children. The entire congregation numbered less than thirty. With the area rug in the big front room rolled to one side, the congregation of women knelt on the bare hardwood floor, their knees aching, enjoying the suffering they believed would bring them closer to their god, while Elder Reeves, Elder Smythe, and Elder Barth sat comfortably in chairs facing them, each awaiting his turn to stand and proselytize.

At least now I can do something about the sore knees, Kathy thinks, and stands up. Add one of those foam garden kneeling pads to the list for the next trip to RONA, along with gardening gloves and, of course, loppers.

Her shirt's sticking to her, and she wonders if she'll ever get used to the heat. She decides to leave the rest of the weeding and yard work for later, when hopefully it will be cooler. *I'll have a cool bath. Maybe a little nap. Then go to Regina and do some shopping for a desperately needed coffee maker.* Her mother's old electric percolator takes half an hour. Who can wait that long?

She goes inside and upstairs to the bathroom, stripping as she runs water in the tub. She can almost visualize her father at the sink shaving, and thinks back to when he went away. Had she started school yet? She remembers the conversations she'd had with her mother.

"When is Daddy coming home?"

"He isn't." And "Dirty! He was a dirty man!" And "What are you sniveling about?"

"I miss Daddy."

"Well stop it! He doesn't miss you."

She didn't understand how he could be dirty when he seemed so clean. His face, at least, was clean. It had to be, with all the soap she watched him put on it every day. Maybe some part of him she couldn't see? But he always smelled nice. And even if he was dirty, why didn't he come home? But asking about him made her mother angry, so she stopped, and just waited and hoped.

She spent hours sitting on the stairs next to the landing, the itchy runner prickling her legs. She chewed her nails down to stubs and picked her cuticles until they bled, unable to stop, even knowing that when her mother saw them, she'd sprinkle Tabasco on them to get her to quit that bad habit. Listening to noises from the kitchen as her mother made supper. Watching dust motes swirl in the colored light from the leaded-glass windows. Hoping he would come through the door.

Of course, he never did. All these years later, she still doesn't understand.

On her arrival back in Pillerton, Kathy had gone through the house, room by room. She'd been away for twenty years. It was familiar, of course, but there had to be changes too. Were there clues to how her mother lived her last years?

Her mother's bedroom at the front of the second story was still full of her things, as was her bathroom next to it. The two smaller bedrooms and Kathy's room at the back, though, held nothing other than the old furniture.

The small door leading to the attic was still padlocked as she remembered. She'd never been allowed up there. Now there was no one to stop her! A twinge of guilt was quickly replaced with anticipation. She looked for the key in all the logical places (the junk drawer, the bowl of odds and ends on the dresser, the row of hooks on the wall by the back door where all the other keys were hanging, even the tiny freezer compartment at the top of the old fridge) but found nothing. Well, nothing except a screwdriver. She used that to take the hasp off. Then she took a deep breath, pulled the door open on a narrow, steep staircase, and up she went.

There was enough light from the small window in the dormer to see old furniture and a pile of dusty shoes, but mostly, stacks of cardboard boxes. A couple of antique-looking trunks might be worth something, but there didn't appear to be anything else of value. Nothing she could see was worth locking up.

"What? No dressmaker's dummy?" she'd said out loud and then giggled at her own joke.

But the attic was dusty and hot, seemingly ten degrees hotter than the rest of the house; in minutes, she was sweating and happy to leave.

The main floor's large country kitchen was unchanged except for one surprisingly modern touch: a dishwasher was retrofitted into the chipped and battered cabinets, incongruous beside the stained white enamel sink, the fifties electric stove, and the old refrigerator that rattled noisily when the compressor kicked in.

She'd forgotten how impressive the long butcher block in the center was, even distressed by decades of slicing and dicing, with the same collection of pots and pans hanging from the rack over it. But it was the only appealing thing about an otherwise ugly old kitchen. The chrome table and chairs, which needed the torn vinyl seats and the Arborite top replaced, added to the house's overall impression of decay.

In the enclosed back stoop, her mother's rubber boots stood at attention on a rubber mat. The small powder room by the back door, decades ahead of its time when built, now ugly with its worn, dated fixtures. No personal effects there, just a threadbare hand towel on the ring by the sink and a plastic-wrapped bale of Kirkland toilet paper rolls under it.

A built-in cabinet with carving to match the mantel divided the living room from the dining room. Leaded glass in the doors allowed peeks at proudly displayed rose-patterned dishes her mother collected out of laundry detergent. What was it called? Extra? Or bonus? Such cheap dishes beside dozens of wineglasses.

Worn hall runners. Dingy battleship linoleum. Worn area rug in the living room.

She'd opened the door leading from the kitchen to the basement, but the light switch didn't turn on any lights. As a child, she was afraid to go down there. The stairs were steep, with no handrails. Anytime she did go down, she was overcome with fear something under the stairs would reach through and grab her ankle. When she was about nine or ten, she realized the dirty man who lurked there, waiting to catch little girls and do unspeakable things to them, was no more real than any of the others her mother warned her about. Even so, decades later the old fear flooded her, and she couldn't force herself to go down. No hurry. When Penny's here and it's daylight, that will be soon enough. Safety in numbers and all that.

Now Kathy runs the water until it's cold, too cold even for the cool-down bath she wanted, and still there's less than six inches of water. At least sitting in it brings the water level up somewhat; she washes with a washcloth and then lies down to wet her hair. Up to shampoo. Down again several times to rinse.

She wonders if it's wise to replace the water heater that clunks away in the basement loud enough to wake her. All that noise and hardly any hot water! Maybe it's a real old-timer. Maybe even leaking. *I really should go down there and take a look at it*, she thinks, *but not until Penny gets here tomorrow.* And Penny will say it's not worth spending any money on until she knows the house is going to be hers.

She pulls the plug and gets out of the tub. The towel on the bar is worn through in a couple of places, but she hadn't thought to search for a better one before she got in the bath. So she uses it, toweling all over before wrapping her hair in it.

What a crummy little bathroom, she thinks. Everything's so old, so worn. The lion-footed tub suits the house, but the enamel finish is gone, worn right through to black in places. There's a wall-hung sink, no vanity, and just a tiny recessed medicine cabinet with a slot in the back where her father discarded his razor blades. She thinks again of watching him lather up his face and scrape it off while carefully studying what he was doing in the mirror, the smell of shaving soap filling the room. Every day she told him it smelled nice, and every day he told her it was English Leather. Then they laughed together because it wasn't leather but soap, and he'd give her a tickle under the arm. Like the dab of lather on her nose, it was their little joke that never got old.

Now the silvering is eroding from the mirror to the point there's only a small area in the center where she can actually see herself. Should she spend money on renovating? Or is the house doomed to be torn down anyway? To make room for a new Children of Noah meeting hall, maybe?

The worn toothbrush in the toothbrush holder seizes her attention. The sight of such an intensely personal item unexpectedly causes her throat to ache, and she tears up. Then she gives herself a mental shake and reminds herself she lost her mother a long time ago. She snatches the toothbrush from the holder and drops it in the wastebasket.

Then she opens the door to the medicine cabinet and hurriedly dumps its contents: corn plasters, suppositories, Preparation H, generic Vaseline, iodine (seriously, iodine?), Band-Aids, worn-out emery boards, and toenail clippers rusting where the chrome's peeling off. She stops for a second, realizing it's foolish to throw good stuff away. She retrieves the Band-Aids, using one to wrap the thumbnail she'd chewed raw, then leaves the bathroom and heads down the hall to her childhood bedroom.

She hasn't slept well in her mother's room. It's the largest and nicest of the bedrooms with a big bay window overlooking the street. It's next to the bathroom, handy for those middle-of-the-night trips to pee, and the bed's bigger, but the water heater clanking is louder there. So she's moving into her old room overlooking the backyard, the small garage, all the vacant lots, and farther, the rest of Pillerton.

She bumps the door as she walks in and hears an odd rattle or clunk. On closer inspection, she sees a barrel-bolt latch just under the doorknob. It lines up with a hole in the jamb so the door can be locked from outside. *I don't remember that*, she thinks. *It must be something added lately, but what would its purpose be?*

Otherwise, her room is unchanged, dominated by the old brown metal headboard with its fading tole-painted roses. The bed is made up with her pink chenille spread, but nothing else remains of her old life. The dresser drawers, wardrobe, and nightstand are all empty. *My mother gave up on me a long time ago too*, she realizes.

The room smells of dust and stagnant air. She opens the window, allowing the slight breeze from the shady side of the house to glide sensually across her still-moist skin; then she lies down on the soft chenille, finally cool.

But instead of drifting off to sleep, memories of her first boyfriend parade through her brain like a slide show. He was the school jock, the school heartthrob, so handsome with that sandy forelock over his intense blue eyes. Little scar in one eyebrow. Lips finely drawn, wide mouth always on the edge of a grin. Strong and lean and so male. How he made her heart race! Since then, nothing has come close to it. Was it just the intensity of youthful emotions? What's that song—no more highs, no more lows, where do the all the feelings go? Well, the feelings haven't gone; there are still lows, just no highs.

In high school, Kathy had a few awkward dates, but until grade twelve, never an actual boyfriend. That's when he came along. She knew who he was, of course; it's a small town, and they'd gone to the same schools since kindergarten. But saying they didn't travel in the same circles would be an understatement. He and his buddies were on top of the social heap. She and Penny were barely even in the heap, squished out the bottom like fresh dog shit under a boot. Everyone in school, probably everyone in town, was surprised when he asked her to the Valentine's Day dance. She knew the popular girls giggled behind hands that he'd only done it on a dare, but she ignored them and went anyway. Then there was another date. And then they were going together. But it didn't last. Much too soon, it was one of the popular girls he was cruising with.

Water under the bridge. No point regurgitating it now.

The doorbell chimes its lengthy series of notes, and Kathy leaps up, surprised that she'd dozed off. She can't remember where her robe is and can't possibly get dressed in time to answer the door, so she decides to ignore it.

Then there is loud, insistent knocking on the front door, as if someone's opened the screen door and is pounding on the door behind it. *That's how cops knock, at least in TV shows,* she thinks. *Who could possibly be that eager to see me?*

She goes to the front bedroom window to look out, hiding her nakedness behind the curtain. But it's not a cop car she glimpses through the bushes, just a late-model gray Honda or Toyota. *Most likely Elder Reeves again. Well, he can wait.*

After a moment, a man, a small man, walks out from under the veranda and into view. He's wearing light gray pants. Suit pants? A long-sleeved dress shirt. And an odd hat, a kind of wide-brimmed, outdoorsy hat. Tilley maybe. *An odd choice to wear with a suit,* she thinks, *especially in this heat.*

The hat effectively blocks his face from anyone looking down on him, as she is, though. Still, nothing about him reminds her of Elder Reeves.

He stops on the cracked and heaved concrete walk and seems to be looking at the flower bed by the pile of weeds she left there earlier. He goes out of view from her vantage point, behind the veranda roof, as if he's gone into the flower bed. When he returns to view on the walkway, she sees he has weeds in one hand, and he adds them to the pile.

Is he wearing gloves?

He walks toward the side of the house but reappears moments later and looks up, right at the window where she's standing.

She quickly drops the curtain and hopes he didn't see her. Peering out through the small space between the curtain and the window frame, she sees he's still looking up at the window, and she has a clear view of his face. Definitely not Elder Reeves. His small beard—a goatee?—is light blond or maybe even white. Wraparound sunglasses coupled with the hat hide the top half of his face. He's covered from head to toe, she realizes, all except for the bottom half of his face. He's small for a man, but there's an impression of heavy muscling. Power.

He turns and goes to his car. As he drives away, she gets a fleeting glimpse of a green bumper sticker but can't make out what it's for. "Hmmpff," she shrugs. "I brake for Unicorns" or "Proud Parent of a Pillerton High Honor Student" or maybe something commercial like Amway. She pushes it out of her mind.

Thinks about where she'll shop.

Decides on Costco.

They have the best price on coffee makers.

Elder Reeves strolls through Pillerton's Royal Canadian Mounted Police Detachment, smiling, saying hello, and calling everyone by name. The door to Chief Johannsen's office is closed. He pushes it open and raps on the doorframe. "You awake, Selmer?" he says. He walks in and closes the door behind him.

Chief Johannsen is at his desk, back to the door and feet up on the credenza. "I am now," he says, sitting up and swiveling his chair around. He hoists his belly so he half stands and sticks out his hand. "Hey, Nick."

"Hey." Nick gives the chief's hand a quick shake and then sits in the chair facing the desk. "How's your grandson? What's his name again? Wilson?"

"Jaxon, his name's Jaxon. 'N' don't call him Jack or Melissa'll bite your head off." He snorts and scratches a large, angry-looking patch of psoriasis on his elbow. "He's a good kid. Starts high school this fall, can you believe it?"

"Tsk," Nick says, "where's the time go? Seems like just yesterday we were getting drunk at your bachelor party. Good times, eh?"

"Yup, we had the world by the short 'n' curlies then, didn't we?"

"Still do, Selmer, still do."

"Oh yeah? Now the high point of my day is having a good dump, not bangin' the twin cheerleaders," Chief Johannsen clucks. "What brings you here today?"

"I have a favor to ask."

"Anything, Nick, you know that."

"You know the house where my congregation meets?"

"Of course."

"Well, the owner gave it to the church. Now she's passed, and her daughter's moved in. We're worried she has no plans to move back out. We need her gone. Can you evict her?"

"If she's living there"—he whistles tunelessly under his breath while he considers it—"it's not that easy."

"It would be worth your while."

"It's not that. I'd do it. You know that. But I'm already on report for that other deal."

"Oh. Yeah. Sorry that blew back on you."

"I can ride it out. But I have to tread carefully. I ain't financially ready for early retirement thanks to the ho and her lawyer."

"That bad, eh? Well, we won't hang you out to dry, Selmer. We have some influence. And we'd always be able to find, er, a position for you."

"I know, and I appreciate it. But I like being king shit of turd island. Least it's my turd island. I ain't ready to bow out yet."

"I get that." Nick studies his old friend's face. He notes the high color in his cheeks and wonders how far away he is from a coronary, if he'll actually bow out before he drops dead. He suppresses a chuckle at the thought that Selmer actually thinks Pillerton is *his* turd island. He makes a mental note to put some feelers out to determine who might best replace him. Then he returns his focus to the conversation. "You're absolutely right. So. You can't do anything?"

"We can call her a squatter or a trespasser, but there's still a legal process to get her out. I'm not a hunert percent sure how it works." More scratching sends flakes like the icing off glazed doughnuts onto his desk blotter. "Was it left to your church in a will?"

"No. There was no will."

"So the daughter thinks it's hers by right of survivorship?"

"I don't know. The parishioner in question transferred the property to us a few years before she died."

"Oh, that might change things." Now the chief scratches his head vigorously, then pats the thin strands of hair back in place. "Well, Nick, you know I'll help if I can. But you gotta help me help you. Get your lawyer to get it in front of a judge. Bring me something I can work with."

Nick's cheeks puff as he exhales a large breath through his mouth. "Yeah, okay. Meantime, though, if you get any calls reporting any goings-on at the house, can you just make sure nobody pays attention? Tell 'em it's just a paranoid city girl afraid of being in the big ol' house alone."

"Sure, that I can do."

Nick stands, thanks him as he shakes his hand, and leaves the office wondering why he feels so itchy.

Rick lifts his glass and takes several cool, satisfying swallows of draft Labatt's Blue; then he puts the glass down and reaches for the last clump of chips on the share-sized plate of nachos in the center of the battered table. Marty and Donnie, guys he's known all his life, both growl. "What?" he asks. "You both wanted this?" He teasingly holds out the chips, scoops the remains of salsa and sour cream onto them, and shoves the lot into his mouth with a grin.

He loves this pub. He and his buddies have been coming to Al's Place since before they were of legal age to drink. The previous owner didn't care. The new one does, probably because the liquor board's threatened to close it down, but it's been a couple of decades since Rick and his friends would have been tossed out. *That's got to be the only upside to getting older*, he thinks, as he takes another swig of beer.

The new grease monkey from Sloan's Garage is at the table next to them. Donnie leans over to talk to him, and Rick hears him telling the newcomer the history of their town. "Pillerton's on the Soo Railway," Donnie says, "the Chicago connection. Al Capone spent a lot of time here. That's why they named the pub after him. He had a sweet little business going, buying legal Canadian liquor, loading it onto freight cars here, and selling it in Chicago at a massive profit. Prohibition made millionaires outta them guys. Doubt there'd be Mafia in North America otherwise."

Rick's thoughts turn to the Al Capone tunnels that undermine so much of Pillerton. Parts of them have been reinforced and are deemed safe, so they're open to tourists. There's a gun room, poker room, dining room, bunk rooms. And the largest, the Entertainment Room. The only access to the tunnel system and the starting point of the tours is in the basement of the three-story sandstone hotel they're in. Rooms haven't been rented for decades. If it wasn't for Al's Place and the tunnel tours, the whole building would have been boarded up years ago.

He took the tunnel tour once or twice and likes to go to the Entertainment Room on the rare occasion he has a date he wants his friends to meet. There's a piano player, and the crowd's usually happy and lively, singing along to Roaring Twenties songs and dancing the Charleston.

But the tunnels have a dark side too; there are rumors they're haunted, and everyone's heard stories of kids getting into them and never being seen again. People swear they've heard screams, even babies crying. The rumors are officially denied but not too vehemently. It's good advertising, and Lord knows, Pillerton can use the exposure. The tunnels and Al's Place are the only thriving businesses in town. Even the curling rink's closed.

Over the years there's been talk of this developer or that buying the hotel, spending money on updates, and renting rooms again, but the building code makes it financially unattractive. It's even less viable now, with competition from the new Holiday Inn just twenty minutes away and right on the highway.

Added to that, there's the bylaw prohibiting excavating, jackhammering, and blasting, intended to protect the tunnel system and, of course, the buildings they lie under. The alternative is to reinforce the tunnels, but that would be expensive. There's endless controversy over who actually owns them. Who should pay for the reinforcements, or the lawsuits when houses suddenly drop into a sinkhole? The town? The province? Are they a national historic site? Lawyers are studying it. So the answer is probably years off.

"How's yer hay this year, Rick? Get a good second cut?" Marty's question stirs Rick from his reverie.

"It's good 'n' thick, nice quality. Might get a third cut if it doesn't start raining too early. How's yours?"

"Not bad. Got a lot of foxtail in that back field 'n' got hit with a weed notice, so I hadda spray the toadflax. Guess I'll have to rip that field out and replant next year. Thought I'd get a few more years outta it but ..." He shrugs and empties his glass.

"Yup, always something. Our canola's mediocre. Next year I think I'll go back to lentils. Or maybe barley. Or something else the cattle can eat."

"I think I'm just gonna quit cattle all together," Marty says. "My ball 'n' chain wants to go south for a couple months in the winter. Can't do that if you have cattle."

Four o'clock signals the start of happy hour. More customers drift in—tourists back after an earlier tour of the tunnels, couples looking for bargain beer and free peanuts in the air-conditioned pub.

Marty says, "I better haul ass or my ol' ball 'n' chain'll come after me."

"Ball 'n' chain. You're lucky she didn't kick you to the curb years ago," Rick tells him.

"Well, you know, it's too far from the ground to feed itself."

"Don't think it'd take her long to find someone else to feed it. She still looks like she did in high school, 'n' you look like her dad."

"Yup. Distinguished."

"Distinguished, eh?" Donnie says, turning back to his friends. "Time you're fifty, you're both gonna look like worn-out boots."

"At least we'll be worn-out boots with hair," Rick says.

"Ow! A shot!" Donnie exclaims, then shakes his head and grins. "You know what they say, you can grow hair or you can grow brains, not both!" He lifts his Saskatchewan Roughriders ball cap and scratches a mole on his balding head with the three remaining fingers on his right hand before settling back down. "One more for the road?"

"Fine by me," Rick says as he looks at Marty. "What about you?"

"Oh, what the hell," Marty says. "Why not?"

Rick half stands and waves at Carl, who's busy behind the bar; then he sits again when he sees the small gathering of tourists surrounding him. It has always struck him as comical that Carl dresses like a twenties gangster—complete with fedora, armbands, and suspenders holding up his wide pleated pants—and entertains the tourists with stories of Al Capone's exploits. He's in the middle of a performance now, holding forth to the sunburned flock sucking back their four-dollars-a-bottle beer as they cluster around the bar.

One of the tourists says, "Someone told us Al Capone lived in that big old house in the next block."

"Not true!" Carl says, laying on his English accent. "This hotel was *some* swanky in the twenties! Why would he live there when he had room service here? Ol' Al, he had a flat upstairs fit for a prince! Never had nuffink but the finest meals: Steak! Prime rib! Rack of lamb! And talk about the birds!" He gives a loud wolf whistle. "Nuffink but the finest birds too. Lots of 'em, and every one gorgeous, believe it. Did a lot of his business"—he makes air quotation marks—"up there." His audience laughs, right on cue.

Carl, always to be depended on for the male lead in the local dinner theater group, is just warming up. "And if the G-men came, he had his bolt hole into the tunnels handy. Of course the entrance to the tunnels was hidden then. And there was no gift shop."

The tourists laugh again. The locals have all heard his routine many times, so it's just background noise, but Carl always puts his heart into it and can't be interrupted to do any bartending. Finally Donnie picks up the dirty plate and empty pitcher, goes behind the bar, dumps the plate in the dish pit, and pulls the beer himself.

"Dunno why Carl doesn't have Marge come in to cover happy hour," he says on his return as he pours them each a glass. "She has to come in later, anyway, when he goes down to the Entertainment Room. 'N' she could use the extra hours."

"Carl's cheap, you know that," Marty says. "Didn't get rich payin' wages when he doesn't have to."

They all take long drinks of the fresh beer.

"Hey, Donnie, speakin' of gettin' rich. How's the ol' Prairie Equity and Wealth Management doin' these days?" Rick asks. "Must be okay. I see they've done a nice reno on the building, and you've got a brand-new truck."

"Yup, three kilometers on it when I took delivery. That paint job's a three-thousand-dollar option. You see how the color changes depending on the light?" Donnie takes another good swig of his beer, wipes the froth off his upper lip on the back of his hand, puts the mug down, and leans forward, elbows on the table. "But to answer your question. Company's doin' great. I got a big commission check. Get new clients all the time 'cause we make money for people. Any time you guys want to get in on it, you know where to find me."

"Dunno 'bout Rick, but I got no wealth for you to manage." Marty frowns.

"Me neither," Rick says, "but I always wondered. Seems more like a big-city business."

"We been around for a long time 'n' we're careful with our assets," Donnie explains. "We got rentals. You might not be able to buy a high-rise apartment building on your own, but through us you can buy a piece of one in Toronto or Vancouver and start rakin' in a share of the rents. And we hold mortgages."

"Isn't that risky? Mortgages, I mean?" Rick says. "You hear about the housing market, the bubble about to bust or—"

"Nope, very minimal risk. Like I said, we're careful. Never take nuthin' but first mortgage position, and never for more than eighty-five percent of appraisal. And our rates are higher than the banks."

"People go for that?"

"Well, folks who come to us for mortgages, they can't get 'em anywhere else. They use our mortgage to reestablish their credit and pay us out as soon as they can refinance. Works like this: if we lend three hundred and fifty thousand dollars at nine-point-five percent, plus earn a one percent fee of three thousand five hundred dollars, and then get paid out, say in six months, it pretty well makes the one-percent fee into a two-percent annualized fee ... Oh, here's where your eyes start rollin' back in your head."

"Yup, you lost me," Rick says. "That's why you're the money guy at Prairie Equity and I'm on the farm."

"I'm with you." Marty glances out the window and then takes a better look. "Fuck! Lookit them black clouds up north. It ain't supposed to rain till Thursday! I got fifteen acres ready to bale tomorrow."

"It ain't gonna rain tonight," Donnie opines.

"Oh, and you know this how? Yer ol' football injury ain't painin' you?"

"Shit no. I got an iPhone."

"Well, so do I 'n' the fuckin' forecast's changed every time you look at it," Marty says as he pushes his chair back and stands. "I'm gonna see if I can git 'er off the field tonight, just in case." He pulls a couple of crumpled bills and some coins out of the front pocket of his jeans and tosses the money on the table. "See you guys," he says, and weaves his way through tables to the door.

"Yeah, I gotta go too," Donnie says, pouring the last of the beer more or less equally between his and Rick's glasses. "He won't get fifteen acres in the barn before the dew falls."

"No. I should go help."

"Mmm." Donnie swigs his beer. "Off topic, but you seen her yet?"

"Seen who?"

"Kathy Klein. A client told me there's a glitch with some real estate deal. She's involved somehow. Said she's in town to take care of it."

"Kathy Klein!" Rick's mind spins. He gulps his beer to hide his shock and then says, "Didn't know she ever visited."

"Well, her mother probably never died before."

"Oh?"

"You don't read the community newsletter?"

Rick shrugs and shakes his head. "It's online, isn't it?"

"Yeah. So?"

"There's your answer."

"Anyway, you gonna see her?"

Rick frowns, abruptly pushes his chair back, and stands, leaving his glass three-quarters full. He calls out, "Hey, Carl! Whadda we owe ya?"

Carl breaks away from his audience long enough to consult his notepad. "Forty-five thirty. Make it forty-five."

Donnie picks up the two five-dollar bills and coins Marty left and says, "Goddamn that cheap bastard! He done it again! Like his share is ten dollars and fifty cents!"

"Well, it's close."

"Close, hell! 'N' don't Carl get nuthin'?"

They each toss in a twenty and a couple of loonies. Then Donnie chugalugs the rest of his beer, gets to his feet, and follows Rick out into the late-afternoon heat.

"That goddamned Masterson! How's he do it? How many times has he been in the shitter when the bill comes?"

Rick shrugs. "Come on, Donnie. You bitchin' about subsidizing us poor farmers? With your money?"

"Yeah, you poor farmers. Isn't that a new pickup?" Donnie asks, pointing to the green Silverado LTZ double cab.

"Lease return. Only thirty thousand kilometers on it when I got it. I got them to throw in the paint."

"Smart-ass." Donnie scowls and shrugs. "Fuckin' Marty, though. It's the principle. Sometimes makes me wanna beat the snot outta him." He exhales loudly. "Next time we'll let him run his own tab."

They slap-shake hands and go to their vehicles. Donnie climbs into his metallic-red Escalade, starts it, backs out of the angle parking spot into the street, and drives off.

Rick fusses with the stereo as he watches Donnie drive away. Not for the first time, he relives the memory of Kathy Klein, so out of place in her plain, dark dress among all the fancy ones at the Valentine's Day dance, but her face was glowing, her brown eyes as big as saucers, oblivious to the smirks and giggles at her expense. He feels a rush of shame remembering how breathless she was when he kissed her good night at the door, and then he'd gone and picked up Tina to take her to the after-party that lasted all night. But there were weekly dates with Kathy after that. Tina had dropped out of school and was taking a hairdressing course in Regina, so it wasn't too difficult juggling them. He just had to be careful not to be too friendly with Kathy at school. There was no hand-holding or even walking together, and somehow Kathy accepted that. Still, about the time he realized he was starting to like Kathy, and like her a lot, inevitably Tina found out. They married a few weeks after graduation, and Sarah was born in November. *I thought I was so goddamned cool*, he thinks. *What a fool.*

When he sees the Escalade out on the highway, he pulls away from the curb, drives around the block, and turns onto Front Street, slowing as he approaches number ten.

Kathy's standing next to a pile of weeds on the walkway, looking down at the flower bed. Wearing shorts and a white halter top, she looks trim and fit. Her shoulder-length dark hair is swept back into some kind of sparkling clip. She has her hand to her mouth, as if she's chewing her nails.

Damn! he thinks. *It could be twenty years ago, with her waiting out front for me to pick her up. It would've been so much easier to drive by if she didn't still look like I remember.*

He wishes she'd turn his way so he could see her face but realizes he doesn't really want her to if it means she'll see him cruising slowly past her house. "Now I'm a goddamned stalker," he mutters.

She starts to turn her head.

For a split second, he thinks about gunning the engine and heading to Marty's.

Then he pulls across the oncoming lane and parks, driver's side at the curb. He slides out onto the sidewalk, closes the door behind him, and walks the few steps through the gate toward her. She turns as he approaches.

"Hi, Kathy," he says.

"Oh my God! Rick!"

Clarence stands facing three red-robed, hooded men seated on the far side of the table. It's a dark, windowless room, and fresh paint smells coupled with the unpleasant, buzzing blue light from the overhead fluorescents are giving him a headache.

"How's the hand, Brother Weaver?" one of the tribunal asks as he shrugs the hood onto his shoulders, exposing his bald head. The mole in the middle has a few hairs sprouting from it. He scratches it absently.

Clarence peels back the bandages and holds up his hand to display the short, raw stump of his index finger, bristling with black stitches. "It's healing. Dr. Benzi did a good job, but there's a ways to go yet."

"Good. Good," the man in the middle says.

"What about your wife?" the man on the left asks. "Where's she on joining with us? And your mother-in-law?"

Clarence looks at the floor.

"They haven't come around yet?"

He shakes his head slowly but doesn't look up.

All is quiet. Clarence's missing finger begins to itch. He badly wants to rewrap his hand, take a couple of the oxycodone tablets Dr. Benzi gave him, and go back to his bunk.

"Maybe another sacrifice?" suggests the bald man.

At this, Clarence looks up and frowns. "But Donnie! They're only women! Mutti's old, and Jeanie's pregnant! Neither of them would ever be able to—"

"I wasn't talking to you," Donnie snaps, "and I'm Exalted Leader! Got it?"

"Sorry," Clarence mumbles, head bowed.

"But since you brought it up, when's that baby due?"

"The baby?"

"You want to be right with the Lord, don't you?" the middle man asks. "You have paid attention to my sermons, our teachings, haven't you? You've read the True Bible we gave you as you began your purification, haven't you? As is written in Leviticus 26:29, the Lord commands, 'Ye shall eat the flesh of your sons and the flesh of your daughters shall ye eat.'"

"I ... I haven't gotten through it all, Imperial Leader. But I remember your sermons," Clarence says, taking a deep breath. "It's due in a few weeks. Maybe a month."

"You know how the Lord favors us and what we are able to do for you because of his favors?"

"Yes, Imperial Leader."

"You know the favor you came to us for is a big one, don't you?"

"Yes, Imperial Leader."

"Say it. Tell us why you need a favor."

"Well ... well, I, uh—"

"He can't own up to it," Exalted Leader snarls. "Maybe we should reassess."

"No!" His headache pounding now, Clarence is sweating, despite the coolness of the room.

"Brother Weaver," Imperial Leader says, "you must own your transgressions in order for the Lord to forgive you. If you don't ... if you make excuses or blame others, there is no forgiveness in the Lord."

Clarence wonders why the other two leaders suddenly lean forward, bringing their hoods over their heads again, and why they're leaning their elbows on the table with their hands covering their faces. He sees Imperial Leader watching him with narrowed eyes.

"But ... but I already told D-Don ... I mean Exalted Leader."

"Now you must tell us all, and we may ask you to tell us as many times as it takes until we are satisfied you are truly remorseful," Imperial Leader says. "Your hope is not in you. It is in the Lord! Your weakness is united to His might. Your ignorance to His omniscience. Your frailty to His enduring omnipotence."

"I know, Imperial Leader! Forgive me! I'll tell you!" He fidgets, licking his lips. "I, uh, took money. Not from people! Just from the bank. Then I had to take more to cover it, and then more to cover that. So far I've been able to cover up everything. Now the branch is scheduled for a major audit in November. Independent auditors from Toronto. They're bound to find out. I'll lose everything! I'll go to jail!"

"You're an embezzler," Donnie says, dropping his hands to the table and sitting up straight again. "Say it."

Clarence flushes. "I'm an embezzler," he says quietly.

"What?"

"Embezzler."

"Louder."

"I'm an embezzler!"

"What did you do with the money you embezzled?"

"Well, really," Clarence begins, taking a deep, calming breath. *I can talk my way out of this*, he thinks. "The bank got most of it back in interest payments on the phony loans. Greedy bastards! Ridiculous interest rates! I bought the house ... and the condo I already signed over to you. And there's a girl, Monica."

Imperial Leader frowns. "That's it? You took a chance on going to jail for a couple of houses and a ho?"

"Well ... also a couple of cars. A few cars. You know, my Lexus wasn't cheap. Clothes. A couple of vacations. Monica likes to travel."

"You're thinking with your dirty man part like the unclean man you are."

"Yes, Imperial Leader."

"When you have completed your purification, you will no longer be unclean. You will be purified and sanctified."

"Um ... yes, Imperial Leader. I remember your teachings."

"I am only a humble servant of the Lord. They are not my teachings, but His. He speaks through me."

"Yes, Imperial Leader. Sorry, Imperial Leader."

"So, as to the money business. You were given two hundred thousand dollars after the first part of your purification." He turns to the bald man on his left. "Exalted Leader, what is the ask?"

"Two point five million."

Clarence mentally calculates what he needs to cover the phony accounts and thinks, *I should add something for myself. I've earned it. They owe me! My finger alone is worth more than that.* So he says, "That's wrong, Donnie! It's *three* point five million."

The three at the table exchange looks. Donnie bristles and emits a low growl, but Imperial Leader silences him with a wave of his hand. He frowns at Clarence and says, "Leave us. Wait in the hall. We'll call you when we want you back in."

Clarence gives a nod to show he's obsequious and scurries out the door. Once outside, he stands in the hallway as close to the meeting room door as possible. As close as the van driver—standing with legs wide apart, hands held still in front of him, and his back against the door—will allow.

He must think he's the damned Secret Service, Clarence thinks. *Sunglasses? In here? And all in black so he practically blends into the walls? Cowboy boots and a leather vest?* But the asshole won't let him any closer, and he's not nearly close enough to hear what they're talking about inside.

He shifts his weight from one foot to the other and farts. It's more of a trumpet blast than he expected, and it reverberates in the short, featureless hall. *This idiot must've heard that,* he thinks. He's embarrassed but reminds himself he doesn't care about the big, muscle-bound jerk. He only cares about the Illustrious Ones, and if he can't hear them, they can't hear him.

After what seems like an eternity, Regal Leader opens the door and beckons him back in.

"That's a lot of money," Imperial Leader declares when Clarence is once more standing in front of him. "You think this comes without sacrifice?"

"But ... but the baby?"

"We have all had to make sacrifices. You know babies are innocent. When they pass on, they are all with the Lord."

Clarence nods. "Yes, Imperial Leader. I know that. I *believe* that!"

"Your wife is proving stubborn. You're not trying hard enough. You get her turned around, and the Lord may not make that demand of you. But the deed to your house—"

"But ..."

"Another 'but'?"

"Well, it's just ... I already gave you the condo in Regina. It's assessed at three hundred thousand dollars. I paid more than that for it. And you've only given me two hundred thousand."

"Have you heard the term 'forced sale value'?" Exalted Leader snickers.

Clarence looks at the floor. "So ... my houses *and* my finger?" he mutters.

Imperial Leader says, "You're welcome to withdraw at any time. Actually, I'm thinking you show such reluctance, maybe we should discontinue."

"No! You can't back out now!"

"We can, actually," Regal Leader says.

"No! You can't! We have a deal! And I've got proof! Look at my hand! I've been mutilated! And besides, that skeleton. Think the cops might have a missing person file for that?" He sets his jaw.

"Go to the police, Clarence. What will you tell them? That you ate your own finger? We made soup out of it? Don't be ridiculous." His voice has risen to the booming baritone of his sermons.

"Still the fact remains, I'm missing a finger!" He holds up his hand again as if to prove it.

"A time-honored ritual. We're a recognized religion, remember. As such, we have certain ... protections." Imperial Leader leans back, makes a tent with his hands, and swivels his chair side to side. "And we have the video of you saying you were participating of your own free will."

"You recorded that?"

"Of course." Imperial Leader raises his own three-fingered right hand and strokes his chin with his middle finger, prominently displaying the large gold and cabochon ruby ring, symbol of the Children of Noah's highest office. "So. Enough blubbering. Do you want to continue or not?"

Clarence slouches, heaves a sigh, and mutters, "Yeah."

"Your family home. Is there a mortgage on that?"

"No. Don't tell my wife though. She thinks we have a mortgage, and a big one. So my paycheck is mine. She whines she needs new winter boots, I remind her of the big mortgage payments. She knows her place. You know the old saying, 'Keep 'em pregnant in summer and barefoot in winter'!" Standing taller now, he taps his head with his left index finger and grins. "Just usin' the ol' noggin!"

But there's no answering grin on Imperial Leader's face. "You're going to have to get your wife to join us and sign over the title to your home," he says.

"But her name's not even on the title! I'm the one who bought the house."

"Yeah, smart weren't you," Donnie says. "You ever hear of dower rights?"

Clarence shakes his head.

"Some loans officer you are! She's your wife, and she lives there. You can't sell it out from under her. You can't even give it as security for a loan without her agreement—and then only after she gets independent legal advice."

"No!" Clarence shakes his head.

"Yes."

"Okay." He ruminates for a moment and then says, "Not a big problem. But where will we live?"

"You'll stay in the house, of course. We're not unreasonable men," Imperial Leader snorts. "Now leave us. Return to your bunk to await the last phase of your purification tonight."

"I won't come into this as one of the kneelers!" Clarence declares.

Imperial Leader tilts his head to the side, narrows his eyes, and says, "Oh, you *won't?*"

"I mean … I mean I don't want to." Clarence's shoulders slump. Another small fart.

"Leave us! And close the door." Imperial leader's booming voice resonates through the windowless room they'd thrown up inside the old curling rink when they lost the use of 10 Front Street.

Clarence scurries to the door, closing it behind him as instructed.

The three leaders sit quietly until they hear the outer door slam shut.

Then Imperial Leader says, "Goddamn, what a weasel! I think he's actually considering cannibalizing his own child. And he threatens us. *Us!*"

"He's even embezzling from his wife," Donnie says.

"Come on, Donnie," Nick chides, "we've all got plenty we don't tell our wives about."

"I just meant … well, regardless, if we ever had any idea this asshole—bank manager or loans officer or whatever the fuck he calls himself—might work for Prairie Equity, I'd say, no fuckin' way!"

"Aside from being such a weasel, didn't you tell me he left his last job under some, er, *questionable* circumstances?"

"Not exactly. Just his background check. We couldn't trace him back further than half a dozen years or so. Before he started at the bank, he was running some sketchy online investment deal. Long gone. I didn't care, really. We're not loaning him money or hiring him. Anyway, I figured the bank must've checked it out."

"Maybe we should revisit that," Nick says, squirming and tugging his pant leg down. "Might be something there we could leverage him with, in case we need it sometime down the road."

"Wish goddamned Schoenfeld wasn't such a fuckin' mule. He could talk sense to his sister. She'd listen to him," Donnie says. "Plus, he was fucking Klein back in the day. He could help us with both these problems."

"Oh, that's right, I knew your buddy was Weaver's brother-in-law, but I didn't know he and Klein were knocking boots," Nick says. "Before or after Tina?"

"Hmm, not sure. Maybe at the same time. In high school, anyway."

"Yeah, I seem to remember he was a young man with quite a reputation as a stud." Nick chuckles. "See what these small towns are like, Marcus? Everyone knows who's fucking who. Or everyone's related to everyone else." He turns his attention back to Donnie. "We need him to join. How come he hasn't?"

"Stubborn as a goat! I'm workin' on him."

"What if we made it worth his while?" Marcus asks.

"Maybe if he needed cash. But I run credit checks on him every once in a while, 'n' he's got his shit together. 'N' I just told you, I'm workin' on him, 'n' offering him a bribe would piss him off." Donnie turns to Nick. "Back to Weaver. I'd like to know exactly how much that fat fuck actually embezzled. The guy we sent in to cover his desk while he was our guest, when I talked to him earlier, said he's made a start but needs more time. Can we make it so Weaver doesn't go back to work for another week? This increase in the ask stinks worse than his farts."

"I'll get Doc to tell him he needs more rest, or—I don't know." Nick rocks back in his chair, weaves his fingers together behind his neck, and rests his head on them, with his eyes closed, thinking. "Something. Write him a scrip for stronger painkillers. Get his boss to make sure his medical leave is extended. I bet he'd be happy to lie around enjoying the drugs."

"We sure about the original ask?" Marcus wonders.

"What do you think?" Donnie scowls. "I forget things like that?"

"Of course not," Nick says, bringing his arms down again. "And he won't come in as a kneeler? He thinks he's in a position to bargain? What does he think he's going to come in as? A replacement for one of us?"

"Can we even do three point five million?" Marcus asks.

"It's a lot. Two point five was gonna seriously tax our cash flow. For sure we'll need some time to get that much in cash." Donnie drums his fingers on the table. "Hmm, I wonder if we have to give him that much. We might get the farm signed over without paying for it, no? Or maybe just a dollar, like Ten Front Street."

"Too bad Mrs. Schoenfeld isn't a member, so we'd be able to get a feel for how receptive she might be to signing over her property," Nick says.

"She's been a widow for years, Nick. Maybe you should go introduce yourself. Be real nice to her," Donnie leers.

"Goddamn, we're not *that* desperate!" Nick snorts. "Anyway, Weaver's still in play, and without the cash, he's in big trouble."

"I could give a shit if that asshole goes to jail. He might really like it. He'd be popular, with that jiggly, girly ass. Probably has man tits too. Unless he's as stupid as he looks, he's worryin' about it," Donnie says.

"Still, we're a ways off from gettin' even just his house. The wife needs to come in. Just signing away her dower rights won't do."

"No?" Imperial Leader asks.

"No. She'd have to have independent legal advice or it wouldn't hold water. What lawyer would advise her to do that, just so her husband can sign the house over to us?"

"Well," Marcus says, "he might talk his way out of that. He's hoodwinked her this far. Or, depending on how, er, *obedient* she is, he might get her to sign despite some lawyer telling her it's a bad idea."

"Hmm. Well, somehow, unless she agrees to donate the house, she *has* to sign. If it was a mortgage, wouldn't need independent legal advice. But he's got her believing they already have a mortgage. Maybe he outsmarted himself," Donnie says. "He's the only one who can lean on her to join, and she's the only one who can convince her mother to come in and sign over that farm. Even without the lease income from the potash plant, it's seven sections of good farmland. Worth way more than these rinky-dink houses. I don't like giving lard-ass three point five million on the off chance the mother-in-law will sign the property over, when we can only recover assets of a fraction of that for his two properties now."

"We've always been patient, remember," Nick says. "It's a lengthy process, takes time to make them see they should give their property to us even after they've joined. But we've always taken the long view."

"Still, it all hinges on ol' lady Schoenfeld. It's risky."

They all think about that for a moment.

"We're sure there's no mortgages or other liens?" Marcus asks.

"You think I don't run title searches?" Donnie snaps. "The house is free 'n' clear. The farm has a collateral mortgage for their line of credit. That's nuthin'."

"Donnie's always careful about that, Marcus," Nick says. "I knew there was no mortgage when I asked Weaver about it. I was just testing him." He drums his fingers on the table and shifts in his chair. "Maybe the old lady passes on sooner rather than later. Weaver's wife would inherit, no?"

"Only if she had a will 'n' left it to her. More likely she'd leave it to Rick or to both. If she doesn't have a will, there's the grandchildren. 'N' the old man, the grandfather, he's still alive. Not sure, but he might be entitled. Anyway, there's a lot of people in the way."

"Je-sus!" Marcus exclaims. "How'd we ever think this was going to work?"

"Oh, don't get your panties in a bunch." Donnie turns to face Marcus, eyes narrowed. "We're only in for two hundred K, and he wants more. If he doesn't bring his wife in or at least get her to sign the house over, we won't give him more. He's under a time crunch."

"For sure," Nick says, "what you might call highly motivated. Okay?"

"Okay." Marcus nods.

"Good. Any more questions?" Donnie scowls at Marcus and scratches the mole on his head again. When Marcus shakes his head, he continues, "What about this other problem? How're we going to get Klein out of the house? Meeting in this fucking old curling rink is only workable until we need the tunnel again. Just lucky she didn't show up till after the first part of Weaver's purification."

"I was wondering," Marcus says, "why'd you let her in the house anyway, Nick?"

Donnie snorts and throws up his hands.

"I had no choice," Nick responds, shutting Donnie down with a glare. "Her mother transferred the title to the house, but she's still entitled to the contents. I offered to have the whole house packed up and shipped to her at our cost, but she didn't bite. So I had to let her in to pack, don't you think? If I didn't, she'd really be suspicious. Plus, she showed up unexpectedly. We might have been able to have everything packed and ready to go out the door when she came."

"Well," Marcus says and shrugs, "I see how you had to let her in. If we had the place packed up, who knows how she'd have taken that? Might've been worse."

"Couldn't be worse! Her packin' by herself, it'll take weeks. Even if she gets a crew, there's a shitload of stuff in that house. Max says he didn't see any signs she's packing anything. So," Donnie says, "she's there, 'n' until we see a moving truck, we gotta assume she ain't plannin' on leaving. Dunno what it's gonna take to spook her so she doesn't want to be there. So far Max banging and clanging in the basement and rattling the screen door doesn't seem to bother her."

"It's only been a couple of nights," Nick says, rubbing his temples, "but we may have to up the ante. The rat Max left when he planted the bug, if she found it, didn't make her want to leave either. Maybe dump in some live rats? Would that be enough?"

"She'd just call an exterminator." Marcus shakes his head.

"Wouldn't want that!" Nick whistles under his breath while he thinks and then says, "What about your friend, Donnie? Would he go in on some pretext, like maybe just dropping in to say a friendly hello for old times' sake? Maybe leave a few bloody handprints around the place or something? Maybe he'd at least do that for a price?"

"Are you nuts? You didn't see his face when I told him she was back in town. Even if they don't hook up, he wouldn't think it's funny, 'n' he sure as hell won't help us terrorize her. He's suspicious of us as it is. Back in the day, I tried to get him to come to us when he needed a loan for all that new equipment, but he wouldn't even talk. His old man 'n' him got some big fuckin', farmer-lovin' bank in Regina to give 'em a government-backed loan, 'n' now even without the old bastard in the picture, they're financing his new house. Pisses me off."

"Pisses you off? What about Clarence? He didn't get the mortgage through him?"

"If Clarence was drownin' in shit, Rick would throw him an anvil."

"Huh. A job for Max then. We've got the bug. Have him watch her, watch the house. Make sure she hears the rumor that the place is haunted. Then, instead of just banging and clanging, start moving some stuff." Nick stretches and yawns. "Not too much. At least not the first time. He knows the drill. Meantime, we'll set our sights on Clarence's wife and her bringing the mother in. Prairie Equity hasn't been in business since Mr. Capone by being impatient." He stands, shrugs off his robe, and tugs his pants away from his crotch. "These goddamned tight pants you guys had to have as part of these outfits are like a cheap mansion—no ballroom. I'm going back to my own," he grouses, "and for now, let's just hope Ms. Klein and Mr. Schoenfeld don't hook up. You know women. She might think she's in love and never leave."

"Maybe we should build a new access," Marcus says. "I've looked at the town maps showing the tunnels, what properties they're under. We have two houses right on top of other unused branches and more that are close enough to connect with a small amount of tunneling. We could just abandon Ten Front Street."

Donnie shoves his chair back and stands. "There's no other tunnel that links up with the ceremonial crypt."

"Do we really need a crypt that big? Couldn't we just make a new tunnel a little wider?" Marcus says.

"Why should we go to a lot of fuckin' trouble and expense to make something not as good?"

"Well, it might be worth it to stay anonymous. Stay under the radar. Hard enough keeping everything under wraps with the number of True Believers we already have."

"No one's gonna talk. You think any of them wanna give up communion? Or have anyone find out what they do at communion? And need it or not, that fuckin' property's ours. Why can't we get the cops to toss the stinky out?" Donnie asks.

"I talked to Chief Johannsen this morning. He'll help, of course, but there's something about squatter's rights or right of survivorship or something. May need a court order. I have to see what our lawyers say. Got an appointment tomorrow." Nick sighs. "I also told Johannsen she might report a prowler. He'll make sure the rank and file know it's just a neurotic big-city girl with an overactive imagination." He chuckles. "By the way, we got hookers for tonight?"

"Just the boy," Marcus replies. "The one the ladies said they wanted. Apparently he has a big dick and knows how to use it. And oh, Max says he's in. I didn't know he was purified."

"He's not. It's one of the perks of his job," Nick says. "Don't worry, he won't join the queue; he knows I'd knock his head off if he did, but he likes the Mingling, and he's always popular. As long as everyone thinks he's purified, he's welcome to take part."

"Pretty sure they know the boy with the big dick isn't purified," Marcus chuckles, "and they don't seem fussy about that! And for ladies, a dozen or so are eager to take communion."

"All fat old bags?" Donnie asks.

"Not all," Marcus responds. "Anyhow, put the hoods over their faces and it doesn't make a difference. The fat ones are nice and soft."

They're all standing now, chuckling.

Donnie and Marcus shed their robes.

"We reconvene here at ten o'clock. I'm going home. Dinner with my wife," Nick says. "Put the cushions out, would you, guys?"

Rick leans his elbow on the table. He's listening to Gramps speak but can't take his eyes off Kathy, who, at the table across from him, is even more alluring than she was twenty years ago. If he didn't know better, he'd swear she couldn't be older than twenty-five. How is that possible? Where are her crow's feet? He barely hears Gramps say, "I remember that old house of yours. It was the talk of the town back in the day, a mansion when it was built. I was a baby myself then. People talked about it for years."

"Oh!" Kathy says. "I knew it had been in my family for generations, but I really don't know more than that. My mother never talked about it. There's a history?"

"A lot of stuff went on there if you can believe what people said. Henry Klein and Al Capone were like this." He crosses his middle finger over his index. "Built that house when Capone's guys were building their tunnels. It was a mansion when it was built. I was a baby myself then, but people talked about it for years."

Rick's mother comes in the back door with a pail of peas and stops short when she sees Kathy. "What's this?" she asks, her mouth set in a hard line.

"You remember Kathy," Rick says, tearing his gaze away from Kathy. "She's going to be in Pillerton, for a while at least. We're going to take a run into town for dinner. Just stopped here to change out of my work clothes." Rick slides his chair back and stands.

"Hello," Kathy says, smiling.

"Yes. Hi." Mutti turns her back and puts the pail on the counter with a clatter.

"They found ol' Hank face down in the river," Gramps says.

"Hank?" Kathy asks, turning back to him.

"Henry Klein. Al Capone's sidekick."

"My great-grandfather drowned?"

"What?" Gramps says.

"My great-grandfather?"

"Your grandfather?" Gramps closes his eyes.

They wait for Gramps to continue. But he takes a deep breath and then looks around with a puzzled expression. He looks up at Rick, his pale blue eyes watery, and asks, "Have we got ice cream?"

"I think so." Rick goes to the freezer and looks inside. "Yup, vanilla and Neapolitan. You want it now or later, Gramps?"

"What?"

"Your ice cream?"

"Ice cream? I never liked ice cream."

"Okay," Rick says. He closes the freezer compartment and turns to Kathy. "I'll just be a couple minutes." He heads into the hall and clomps up the stairs, taking two at a time.

Kathy orders mushroom tortellini and a glass of house white, and scans the near-empty restaurant while Rick orders the chicken special and a beer.

During the twenty minutes or so they were driving to the Holiday Inn from Rick's farm, they caught up on the what-have-you-been-doing-for-the-past-twenty-years small talk, so he knows about her job, and Brent.

And she knows about his ten-year marriage to Tina Audet and their daughter, Sarah, who's been living with him since she was twelve. He told her about spending a year at Olds Agricultural College, the barn fire that killed his father, and the house he's having built.

But they haven't acknowledged the elephant in the room.

"I enjoyed your Gramps," Kathy says.

"I'm surprised he remembered you. But then he's pretty good at remembering things that happened a long time ago, and you haven't changed."

"Well, thank you. I know that's not true. But thank you." Kathy takes a sip of wine. "Your mom seems, how can I put it, like she's miffed at me?"

"Don't take it personally. She seems to be like that, angry, a lot lately." Rick takes a long pull of his beer. "I worry it might be early signs of Alzheimer's and she'll end up like Gramps. If you knew how often she rants about how it's my fault the barn burned. Just can't give it a rest. I should've built my own house years ago, right after Tina got the one in town." He shrugs. "Live 'n' learn. How're you gettin' on in your old house?"

"It's not mine, you know, at least not yet. My mother gave it to the Children of Noah. My friend Penny—remember her from school? She's a lawyer now. Lives near me in Vancouver. She's coming tomorrow, and we're going to look into how that transfer all came about. She thinks I should dispute it."

"Can you?"

"We'll see, I guess. But for now I'm going to live in it. And to answer your question, it's pretty much the same as when I left. Some weird stuff's been happening, though." She tells him about the clanging noises, the screen door banging, the door being unlocked when she was sure she'd locked it, and the strange man pulling weeds.

"Maybe it'd be a good idea to get new locks."

"You're right. Never know how many people have keys. Did you know the Children of Noah hold their meetings there?"

"Yeah. I forgot, though."

"I guess it started when my father left and my mother needed the money."

"Oh. Helped her out, I guess." He takes a piece of his chicken and chews thoughtfully. "Thinking about that guy who was at your place earlier today—I sure don't know anyone in town who looks or dresses like that."

"What about his car?"

"Well, there's about a thousand of those around. If you knew the make, maybe."

"Yeah, that would help. Didn't really get much of a look at it, what with that overgrown hedge. I did notice a bumper sticker, a green bumper sticker, but I couldn't read it."

"What if it was a rental car? They all have bumper stickers. You know anyone who might have had to travel some, maybe fly here for your mother's funeral?"

"Oh, I didn't think of that. But there isn't going to be a funeral. The Children of Noah had my mother cremated before I got here. Elder Reeves has the urn. They had a service." She snuffles, then quickly collects herself and continues, "We have no relatives that I know of, at least I don't remember ever meeting any, and I think her only friends were Children of Noah."

"Maybe someone who left the C-O-N?"

Kathy laughs. "The C-O-N? Is that what you call the Children of Noah?"

"That's what everyone I know calls them." He grins. "Too disrespectful?"

"No, in fact I think it's perfect! Just quit spelling it and call it the Con! My friend Penny's going to love it! But to get back to your question, I've never heard of anyone leaving." Kathy furrows her brow. "But I don't know all that much about it."

"Yeah, I don't understand how people get sucked into that," Rick says, stirring his rice, "but then, my brother-in-law, Clarence, just joined. He was raised in some other crazy fringe religion, so I suppose this one just seems normal to him." He studies her face as he chews, drinking in her dark eyes that seem so large, her smooth, olive-toned skin, and the tiny dimples that form when she favors him with her wide smile. Then his gaze drops to the crystal pendant on a fine chain around her neck and, from there, to the alluring swell of her breasts. He feels a stirring and wonders how it can be that she's grown more lovely over the years, while he's just gotten older.

"Oh, a man? I thought they were all women," she continues, sorting through her tortellini for another mushroom, unaware of his scrutiny. "You know, bored housewives or divorced. Or like my mother, husbands ran off. And widows. All drooling over handsome young Elder Reeves. In a completely puritan way of course! Filled some need, I thought. How

I dreaded those meetings! My mother was so, well, so *into* it. The whole lot of them, batshit crazy. 'Course I didn't realize it at the time. They had me convinced. You might remember me yammering about having to be 'purified.' But then I went away ..." She spears a tortellini and a slice of mushroom. Puts it in her mouth. Chews and washes it down with a sip of wine. "This is really tasty. Where was I going with that ... oh, the Children of Noah. Being purified. When I left Pillerton, it was as if I'd been holding my breath all my life and could finally breathe. There was nothing for me here, so I never came back."

Rick clears his throat. "Yeah, uh, about that, Kathy ... You know, before you left for university ... how we broke up 'n' all—"

"Rick," she says, cutting off his thought, "we were just kids! It was a different life. It's behind me now. Behind *us*." She smiles. "Friends?"

"Okay! Friends," he agrees. His smile crinkles his eyes. "If you want, I mean, if it'll help, I'll go through the house with you when I drop you off. Check out that basement for you."

"Thanks!" She takes a deep breath. "That'd help me feel better."

The wind rises around nine, and a fierce rainstorm begins. By ten, rain is coming down in sheets. There is a respectable turnout at the curling rink despite the storm.

Since Clarence was in this same room earlier, floor cushions have been arranged in rows for the kneelers. The overhead fluorescents are off, so the room's dark but for the candles on the altar against the wall at the front and dimmed LEDs in half a dozen wall sconces down the sides,

Clarence is standing shoulder to shoulder with the Illustrious Ones. Well, if he's honest, not quite shoulder to shoulder. They're equally spaced out along the front wall, about two feet between them. And he's at the end, not in the middle. Exalted Leader is immediately to his left. Then there's the podium, with Imperial Leader and Regal Leader on the other side of that. They each have a cushion on the floor in front of them.

He'd rather be in the middle. Still, he's in a position of importance. His robe is black, though, as if he's ordinary congregation. *That'll change soon*, he thinks, and presses his lips into a smug grin.

It's a little drafty, being naked under the robe. But the polyester material sliding ever so slightly back and forth across his penis feels nice. So nice it's giving him an erection. He knows some in the congregation see it despite the dim lighting. Far from being embarrassed, he's proud. The small one in the front row has looked his way several times. Staring right at it! He gives his hips a little forward and back in her direction. She frowns and quickly looks away.

Clarence narrows his eyes. Knowing what's coming, he thinks, *Look away, will you? You just wait, sweetheart.*

Imperial Leader, Elder Reeves, begins his sermon in Latin, much of it singing in his deep baritone, with the congregation kneeling in front of him, responding, "Amen!" or "Hallelujah!" on cue. Not that Clarence or any of them has a clue what he's saying. If it wasn't for daydreaming about the purification, and if he wasn't standing, Clarence thinks he might doze off.

Then Imperial Leader moves behind the podium and pushes the button to turn on the light that shines down on the book. He places his hands one on each side of the podium and says, "The liturgy on this special evening was written for the purification ritual and Holy Communion. It is taken from the book of Esther, chapter 1: 'Now it came to pass in the days when King Ahasuerus sat on the throne of his kingdom, in the third year of his reign, he made a feast to show the riches of his glorious kingdom and the honor of his excellent majesty. And Vashti the queen made a feast for the women of the royal house, which belonged to King Ahasuerus. On the seventh day, when the heart of the king was merry with wine, he commanded Vashti to come to him …'" *Blah, blah, blah*, Clarence thinks. He's been told about the ritual and fantasizes about what's to come. His penis is throbbing as though it might explode. *Get the fuck on with it, Reeves*, he thinks. *Can't you put a sock in it?* Then his interest is piqued by what he's saying: "And so shall all wives give their husbands honor, both great and small or so shall they be set aside and have no estate according to the law …"

Interesting. Wives shall honor their husbands or be set aside with no estate. *If I take the money for the house and forget about Jeanie, I'd really just be following the rules of the Bible?*

Finally, Elder Reeves closes the prayer book and continues. "Women, obey the statutes and your husbands. Give your husbands honor. All purified men are your husbands. Men, be indulgent with your wives; love and protect them and keep them safe. All purified women are your wives. Remember, we live surrounded by sin. Be sanctified and purify yourselves in Holy Communion. Remember, we are all children in the eyes of the Lord, and by keeping His statutes, the Children of Noah have from the time of Noah been chosen and blessed by the Lord. The Lord promises everlasting life, and by keeping his statutes, we shall be together always in the afterlife. Only those who believe in the Lord and are purified shall be saved.

"Amen."

The congregation responds, "Amen!"

Then Imperial leader sings out, *"Awmindah formishda!"*

And the congregation chants in response, *"Awmindah formishda! Awmindah formishda deya!"*

Latin too, Clarence thinks. But it seems to be just a couple of words, so he'll be able to learn those easily enough.

When Imperial Leader steps away from the podium, the chanting stops, "Those wishing purification see Acolyte Audet for sanctifying," he says.

The black-shrouded figures form a line at Clarence's right. He's pleased to see the first supplicant is the hottie with the long blond hair in the red-trimmed robe who passed him the silver goblet in the first part of his purification. His goddamned asshole brother-in-law's gorgeous ex-wife. Elder Reeves called her Acolyte, and he now understands the reason her robe is different. Fuckwit Rick couldn't keep her, and now he's going to stick his erection in her hot mouth! She kneels before him, and as instructed, he pulls his robe open to expose his nakedness. But instead of taking him in her mouth, she anoints his penis with oil from a silver flask, stroking and squeezing to spread the oil evenly. He fears for a moment it might be enough to make him come, but then she moves over to anoint Exalted Leader. *What? She's leaving? Isn't she supposed to take me in her mouth?*

She anoints all three Illustrious Leaders and doesn't take them in her mouth either, just comes back to stand at Clarence's right hand. It's all right. He'll fuck her during the Mingling.

Each supplicant stands in front of her to be anointed before approaching Clarence. He's curious about how females are anointed, but the first supplicant has her back to him, and whatever they're doing is hidden in her robes. Before he sees anything, he's distracted by her kneeling before him, cupping his genitals, and taking his penis in her mouth.

"Ah-ha-ha-ah!" he sighs.

However, after just a few sucks, she goes to kneel in front of Exalted Leader.

The next supplicant is the small, plain woman who looked away when he thrust his erection at her earlier. After a very tentative lick/suck, she starts to break away. Clarence grabs her head and forces his penis deep into her mouth. Moving his hips forward and back several times, hard, he mutters under his breath, "Fix … you … bitch!" and ejaculates with a loud "Ahhh!" With his eyes shut, he pushes himself against her face, feeling her nose pressed into his pubic hair. He savors the pure, throbbing release, the all-over-body flush.

She's trying to break away from him, her hands pushing his thighs, but he doesn't let go until he feels strong enough to stand straight again. When he takes his hands away from her head, she sags. Gagging and choking, she nearly falls sideways. Her face is tear-streaked. Exalted Leader quickly steadies her, helping her to her feet. He places his hands on her shoulders, and Clarence hears him tell her quietly, "Enough, Sister. You are blessed in the Lord."

And after a moment, she wipes her mouth and her face on her sleeve, gives Exalted Leader a slight bow, and returns to the back of the room without approaching the other leaders.

Clarence is only peripherally aware of this, as he's signaling the next supplicant to come and kneel before him. Despite the number of supplicants, he doesn't get a second erection even though he's rubbing himself vigorously between them. It's awkward, though, since he has to use his left hand.

He's aware the Illustrious Ones have quietly ejaculated, maybe even twice. *They're sucking them longer,* he thinks. *Probably harder too. The lousy bitches aren't doing me right!*

Finally, the congregation is back kneeling. Imperial Leader moves to the center in front of the podium and motions Clarence to join him. He stands behind him and cups his shoulders.

"This man, Brother Weaver, is now purified!" he declares. "He's attained the highest degree of purification! Praise the Lord!"

The congregation answers in unison, "Praise the Lord!"

Imperial Leader turns Clarence to face him and says, "You may now take your place in the congregation, my son."

Clarence's face registers his shock. "Me? There with *them*?"

Imperial Leader gives him an intense, dark, penetrating, unblinking stare that is unmistakably threatening. "I said join them." He raises his arm to point to the congregation.

Clarence's shoulders slump, and he grumbles, "Join the kneelers!" But when he turns to do as he's bidden, he realizes with a jolt no one's kneeling now. They're crawling about, assuming various positions with other congregants. So many nearly naked bodies! Kissing! Fondling! Fucking!

The Illustrious Ones have taken chairs and are sitting back, watching.

Why did I think I'd rather be up there instead of down here? he wonders. He hikes open his robe and, finally erect again, grabs his member.

When the Mingling ends and Clarence joins the queue of those leaving, Regal Leader pulls him aside, saying, "Not you."

He grins. *Of course*, he thinks, *here's where I get my red robe!* He's been wondering when this would happen and was going to ask but then figured it would be at the induction ceremony, which isn't scheduled until late September. A long time to wait! But fortunately, he's been thinking about what title he'd like, so he'll be ready to make suggestions now. Assuming Regal Leader isn't demoted, Distinguished Leader sounds good, but he likes Eminent Leader better.

Once there are only the four of them and the ever-present van driver, Nick says, "Max will take you back to your bunk now. You'd better clean up. A rental car's waiting for you. Leave while it's still dark. Go to Regina and then come home as if you've just come in on the red-eye."

"But ..." Clarence's shoulders droop and he frowns. "Why was I sent to join the kneelers? And anyway, my wife ... she'll want to know why I didn't call her to come and meet my plane!"

"Then drop the car off at the airport and have her pick you up there," Nick says, "and no one ever said you'd be anything other than a kneeler. Be glad you were accepted for the purification ritual. And Clarence? Next time you're fortunate enough to join those at the front? Do not speak or put your hands on a supplicant again."

Clarence feels a surge of anger, squares his shoulders, and bites back an angry retort. Then he clamps his teeth shut and returns Nick's unblinking stare.

At a nod from Nick, Max takes his arm and hurries him to the van. He's pushed in the side door, and the door is slid closed behind him. Max is in the driver's seat and driving away before Clarence even has a chance to get seated and buckled in.

"Ahhh, great communion as always," Nick says, returning to his chair.

Donnie pushes aside the heavily embroidered cloth covering the narrow table that serves as an altar, and gets out a bottle of Crown Royal and three shot glasses. He pours drinks while Marcus rolls the podium into the corner.

Nick takes the drink handed to him and swirls the liquid in his glass for a moment. Then he says, "You always have to get in there and fuck Tina, Donnie?"

"Yeah, well, you little dogs just move over and let the big dog git 'er done!" Donnie gloats. "She's hot."

"And she's your buddy's ex."

Donny shrugs.

"Well, if you have to join the Mingling, fuck some of the others once in a while," Nick continues, "especially your secretary. She looks at you like you're a god. Don't want her to lose that look."

"I can fuck Diana at the office anytime I want. Believe me, we make good use of that suite in the back."

"Okay." Nick drains his glass and holds it out for Donnie to refill.

"Speaking of Diana, that fuckin' Weaver! He damn near choked her. That was assault! Did you see that fuck-you look he gave me when I called him on it?"

Marcus nods, and Donnie says, "He's a dumb shit."

"Well, he sure makes bad decisions," Nick allows. "I mean, you get wobbly-kneed, you lean back against the wall, no need to grab on. And remember how long it took him to find his way out of the tunnel? Two hours? More? We were all pretty well shit-faced by the time he came up. Didn't he remember which way we went in? I know it's dim, but he should've seen the light from the other tunnel even if he didn't remember turning left."

"Well," Marcus says, refilling his glass, "he lost a lot of blood. You notice how pale he was when he finally came up? He was unconscious when we left. Who knows how long it took him to come to. You did botch that amputation, Nick."

"I suppose you could do better?" Donnie scowls.

"No, Donnie, Marcus is right. Too bad old Tommy passed. He was deadly with that cleaver. If I used it, I'd take off half the hand."

"Well, he liked his work more'n you do," Donnie says.

"Yeah. If I'd spent more time with this guy ahead of it, I think even I would've enjoyed it! It's harder than you think, though, cutting through the bone. I got lucky and hit the knuckle, or it would've been even worse. Next time, bolt cutters. Or kitchen shears maybe."

"That'd go over big, ceremonial bolt cutters!" Marcus chuckles.

"Maybe get them engraved or something. Don't need to worry about it now. No one else has come to us with a problem. Just regular folks who can pay off their loans in more conventional ways. But Weaver—I've got an uneasy feeling about this guy. Something's off."

"Dealings I've had with him at work, he's always been an arrogant prick. It's just his asshole personality," Donnie opines.

"I think he has an exaggerated opinion of his own intelligence," Marcus says, "and thinks he can con everyone. He might be a runner."

"Might be," Nick considers it. "He's so goddamned cocky … maybe he *does* think he can take the money and skip before the auditors come, before they even smell the cooked books. Wonder what he did with the first two hundred K, if he even put it against any of the bogus loans. I wouldn't put it past him to slip it into his own pocket."

"Two hundred K isn't enough to run with. He's signed the condo over," Donnie reminds them, "so we're covered. Let's keep our eye on the prize. He's just the beginning of this deal. We get this done—big commission checks."

"That's the name of the game." Nick grins.

Marcus nods and says, "But let's not have him at the front again."

"Absolutely not! Maybe we won't accept him as a True Believer, or allow him to take communion, period. But we won't tell him that just yet." Nick drinks his shot, slams his glass down, and fills it again. "Let him dream about all the head he's going to get and all the ladies just lying around waiting for him to fuck them. I can't wait to see his face when he finds out that after his house is signed over to us, those bogus mortgage payments he's so proud of become real, and he's just kneeling in the congregation with the rest of the sheep."

"I'll drink to that!" Marcus says. They all chuckle and shoot their whiskey.

"You know, I've been thinking," Nick begins as he refills their glasses, "how long's it been since we had a purification ritual for a virgin?"

"Ha!" Marcus snorts. "Can you even find a virgin of consenting age?"

"Yeah, it was better back in the day. They only had to be twelve then, and their parents brought them in," Donnie says. He sees Marcus's giant caterpillar eyebrows shoot up. "What's that pissy look for, Marcus?"

"No twelve-year-olds," Nick intercedes, "eighteen at a minimum. Been that way for decades, since long before you joined, Donnie, and those twelve-year-olds were married off right after. Men had three or four wives then, more even. Actual wives, not just ceremonial. Hell, that went out before *my* time, when the goddamned government stuck their noses in."

"Just sayin'." Donnie quaffs his drink. "Them was the good ol' days."

Marcus snorts and shakes his head. Donnie glares at him.

"Well, we could use some new members," Nick says. "I have a few ideas."

"Who?" Donnie asks.

"I don't want to name names just yet," Nick says, getting to his feet. "Right now I'm taillights."

"By the way, Nick," Marcus says, "if we get new members, let's make sure we don't get any who understand Latin. But you do have a nice singing voice."

The wind has picked up, and rain, in big wind-driven drops, pummels the windshield. Kathy says, "I think I may be sorry I left my umbrella in Vancouver. I didn't expect rain like this!"

"Neither did Environment Canada," Rick says as he steers the pickup to the curb in front of 10 Front Street.

They both get out and hurry through the gate and up to the veranda, stopping by the steps so she can point out the pile of weeds and how everything's been cleared from the window. The strange man's footprints, just barely visible in the weak light from the veranda, are already being obliterated by the rain.

"You didn't weed up there?" Rick asks.

Kathy shakes her head and points to the narrow strip along the sidewalk. "Just along here."

"Window's pretty small. You think someone could've gotten in through it?"

"That's what I was wondering."

"I'd be surprised. But we'll take a look. Let's get out of this rain."

Inside, she pours a glass of wine for herself and hands him a beer. Drinks in hand, they tour the first and second floors, and then go partway up the narrow staircase into the attic. Rick pulls the string that should turn on the light, but nothing happens. "Needs a new light bulb," he says. He pulls out his iPhone and turns on the torch app but sees nothing but a jumble of boxes.

Back in the kitchen, Rick sets his bottle on the table, opens the basement door, and iPhone in hand, goes down the steep stairs without a second thought. Kathy follows carefully.

Rick finds the light and pulls the chain, but as with the attic light, the bulb's burned out. With just the iPhone, there's sufficient light to see a typical old basement. Smelly. Dank. Uneven concrete floor. The beams are so low they have to duck under them, and there are piles of junked furniture in the darkest corner. Near the stairs, there's an old, disused gravity coal furnace and, beside it, a newer forced-air oil furnace. The water heater is behind it.

"Looks okay," Rick says as he examines it. "I'd need a better flashlight to see the date tag, but it doesn't look, you know, ancient. Don't see any leaks. I'll try turning the temperature up, see if that gets you at least enough water for a bath."

Then they check the area around the window. A mismatched washer and dryer are beneath it, with a thick, undisturbed film of dust on them.

"Anyone who did manage to squeeze through that window would've had to land on the washer," Rick points out. "Couldn't've done that without leaving marks in the dust. And it's latched from the inside, so he'd've had to break it."

"Oh! You're right. I'm just letting my imagination run away with me. But still, all that noise at night? I wonder why it's so quiet now."

"Maybe the water heater hasn't kicked in for a while? We should run some hot water, enough that the thing has to take some water and heat it, and see if that sets it off."

"Oh, that makes sense. And I guess I'm going to have to get used to coming down here unless I want to take my dirty clothes to the Laundromat."

"The Laundromat here in town closed years ago, so you'd have to find one in Regina."

"Yup, going to have to get used to coming down here." Kathy sighs. "Just hope these old machines actually work and they're not something else I have to buy. Doesn't look like they've been used in a while."

Near the bottom of the stairs, there's a rough, battered workbench. Rick spots a hammer on it and picks it up. "Can always use a hammer," he says.

"Don't know why I might need it, but at least it's one less thing on my RONA list if I do!"

They go back upstairs, Kathy bolting up ahead of Rick. She goes to the fridge and refills her glass. "Another beer? Coffee maybe?" she asks.

"You have decaf?"

"Yup. Decaf it is." She roots through the cupboards, finds the box she's looking for, puts a pod in the coffee maker, closes the lid, and pushes the brew button. In a minute, the homey scent of freshly brewed coffee fills the kitchen, and she sets the mug on the table.

"Sorry, I don't have cream. I wasn't expecting company. But there's french vanilla and Cinnabon."

"Don't apologize," he says. "I like french vanilla, when there's no half-and-half anyway." He takes the bottle she hands him, flips the lid open, and adds it to his coffee, then picks up his mug and walks to the dining room doorway. He turns back and says, "I don't want to sound like I'm making light of your nervousness about this house, Kathy, but it's beautiful. Needs some updating, but really a heritage home. As Gramps said, it was a mansion in its day."

"Yeah, I know, there's a lot of nice things about it. It would be a good restoration project, and it wouldn't take much. But"—she shudders—"it's just got such a bad feel to it. Such a malevolent feel. I don't know why. When I let it, it makes me shiver. Don't you feel it?"

"Hmm, nope, can't say I do. But if you feel it, that's what counts. You know, if it helps, I could stay a couple of nights. On the couch! If you want. Just so you have someone else in the house until your friend comes."

Kathy considers it. "Yes," she decides, "I'd like you to stay. Maybe you'll recognize the noise if you hear it. It really spooked me last night. I'm not sure now that it *is* the water heater, seeing it's about in the middle of the basement and the noise is loudest in the front bedroom. It seems to be traveling up the old heat duct. You don't have to take the couch. You can sleep there." She sips her wine and wonders why she poured it. "You know," she says, "I think I'll have a decaf too." She puts her glass in the fridge, gets a fresh pod of decaf, and takes it to the coffee maker. When she opens the cabinet under the sink and pulls the garbage can forward to toss in the spent pod, she gives a little squeak of surprise and jumps back.

"A mouse!" she explains.

Looking closer, they see not a mouse but a small rat, dead, in the space between the garbage bin and the side of the cabinet.

Rick picks it up by the tail and pulls it out. "This guy's been here a while."

"Really? Why didn't I see it before? Why is it here? There's nothing in here to attract a rat. And why is it dead?"

"Maybe poisoned. They go for water if they've eaten Warfarin and can even chew through copper pipes to get at it. That may be why it came in here. Still, there's pipes in the basement. Odd it didn't just stay down there." He dumps the rat in the garbage.

"I don't like the idea of poison! What if a cat or a dog or a bird eats a poisoned rat? I'll have to check to make sure there aren't more lying around."

"Might be more live ones too. You might want to get a trap. Or a cat."

"Trap for now, I think," Kathy says. "How'd it get into the cabinets, though?"

"See?" Rick points to the holes for the pipes going through to the basement. "They can squeeze through amazingly small places."

"Hmm. Well, nothing to worry about, I guess. Just so you know, I'm not afraid of mice. Or rats. It's just that they always startle you." She slides onto a chair and puts her mug on the table.

He takes a seat across from her and says, "Of course, that's all it is. They just startle you."

She sees the teasing grin and the crinkles around his eyes, and grins back.

Rain drumming on the window next to the table is louder now, and lightning illuminates the whole sky just a fraction of a second ahead of thunder so loud it rattles the panes and leaves behind the scent of ozone.

"That's close," Rick says. "I hope there's no lightning rods on this house!"

"Lightning rods?"

"Common back in the thirties. According to Gramps, traveling salesmen came around claiming they prevented lightning strikes. Lots of electrical storms on the prairies, you know, so everyone bought them and stuck them up on their roofs, but instead of preventing lightning from striking, they attract it."

"Now that you mention it, I do remember seeing the old farmhouses with those things! So much I've forgotten." Kathy shakes her head. "We sure don't get thunderstorms like this on the coast!"

"Does it bother you?"

"No, it's kind of entertaining if that's the right word. People flock to the west side of Vancouver Island to watch the winter storms. I've been there myself. Of course, there it's just wind, rain, and massive waves crashing up onto the shore. Something about it is mesmerizing, though. Have you been to the coast?"

"Well, Tina and I went to Vancouver on our honeymoon 'n' we took the ferry to Victoria, stayed there a couple days. But no storms, just rain." He sips his coffee while he studies her face. "Incessant, gray, cold rain. For the whole week."

"Well, it *was* your honeymoon," she teases. "Probably didn't want to spend a lot of time outside anyway."

"Yeah, well," he snorts.

She meets his gaze and then breaks eye contact, as she chews a blip off a hangnail on her thumb. "Sorry," she says, "that was overly familiar."

"It's fine." But it's a conversation stopper.

She stifles a yawn. "Tired yet?" she asks.

"A bit. 'N' you definitely are," he says, looking at his watch. "It's after one. Where'd the time go? Let's call it a day."

Rick finishes his coffee and follows Kathy up, stopping at the top of the stairs. She points to the front bedroom and says, "Make yourself at home. Good night."

He nods. "Good night." But he doesn't go into the bedroom or turn away.

Neither does she. She turns her face up, lips slightly parted. Rick leans forward and kisses her mouth. Then her mind whirls back to high school, his good-night kisses at the door. Her mother waiting inside. *Where were you? What were you doing?* Pushes her up against the wall. *I can smell him on you!* With a sharp intake of breath, she stiffens.

"Sorry," he breathes, "now I'm being overly familiar."

She whispers, "Don't be sorry. I'm the one who should apologize."

She steps away and heads to her own room, then turns in the doorway and says, "See you in the morning," and closes the door behind her.

Jeanie drives into the farmyard, skirting puddles from the previous night's fierce rainstorm. The two older boys, who've learned how to release themselves from their car seats, pile out of the van almost before it stops. She goes around to the side door and unbuckles her youngest, giving him a hug and a kiss before setting him on the ground to toddle off after his brothers. They make right for the puddle and splash in it. Jeanie shakes her head and imagines they'll go through several changes of clothing before she returns. At least they're wearing their gum boots.

Mutti appears on the veranda and comes out to greet them. The boys can't manage more than a "Hi, Gramma," as busy as they are trying to make the biggest splashes and channel the water into the smaller puddle next to it.

"So, you say Clarence wants you to pick him up at the airport?" Mutti frowns. "I thought he wasn't coming home until next week. I have things I need to do today."

"I'm sorry, Mutti. I didn't get any notice either. I could take the kids, but if I have to park and go in, it's such a hassle dragging the three of them … and it's so much nicer for them not to have to be in the van for more than an hour."

"It's fine." Mutti scowls. "I'd rather have them here than traipsing into town just to turn around and come back home."

"You know I appreciate it, Mutti." Jeanie sighs and leans from side to side, stretching her back.

"Your brother!" Mutti says. "You know what he did? He brought that girl with him yesterday. You remember the girlfriend he had in high school? Kathy something?"

"Oh, Kathy!" Jeanie says and smiles. "Yes, I remember Kathy. She was nice. She's back in town?"

"Yeah," she snorts. "They said they were going for dinner, but Rick didn't come home until this morning."

"He's an adult, Mutti," Jeanie says.

"But stirring up all those old things again! Mark my words, no good will come of that!" Another snort.

"You can't live other people's lives for them, Mutti," Jeanie tells her. "Well, I gotta run. Clarence was already at the airport when he called. He'll be getting antsy. I should be home in about an hour and half." She goes to the driver's door, gets settled in the seat, and yells, "Thanks!" as she drives away.

Mutti's got such a selective memory, she thinks, *always blamed Kathy for breaking Rick's heart.* How many times has she said he wouldn't have married Tina otherwise? She's forgotten that after meeting Kathy, she told Rick she was impressed with his taste in girlfriends. He had laughed and said something like "Don't worry, Mutti, I know which ones to bring home."

I love him, she thinks, *but now I realize what a cocky creep he was back then. Well, now he's had some life lessons and seems better for it. I wish the same could be said for Clarence.*

Jeanie's more apprehensive than eager about seeing him. He's been gone nearly two weeks, without even a phone call home. It's been peaceful not having his hangdog face at the table, his constant hollering at the kids. *Maybe he'll be less bitchy*, she thinks, *having had a break from the chaos. Funny, a guy who wants unlimited kids can't stand what all kids do—make noise and tumble around. I'd be worried about kids who just played quietly in their rooms like he keeps telling them to.*

Rick's suggestion that she and the kids should come and live with him struck a chord. When she told him she wasn't sure she'd made a mistake marrying Clarence, she wasn't being truthful. If he knew how many times she's thought about divorcing him, kicking him out! But what would she do on her own? Hardly any equity in the house. Big mortgage she couldn't afford even if she had a job and didn't have to pay for childcare. What if he didn't pay child support?

Did she ever think he was attractive? Lust for him? When he was thirty pounds lighter, maybe? Did she ever love him or even like him? She must have, once, but it's hard to remember. She dreads the thought of having intercourse with him again once the baby's born. Fortunately, he never takes very long, but she resents that there's never anything in it for her, except always the risk of pregnancy. *Because of his religion, not mine*, she thinks. *I am going to do something before it comes to that; if not a tubal ligation, definitely the pill.*

I couldn't really live with Rick. Not forever. And as a temporary thing? His house is well under way, but there's still an awful lot to be done before there is actually a "Rick's house." But the farmhouse is big. Maybe move in there when Rick's in his new house?

How can I admit to my family I was stupid to marry Clarence? Was I stupid? Maybe we can get back to whatever it was that attracted us to each other in the first place. I'll try. I'll work on my marriage for a year. If I still feel this way a year from now, I'll pull the plug.

She takes a deep breath and blows it out through her mouth. *I have a plan! I feel so much better! Dr. Laura wouldn't approve. I'm going to quit listening to her radio show.*

Pulling into the arrivals lane at the airport, she sees Clarence standing next to his suitcase on the sidewalk with a scowl on his face and his hand engulfed in a white bandage.

She pulls to the curb, slides out onto the asphalt, and hurries toward him.

He holds up his bandaged hand as if to keep her away.

"What happened?" she demands.

"Just put my bag in the fucking van. I've been standing here waiting long enough. I'll tell you about it on the way home."

Jeanie holds her breath through a Braxton Hicks contraction, rolls the suitcase to the van, and puts it in the side door. She gets back in the driver's seat after settling Clarence in the passenger seat and merges into the traffic headed for the exit.

"Don't you look beautiful," Clarence says, once they've cleared city traffic.

"Aw, thanks, honey!" Jeanie favors him with a wide smile and thinks maybe the time away from home has improved his disposition after all. Absence makes the heart grow fonder, as they say.

Clarence scowls. "I meant, look at you. Is that the best you can do when you go to meet your husband after he's been away for so long?"

Jeanie's smile evaporates. She says quietly, "I don't fit anything else.

I know these are shabby. But we can't afford new maternity clothes, not now, with only four weeks to go."

"Well, you had to have that big fancy house. And I'm talking about your hair. And no makeup?"

"I didn't have time. I was working in the garden when you called." Jeanie sighs and takes a deep breath. "Sorry."

He stares at the long, straight highway.

"About your hand …"

"I fuckin' lost a finger, Jeanie!" he snaps.

"What? You lost a finger?" She's startled, jerks the steering wheel to look at him, drifts over out of her lane, and then straightens when the car in her blind spot lays on the horn. "But how? How could you?"

"In a car door. Fuckin' cabbie took off and my hand …" He's overcome. Sobs. Sniffs. Wipes his nose awkwardly with his left hand. "I'm going to sue. Don't you worry. He took off before I could get any information. I was in shock! It happened so fast! But the company he drives for knows about it." Now he's into serious sobbing, holding his head in his hands. "I can't talk about it!"

"Oh my God, Clarence! How awful! And on your right hand too." She looks as if she's about to burst into tears too.

"I got it fixed up," he says once he's calmer, "but I want Dr. Benzi to look at it, you know, to see what he thinks. That fuckin' immigrant bastard calling himself a surgeon at the hospital in Toronto said I'll still be able to use a computer, once I get used to it. Course he didn't even try to sew the finger back on! Too badly crushed, he said. At least I think that's what he said. Who knows for sure with that thick accent? The pain, Jeanie! You can't even imagine pain like this! I want to see Dr. Benzi. Even if just to document it, you know, for the lawsuit."

"Of course! We can go straight to his office. I'm sure he'll see you right away!"

"Let's do that."

Clarence leans back and closes his eyes. That should do it, he thinks. Right on script. No more detail or explanation required.

In truth, the pain's abated and he hardly notices it. He'll be glad to get the bulky bandage off so he can actually use the hand. But no use admitting that.

In the waiting room at the clinic, he's becoming annoyed at having to sit while the old bags with their miserable little complaints are rotated through. He is almost ready to get up and leave when they're finally ushered into an examination room. He squirms up onto the examination table, and Jeanie squeezes into a chair in the corner at his feet. "Wonder how long I'll have to wait in here now," he grouses.

Dr. Benzi appears promptly, though. "Hello," he says. He gives his pants a tug as though the suspenders can't quite keep them in place and closes the door behind him. "What happened here?" he asks as he takes Clarence's right arm and begins removing the bandage.

"Car door," Clarence tells him.

"Oh no! Well, let's have a look." He finishes removing the bandages and examines the amputation.

Jeanie, sitting in the corner of the tiny examination room, has paled.

"Are you okay?" Dr. Benzi asks her.

She nods, closes her eyes, and turns her head away.

"It's healing quite well, outwardly," Dr. Benzi tells them, "but there's more damage than just the amputation of the finger. Ligament damage. Nerve damage. Tendon damage. You can sit up," he tells Clarence. Then he searches the cabinets and comes up with a felt marker. Holding Clarence's hand, he draws lines on the palm and wrist. "Under these lines are tendons. They've sustained an insult, too, and need time to heal. If you get back to work too soon or use the hand too soon, they might be damaged further. Tear some more. If they build more scar tissue, they may pull the other fingers. See, this tendon here"—he redraws a line on the wrist—"moves those two fingers. If it stiffens up with scar tissue, you could end up with fingers that just curl and won't move, making your right hand nearly useless."

He lets that news sink in for a bit. "I know it's a bitter pill to swallow, Clarence. I know you're anxious to get back to work. I understand you've been away on a seminar? But I can't, in good conscience, recommend it." He puts the pen in his shirt pocket.

"Look," he says gently, "I'll give you a prescription for the pain, which I know must be excruciating even though you're putting on a brave face. I think we've got some samples around here. I'll give you those to tide you over until you can get the prescription filled. And I'll give you a medical letter for your employer." He stands, parts his lab coat so he can give his waistband another tug, opens the door, and starts to leave.

Turning partway back, he says, "Just sit here for as long as you like. But before you go, book an appointment for a day or two from now so I can remove those stitches and have another look. My girl will come in and bandage the hand." With that, he leaves.

Clarence hadn't expected any complications. His legs are like rubber. Jeanie has to physically help him from the doctor's office to the van, and once home, into the house.

She tells him he should lie down in the bedroom, but he heads for the couch, saying, "Just get me a pillow and a blanket."

As she settles him in, she takes off his shoes, remarking how dirty they are. "I'll clean them for you, honey," she says and heads toward the laundry room. As she sets the shoes on the counter above the washing machine, she notices the label inside. Custom? Hand made in Italy?

He yells after her, "Bring me a couple of those pills!"

She leaves the shores and goes back to the living room with a glass of water in one hand and her purse in the other. She sets the glass on the end table, digs the sample pack of pills out of her purse, and reads the label on the oxycodone. "Says here, take one every six hours as needed. Not to exceed four per day. This is heavy-duty stuff, honey."

"I know what I'm doing. I've had these before. One does nothing. It takes two."

Clarence lets her help him lift his shoulders enough to drink and downs the pills. Only once he's settled back does he ask about the boys.

"They're at Mutti's," Jeanie tells him. "You must've missed them! I'll go get them …"

"No. No, not today. They'd just make a racket, and I couldn't take it. You heard Dr. Benzi. I need to rest."

"Will it bother you if I do a few loads of laundry?"

"Yes. And don't bother with my shoes right now. Just go to your mother's. Bring me back a plate at dinnertime."

"Oh, all right." She gives his forearm a rub.

He closes his eyes. "Jeanie, you don't know what it's like. You just don't know how bad it is, the pain!"

"I understand." She gets her purse and car keys, and leaves, careful not to let the door slam behind her.

As he reaches for the TV remote, Clarence thinks, *I have to plan. Those bastards! Those goddamned bastards! They didn't tell me this could happen. And they left me on my own, dragging my bag out to that rental car, driving into Regina to the airport when I wasn't supposed to even be using this hand!*

He recalls actually drumming his bandaged palm on the steering wheel in time with Keith Urban on the radio as he drove along. Who knows what damage that did?

I'll make them pay for this.

I just have to figure out how.

The next morning, Clarence is on his back deck, basking in the afternoon sun. He'd slept in, enjoying a night in his own bed, despite the fact Jeanie hadn't brought him a plate at dinner like he told her to. He'd had to grub in the fridge for leftovers. With Jeanie being an indifferent cook, there was nothing but some kind of macaroni casserole. But then he was out like a light. Well, first he fantasized about that communion ritual, got in the shower and masturbated, and then was out like a light. Remembering that ritual now, his penis becomes tumescent again.

Of course, he woke up when they phoned to say Jeanie was in labor. But he got right back to sleep.

They knew I couldn't go, with my hand. They didn't need to bother me that late, nearly midnight! They can look after it. Mutti loves any excuse to stick her beak in.

Now he's got his second beer, and settles back in his chair with his shirt open to tan his fish-belly white body while his mind races. Half the time he's visualizing how much better his tanned body will look at the next communion. (In his imaginings, his stomach is considerably smaller.) And then he reminds himself there won't be another communion once he gives those bastards their comeuppance. He just has to think of how to do it.

There's no way he could go to work for Prairie Equity and run a bogus loan scam like he did on the bank, so he discards that idea. Even if they did hire him, they'd be wary.

Maybe he'll anonymously tip the cops off to the ceremonial crypt. There's bound to be plenty of blood there, and who knows what else? He didn't see it in the light. There may be more than one skeleton! It will have to be after he gets the rest of the money, though. He won't have to use it to cover what he got from the bank. He can skip out. Maybe go to Costa Rica. Or better, Belize. Start a new life.

But how to get the money? He knows he won't get the full amount but at least the next installment. Is half a million enough? He will have that and more, counting the bank accounts he systematically set up with a fake ID to hide embezzled funds over the past few years, if Jeanie signs over the house. She'll just have to, period. Wouldn't need ol' prune-face Mutti to sign over the farm. He could run a few more bogus loans at the bank before the auditors get there. He'll have a million. Maybe more. That will go a long way in Belize.

Between the beer and the oxycodone, he's getting a pleasant buzz.

There's a crash as if the front door has been smashed in. Heavy footsteps thump through the house, and Rick appears at the open patio door.

"What the ..." Clarence starts to stand.

In two strides Rick's in front of him, grabs him by the shirt, and reefs him up. His chair wobbles and then topples over backward with a clatter.

"You fuckin' piece a shit! Sit here fuckin' drinkin' beer, will you? While Jeanie's delivered another tiny baby girl? 'N' you can't go because your hand hurts?"

He lets go of Clarence's shirt, then steps beside him, puts his arm around him, gives him a pat, and walks him into the dining room.

Clarence squirms away and turns to face him. "You get outta—"

Rick puts his whole weight behind a punch to the gut, propelling the air out of Clarence's lungs. Clarence doubles over, coughing and gasping, feeling as if he might vomit. He turns to get away.

Rick shoves him, propelling him forward onto all fours, and then delivers a kick to his buttocks.

Clarence yelps as he's launched farther into the house, barely missing the corner of the fireplace hearth. Now he's flat on his face, struggling to get up. He makes it up onto all fours, but Rick kicks him again, this time in the side of his torso.

Clarence topples and curls his body protectively. Gasps. Gasps. Gasps. He turns his head to see where Rick is and tries again to get to his feet. This time, he makes it, wobbling slightly. He starts crying but ignores the tears running down his face. He turns to Rick, jabs at him with his left index finger, and sobs, "You get outta my house!"

Rick grabs him and pushes him up against the wall. "You lame excuse for a man! Your wife needed you! *I* took her to the hospital. The baby's barely makin' it. They've been airlifted to the special unit at Royal University Hospital in Saskatoon. I don't give a fuck about your religion! After losing little Winnie and almost dying herself not even a year ago, you couldn't stay off her for a couple of months? At least make sure she didn't get pregnant? 'N' you can't fuckin' get off your ass to be with her now?"

"But I—"

"No buts. You get fuckin' dressed. Get in your fuckin' car. Haul your big fuckin' ass up to Saskatoon."

"I can't! My hand!"

Rick keeps hold of his shirt with one hand, grabs Clarence's right wrist with the other, and thumps the bandaged hand several times against the wall. "Didn't mind usin' it to keep from landin' on your face, did you? The fuckin' thing ... is a long fuckin' way ... from your heart!"

"Ahhhgg! Agg!" Clarence gasps, spewing droplets of spittle. "I'll call the cops!"

"Go ahead. I'll wait. But you'll be in a coma by the time they get here." Rick gives Clarence's hand another thump against the wall. Then he drops him and backs a step away. He's still clenching his fists. "What's it gonna be?"

"I'll go!" Clarence's face contorts. He farts. Then sobs, "I'll *go!*"

Rick's nostrils are flaring. His shoulder and arm muscles are still flexed. But he turns and starts toward the front door before turning back and says, "I'll be outside to make sure you get away in good time. And Clarence? Jeanie gets pregnant again? Ever?" Rick's eyes narrow as he says quietly, "I'll fuckin' kill you."

Max drives his five-liter Mustang out to the Reeves acreage. He doesn't like the gravel roads; they're hell on the paint, but there's no joy driving this winding, hilly road in the plumbing van. Plus, Imperial Leader doesn't want that thing seen in his yard. So it's either his car or his Harley.

He pulls into the driveway. The sprawling split-level with its four-bay garage is set far back behind a beautifully landscaped front yard, flanked by exposed aggregate retaining walls. There's plenty of parking on pavement for those informal meetings of the Illustrious Ones in the downstairs billiards room.

It's the hottest part of the day, and heat waves shimmer across the miles of open prairie, giving everything an ephemeral quality. The land is undulating, arid, treeless. This is the beginning of the badlands. When Max was growing up out there, the townies disparagingly called kids from the badlands "hillbillies." Dressed in ragged hand-me-downs, holes in their socks, holes in their mittens. Or no mittens. Hard scrabble making a living on a quarter section in the hills. The old man always had money for booze, though.

Answering the door is a petite, pretty woman who looks to be in her forties, although Max knows she's at least midfifties.

"Evenin', Mizz Reeves."

"Hi, Max, come on in. Nick's expecting you. He's out on the patio." She gives him a warm smile, grasps his forearm, and gives it a squeeze. Then she stands aside and closes the door behind him.

Max heads down the stairs to the lower level, walks out through sliding doors, and finds Nick sitting in one of the comfortably padded armchairs. The patio is shaded by the huge cottonwoods surrounding it, and he's enjoying a rye with lots of ice while he reads *The Hunt for Red October*.

"Hey, Boss," Max says. "Good book?"

"This is about the fifth time I've read it, so yeah. Classic. This is a first edition, first printing. It's worth some bucks. I should really get it in paperback and read that instead of wearing this one out." Nick shrugs. He dog-ears his page and puts the book on the table next to him.

Indicating the aromatic smoke drifting out of the barbecue with a nod, Max asks, "Cookin' something?"

"Waiting for the grill to come up to temperature and burn the gunk off," Nick explains. "Have a seat. Can I get you something?"

Max sits in a patio chair. "Sure. Whatever you're having."

Nick stands, picks up his glass, and disappears into the family room. He returns with two drinks and hands one to Max. "What's up?" he asks, sinking back into his chair.

"Our target? She had male company."

"As we feared?"

"As we feared. No sign it's permanent. Could be a one-night stand. Now the friend from Vancouver is here." Max slaps at a mosquito on his neck. "She's a butchy-lookin' little stinky."

"I remember. She's a lesbian," Nick says. "Her parents were mortified. We had a ritual, you know: pray away the gay. Didn't work of course. You remember her from school?"

Max's forehead wrinkles. He shakes his head.

"I guess she's quite a bit older than you," Nick concludes. "Well, even if they have a good look around, it's unlikely they'll find anything. No big deal if they do. Can't connect anything to us. I think we're okay." Ice rattles in his glass as he takes a good swig.

Max leans his muscular forearms on his thighs. "Didn't have time to lock up the place again the other night. I should've done it before I rattled the screen door. Didn't think she'd investigate, but she actually had the jam to come down and turn on the lights to take a look. 'N' with the boyfriend staying 'n' the friend there now ..."

"Nope, stand down for now. Take a few days off." Nick sips his drink. "So, should I tell Marlene you'll stay for dinner? I'll just toss another steak on the grill."

"That'd be nice!" Max smiles, a rare thing. He pushes his sunglasses back up on his head, exposing the thin scar running through his left eyebrow, over the bridge of his nose, and ending at the top of his right cheekbone.

"No lady friend waiting on you?'

"Let 'er wait," Max says.

But there is no lady friend, and Max is in no hurry. He enjoys a leisurely dinner of steak, potato, and Caesar salad, and several more drinks before helping Marlene clear up and heading home.

His mastiff cross dog, Delilah, is waiting for him just inside his front door, and once he makes a fuss over her to let her know he missed her too, Max goes out on his back deck for a final cigarette. Delilah goes to the back of the garden to do her business, then returns and lies next to his chair. He absently scratches her ears. She was a rescue, a small, seal-brown puppy that grew into a hundred-and-twenty-pound slobber-puss.

She's fearsome-looking and has a huge bark. She could hurt you. Except for the slobbering, she's just like him.

She loves everyone. And that's not like him. Not at all.

He's a fixture at The Globe, always sitting at the end of the bar affectionately known as "Gynecology Row." Big, good-looking guy and big tipper that he is, Max is popular with the girls, so much so that other patrons get miffed at the amount of time they dance at his end.

Funny how the girls are always turned on by his jailhouse tats. They kid him about the one that reads "Jeanie" and want to know who she is—his first love? His first real girlfriend? Wife, maybe? He never talks about it. He's never had a relationship of more than a few weeks. And never with Jeanie.

Long legs in dark jeans stretched out in front of him, Max slouches in his chair and enjoys the cloudless sky, the millions upon millions of stars. He sends smoke rings up, thinks of the Tibetan monks sending prayers up from those rattle sticks, and decides smoke rings are his version of that. Then he thinks, as he often does, about Jeanie Schoenfeld.

Jeanie, Jeanie, Jeanie.

Kathy picks up one of the many legal documents covering the dining room table. She glances through it and looks over at her friend, who's deep in thought, tapping away at her laptop.

Penny finally says, "Well, there's three Wi-Fi's in range, but they're all locked … alsplace, is that the pub on the next block?"

Kathy nods.

"You know the password?"

"No, sorry. Haven't been there yet."

"We should've gone there instead of sitting here drinking wine," Penny says. "Maybe tomorrow? With your boyfriend?"

Kathy feels heat rising up her neck and into her cheeks. "He's not my boyfriend. That is, he was my boyfriend back in the day. Briefly. But we haven't hooked up. At least not yet."

Penny studies her friend's face and grins. "Well, when do I get to meet him? Renew our acquaintance, that is."

"Tomorrow. He wanted to be here tonight, but … family issues. His sister had a premature baby last night, and they moved her from Regina to Saskatoon, so he drove his mother up today."

"Ohhh. Is it … bad?"

"Worrisome, anyway. She had a preemie last year. Died after only a few hours. So everyone's anxious about this one."

"Of course."

"Well, there's nothing we can do," Kathy says. "Let's have a glass of wine on the veranda before dinner."

"Sounds perfect!"

Kathy opens the fridge and fills two glasses from the box, then hands one to Penny, who chuckles. "Mmm, Cardbordeaux!"

"Yup, nice fresh wine in a box, although I'm not sure Cardbordeaux's appropriate for Riesling." She leads the way onto the shaded front veranda, puts her glass on the railing, and hops up beside it. "You take the swing, Penny. Two people drinking wine on it—we'd probably waste a lot."

Penny sits, careful to keep her wine from slopping over, and waits for the swing to still before taking a sip. "Mmm, I've been looking forward to this all day! Perfect way to start my vacation."

"Is this what you call a vacation? Coming here to work on my schmozzle?"

"Yup, no work-play balance in my life. But you should talk!"

"At least you've got a career, and I wouldn't have worked all the extra hours if I didn't need the money." Kathy sighs. "In fact, lately I've been thinking about what's in my life I'd be better off without. Or what isn't in my life, that should be. One thing I regret is not coming back here sooner. I should've at least tried to reconnect with my mother. I know so little about her life, the last twenty years of her life, and now I'm packing it up. It's pitiful, really, how little she had. How old and crappy her stuff is. I guess it was pretty tough, her only income being what the Children of Noah paid for using the house."

"I know what you mean. My folks had even less. No house. Renters." Penny takes another swallow.

"Really? That little house you grew up in was a rental?"

"Yup. They rented it for thirty-eight years. Could've paid for it twice over. Landlord never fixed a damn thing, other than the roof, and then only because it rained inside almost as bad as outside. Guess who the landlord was. Children of Noah."

"No!"

"Yes. Someday I should check land titles and see just how many properties they own. Although I suppose by now they've got them all in numbered holding companies. More proof that calling them the Con is appropriate. Nothing but self-serving takers." Penny shakes her head. "Oh, I just remembered. I haven't told you yet! This property of your mother's? You think it's just the house? She owned every lot on this block. So the property's actually this house on this lot and the nine vacant lots."

Kathy's eyes widen as her brows lift. "You kiddin' me?"

"Nope, not kidding. I had my secretary get title searches, historical title searches, before I left. That's in the mess of papers I dumped out on the dining room table. So, she could've sold the lots, even if she kept the ones adjacent to the house, and lived pretty damn well."

"But why would there be ... who would buy a whole block?"

"Your great-grandfather, although he probably didn't buy it, exactly. It was likely a homestead. It was common back then for landowners to donate property for a school, maybe also for a post office. This would've been an ideal location with the railway right there, and Front Street was the main highway to Regina up until the Sixties. Other businesses start to move in. Presto! You've got a town. And you got rich in the process. Something like that. He didn't build the house until 1927."

"Huh! That's really something. I knew the house was always in the Klein family, but I didn't know they had more than that. They must've been well off. Rick's grandfather said the house was a mansion for the time and that my great-grandfather was a close friend of Al Capone's."

"Really? You think your great-grandfather might've been a gangster too?"

"You know, I didn't put much stock in it when Rick's grandfather said it. I thought it was likely just gossip back then. And with the Alzheimer's, well, his memory might be a bit jumbled. But maybe there's more to it. I'll have to do some research once I get Internet."

They sip their wine in silence for a few moments. Then Kathy asks, "What's the first step then, Penny? To challenge the title transfer?"

"Well, we'll need a lawyer here to be counsel of record. I can draft the pleadings, but we'll need a lawyer licensed in this province. This won't be wrapped up while I'm here, and doing everything from the West Coast would be clumsy. And if you noticed, the Con's lawyer is a senior partner in a big firm here—one of the Robertsons in Robertson, Robertson, McKinley, et al. They got the big guns. Must have some bucks behind them, and probably think they can wear us down with delays, mountains of paperwork, costly stuff. They'll be asking, who has more money, them or you."

"Well, we know the answer to that! I have nothing. So is it a fool's errand? Trying to set aside my mother's will?"

"It wasn't left to them in a will. I had my secretary do a will search, remember, and got no hits. That's why Elder Reeves didn't e-mail you the will. Unless there was an unregistered will, they don't have one to give you a copy of. Your mother gave them the property last year. I don't know why he didn't just tell you that. There's a life estate on title, so she was to live here until she died."

"But the Con's congregation's tiny. Have they actually got money? To hire expensive lawyers? If they own rentals, I guess they must have other income besides the collection plate, but then why would they meet here?"

"I don't get it either. It's puzzling."

"And anyway, how could my mother sign the property over to the Con? What about my father? It was his family home. We don't know what happened to him. He could still be alive. She'd have to get him to sign too, wouldn't she?"

"Aren't you clever! I didn't even think of that. I think she was the sole registered owner, but how could she be? Let's look at the title." Penny swigs the last of her wine, rises, and goes back inside with Kathy right behind her. She shuffles through the papers and comes up with the historical title search. "Okay. See? He was the sole registered owner until five years ago, when the title was transferred to her. She must've had him declared dead."

"How could she? Wouldn't she have to try to find him first?"

"Yes." Penny nods. "She'd have to prove sufficient efforts had been made to locate him. There must be a court record. We can go to the courthouse and do some research ourselves." She picks up her empty wineglass and wiggles it at Kathy. "Assume there's more of this?"

"Yup. And let's dish up some salads to go with it." She takes Penny's glass to the kitchen.

"Want me to clear this stuff off the dining room table?" Penny calls after her.

"No," Kathy says, "that'll be our office. If you don't mind eating in the kitchen."

They sit down with plates of green salad, potato salad, and fresh glasses of wine.

"Mmm," Penny says as she chews, "love the black beans in the salad. Potato salad's yummy too. You made it?"

"In honor of your visit, I actually cooked ... if you call making a couple of salads cooking. Well, I did boil the potatoes."

"Atta girl!" Penny says and takes a sip of wine. Then she blurts out, "Ohmygawd! Wills!"

"Wills?"

"If your father just disappeared, how likely is it he'd've planned ahead and made a will?"

"Doesn't seem likely."

"I didn't even think to do a will search for your father! And we need to know if he had one. Depending on what it says, we may have an uphill battle. But if he didn't have a will, and no one ever contacted you, this would've been around the time his name was taken off the title? To see if he'd been in contact with you? If not, and if he died intestate, or if he was just presumed dead, we have sound legal grounds to challenge the declaration of death and the title transfer. You're entitled to a share of his assets. Not sure how much. I'll see if the Saskatchewan intestate succession law is online." Penny's eyes are bright.

Kathy puts down her fork. "He must've been reported missing. Could she have him declared dead based on the police never finding him?"

"Hmm." Penny gives her head a scratch and then finger-combs her short coppery hair. "That would be part of the documentation in support of the application for the death certificate."

"How can we find out?"

"Must be a record of the court case." Penny slides her chair back. She stands, picks up Kathy's plate, and takes it with her own to the dishwasher. "We need a plan," Penny continues. "For starters, tomorrow we'll get a lawyer, have them do the will search, and put things in motion to have the legal presumption of death, or declaration of death, whatever they call it here, set aside. We don't have to prove anything, just make the allegations. At least get the complaint filed. Make sure that if they're planning on getting a court order to have you evicted, the judge knows about this challenge. That'll put the brakes on it. For tonight, though, let's see if we can find some wills."

"Starting where? There's no desk. Maybe the drawers in the sideboard."

"You start there. I'll see if there's anything in these cupboards."

Kathy heads into the dining room. The room divider has a row of cabinets above the pass-through to the living room. She starts with those. There are shoeboxes full of papers, photographs, letters, empty envelopes covered with shopping lists, and old two- and three-digit phone numbers.

"I'll be here all night!" she calls out to Penny. With nine-foot ceilings and built-ins right to the top, there's a lot of storage space for things not often used.

"Same here!" Penny answers from the kitchen. "But you don't have to open every envelope. Wills are usually folded and put in an open-ended sleeve, or at least have a heavier, colored title paper with the name and date on it.

"And tomorrow, when it's daylight, you can give me a full tour of the house, basement included. You need to do laundry sometime. If nothing else, you need to know where the electrical panel is in case you overload a circuit with all that cooking."

Their search turns up nothing of interest, and they call it quits when Penny says she's had a long day and would like a fresh start in the morning. Kathy shows her to the bedroom next to hers.

The next morning dawns clear with the promise of another hot day. It's pleasant on the veranda, though, so they have a relaxing breakfast of coffee and toasted bagels there. While she eats, Penny is on her laptop booking an appointment with a lawyer.

They have just enough time to check out the basement before going to Regina for their meeting with the lawyer. After they dress, they go down the narrow staircase into the basement. It's much as Kathy remembered from her brief tour with Rick: smelly and dungeon-like. The one small window provides a surprising amount of light, and she's easily able to bat spiderwebs away and replace the burned-out light bulbs.

"Should've done this before we got into our go-to-town clothes! Don't think anyone would store any paperwork down here, though. It smells like a cave! I'm surprised they'd put that stuff here," Penny says, ducking beams to get to the far end of the basement where there's a pile of broken chairs, an ancient dresser with missing drawers, and mattresses leaning up against the wall. She goes to a battered wardrobe. "This sure isn't as nice as the rest of the antiques," she says, unlatching the door and reefing it open. "Whew! No one's opened this for a while!"

She sticks her head inside. "Nothing in here but some pieces of crayon and rat poop. Someone scribbled on the sides."

Kathy starts toward Penny, looks at the wardrobe, and is jolted as if struck. Suddenly she feels as if everything's gone dark and she's afraid ... but of what? She stops in her tracks as adrenaline courses through her. She draws several deep breaths and realizes it's just her old, irrational fear of the fictional dirty man.

"What is it?" Penny asks.

"It's nothing. I just ... for some reason, I got the heebie-jeebies." Kathy shakes her head. "The whole frickin' basement gives me the heebie-jeebies, actually."

Penny looks puzzled. She shrugs, closes the wardrobe door, and comes back to the front part of the basement. "So much stuff, big stuff too, to get rid of. I don't envy you the job."

"Maybe I'll just leave everything where it is." Kathy grimaces. "I sure hope the furnace still works. It looks pretty old too. I'm going to have to get insurance on this place, and I bet I'll have to get a new fuel tank before any insurance company will insure it. Sure won't be able to get the old one out. It'll just have to stay here. Funny how nobody thought about that when they put it in."

"Wonder how they got it in here in the first place."

"There used to be a door to the outside. Concrete stairs outside. Good place to hide when we were playing hide-and-seek, remember? Or you could sit down there and let the older boys look up your dress! Ha! Remember Allie Bogs?"

"Vaguely. Trisomy twenty-one?"

"Down syndrome, yes. Back then my mother called her 'that drooling Mongoloid,' and I wasn't allowed to play with her. If my mother caught her in the yard, she'd get her stick and chase her away. Still, Allie kept coming back. She spent a lot of time in the stairwell, usually with the boys. Remember, she never wore panties?"

"Poor little Allie. Wonder what she's doing now." Penny clucks and shakes her head. "I don't remember you ever talking about your childhood. Is being in the old house stirring your memory?"

"Yeah, funny, I haven't thought about Allie for years." Then she points out a rectangle of concrete blocks, with poured concrete walls on both sides. "That's where the door was. I wonder why my mother had the stairwell filled in and that doorway bricked up. You'd think it would be handy having that access."

"You would've thought she'd at least have the old coal furnace taken out before she did that, wouldn't you?" Penny says as they walk around it, examining the twelve-inch-diameter pipes sprouting from it. "It's such a big monster, really takes up a lot of space. But I guess she had no use for the basement, anyway."

Kathy tries the door to the combustion chamber, but it refuses to open. There is a sliding grate on it to allow more air in. It won't budge either. "Stuck."

"Why would you want to open it, anyway?" Penny asks. "If there's bogey men in there, I say leave 'em sealed in! Unless you think they can climb up through the pipes. Maybe that's the noise you've been hearing."

"Ha-ha!" Kathy fake chuckles. "Very funny. You know, that noise hasn't returned. It was just the first few nights. Not a sound when Rick stayed over."

"Rick stayed over … but you haven't hooked up," Penny teases.

"No, we haven't hooked up. Separate beds. Separate rooms!" Kathy says. "Really. So, the noise. Maybe just because the water pipes hadn't been used for a while? Maybe air in them? Water hammer?"

"If you say so! Let's just hope that's the end of it."

They move over to a rough workbench. There's a vice bolted to it and odds and ends of rusting hand tools on it, including the hammer Rick had pointed out.

"Some of this stuff might come in handy," Kathy says, picking up a pry bar.

"Oh yeah? What for?"

"I don't know. I guess maybe just the hammer, in case I want to hang pictures."

"You *will* want to hang pictures, Kathy, once the house is yours. Power of positive thinking!"

There's a small area of wooden floor against the wall across from the stairs. It has a removable center section, with a couple of handles on it.

"Wonder what this is," Penny says. "Oh, something's written on it."

Sump Pump is neatly lettered on the rough wood.

"A seepage problem? Here? That's surprising," Kathy says. "I should have this stuff serviced, I guess." She takes the handles and tries to lift the removable section, but it's heavy and firmly wedged in place.

"Nothing interesting about a sump pump anyway, Kathy, and look at the time!" Penny says. "We'd better go. Don't want to be late for our appointment!"

They locate the electric panel near the water heater and behind the oil furnace, turn off the lights, and go back upstairs. Penny gathers up all the documents and slides them into her portfolio. Then they lock up and leave.

athy takes a deep breath as she walks behind Penny into the law offices of Stanton, McCafferty, and Prowse. The office is in a strip mall, the ground level given over to commercial storefronts and the second story, offices. It's just one flight up, but there's an elevator, and even the outer hallway smacks of good taste. She doesn't know why she's feeling nervous. She takes another deep breath and walks up to the reception desk. The receptionist, an older woman with glasses on a chain around her neck, looks up with a smile and says hello.

"Hello," Kathy responds, returning the smile. "We have an appointment with Reese McCabe. I think we're a bit early."

"She's with a client right now, but I don't think she'll be long. Please have a seat."

Kathy and Penny head for the stylish upholstered chairs near the door to wait. "Reese is a woman," Kathy whispers.

"Good," Penny says. She picks up a *Regina Today!* magazine and starts leafing through it, while Kathy eyes the spacious, tastefully decorated waiting area. She thinks how poorly the waiting area at the insurance office where she works compares. Penny, on the other hand, takes it in stride and seems to barely notice the gleaming wood paneling and original artwork.

Soon a young woman leaves, and after a short wait, they're ushered into an office so small the desk nearly fills it. It's the junior partner-size office, Reese McCabe explains as she introduces herself. No neat freak, she has to move a stack of bulging files from one of the chairs before Kathy and Penny can sit facing the desk.

"The note from my assistant says you're a lawyer, and you're from Vancouver. What area of law do you practice, Penny?" Reese goes around to take her chair behind the desk and unbuttons the jacket of her stylish navy pantsuit as she sits.

"Insurance defense, mostly. I won't be counsel of record of course. I'm just a friend. Anyway, it's a bit out of my experience to be plaintiff's counsel, as is dealing with a fraudulent declaration of death and transfer of property."

"Well, it sure isn't something that comes along every day!" Reese says. "Very intriguing! Let me just make a few notes while we chat." She leans over a yellow foolscap pad, ready to make notes.

"I e-mailed your assistant with the details earlier," Penny says.

"Oh, okay. Let me take a look," Reese says, putting her pen down and turning to tap her keyboard. "Okay. I see it. So you want the title transfer set aside because your mother, Kathy, didn't have standing to assign it?"

Kathy looks at Penny, who responds, "Yes. Kathy was never contacted to see if her father had been in touch with her. But even if the declaration of death is legitimate, without a will, Kathy is entitled to a share of his estate."

"There's no will?"

"Not that we know of," Kathy says. "We're still looking."

"My office ran a search for Louise Klein's will and found nothing, but I didn't think to search for Gilbert Klein," Penny says.

"Okay, just a search for your father's will then," Reese says to Kathy as she pushes the pad and a pen across the desk to her. "Print your father's full name and his date of birth for me, please." Then she looks up and grins at Penny.

Kathy prints "Gilbert Klein" and pushes the pad back to Reese. "I never knew his middle name or even if he had one," she says apologetically. "Never knew his date of birth either."

"Oh, I see. Well, how many Gilbert Kleins can there be? No more than a couple of thousand, I don't imagine!" She grins. "Do you know his approximate age? Even that would help."

"Oh … probably twenty or thirty years older than me, so fifty-five to sixty-five?"

"In the meantime," Penny says, "the church elders keep reminding Kathy they want her out of the house. We want to be sure they can't get an eviction order."

"So, let's get a statement of claim filed. I'll see if we can have a caveat registered on the title, but in the meantime, I'll let Mr. Robertson know about this. Maybe I can get his undertaking not to take any action until the challenge is heard. But," Reese warns, "he's never cooperative. Misogynist! Or maybe junior partners of small firms are beneath his notice. But don't worry. I'll do my best for you. This will irritate the hell out of him. I'm looking forward to it!"

Then she lowers her voice to a conspiratorial tone. "Just so you know, and you didn't hear it from me, around here we call him Mr. Big Balls."

They share a chuckle.

"I'll get my assistant to do a search, see if there is a will registered, but that takes a few days, and there is a small fee. Meanwhile, keep looking through your mother's papers. There may be a handwritten or unregistered will somewhere. A holographic will can still be legal and binding."

"Okay," Kathy agrees. "By the way, just so you know ... the house is nearly a hundred years old and needs some work, but it's heritage and worth something. All the vacant lots are definitely worth something. So the property has value, but I don't have a big budget."

"Noted. Today's your free fifteen-minute initial consultation, except there'll be a cost to register a caveat against the title and for the will search. For your notice of claim, I'll just have my secretary copy Penny's notes and print the documents for you. Are you satisfied with what you put in your e-mail, Penny?"

Penny nods.

"Good. And I'll keep my time to a minimum, use one of the articling students whenever possible. Can we agree to a thousand-dollar retainer?"

"Oh. Could it be in instalments?"

"Well. How about five hundred now, and five at the end of the month?"

Kathy thinks for a moment, then nods.

"Give my secretary a couple of checks, then. I have both your cell numbers. Kathy, you let me know when you get your Internet hooked up. I'll have my assistant leave the statement of claim at the reception desk. If you have something else to do, shopping maybe, you could come back in an hour, or better yet, I'll text you when it's ready for you to pick up." Reese comes around her desk and takes the few steps to her office door to shake hands with Kathy, then Penny. She holds Penny's hand, looks into her eyes just a little too long, and says, "Let's keep in touch."

At the front desk, Kathy makes out the checks for the retainer and hands them to the receptionist, then they leave the cool office and are back out on the hot sidewalk. "Whew! What a shocker after the air-conditioned office!" Kathy says.

"Well," Penny looks around, "I see there's a Starbucks across the street. It's bound to be air-conditioned. Let's go there to wait for Reese's text."

In a few minutes, they're on stools at the narrow counter with iced soymilk lattes, looking out into the street, watching the ebb and flow of vehicles and pedestrians.

"When we get the statement of claim, then what do we do?" Kathy asks.

"Well, we have to go to the courthouse and get it registered, then serve it on the Con. Not themselves, just their registered office, which is just down the street."

"Is that ... you know ... risky?"

"No. We could get a process server, but they charge about a hundred dollars, and it's a simple thing to do ourselves since we're so close anyway. Then we go back to the courthouse and file the affidavit of service and wait for them to respond." Penny breaks off a piece of her lemon-poppy seed loaf and pops it in her mouth.

"So," Kathy continues, "sounds simple enough. By the way, what did you think of Reese?"

"She's nice. And a thousand-dollar retainer? That's nothing. She's giving you a deal."

"Well, if she did, it's thanks to you. Wasn't your gaydar pinging like crazy? Mine was. She hardly looked at me. I think she likes you."

"What's not to like?" Penny shrugs. But she looks down at her latte and a tinge of red creeps into her cheeks.

"Well, I'm sure you can handle any further meetings with her." Kathy grins, nudging her friend with an elbow. "That wasn't as difficult as I expected. I don't know why I felt so nervous about doing it. But you think Reese can take on Mr. Big Balls?"

"Mmm, I think so. She seems pretty feisty. Plus, she's what you can afford." Penny pushes up her dark-rimmed glasses. "You can bet the Con won't take it well. The allegations are damning. But it's bought us time. The ball will be in their court."

"What's next?"

"For now, they just deny everything. Then we wait to be notified of a court date. Likely a settlement conference first." She tilts her head to the side, deep in thought. "That can be uncomfortable. But it's a long way off, months at least. Don't know how long it takes to get a court date here, but in Vancouver it can be a couple of years." Penny's face turns serious. "I wonder if the Con is inclined to wait for due process."

"You don't think they might try something else to get me out of the house? What could they do? Have a bad guy come and rough me up?" Kathy chuckles. "What am I thinking? It's a *church* for crying out loud."

"Yes, a church with very deep pockets, judging by the five-hundred-dollar-an-hour Mr. Big Balls Robertson."

"Oh!" Kathy's forehead creases. "I don't know if I can do this, Penny!"

"You can do it."

"But they've been in Pillerton so long. They're established. There's a whole bunch of them, and their high-priced lawyers to boot, against me. They've got money, and I don't. You said it yourself: they could just wear me down with delays, legal stuff …"

"It's not just them against you, Kathy. It's them against you *and* me."

"But they've got the money."

"Apparently. But don't give that too much weight. If it goes to court, and I mean *if*, because only a fraction of suits actually get that far, you will be a very sympathetic plaintiff. And the judge wouldn't be ignorant of the fact they've got high-priced help and might be inclined to wonder how they can afford it. It really is quite remarkable given they have such a small congregation, and every other church pretty well everywhere relies on bingo and hall rentals to stay afloat."

Kathy knits her brow. "You think there's something fishy?"

"Don't you?" Penny frowns. "I think we need to quit thinking of it as a church and call it what it is, a cult. Remember Jimmy Jones? The Branch Davidians? Especially the Branch Davidians. The standoff with the ATF lasted nearly two months and finally ended with a gun battle worthy of a war."

"I remember."

"And I need to quit calling them the Children of Noah, as if they're some benign, innocent little beings. The Con is certainly appropriate, maybe even too kind. We don't know what they're capable of. There is, after all, property worth about a million dollars on the line."

"But, Penny, in Pillerton? This isn't the south side of Chicago! And we've known Elder Reeves all our lives."

"So we trust that *Schweinhünd*?" Penny's lips are pursed. Her brow furrows. "You weren't treated to the virgin purification ritual, were you." It isn't a question.

"Virgin purification ritual?"

Penny's phone pings. She looks at it and stands abruptly. "The statement of claim's ready. Let's go do our errands and get back to Pillerton. We still have a lot of searching to do."

Puzzled, Kathy gets to her feet and follows her friend.

Once they've taken care of their errands, they return to Kathy's rented car, leave the parkade, and drive back through the city and onto the highway leading to Pillerton. As they approach 10 Front Street, Kathy sees Rick's pickup, with him in it, parked at the curb. She pulls up behind him and parks.

"Hey, Penny," he says once they're all on the sidewalk, "long time no see."

She extends her hand, and he takes it. "Yes. Years! You and Kathy were still juniors in high school when I moved away."

"Well, you haven't changed."

"Oh, you always were a silver-tongued devil," Penny says, "but thank you. You're looking good too."

"Ha! I was recently told, by a friend mind you, I look like a worn-out boot." He chuckles. "Sure feel like one some days." He drops an arm lightly around Kathy's shoulders and gives her a brief squeeze. "I thought you two might want to walk over to the pub for a drink and some pub grub."

"Best idea I've heard all day!" Penny says.

They head down the sidewalk to the old hotel building a block away. Happy hour at Al's Place is under way. They find a table in the back and slide into chairs. Carl notices them and works his way over.

"Hey, Carl," Rick says, "meet Kathy and Penny. Kathy's living in the house up the street. You'll likely be seeing a lot of her, the way she likes to drink wine and doesn't like to cook!"

"Ha-ha! Very funny," Kathy says, giving Carl one of her winning smiles. "He doesn't know me that well."

"Am I wrong?" Rick asks.

"No, you're not wrong, dammit! Seems like I told you too much about myself the other night." She chuckles and turns back to Carl. "He's right. I'll probably be a regular. This place is just stumbling distance from the house."

"Welcome. I look forward to it! You ever do any acting? We could use you in our amateur theater group," Carl says.

"Nope. Never. But I might give it a try."

"Great! And Penny? You live there too?"

"No, I'm just a houseguest."

"Well, enjoy your stay. What can I get for you?"

They order a liter of house white for the ladies and a mug of Steamboat Pilsner for Rick.

"He always plays the leading man," Rick says after Carl's gone to get their drinks. "Probably sizing you up as a new leading lady. You know, for the stage kisses."

"Thankfully he's not hard to look at." Kathy blushes. "A young Pierce Brosnan, English accent 'n' all."

"And don't think he doesn't play that up!"

"What news of Jeanie and the baby, Rick?" Penny asks.

"Well, not as bad for Jeanie as last time, at least. She had something called preeclampsia again. The baby being born is the best treatment for that, they tell us, although as a preemie, not great for baby. She's tiny, under three pounds, but her lungs are quite well developed so she should be able to breathe on her own soon. She can suck, so she's feeding."

"That's so good," Penny says. "I Googled the hospital when Kathy told me they'd moved them there. It's supposed to be the best neonatal intensive care unit in Saskatchewan."

"They've been great," Rick says.

"Imagine, a little human not even three pounds! Is her husband with her?" Kathy asks. "Will they be staying in Saskatoon while the baby's there?"

"Clarence went up yesterday but only stayed a couple hours. Came back last night. He has a phobia about hospitals, Jeanie says. Also, he had an appointment for his hand today."

"His hand?"

"Yeah. He somehow managed to squash it in a car door when he was in Toronto. Took off most of one finger."

"Eww. That's grim."

"Jeanie's going to stay with the baby. She's needed there, of course, and is hoping she can breast-feed her soon. When that happens, they'll transfer the baby back to Regina."

"Do they have other kids?" Penny asks.

"Yup, three boys. They're out at the farm. They miss their mommy but love being there, and between my mother and my daughter, there's always someone riding herd on them."

Carl returns with their drinks.

"We'll run a tab," Rick tells him. "We'd like menus when you get a chance."

"Will do. Today's specials are on the board." He points to the signboard over the bar and scurries off to deliver the rest of the drinks on his tray.

"Ugh!" Penny says with a shudder. "Steak 'n' kidney pie?"

"The fish 'n' chips is good," Rick tells them. "Or are you both vegans?"

Seeing their nods, he continues, "Well, maybe there's a veggie burger or something on the menu. If we ever get menus." He scans the room and notes Carl is busy taking an order from a large group. "Let's hope the tourists don't ask him about the tunnels," he says. "Service really grinds to a halt when that happens." He takes a draft of his beer before leaning forward and lowering his voice. "Kathy, that guy you said was skulking around your place? With the big hat? I saw him today."

"Oh! You did? Where?"

"At your house. He was on the veranda. I think he was trying to look in through the living room window. He spooked 'n' ran around to the back when I pulled up. Drove away in a hurry, raised a big cloud of dust down the lane." He leans back and grins. "You should do him a favor 'n' open the curtains in that bay window so he can see in."

"Oh sure. Maybe leave one of those windows open too?" Kathy chuckles.

Penny snorts. "Not funny!" she says. "Surely he was trying to get in, not just look."

"True," Rick agrees, "but you'd think it'd be easier to just kick in the door."

"It would be. But he may not want anyone to know he's been in."

"Why? If he's going to break in, why would he care if anyone knew?" Kathy asks.

Penny's eyes narrow, and she cocks her head. "Maybe he's after something in particular and doesn't know where it is."

"So he might come back? That's a scary thought! Maybe he's the one who's been making the noise in the basement! But what could he possibly be looking for?" Kathy asks. "There's nothing in the house worth anything."

"Well, maybe he knows something we don't. Or he's at the wrong house. In any case, he's up to no good," Penny says. "If it was him down in the basement … that's puzzling. Both times we know for sure he was there, it's been during the day when it's least likely anyone will be home."

"But he knocked," Kathy points out.

"Yes. And if you'd answered the door, he'd've come up with some story like he's selling magazine subscriptions, or which way is it to Pangman, or the company he represents is in the neighborhood cleaning carpets and they can do yours for a reduced charge." Penny pushes up her glasses.

"So he knocks first to make sure no one's home before he breaks in? Then why didn't he come in the day I saw him?"

"Did he see you?"

"No." Kathy says and then thinks for a moment. "Maybe. He looked up at the window. Maybe he saw me. Hope not! I was naked, hiding behind the curtain. I dropped it when he looked up. Maybe he saw it move."

"He might be watching to see when you leave," Penny says. "Guys, let's get our food to go. Just in case."

Nick's behind the bar getting a fresh beer and watching Max trounce Donnie in the third of a best-of-five eight-ball competition, when he sees Marcus trotting around the corner and down the steps onto the patio. The doors are open to the cool of the evening, so Marcus comes right in.

"Hey," he says.

"Hey, Marcus," Nick says, "what held you up? We're waitin' on you. Beer?"

He nods and takes the beer Nick hands him. "Sorry. Can never predict how long the fuckin' in-camera sessions will go on for."

"Always something," Donnie mutters, missing his shot despite vigorous chalking of his cue.

Marcus gives Donnie a sour look but doesn't respond, asking Nick instead, "So what's the emergency?"

Nick snorts, "Not really an emergency, just a couple of, er, *untoward* developments. Tell him, Max."

Max is surveying the lay of the balls ahead of his shot. He picks up the chalk and works it on the tip of his cue. "Two things. There's some weirdo snoopin' around the house. Peerin' in windows. Dunno what his deal is."

"You think it's that same jerk-off you seen before?" Donnie asks.

"Think so."

"Doesn't seem to be able to stay away," Nick says. "Well, next time you see him, pick him up. We'll find out what his deal is. But more important, Max heard the two stinkies planning to have the transfer of property at Ten Front Street declared illegal."

"Oh?" Marcus says.

"Yeah," Max nods. "Didn't pick up everything. There was a lot of paper rustling, water running, dish noises. Maybe under the kitchen sink wasn't the best place for the bug. But I heard enough." He bends over the table, takes his shot, and sinks one of his balls. He's set up for his next shot and moves around the table to line it up. "The butchy friend? She's smart." He sinks another ball.

"Max came to me with this earlier," Nick says. "Then just before dinnertime, our lawyer called. Hope the hell he doesn't think calling ten minutes after five entitles him to overtime!"

They share a chuckle, but it's humorless.

"We, meaning them as our registered office, got served papers this afternoon. A statement of claim disputing the declaration of death for Gilbert Klein. Which means if they're successful, his property has to be restored to him. And the crazy ol' bitch Louise Klein couldn't have legally transferred the title to us."

"Ho-lee shit!" Marcus puts his bottle down.

"It gets worse. Even if they don't get the declaration of death set aside, unless Gilbert had a will leaving his property to his wife, Klein's entitled to a share. A pretty big share. Half of everything over a hundred K. So, a lot."

"Can that fly?"

"Yeah," Nick says. "Robertson says it can fly."

"So," Donnie says, "it was a mistake not to contact Ms. Klein to ask if she'd heard from her father."

"That was stupid!" Marcus blurts out. "Why didn't you?"

"Stupid? For fuck's sake, Marcus! You gonna second-guess every fuckin' thing we done before you came on board?" Donnie slams his cue down on the table. It rolls, knocking balls out of position, and he takes several strides toward the bar where Marcus sits.

Nick puts his arm out in front of him and holds him back. "Easy, Donnie. Marcus just needs to be brought up to speed."

"Sorry," Marcus says, "poor choice of words."

Donnie swallows. Takes a few deep breaths. "Okay." He shrugs

Nick's hand off him. "We didn't think we needed to. She hadn't been in touch for twenty years. She wouldn't ever've found out. Shouldn't've found out."

"I made the decision, Marcus," Nick says. "We didn't contact her because it was in our best interest for Louise Klein to be the sole owner. No one knew where the daughter was, and if we did locate her? Big complication. She wouldn't sign away her share of the estate without getting something in return, and maybe not at all. We took a chance. And it would've worked, except some do-gooder posted an obit in the community newsletter. That must be how she found out about her mother's death so soon. We figured she'd find out sometime, but she'd just think the house was willed to us, end of story. Didn't think she'd decide to come here and snoop around. Or that she'd even think about how her mother could've transferred the property without her father's signature."

"Has to be that Meier cunt's doing," Donnie says. "Another *untoward* development. She disappeared years ago too. We never even thought about her 'n' sure never knew them two were together."

"So, where *is* her father? He just, what, ran away with his secretary?" Marcus asks.

"Nope, he's dead as a nit," Donnie says. "Body was never found. It was just put around town that he ran off. I barely remember it. I was just a kid myself. I just remember the adults laughing about it."

"Well, I remember it," Nick says. "I was Regal Leader then, I mean, when Gilbert Klein 'ran off'." He chuckles. "The ol' 'he went to the store for a pack of cigarettes and never came home' story. Cops never bothered investigating."

Marcus leans his forearms on his thighs, swirling the beer around in his bottle. "We took him out?"

"Shit, no!" Nicks says. "The lovely and talented Louise Klein took care of that! We just cleaned up the mess." He gets down off his barstool, wincing at the needle of pain that shoots through his knee. *Probably have all that goddamned kneeling in my youth to thank for that*, he thinks. He takes the cue off the table and racks up the balls before continuing. "Called up all in a dither. She'd cut his dick off and caved his head in. Not sure in what order!" He chuckles. "Hey, you guys only knew her these past few years, but she was good-lookin' back then. Big brown eyes. Nice ass. Like her daughter. Crazy as a shithouse rat, but a more fervent and committed True Believer there never was."

"Really? I don't remember … Were you fuckin' her?" Donnie asks. "Back in the day, I mean, before she turned into a raisin?"

"Well, that's the funny thing. She never fucked anyone. Didn't even want to be diddled. But what a gobbler! She'd blow me anywhere. She actually got demanding about it. She was a hot number. Who wouldn't want some of that? But Jesus H. Christ, cross her and she'd turn into a Tasmanian devil! I'd've called a halt to it years ago otherwise. Toward the end, I had to close my eyes and fantasize about my wife, for Chrissake!"

They all chuckle, and Nick continues. "She was starting to scare me. Startin' to take the ceremonial wife thing too seriously. And listen to this: she had a list of men around Pillerton who she said needed purification. Had a plan for us to start rounding them up and purifying them. If they didn't go along with it, castration in lieu of. I guess that's more or less what happened to Gilbert when he refused, or maybe he wanted something other than a blow job that night."

"Gaww!" Max gasps and shudders noticeably.

"So actually, it was lucky she kicked off when she did," Nick says, "a big relief."

"Just lucky?" Marcus asks.

"Well, a little luck," Nick chuckles, "and a little Dr. Benzi."

"Yup," Donnie chuckles, "amazing how many of the old bags go for a dirt nap as soon as they sign their houses over. Hardly make any use of that life estate at all."

Marcus frowns at Donnie and asks, "So, Klein's the skeleton in the tunnel?"

"Fuck no." Nick grins. "You thought that skeleton was real? Marcus! It's just a stage prop. But don't let on you know. Adds to the mystique of the rituals. Ol' Gilbert's in the coal furnace."

"In the house?"

"Yup. Who's next?"

"I was runnin' the table, boss," Max says, glaring at Donnie.

"Donnie, you're disqualified. Okay, Max and me." He turns to Max. "You break."

Max sinks a stripe on the break and runs three other balls before he misses. But he leaves the cue ball buried.

"Yeah, I should know better than to let him break," Nick says. "The good and the bad thing about playing against Max is that you have plenty of time to drink between turns."

"Misspent youth," Max says quietly.

"Okay, so back to our problem with Ms. Klein. Been here what? Two weeks give or take? 'N' already she's really gettin' on my wick. How do we get her out? I mean, permanently?" Nick chalks his cue, takes his shot and misses, then sits while Max sinks two more balls.

"If she's scared enough, she might still give up and go home," Marcus says. "Maybe she doesn't even like the old house. She's living on the coast, right? She might be happy to take a buyout. Maybe she doesn't know about all the other properties."

"Yup, maybe she'll leave on her own. And maybe pigs can fly." Donnie frowns at Marcus. "But say she doesn't leave. Say she doesn't accept a buyout and decides to stay permanently. I'm wondering. What would Brother Weaver do for us if he didn't have to bring in his wife or his mother-in-law to get the rest of the money?"

"Shit, Donnie. You sayin' what I think you're sayin'? We can take out a hit for a lot less than three point five million!" Nick says.

"Sure, but then we'd be dealing with some pretty nasty characters, and we'd have to pay. If Brother Weaver looks after it, we won't have to. Will we."

"I'm going to have to start a compost pile out in the yard somewhere," Kathy says as she pulls the garbage can out from under the sink and drops the empty takeout containers in it. "I should get one of those black plastic composting bins next time I'm at RONA. I guess Pillerton is just too small to have compost collection. Penny, would you believe they don't even collect recyclables? You have to take them to the collection bin yourself."

"I apologize for Pillerton's evil ways, but people still put that stuff in the garbage," Rick says. "Maybe once this house doesn't qualify for the church exemption and you have to start paying property taxes, the town can afford some of the big city services you two are used to!"

Kathy sees the twinkle in his eyes and smiles. "Hmm. Collecting everyone's stinky compost. Maybe a business opportunity for the Con," she suggests.

"Don't knock it," Penny says. "Waste management's an honored profession in organized crime." She goes to the stack of boxes she and Kathy had pulled out of the topmost cupboards before going into town that morning and brings back a box for each of them.

"What exactly are we hoping to find?" Rick asks.

"Well, possibly, Gilbert Klein's will," Penny says, "but I doubt we'll be that lucky. Or unlucky, as the case may be. So just anything about his disappearance. Any legal paperwork. Maybe details of what investigations were done in order to obtain the declaration of death."

"It's a long shot." Kathy shrugs. "But I need to go through all this stuff and pack it all up sometime, even if I get the house."

"Looks like this dates back to the Depression," Rick says as he examines a clutch of papers from the box Penny gave him. "Here's a handwritten invoice from Sears Roebuck for a bedroom suite. Two hundred dollars, including rail freight from Chicago. No import duty and no sales tax!"

"I guess the Kleins never threw anything away. Must have been what we call hoarders nowadays," Penny says. "At least it's all tucked away nice 'n' tidy."

"I wonder if that bedroom suite is actually worth something then." Kathy closes up the box she's working on. "You know, with the original receipt. But still. Cheap catalog furniture."

"Not so cheap! Two hundred bucks was a lot of money back then," Rick says. "Fifty cents for a good pair of work boots then, you know, and only a penny to mail a letter!"

"You been talking to your grandfather?" Kathy asks.

"Yup. He talks about those good old days a lot. Sometimes I pay attention." Rick gives Kathy a grin, stops rooting through the box, and pulls out a yellowing newspaper clipping. "Nothing big enough in this box to be a will, I don't think, but interesting stuff! Here's an old newspaper clipping." He unfolds it. "Regina Leader Post. Can't make out the date. Maybe 1930? Oh, Kathy, it's about Henry Klein. That must be a relative ... Isn't that your great-grandfather? Isn't that the name Gramps mentioned?"

Kathy and Penny come and stand on either side of Rick, reading over his shoulder.

Kathy reads aloud, "Gangland Slaying ... Local trucking magnate with ties to Chicago crime syndicate shot."

"Wow, girlfriend," Penny says, "you *do* have gangster genes!"

"How could they print libelous stuff like that?" Kathy wonders aloud. She takes the clipping from Rick and sits down to read it.

"The more salacious the better in those days. They even printed pictures of dead people covered in blood. Don't you remember seeing photos of Bonnie and Clyde riddled with bullets? News and entertainment camouflaged as proof of death. No TV, you know. Plus, no one ever sued anyone for anything back then," Penny says. "Lucky that's changed or I wouldn't have a job!" She heads back into the kitchen, calling over her shoulder, "Want your wine topped up, Kathy? Another beer, Rick?"

"No thanks." Rick pushes papers to one end of the box and fishes something out. Gives a short whistle. Holds up a coin. "Lookit this! A gold coin. Says United States of America, twenty dollars. A US twenty-dollar gold piece!"

Kathy and Penny both come back to look.

Rick drops it in Kathy's hand. "Oh my God! It's heavy for something so small. But how beautiful! A bird ... probably an eagle." She turns it over. "On this side, a woman like the one at the intro of the movies. Is it MGM?"

"No, that's a lion," Penny says as Kathy hands her the coin. "I know what you mean, though. It's like the Columbia woman, maybe. It's really beautiful. I can see why people made these into pendants."

"It's a little worn, but I'll bet it's worth a lot more than twenty dollars today," Rick says. He digs through to the bottom of the box and pulls out dozens of other old coins, including inch-diameter pennies, but no more gold.

Still, it's enough that they search with renewed interest.

"A few of those'd make a nice early retirement fund, Kathy," Penny says.

"Make a start on paying my legal bills, anyway."

But no more coins are found. No helpful paperwork either.

Soon Rick says, "Well, that's it for me, ladies. I got horses to feed 'n' I'm already late. They'll be gettin' frantic." He stands and stretches before slowly making his way to the door.

"Good night. Thanks for dinner!" Penny says. She makes eye contact with Kathy and jerks her head in Rick's direction.

"Yes, thanks." Kathy gets up and follows him to the door.

In the foyer, he turns to her and says quietly, "Can I see you tomorrow night?"

"Tomorrow night." She smiles and turns her face up, and then his lips brush hers. He looks at her for a moment before giving a half shake of his head and going out the door. She latches the screen door behind him, closes the inner door, and sets the deadbolt.

When she returns to the dining room, Penny says, "That didn't take long."

"I told you, we haven't hooked up. So no 'mushing' as my mother used to call it."

"Well, I'd say judging by how he looks at you, he wants to hook up, but if you don't want him, pass him over to me!" Penny giggles. "Hellish good-looking! Either I'd forgotten or he's gotten better with age. He sure fills out those jeans in a most attractive way, and those eyes! I'll 'mush' with him any day!"

"Ha-ha!" Kathy says. "Since when do you 'mush' with guys?"

"I'm open to it!"

"Oh, you're AC-DC now? Anyway, I'm not sure where it's going or even *if* it's going. I'm still married, remember."

"Of course. Which is it now, husband number four?"

"No, Penny. I didn't marry the others. And you should talk!"

"You're right. I'm no good at relationships either."

"Plus ..." Kathy goes to the kitchen and brings the half-empty wine box to the dining room to top up both glasses. "Plus, I keep having these flashbacks, really vivid flashbacks, to when we were dating in high school. Almost like I'm transported back in time. It's off-putting, my mother interrogating me the second I stepped through the door. I guess all mothers do that, but she just seemed … I don't know …"

"Like the gestapo?" Penny offers.

"Gestapo. Yes. Aggressive."

"She ever get … well, *physical?*"

"Hmm. No. Well, no more than sort of pinning me against the wall. And warning me that she could smell him on me. What the hell, eh?"

Penny busies herself sorting papers. Then she stops, looks up, and says, "She's not here, Kathy. And you're both consenting adults. You don't have to marry him, and you don't have to tell your *Arschlöch* husband."

"Brent's not that bad," Kathy says quietly.

"No? So why have you been thinking of divorcing him if he's *not that bad?*" Penny closes up the box she's been sorting through, then straightens and pushes up her glasses. "You know, Kathy, *not that bad* isn't exactly a ringing endorsement. And he *is* an asshole."

Kathy puts the box she's been sorting through up on the window ledge, leans back against the wall, and studies the floor.

"Okay," Penny says, dusting one hand against the other. "Let's leave this for now. How about taking a look in your mother's room? We could pack up her clothes while we're at it."

"Oh, sure. I guess. No reason to put it off any longer." Kathy goes to the back porch and returns with a bundle of flattened boxes and the tape gun; then they go upstairs and into the front bedroom. Kathy folds a box together, tapes the bottom, and sets it on the floor next to the wardrobe.

Penny opens the wardrobe door. "Jeez, I was thinking she might've stashed stuff in her dresser. But here? In this dinky little wardrobe? What do I find? More shoeboxes." She points to the shelf above the clothes rod.

"Well, if they're not full of shoes, let's hope at least there's more of those gold coins!" Kathy chuckles. "But for now, the clothes." She pushes the hangers along the rod and has a quick look. "Don't think we need more than one box for clothes. There sure isn't much here." She pulls out a hanger with a plain navy dress on it, folds it in half, and puts it in the box.

Then she notices a long black garment and pulls it out. Puzzled, she cocks her head. "What's this?"

Penny folds her arms across her chest and gives Kathy a penetrating look. "You don't remember?"

"Remember what?" Kathy furrows her brow.

"Remember the whole bunch of 'em in those robes?"

"Uh, no. Like a choir?"

"Nothing like a choir! Remember when we were supposed to be in bed? Up in your room? When we sneaked out onto the stairs and watched them? The whole scheißen bunch in robes. Chanting. Some kneeling in front of the elders. How furious your mother was when she looked up and saw us? Chased us back into your room and walloped us? 'N' after that, we were locked in?"

"Penny! That's awful!"

"Yes, awful. You were very small. And if you've forgotten it, I'm sorry I reminded you."

Kathy sinks to the bed, bows her head, and studies her clasped hands. "That's why there's that lock on my bedroom door," she says.

Penny sits next to her.

They're quiet for a few moments.

Then Kathy asks, "There's more, isn't there?"

Penny nods.

"Can you tell me?" she whispers.

Penny leans forward, staring unseeingly at the faded roses in the Aubusson rug. Finally, she answers quietly, "Maybe someday."

Kathy's sitting in the lobby of the Pillerton Police Department. She's been waiting for about fifteen minutes, plenty of time to have taken in all the details of the tiny room, from the small safety glass window the civilian receptionist sits behind to the tattered chairs and the stuffed buffalo head, symbol of the Royal Canadian Mounted Police, on the wall above the coat of arms.

Finally, the receptionist tells her she can go in, and the security door to the office area buzzes. When she pushes through it, she sees half a dozen desks piled with papers, computer monitors, and phones.

There are only two officers, though, and one is waving at her. When she gets to his desk, he leaves her standing while he studies his monitor for a few moments. Then he says, "Have a seat," and indicates the chair at the next desk. She pulls it over and sits. It's another moment or two before he looks at her.

"I'm Constable Grogan," he says.

"Kathy Klein. Pleased to meet you."

"So," he begins, "you want to report a stalker or a prowler."

"Yes."

"Which is it?"

Kathy frowns. "Well, I don't really know. He's been poking around my house, looking in my windows. I haven't noticed him anywhere else, like following me, so I guess he's a prowler. He's up to something, and it worries me."

"Okay." Grogan taps at his keyboard for a bit. "Name?" he asks.

"Kathy Klein. K-l-e-i-n."

"Address?"

"Ten Front Street. Here in town."

"Postal code?"

"I'd have to look it up. Can't we just get to the point? Someone's been poking around the house. Pulled weeds so he could look in the basement window even."

"Pulled weeds?"

"Yes, pulled weeds."

"That really *is* suspicious."

Kathy sits up straighter and studies the constable, wondering if that was supposed to be a joke. But there's no trace of humor on his face; he's fixated on his computer monitor, and doesn't make eye contact.

"Okay," Kathy says. "Please just make note of my complaint. He's short for a man, I'd say about five foot six or seven. Burly looking. Well dressed. Very light complexion. White or light blond goatee. Wears a wide-brimmed hat like an Aussie Outback hat. His vehicle's a gray Honda or Toyota, looks new, with a green bumper sticker. Might be a rental. I'd like it on record that I've reported it." She exhales loudly. "But I'm also here to inquire about a missing person."

"Oh? A child? Today?" This seems to arouse Grogan's interest, and he starts to stand.

"No, an adult, about thirty years ago."

Constable Grogan relaxes back in his chair. "Oh. Good!" he says. "A bit late to be reporting it, though, aren't you?"

"It's my father, and I couldn't have reported it when it happened. I wasn't even eight years old! But someone must've reported at the time. I just want to know the status, being as he's never been located. Is anyone working the case still? I mean, I know it's cold, but ..."

"His name?"

"Gilbert Klein."

Constable Grogan makes another entry in the computer and then says, without looking up, "No file here." He swivels his chair so he's looking directly at her. "But we don't have a lot of resources, even less back then. It might've been sent to Regina. And naturally we have no one still on staff from that long ago."

"Oh," Kathy sighs, "well, even if it was sent to another detachment, wouldn't there be a record of it? Is there a file number? Maybe microfiche? Paper files? I can search through old records myself, wouldn't need any of you to do it, if that helps."

Constable Grogan drums his fingers on his desk and says, "I'll ask around. Be back in a few minutes. Can you wait?"

"Yes, of course." Kathy nods, then watches as he heaves himself up out of his chair and weaves his way through the desks into a rear hallway.

While she waits, Kathy checks her phone for e-mails, exchanges text messages with Penny, updates her Facebook status, and still has time to wonder why his desk, alone, is clear of paperwork.

When Constable Grogan returns, he doesn't sit. He just says, "Well, no microfiche, and nobody knows anything. But it'll be in the daily orders so everyone will be made aware at roll call. Also about the guy in the hat. We'll have a car cruise by a few times. Call nine-one-one if he shows up again. We can be there in ten minutes." Then he tosses his pen onto his desk.

My cue to leave, she thinks. *Bet he doesn't know he has icing sugar on his moustache.*

She walks the short distance back to 10 Front Street. Penny isn't due home from Regina for a while, so Kathy changes into her gardening clothes and does some more weeding and tidying up around the yard, staying in the shade as much as possible.

When Penny pulls into the backyard beside the garage, Kathy takes off her gardening gloves and goes to meet her. "You were gone awhile. No luck?"

"No, I got what I wanted at the Court Registry Office almost right away. They were really helpful." Penny's face colors slightly and she smiles. "I stopped in at Stanton, McCafferty, and Prowse and had coffee with Reese." She pulls her small case out from behind the seat and locks the car.

Inside, Kathy makes them each a cup of tea and says, "Nothing much to report at my end. The lard-ass cop, Constable Grogan, hardly paid attention when I told him about Hat Man, and I think he went to the lunchroom for coffee and a doughnut when he said he was looking for my father's file."

Penny shakes her head. "Lazy. Useless. Arschlöch. To serve and protect, my fat fanny. Maybe next time ask if you can please suck his dick!"

"Penny!"

"Don't look so shocked. You know what they say in the military: it's not what you know, it's who you blow. Probably works for cops too."

"What a jaundiced viewpoint! You are so jaded!" Kathy chides.

"Walk a kilometer in my pumps and see how long it takes before you feel the same," Penny says. She starts laying out documents on the dining room table. "Anyway, I made headway, and I didn't have to blow anyone. Come look at this." She turns to Kathy and frowns. "I can't believe you. You hardly brought any clothes and yet you have those ratty old jeans?"

"I didn't bring them. I bought them at a thrift shop here. When I packed, I didn't think about needing work clothes. If you didn't notice, I did some more weeding around the house while I was waiting for you to get back."

"Sorry. I didn't notice."

"Well, it is kind of a drop in the bucket," Kathy clucks. "Anyway, let's see what you got."

Penny hands her the reasons for judgment document. She sits and reads. Louise Klein, with Mr. Big Balls Robertson in attendance, told the court she'd attempted notification by publication in all the major newspapers across the country, and she submitted documentation to substantiate it. She also produced bank records showing Gilbert Klein's accounts hadn't been accessed since his disappearance and his credit cards hadn't been used. She said he had no reason to abandon her, as they had a loving relationship and seldom quarreled, and there had been no quarrel at the time of his disappearance. And she, Louise Klein, was his only relative.

Her lawyer told the court the only conclusion to be inferred from the evidence was that Gilbert Klein had fallen victim to foul play or had an accident. He was an avid amateur naturalist and often hiked in the badlands alone, Mr. Robertson said, so it was conceivable he had an accident or got lost there. No, he hadn't told his wife he was going hiking on the day of his disappearance, but that wasn't unusual, as he often left while she was still asleep. He was reported missing when he didn't return home for dinner. No clues as to his disappearance were ever found. He stressed twenty-five years was long enough for Mrs. Klein to wait.

The judge agreed and ordered issuance of the death certificate, imposing no restrictions on disposition of his property.

"So … does it look okay?"

"They've crossed their t's and dotted their i's, plus Big Balls probably has a lot of cachet with the judges," Penny says. "But the bald-faced lie about there being no other surviving relatives? I don't know how she could stand there in front of a judge and deny your existence."

"Well, we did have quite a set-to when I left. She said I needed to be purified so I could be saved. Otherwise, we couldn't be together in the afterlife and I would be dead to her."

"I suppose she may have believed it." Penny frowns. "A person's memory can play tricks on them."

"Yeah, false memories. Tell a lie often enough and you can start to believe it yourself," Kathy sighs. "I suppose she could've argued I was legally dead. No contact for nearly twenty years, after all. And I wasn't reading newspapers to see if anyone was trying to find me. Who does? Although my bank account, and especially my credit cards, were being well used."

Penny studies her friend's face as if expecting her to say more and then slowly shakes her head. "Best argument I've heard in a while for running up debt!" She smiles. "So I'll scan these into my computer, and we'll also have a hard copy file here. You need to get your computer, and Internet."

"Already in the works. It's a week before the cable company installer can come."

"Too late to help me this time."

"Oh, Penny, I wish you didn't have to go back so soon."

"You still nervous about being here alone?"

"Well, partly that. But also I'll miss you. I don't blame you for going, though. Not having a shower sucks!"

"Yeah, can you do something about that? But seriously, I'll miss you too. And this is such an adventure! But it's a busy time for me at work, and I left without much preparation. I'll book more time off in a month or so and come back then. For sure! 'N' we'll be texting and phoning often. Meantime, I think Mr. Schoenfeld would be happy to be of service!" She nudges her friend with an elbow. "So to speak!"

"Now that you've pointed out how gorgeous he is, I'm seriously considering it!" Kathy grins.

"Yeah, I imagine you didn't notice before."

"I've been thinking, though. Maybe I should fly back with you. I could get my car, then drive back so I'd have it here. I could get my computer, and more of my things, and I need to turn in the rental car. If it's okay to be away right now, with everything. You know."

"Nothing happening here. We know they're going to file their reply on time and what it'll say. So there's nothing more to be done in that department."

"I was thinking about that, but also about that guy who's been skulking around."

"Oh. Well, suppose he was to pry a window open and come in while you're away. Is there anything here you care if he takes?"

"Other than that gold coin, nothing."

"So take that with you, and there's nothing to worry about. It makes sense for you to have your car here instead of keeping that rental. What's it costing you? Thirty dollars a day?"

Kathy nods. "Thirty-eight something with tax. An expense I sure don't need. It would pay for the plane ticket pretty fast, I think. How much is it?"

"I'll give you some of my frequent flyer points."

"Oh, Penny! I couldn't!"

"You could. And will." Penny goes into the dining room and flips open her laptop. "Let's book another ticket. You still got that matchbook from Al's Place with the Wi-Fi password?"

Kathy goes to the catchall bowl on the hall table and comes back with the matchbook. She stands beside Penny's chair, where she can see the screen, and reads out the password.

"They couldn't have just come up with something like 'good booze'?" Penny says as she taps in the series of letters and numbers. "Okay, it's a weak signal, but I'm in. I'm on the twelve fifteen flight. There are still seats available. There's two together a few rows back of the one I've booked. I'll cancel my seat selection, and we'll take those two instead."

eanie's packing some extra clothes to take back to Saskatoon. There isn't much to pack; so few of her prepregnancy clothes fit since she still has the baby tummy, and if it's the same as last time, she won't lose it for a while. Of course, last time she got pregnant before she had a chance to lose it. This time will be different.

It's an hour before Clarence is due home from work, so she takes advantage of his absence to kneel down and examine his shoes. His feet sweat, so there's a musty, gym-locker odor coming from them that permeates the closet. *Need to get some Odor Eaters*, she thinks. She pushes that thought aside and fumes at the row of expensive-looking footwear. *The asshole has more shoes than I do*, she thinks, *and they're better than mine too*. She'd filled some of the waiting time at the NICU poking around on the Internet and now knows one pair of Clarence's custom shoes costs more than all of hers put together.

She gets to her feet and examines the labels in his other clothes. No Wal-Mart George, Eddie Bauer, or even Tip Top Tailors brands here. How many times has he said it's important for him to dress well? Clothes make the man, according to Clarence. Upwardly mobile, that's him. She feels boiling resentment thinking of his complaints about her spending.

A big part of working on our marriage is going to be confronting him on this, she thinks, *and it won't be a pleasant discussion. Whenever I ask him about money, he starts screaming, and I back down. I'm going to have to be prepared for him to scream and not let him off the hook until I get an answer. This is more than just a question of money. It's about this huge lie. He has, well, everything while the kids and I struggle to get by. Is there any reason for this? Anything he can say that will make sense, make me think I should stay married to this man? I made a pact with myself to give our marriage a year. I will have to be ready to pull the plug sooner, depending on how the discussion goes. But I haven't got the energy to get into it now. When the baby's better, and we're back from Saskatoon. Right now, I don't even want to see him.*

The garage door opener hums. *Damn*, she thinks, *he's home early. I'll just say a quick hello, finish packing, and leave.*

She pulls out a couple of blouses from her side of the closet and takes them to the bed to fold them and put them in her suitcase. Then she gets a clean nightgown and underwear from the dresser.

Clarence comes into the bedroom.

"Hi," she says, but she doesn't look up.

"Good, you're still here."

"Not for long. I have to run. I've already missed a bunch of my—our—baby's feedings. I was late getting here. I spent longer than I expected with the boys." She folds the nightgown and lays it in the suitcase. "I miss them," she says quietly.

Clarence comes up behind her, cups her shoulders, and nuzzles her neck. "Miss me too?" he whispers, reaching around under her arms and squeezing her engorged breasts. "Grrrrr!" he growls in her ear. "You know how much I've always loved these when they're like this ... I'm glad you're here, baby. Mr. Johnson missed you." He pushes his erection against her.

She winces and feels the breast milk begin to trickle, knowing now she'll have another delay to deal with that. She shrugs him off and continues packing.

"What's wrong?" he asks.

She shakes her head. "Nothing."

"Good. Nothing's wrong." He steps away from her, takes off his suit jacket, tosses it on the bed, and loosens his tie. "As usual. Nothing's wrong." He leaves the bedroom and clumps down the stairs. She hears him go into the fridge and then snap open a beer.

Pissed off and grouchy as always, she thinks. Odd. Instead of feeling intimidated, she's disgusted. She realizes her adrenaline's up, though, and feels an urgent need to get away. Instead of taking the time to go into the bathroom and drain her breasts, she just changes the pads in her nursing bra, finishes packing, closes her suitcase, and lugs it down to the front entry.

Clarence is sitting in the recliner in the family room. He puts his beer down and sits up when she comes in. "Well, it's good I caught you," he says. "You need to sign some paperwork. For the new mortgage on the house."

"New mortgage?"

"You know how hard it's been to keep up with the payments? Because of the high interest rate?"

She nods.

"Well, Prairie Equity has a better deal than even I can get at the bank."

"Why didn't we get a better deal from your bank, anyway?"

"Let's not rehash all that, Jeanie ..."

"But I've been wondering ... with the banks all advertising such low mortgage rates ..."

"You don't look after these things, I do, remember? But since you ask, you do remember we had basically no down payment? We were lucky to get a mortgage at all. We wouldn't have gotten it if it wasn't for me, for my good connections at the bank."

"Oh."

"Anyway, Prairie Equity is offering a lower rate and longer amortization. You have any clue what amortization is?"

She shakes her head. "What? Longer term?"

"No, same term." He clucks and shakes his head. "This is why I look after these things," he says. "All you need to know is that it makes our payments lower. Why would they do that? Because they're head-hunting me. Head-hunting means they want me to come to work for them."

"They offered you a job?"

"Well no, not yet. They don't have a position open now. But there's not a lot of people around with my qualifications and experience, you know. Your husband is sought after! So they've offered this sweet mortgage deal, hoping that when they do offer me a job, I'll switch horses, so to speak. They'll have to come up with a really good job offer, of course, now that I'm due for a promotion at the bank. But, in the meantime, this will make life a lot easier. I can give you more household money. That'll be a help with the extra expenses, new baby and all."

"Oh, really." Jeanie's shoulders relax. She perches on a barstool. "Well, that *is* good news. But I thought we had a five-year mortgage."

"There's no prepayment penalty, so it makes sense to switch now."

"And I have to sign something?"

"Yes, the new mortgage documents."

"But I didn't have to sign anything before."

"That was different."

"Different how?"

"Look, Jeanie, I've always taken care of all the finances, you know that!" He leaps to his feet and takes several steps toward her. His voice has risen several decibels, his eyes are narrowing, and his face is turning red. "All I need from you is for you to sign the documents!"

Jeanie shrinks. She asks quietly, "Where do we go to do that?"

"You know where the Prairie Equity office is. Just go in and ask to see Donnie Jeffs. You know Donnie. Your brother's buddy. He's got everything all set up."

"You're not going with me?"

"I've already signed. I wanted to get ink on the deal before they reconsidered!" He taps his forehead with his left index finger and grins. "Usin' the ol' noggin!"

"But their office is closed."

"You can do it first thing in the morning. I would go with you, but I have to work. Still pretty backlogged because of being away." Clarence comes to stand over her.

She shrinks some more, but now his shoulders relax and he smiles. He takes her face in his hands and kisses her gently. "We can use some time, just the two of us." Another gentle kiss. "What we've been through these past few weeks! We haven't been to the new Holiday Inn yet. I hear the restaurant's decent. Let's go up there and have a nice dinner."

She takes several deep breaths and sits up straighter. "I'll have to let the hospital know ..."

"It shouldn't be a problem, should it?"

"No. I guess not. They've actually suggested I take a break."

"Okay! It's all set. You go have a nice relaxing bath and change. Put on some makeup. And wear that pretty pink blouse."

Jeanie nods. She thinks, *Yes, my pretty thrift-store blouse.* But she gets off the barstool.

Clarence draws her into his arms, kisses her forehead, looks her in the eye, and says, "Honey, I know it's been hard on you, making do with so little household money. I don't know how you've managed. This is going to be good for us." He kisses her mouth oh so gently before releasing her.

Jeanie studies his face. Where did the red-faced, "all I need from you is for you to sign the documents" Clarence disappear to so suddenly? *Can I trust this change? He didn't keep screaming when I pressed him about the mortgage,* she thinks, *or at least he got himself under control quickly. And he seems so much gentler than when he came into the bedroom, or when he nearly launched himself out of his chair minutes earlier—more like the Clarence I married. Maybe some time alone together will be just what the doctor ordered.*

She goes back upstairs and runs water in the tub.

Donnie's at his desk with his third coffee of the morning, nursing a wicked hangover and cursing the noise from Diana slamming file cabinet drawers just outside his office. *I've told her about that! She never fuckin' learns. Maybe I'll send her to the mailroom and get someone better looking at the front desk. Maybe Tina. She's complained about hating hairdressing, being on her feet all day,* he thinks. *'Course she can't type, but she can make up for it in the suite … I'm going to have to get rid of all the glass around my office too. Just build solid, noise-proof walls. Besides all the racket, I'm like a fuckin' goldfish in here. But then, if I had Tina instead of Diana to look at …*

"So, near as I can figure, he's overstated what he embezzled. It looks like it's actually under two million," the thin, bespectacled man seated across from him interrupts his reverie. He rustles through papers and then shoves a document toward him.

"I don't need to look fer Chrissake, Jim!" Donnie snaps. "Just gimme the bottom line, okay?"

"Okay. It's under two million."

"Did you talk to Evan about it?"

"Yup. Per your instructions. He isn't going to fire him or bring charges right away. He'll wait for the forensic audit. He's going to reduce his lending limit and approve every loan himself. Of course, he's worried about his own job when his bosses find out how long he's known about this and didn't blow the whistle. Oh, and you wanted to know who the independent auditors are. I'll e-mail you the contact details."

"Okay." Donnie roots through his desk drawer, comes up with an aspirin bottle, shakes three into his hand, and washes them down with coffee. Movement at the front counter attracts his attention; he looks up and sees a pretty woman with a mass of dark blond curls at the reception desk. He nods in her direction. "That's Mrs. Weaver now." He picks up a file folder from the side of his desk, shoves everything else aside, and puts it front and center.

"The other thing," Jim says, getting to his feet and going to the door, "I don't know what he did with his first payment, but there's no sign any of it went against the bogus loans. They're all in arrears. And they have less than a hundred bucks in their checking account."

Donnie shakes his head. "Stupid bastard," he mutters. "He's stashed the cash somewhere."

"Looks that way." Jim opens the door, holds it, and says, "I'll send Mrs. Weaver in." Then he turns and walks to the reception desk and points Jeanie to Donnie's office.

"Jeanie! Nice to see you. It's been too long." Donnie stands and extends his hand as she comes into his office. "Please have a seat."

Jeanie gives his hand a quick shake and smiles. "Hello," she says, as she drops into the chair just vacated by Jim.

She looks tired, Donnie thinks, *those big dark circles under her eyes*. He has a brief twinge of regret that she's about to sign away her home but then reminds himself of the nice commission check he'll get out of it. He smiles. "Thanks for coming in. I won't take much of your time." He sits and opens the file with the documents inside, pushes them across the desk, and hands her a pen. "I've got the pages ready so all you have to do is sign next to your husband's signatures."

The papers are folded so all that shows is the signature block, where

Clarence has already signed. Jeanie sits back, unfolds the top document, and begins reading.

"Jeanie," Donnie says, "these documents are complicated, and your husband's already given them a good going over. He's very familiar with these legal documents. All the lawyerspeak. Gibberish! But he understands it." He stands and reaches across the desk to take the document from her. He refolds it and lays it on the desk in front of her again, pointing to the red *X* where she's supposed to sign.

"By the way, pink's really your color."

"Thank you." Jeanie frowns and looks at the papers.

"Go ahead," Donnie says. *Jesus*, he thinks. *Her lard-ass husband said she'd just sign because he told her to. Now I have to suck hole to her?*

He stabs at the signature line again, sees her startled look, and realizes that was too forceful. He fixes a mild expression on his face and says, "Just a couple of signatures 'n' you can be on your way. I understand you're eager to get back to your new baby. How's she doing, anyway?"

"She's coming along," Jeanie says.

"What did you name her?"

Jeanie shakes her head. "Haven't yet." Then she shuffles the papers into one pile, picks them up, and stands. "You know, I'm going to have to read these. I don't have time right now. I'll get them back to you in a day or two. Thank you."

She turns and goes out the door.

Donnie jumps to his feet and scurries out from behind his desk to follow. "Jeanie! Is there something you don't understand? Can I help?"

"I'll get back to you," she says, but she doesn't turn.

Short of tackling her, there's nothing he can do to stop her. He sees Max coming into the reception area with a Starbucks paper cup. He waves at him frantically and points at Jeanie.

Max stops short.

Jeanie hurries into the reception area, glances at Max, then stops and faces him.

"Max!" she exclaims.

"Jeanie! Hi!" Max answers. He sets his coffee down on the reception desk and reaches out a hand. "How're you?"

"Pretty good, all things considered," she says. She takes his right hand with her left, then stretches up to give him a friendly hug. She steps back and smiles. "You look good! When did you get back in town?"

"Well, I live in White City, not Pillerton, but it's been a couple years now."

"A couple years? And you haven't called me?"

"Well, you know, you're married 'n' all."

"How does that matter? We're friends from way back!" She shakes her head. "But what about you? Some smart cookie snapped you up?"

"I'd say it'd take a dumb cookie, not a smart one."

"Oh, Max!" Jeanie chuckles and soft punches his bicep. "You here for a loan?"

"No, I work here. Well, that is, I work for the company. But I'm usually on the road."

"You by any chance have a black Mustang?"

"I do."

"I thought it might've been you. Nice ride! Suits you!" Jeanie smiles. "I've seen you around. Wasn't sure, but I thought it looked like you!" She gives his forearm a rub. "I'm sorry I'm in such a hurry right now. But we have to get together for a coffee and catch up, maybe in a week or two? My baby's in hospital in Saskatoon. I have to get back. But it's good to see you!"

"Good to see you too! I hope your baby's okay," Max says, stepping aside to let her walk past him and out the door. He watches her until she gets in her van, waves at him, and drives away.

Donnie beckons Max into his office. "You didn't stop her!" he hisses.

Max gives him a dark look and says, "How could I?"

"Fuck!" Donnie drops into his chair. He leans back and throws up his hands. "I guess you couldn't. She not only didn't sign, but she also took the fuckin' paperwork with her."

"So?"

"So she'll realize if she signs, bye-bye house. And that we, and her loving husband, were going to fuck her over. Fuck, fuck, fuck!" He pounds his desktop with a fist. "He was so sure she'd just do what he told her to."

Then Donnie sits quietly, deep in thought.

Max remains standing in the doorway, watching, waiting for him to continue.

Finally, Donnie looks up and says, "Well, the wheels haven't fallen off this deal yet. We'll have a talk with Mrs. Weaver. Enlighten her about her husband, the fact he lied about the house having a mortgage. Tell her he embezzled the money to buy it. Now he needs the money to pay it back, or he'll go to jail and they'll be out in the street." He exhales loudly. "Yup, that should work. You go after her, Max. Pick her up and take her to the curling rink. We'll have a nice private interview. Phone me when you've got her. I'll call Nick and Marcus. We'll meet you there." Donnie picks up his phone and looks up to see Max hasn't moved.

"Something you need?" He scowls.

Max says, "Nope," turns, and heads for the door.

But Max doesn't go after Jeanie.

He walks to his car angle-parked in front of the building, opens the driver's side door, and stands looking back. The front of the old building has been fixed up with new windows, rock facing, and heavy timber post-and-beam trim. *Prairie Equity* gleams in tall brass letters over the door. *All new and shiny on the outside*, he thinks, *but same old rot on the inside*. He realizes he's had enough of these assholes. More than enough. Threatening Jeanie crosses the line.

"I can't help you, Jeanie," he mutters, "but I'll be fucked if I'll help *them*." He gets into his Mustang and drives to his house.

Once home, he fills garbage bags with his clothes, opens the floor safe, and empties the contents into a duffel bag.

Then he makes a phone call. "Hey, Arnie. Got a favor to ask. I'm goin' away for a while. My hog's in the driveway. You know where the keys are. Can you guys swing by and pick it up? Yeah, today. Right now if you can. The shop? Yeah, that'd be good … I'll let you know … Thanks, buddy."

He turns the phone off and lays it on the kitchen counter. Divesting himself of the company phone, symbolically severing ties, lifts a weight off his shoulders. "Consider this my letter of resignation," he says to no one.

When his bags are stuffed in the trunk, he gets Delilah to hop in the back and settles himself in the driver's seat. He drives out to the Trans Canada Highway and heads west.

Jeanie's mind is in turmoil throughout the drive to Saskatoon. Clarence was so like his old self the night before, once he got past the idea she had no interest in having him fondle her. And definitely no interest in Mr. Johnson. *He must be nuts*, she thinks, *if he really thought I would welcome sex.*

Then like a switch flipped, he turns nice. Says let's go for dinner. And they *did* have a nice time. She talked about the baby, the boys, and he stayed engaged in the conversation. He only disengaged when she pressed him for details about what he'd done in Toronto. If he had a lawyer for his lawsuit against the cab company. If he'd seen any of the sights. CN Tower, maybe? Who had he spent time with there, some of the bank bigwigs? Maybe had time to take in a play?

He had so little to say about Toronto and the lawsuit for his injury, it seemed out of character. He kept bringing the conversation back to how much better it would be for them, for their family, once they had smaller mortgage payments. The smaller payments would start as soon as she signed the new mortgage.

If he seemed to be holding something back, she pushed it out of her mind. He was his old witty, funny self. They even slept together, just cuddling. Cuddling!

And now she knows why.

Once back at the hospital, hunger pangs tell her it's lunchtime. She buys a sandwich and a bottle of water at the kiosk in the lobby and goes upstairs to spend some time with her baby, marveling again at how perfect she is even though so tiny. She's breast-feeding now. The NICU nurses are supportive. The pediatrician tells her the baby is doing well enough to transfer to the Regina hospital and that she won't need to be there for very long. *I'm going to have to name her soon*, she thinks, *now that she's out of the woods. My beautiful little girl!*

Then she settles into the armchair next to the incubator, unwraps her sandwich, and digs out the documents. She munches tuna and lettuce on multigrain while she reads.

What she'd caught a glimpse of in Donnie's office, what made her realize she had to read the documents thoroughly, were the words "Children of Noah," which didn't seem to have any place in a mortgage with Prairie Equity.

And now she sees the funds are payable to Clarence.

The implications flood her brain. She thinks, *If I hadn't unfolded that document! And Clarence, being the one who knows all about these legal documents, signed this?*

So much for working on my marriage.

Clarence comes back to his desk after a lengthy, unpleasant lunch with Monica. He still hasn't had a phone call from Donnie telling him that Jeanie signed the documents, and there's no message about it on his office phone either. Asshole! He's done his part. What's the holdup? He told them this was going to go down! They had plenty of time to get the money ready.

Then he sees an untidy pile of papers on his desk blotter. He picks them up and finds they're the documents for new loans he'd set up earlier in the week, back on his desk and all stamped "Declined." He flips through them but can't see anything out of order. There's nothing that should've set off any alarm bells. He picks up the sheaf of papers and marches into the manager's office.

"Hey, Evan," he blurts out, even though Evan's on the phone, "what's this?" He shakes the papers.

Evan frowns at him and speaks into the receiver, "Something's come up. I'll call you back. Five minutes." He puts the receiver back in its cradle. "What is it, Clarence?"

"All these loans. Declined. Why? My customers are gonna be furious! They already made deals based on getting this financing."

"Oh, of course. Well, new regs. Your lending authority is reduced to twenty-five K. Too many past-due loans and loans in default. You have to be more careful, Clarence. More selective. So now all loans have to be approved by Regional Office, and I have to sign off on them before they get sent up the chain. These will all have to be done up as RO applications."

"But that takes time! And twenty-five K? You can't even buy a decent car for that!"

"I know. It sucks. But I'm sure you can explain it to your customers in a way they'll understand. You're good with people."

Clarence studies Evan's face. Was that a smirk? He decides it's only his usual befuddled expression, as if he just woke up in the rain.

Evan picks up the phone again. "Oh, and by the way, I had Sherry pull the files for the loans in default. They're on your desk. Some are already close to being categorized as bad debts and will be by year-end. You need to phone those borrowers and see if they can't at least make a payment, or we'll have to call them."

"No, don't call the loans. These people are farmers. You know, salt of the earth. There's got to be a good reason why they're in default. They likely just need to ship some grain or sell a cow or something. I'll talk to them."

Clarence turns and scurries back to his desk.

How am I going to get another million before I disappear, he wonders, *at twenty-five K a pop? It would really look suspicious if I wrote all those loans in a few days. Even dim-bulb Evan would catch on.*

He feels sweat trickling down his armpits. He sheds his jacket. His face feels hot, and when he wipes his hand across his forehead, it's sweaty too. He rubs his hands down his pants to dry his palms, sits at his desk, and picks up his telephone receiver to begin the pretense of phoning customers. Then he thinks better of it, stands, and gathers up the stack of files. With his jacket over his arm, he heads for the door.

"Sherry," he says to the receptionist as he goes by her desk, "I'm gonna work from home this afternoon. Might have to take off to go up to Saskatoon. You know, because of the baby."

"Something wrong?" she calls after him. But he pushes out the door without replying.

He calls Donnie from his car.

It rings and rings and then goes to voice mail.

Rick and Jeanie sit at a table near the Hospital Auxiliary coffee kiosk in the lobby of the hospital. They've both got tall coffees. Rick has a cheese Danish.

"That's not a substitute for dinner, you know, even with the so-called cheese in it," Jeanie tells him.

"Yes, Mutti." He grins. He takes a bite and washes it down with coffee. "We can go to the Tim Horton's across the street if you want."

"No ... I really ... Well, I had a sandwich at lunchtime, and it's still sitting like a lump in my stomach. I'm just so rattled with this whole thing. That's why I called you. I know it's a lot to ask of you, to make the drive up, I just needed—"

"Take a deep breath, muffin. Put it out of your mind for a few minutes." He takes a few more bites of his pastry, demolishing most of it, and says, "I think our little munchkin's grown since the last time I saw her."

"Yup. She's gained four ounces. I'm trying to think of a name for her. Can't keep calling her Munchkin."

"How about Rickie? After her uncle."

"I was thinking more of Hermine. After her grandmother." She laughs at the moue of distaste that crosses her brother's face.

Seeing he's nearly finished eating, she digs through her satchel for the papers and lays them on the small table in front of him. "Here's what they wanted me to sign."

Rick stuffs the rest of his Danish in his mouth, wipes his hands on the paper napkin, and starts flipping pages. "I see what you're talkin' about," he says. "He's selling your house to the Con! And for less than it's worth, from what you've told me."

"Less than we paid for it," she sighs. "Well, if I can believe what Clarence told me."

"Muffin, this is wrong. So wrong! How could he do that, try to hoodwink you? 'N' the fuckin' Con! I wonder how they're connected to Prairie Equity."

"I don't understand that either. I thought maybe they were just going to hold the mortgage, like an investment, which would be fine. Except the money doesn't go to pay out the old mortgage, it goes to Clarence. And if it was a second mortgage, wouldn't it say that somewhere?"

"I think so." He studies the documents more closely. "But then ... I'm sure Donnie said Prairie Equity doesn't do second mortgages. And anyway, if you already have a big mortgage, why would they loan you another four hundred thousand on top? Is your house worth that much?"

"Close to a million? Hell no! Clarence says we have hardly any equity, that if we sold it, we wouldn't get any money, and he certainly never said anything about getting four hundred thousand cash! Which can only mean there was no mortgage all this time. How could that be? And where did he get the money to buy the house in the first place? I really don't understand all this." She sits back and closes her eyes for a moment, then takes a deep breath. "I suppose you're going to say you were right about him all along."

"Aw, muffin."

"Well, you were! But I still can't believe he'd stoop to this. And there's more. The kids 'n' I've been living on crumbs while he's been buying five-hundred-dollar shoes. I guess he had a lot of disposable income, not having to actually make those big mortgage payments he always grumbled about."

"Five-hundred-dollar shoes?"

"Yeah, custom-made shoes. The first time I really looked at them ... when he came home from Toronto, they were dirty. Muddy. Where'd he get mud in Toronto? Why would it still be on his shoes after he'd been through airports and on the plane? But that's aside from the fact the damn things cost five hundred dollars a pair, and up. I was cleaning them when I noticed the logo."

"Doesn't make sense." Rick shakes his head. "I don't know about shoes. That sounds ridiculous. But this fake mortgage scam—I can't believe my ol' buddy Donnie's part of this. Two-faced, lying bastard!"

"He actually took the papers out of my hands when I picked them up to read them. Then he said Clarence is the one who understands all this legal stuff. He's already signed. So just go ahead. Pfft!" Jeanie hisses. "Yeah, Clarence knows, all right! The thing is, I don't know what to do, where to go from here."

"Well, you're not signing the house away just to give dickhead the money—that's for goddamned sure. We need a lawyer." He looks at his coffee, now cold, with the cream forming a scummy ring inside the paper cup, and pushes it away. "You aren't going to stay married to him, are you?"

"No! Absolutely not! I was close to ending the marriage before I knew all this. Now there's no way I ever want him near me again. But how do I get him out of the house? What if he takes the boys while I'm here? I don't think he wants them, but with what he's done ... he might take them just to get at me. People do awful things! You hear of awful things! I'm scared, Rick!"

"Right now, nobody knows you're not going to sign. So I'll call Mutti and tell her there's a problem and, if Clarence shows up, not to let him in the house and definitely not to let him take the kids anywhere. Sarah's there too, and where she is, those two big boys will be. So, our boys are well protected. He won't be able to grab them tonight. Tomorrow, maybe they go to visit Aunt Waltraud for a while? She's alone in that big house ... Clarence doesn't know where Waltraud lives, does he?"

"I doubt it. I don't think he's ever gone there with us. But the kids don't know her very well either. It would be awfully hard on them."

"You know her place is close to the Regina hospital, right? If your baby gets transferred back there, you could stay with them. It would be handy. So it's something to think about. We'll wait 'n' see on that. Meantime, we'll make sure someone's with them at all times. Okay?"

Jeanie nods.

"You know," Rick continues, "the Con cheated Kathy out of her inheritance. Somehow they got her mother to give them that house. Maybe this is just business as usual for them."

They stand, and Jeanie gathers her things. The intense feeling of angst is abating, replaced with relief now that her big brother's here to help. She tears up.

Rick pulls her to him for a hug, rubs her back, and says, "Don't worry, muffin. We'll work this out. Have faith."

12

onstable Grogan is cruising around Pillerton, thinking about finding a secluded spot for a nap. Just for a lark, he drives past 10 Front Street. He thinks, *Boy, it really is a spooky-looking old place. Can hardly see the house through the overgrown hedge. Just a glimpse through the front gate.* He decides to go around to the back lane and park in the shade behind the house. Number Ten being the only house on the block, no one ever uses that lane, and it's surrounded by bushes, so if someone did drive by, his cruiser wouldn't even be seen. He wonders why he never thought of it before. Once the problem with the girl is solved and the house is vacant again, he'll definitely use it a lot.

But as he approaches the dilapidated single-car garage, he sees a gray Toyota Corolla with a green Economy Car Rentals bumper sticker, not parked in the short driveway access to the garage, but tucked behind the hedge.

"I'll be goddamned," he mutters. He parks blocking the other car, picks up his radio, and tells dispatch to send backup. In minutes the other cruiser pulls up. He sees it's Constable Peets and goes to the driver's window.

"This car doesn't belong here," he tells her. "Go around to the front. I'll take the back. Might be nothing, but could be someone who's not supposed to be there is in the house."

Once Constable Peets drives away, Grogan walks purposefully around the rental car and through the tall, dry weeds of the backyard, but he sees no one. He lifts his hat and wipes his sweaty forehead on a sleeve, hoping it's nothing, that there's no one here who shouldn't be and if there is, it's not one who runs. He decides if it's a runner, Peets can take it, or maybe he'll just shoot the son of a bitch.

He's on the broken concrete walk beside the house when he hears Peets call out, "Halt! Police!"

"Damn!" he snarls. The man Kathy Klein described to him bursts out around the corner with Constable Peets right behind and almost runs right into him.

"Whoa! Whoa! Whoa!" Constable Grogan says as he grabs him by the clothes, spins him around, and shoves him up against the house. He pushes the smaller man's face hard into the wall, breaking his sunglasses and knocking them and his hat off.

"Ahhh!" he cries. He's thrashing, but Grogan leans his much greater weight against him and pins him to the wall.

"What're you in such a hurry for?" Grogan asks. "Why'd you wanna run away from my lovely coworker, eh?"

"He's got tools," Peets says. "He was usin' 'em on the door."

"Lost your keys, did you?"

Nothing.

"Okay. I'm gonna let you go now. You run again, you'll get shot. Okay? Get your gun out, Peets."

Constable Peets opens her holster and pulls out her service revolver, leveling it at the man who's squashed against the wall.

Constable Grogan turns his attention back to the small man as he releases him by taking a step away. His hair's white, but he's strong. Not elderly. "No, keep lookin' at the wall. Put your hands up against it. I'm gonna pat you down and empty your pockets. You got any sharps on you? Anything I might stick myself with?"

Again, no reply.

Grogan does the pat-down, pulling a wallet out of the man's hip pocket. He opens it and finds his driver's license. "Okay, Alphonse Baron of Chicago. Let's have your hands."

Baron drops his arms, and Grogan grabs them, pulls them behind Baron's back, and puts the handcuffs on before he lets him turn around.

"What're you up to there?"

Baron just looks at him with an insolent, unblinking stare. Those strange, colorless eyes seem to see right through him. He's mildly put off and notices Peets shudder when he turns and fixes his impudent stare on her.

"Still got nothing to say? Well, tell you what. Let's go down to the station house and see if we can think of something to talk about." He marches the man out to his squad car, opens the door to the back seat, places a hand on his head, and pushes him in, slamming the door behind him.

"Hey, gorgeous," he says to Peets, "thanks. I'll take it from here."

"Sure," she says. She hands him the man's hat and the broken sunglasses, as well as the little packet of lock-picking tools. "See you in a bit."

Constable Grogan slides into the driver's seat and makes a phone call. "Yeah, Chief. That guy Mr. Reeves wanted to talk to? He's in my cruiser right now … A bag? Okay. Tell Mr. Reeves I'll meet him there."

The three Illustrious Ones huddle around the altar inside the temporary communion room. Donnie says, "Max was supposed to pick up Jeanie Weaver and bring her here. That was hours ago. I haven't heard from him since he left. He's not answering his phone."

"When did he leave?"

"This morning. Maybe about ten. She was on her way to Saskatoon. He was supposed to intercept her."

"I'll try calling him." Nick touches Max's number on his phone, listens, and then says, "Hey, Max, why aren't you here? We're waitin', 'n' Donnie says he's left quite a few fuckin' messages. Get back to me ASAP."

He turns to the other two men. "Nope, voice mail again. Where the fuck is he?"

"Maybe he couldn't intercept her 'n' had to go all the way to Saskatoon," Marcus says.

"Still. What's that—a couple hours each way? He should be here by now. And he goddamned sure should be answering his phone."

"Looked to me like he has the hots for her. Maybe they stopped somewhere to fuck," Donnie says. "But he better fuckin' show up soon. Even without her. We need him for this guy." He nods his head in the direction of the man with a brown paper bag over his head, tied to a chair in the middle of the room.

"Donnie, fer Chrissake, she just had a baby. You think she wants to fuck? I mean, anyone?" Marcus shakes his head.

"What else could be keeping him?"

"Accident, maybe," Marcus suggests.

"Never mind, you two. We got a problem," Nick says. "We been relying on Max too much. This is a wake-up call. We gotta get some depth in the security department." He scratches his neck and then stands arms akimbo. "Marcus, you come with me. We'll go to Max's place and see if that gives us any answers. Donnie, you mind our guest."

Nick and Marcus head out the door.

Donnie walks over to the captive and lifts the bag off his head.

"Wow, that's some white hair you got, eh? Albino?" Donnie goes back to his chair and reaches for the Crown Royal and a shot glass from under the altar. He fills the little glass and salutes the man in the chair with it, saying, "Just you 'n' me, Alfie. Here's lookin' up your old address."

His phone rings. He pulls his jacket off the chair back and fishes the phone out of the pocket. Sees the caller is Clarence, again, and touches Decline.

Nick steers his Range Rover into the driveway at Max's house and turns off the ignition. "No vehicle," he says. "Check the garage."

He and Marcus get out. Marcus goes to the window on the side of the garage and looks in. "Nothin' here," he calls back.

Nick climbs the steps to the front door and rings the bell. He can hear the chiming inside but no footfalls coming to answer, and no barking dog either. "Delilah's not here," he says. "This isn't good."

He pulls a ring of keys out of his pocket, sorts through them, and finding the one he wants, unlocks the door. He steps into the foyer, calling, "Max? Hello! Max?"

Marcus comes into the house behind him.

"No one here," Nick tells him. "Could've taken the dog to the park or something, though. Go upstairs. Check the closets. Bathroom."

Marcus nods and heads up the stairway.

Nick goes through to the kitchen and notes the accumulation of dirty dishes and empty Chinese takeout containers on the counter above the dishwasher. He opens the refrigerator and sees there's isn't much food, but that's not unusual for a bachelor—just three grilled hamburger patties under stretch wrap on a plate, a couple of slices of desiccated pizza, and the usual condiments. There's no beer, but that could be explained by the impressive stack of empties in the dining room next to the weight bench.

He looks out the patio doors into the backyard but sees nothing out of the ordinary.

"He's in the wind," Marcus calls as he thumps back down the stairs. "Emptied all the drawers and closets. No shavin' stuff."

Nick shakes his head. Takes a deep breath. Paces a few steps. Then punches the wall. "Fuckin' shit!" he says, shaking his hand. "Fuckin' last guy I'd've thought would go AWOL."

"Left his phone." Marcus goes over to the peninsula counter to pick it up. He turns it on. "Password protected."

"Pass code's the same as the lock on the curling rink."

Marcus enters it and says, "I'm in."

He touches the phone icon and then Recents.

"Looks like he called some guy named Arnie Anderson about the time Donnie said he should've been headin' up to Saskatoon."

"Let me call Arnie and see what he can tell us."

Nick takes the phone from Marcus and touches the screen. It dials Arnie.

"Hey, Max," a man says, "where you at?"

"Arnie?"

"Yeah?"

"This is Nick Reeves. I've got Max's phone. You're the last person he called. I don't know where he is, and it sounds like you don't either."

Other than the sound of Arnie exhaling smoke, it's quiet on the other end.

"Arnie?"

"Yeah?"

135

"Max works for me. I get nervous when I can't get ahold of him. Plus, he forgot his phone. Any idea where he is?"

"Nope."

"Okay." Nick paces across the kitchen and back. "Okay, Arnie. You by any chance lookin' to pick up a few bucks? Help me out with a little problem?"

"Maybe," Arnie says. "What you got in mind?"

"Can we meet?"

"I guess."

"I'm at Max's house. How soon can you be here?"

"Uh, half an hour."

"Make it fifteen minutes," Nick says and hits End.

Marcus flops down on the couch, picks up the remote, turns on the TV, and starts scrolling through the guide. Nick checks all the cupboards, comes out with a jar of peanut butter, and perches on a barstool at the kitchen peninsula with a spoon. He eats out of the jar while watching Marcus flip through the channels.

"Four hundred channels 'n' nuthin' on," Marcus says. He settles on a Showtime rerun of *Gone Girl*, although it's already halfway through.

They watch for a while, and then Nick says, "He's fuckin' late." He gets to his feet and paces back and forth between the front and side windows.

At the half-hour mark, there's the roar of motorcycles. Nick watches four Harleys pull up, stop, and back against the curb to park. The riders dismount and take off their German outlaw helmets, and the one with the blond dreadlocks pulled back into a ponytail comes to the door.

Nick opens it. "You must be Arnie," he says, sticking his hand out.

Arnie shakes it.

"I'm Nick. Come in. Bring your buddies if you want."

Arnie turns and waves the others in.

Nick stands aside to let them pass.

"This is Marcus," Nick says.

They all nod and mumble greetings.

"Sorry," Nick says. "I'd offer you a drink, but Max seems to be outta booze."

Arnie stands with Nick. Two of the others perch here and there around the room, and one stands with his back against the door.

"Okay. So. No news about Max?" Nick begins.

Arnie tucks a strand of hair that's escaped his ponytail back behind his ear, and says, "Why d'you wanna know?"

"Let's sit," Nick says, leading him to the stools at the peninsula. "As I told you on the phone," he says quietly, "he works for me. I got a couple things going on I need him for. Looks like he's bugged out. I still got those couple things. Max may come back or he may not. Regardless, those couple things I'm talking about can't wait. You interested?"

"What's it worth?"

"You ever hear Max complain he wasn't paid well enough?"

Arnie's eyes narrow. He swivels his stool around, leans an elbow back on the counter, and looks around the room at his friends. Then he scratches the blond stubble on his jaw and says, "Okay. Say we're interested. What's the job?"

"Well, it's pretty simple, really. We got a guy who won't talk. And a stinky who won't sign. Any ideas on how to convince these two they'd be better off cooperating?"

Arnie snorts, "Sounds simple enough. When do we start?"

"Tonight."

Arnie looks at his friends, then shrugs and nods.

They leave by the front door. Nick turns out the lights and locks up. "You know the old curling rink in Pillerton?" he asks. The bikers all shake their heads. The gray-bearded one says, "I know where Pillerton is. Never drove in off the highway to go take a gander, though."

"Okay. You can go ahead and wait for me at the turnoff, or follow me." Nick and Marcus get into the Range Rover and head out. The motorcycles fall in behind.

When they get to the curling rink, they find Baron is disoriented and barely conscious. He's bleeding from his nose and split lip and has a rapidly blackening eye.

Donnie's got an ice cream bucket of ice water on the altar and is soaking his fist in it.

"I see you started without us," Nick says.

"Yeah, well, thought I'd make use of the time while I was waitin'."

"Did he say anything?"

Donnie shakes his head and stands to greet the four men who've followed Nick and Marcus inside.

Nick makes introductions, then goes over to Baron and squats beside his chair. "Look, Alphonse. It's really very simple. Tell us why you're so fuckin' interested in that house and you're free to go. You'd like that, wouldn't you? I mean, nice-lookin' guy like you. Don't want that face messed up, do you?"

Baron sits up straighter and looks askance at the bikers lounging around the altar ten feet away. Donnie's offered them the bottle of rye, and they're pouring shots.

"What about it, Alphonse? Why you wanna get into Ten Front Street so bad?"

Baron spits.

Nick jerks back.

Arnie snaps to attention. He thumps his glass down on the altar, strides across the floor, plants his feet, and delivers a hard punch to Baron's belly followed by a couple of quick jabs to his face.

With the first punch, Baron falls over into his restraints. Then his head snaps back with the punches to his face.

"Gaahh! Ahhh!" he cries.

Nick holds up his hand. "Okay, Baron, isn't that enough?"

Baron glares at him through eyes rapidly swelling shut. A stream of urine runs down his pant leg and forms a puddle under his chair.

"Now look what you did, Baron. You pissed your nice pants. I think your nice shirt's ruined, what with the blood you're leaking too," Nick says.

"Let's help him outta them wet pants." Arnie says. Signaling his friends to come and hold him up, he unties Baron, unbuckles his belt, zips down the fly, and tugs the pants so they fall around his feet. He pulls his underpants down as well.

"Well, lookit this!" Arnie says. "White pubes! 'N' tiny li'l white nuts. Steroids?" He pulls a knife out of his boot. Uses the tip to lift Baron's testicles. "Don't jiggle now. Don't want the knife to slip 'n' damage what little misters you got ... Yup, we'll still be able to attach the electrodes to 'em." He motions to one of the other men and stands aside while he gives him several punches to the gut.

"Wanna talk now?" Arnie asks. "Before the electrodes come out?"

Baron spits again. Bloody slime runs down Arnie's cheek.

The fourth man sets to work again, punching his gut and his chest right above the heart, and then he delivers a couple more hits to the face.

Baron's body sags. He's lost consciousness. They dump him onto the chair.

Arnie turns to Donnie and says, "We could use that water you got there, bro."

Donnie gets to his feet and takes the bucket to Arnie, who pours it over Baron's head.

Baron coughs. Gasps. Opens his eyes.

"Okay," Arnie says to him, "you know, there's enough of us to keep asking questions for a long time. You'll be tired of it long before we are, I guarantee it. Might as well save yourself some hurtin' 'n' tell us now."

"I have friends," Baron rasps. "You'll be sorry."

Arnie shrugs. "You really think your friends're gonna help you?"

"They know where I am. You kill me," he rasps, "they'll come for you."

Nick comes up to squat next to Baron again. "Oh, they know you're here? Right here? I'll bet you don't even know where you are right now."

"They know I was coming to Pillerton. The cops'll … cops'll have a record."

"See, now, that's where you're wrong. You didn't see the inside of the cop shop, did you? And your 'friends'. Did you tell 'em why you were coming to Pillerton?"

"They know why. I've told 'em all about your … operation."

"Oh, our operation? We're not talking about our operation. We're talking about the house you can't seem to stay away from."

"They know why …"

"Well, I sure as fuck don't know why, so please, enlighten me!"

Baron shakes his head and tries to stand.

Nick straightens and steps away, motioning Arnie and his friends to continue. After more hard blows, he passes out again, and Donnie's sent to the kitchen in the old part of the curling rink for more water.

Baron is revived again, but he's still only barely conscious. He topples off the chair and lies prone on the cold concrete floor, shivering, teeth chattering.

Two of the men deliver sporadic heavy motorcycle boot kicks to his gut. Kidneys. Head.

"Okay! Okay!" he gasps. "I'll tell you! Aggh. Aggh. I'll tell you."

He whispers something in his raspy, ruined voice.

"Speak up," Nick says. They all move in closer.

"The money," he coughs.

"What money?"

Baron gags and then continues, "The money ... stole ... from ... great-grandfather. Never found ... still in the house ..." He gags and vomits, splattering Arnie's boots.

"Fuck! What a mess!" Arnie growls. He gives the prone man another kick to the torso.

"Who's your great-grandfather?" Nick asks. "And when ... what're you talkin' about?"

"Long ... ago. Money ... never found. He told my grandfather ..."

"Who? Who?" He grabs Baron's shirt and shakes him.

"Al ... Cap ..." And then he passes out again.

"Well," Arnie says, "might need electrodes yet."

"You think he means Al Capone? Could this be on the level?" Marcus asks.

"I don't know," Nick says, shaking his head. "I really don't know."

"Al Capone? Did he even have kids?" Donnie asks.

"Yeah," Nick says, "one anyway. Sonny."

"Naw, that sounds fake. Who names their kid Sonny?"

Nick looks at Donnie and shakes his head.

"Al Capone? How the fuck would Al Capone's money wind up in this pissant little town?" Arnie asks.

"Don't tell me you haven't been through the Al Capone tunnels," Donnie says. "Capone spent a lot of time here during Prohibition, running Canadian booze down into the US."

"Well, fuck me!" Arnie says, swaggering over to where his friends stand. "I got new respect for the little bastard!"

"A lot easier to earn back in them days, eh?" one of the others says to a chorus of agreement. They share a chuckle.

Baron is stirring. Nick goes and squats beside his head. "Okay, friend. The money's in the house. Where?"

"Don't … know."

"Don't know?" Arnie gives him another boot, this time to the chest. Expels the air out of his lungs. Baron sucks in huge breaths, gasping, trying to refill his lungs.

When he's finally breathing, raggedly, but able to speak, Nick says, "Once again, where is the money?"

"Don't know, Reeves! Told you … don't know!" Blood runs freely from his mouth and nose.

Arnie winds up for another kick but holds up when Baron croaks in a rush, "If I knew, I'd have it! Only know Klein had it … hid … died."

"He could've spent it."

"No … died."

"Died?"

"Whacked."

"Hmm. Whacked? So how were you gonna find it?" Nick asks.

"Just … just been lookin'," he gasps.

"How much money?"

"D-d-depends."

"Depends on what?"

"Gold … price … of gold."

"It's gold?"

"A-Am-merican …" His voice is barely a croak.

"American what?" Nick shakes him. "American what?"

Baron turns his face to the floor and shuts his eyes. With a great sigh, he shudders and goes limp.

Nick stands and goes to talk to the other two leaders. "What do you think?"

"Sounds like it could be real," Marcus says.

"You?" He nods to Donnie.

"It could be, I guess."

"Okay." Nick approaches Arnie, who's standing with his friends.

He pulls out a wad of bills, peels some off, and hands them to Arnie. "Satisfactory?"

Arnie reaches over and selects a few more bills off the wad. "Now it is." He nods.

"Okay." Nick scowls and shoves his roll back in his pocket. "We'll have more work for you. But right now, pack this bastard into the rental car outside. We'll take it from here. I got your cell number. I'll call you about the other problem. Or problems, as it may be. 'N' Arnie? This never happened."

"What never happened?" Arnie grins, lights a cigarette, and sticks out his hand. "Pleasure doin' business with you, man."

Two of the bikers haul Baron out, dragging him between them, pants still around his ankles. A few minutes later, the motorcycles roar away.

"You don't think he could actually be mobbed up, do you?" Donnie asks.

"Naw." Nick shakes his head. "Even if he was, they'd never be able to connect him to us."

"I don't like it," Marcus says. "He's gonna talk. He may not know who we are, but he'll remember the cops picking him up."

Nick paces around the room. Then he kicks the chair and says, "Did he call me by name? I think he called me by name."

"Did he?" Marcus asks. "How would he know …"

"I don't know, goddamn it!" Nick says. "Goddamn it!" He throws himself into a chair and pours a shot glass of Crown Royal. Tosses it back. "We can't let him go. He has to have an accident. Put him in the driver's seat and push the car over the bank into the ravine."

"Nick," Marcus chides, "you know it would have to be something severe enough he couldn't survive. Something that would account for his injuries. We can't just roll him over one of the little cliffs we've got around here. For that to work, we'd have to take him all the way into the mountains."

"Okay. So we have to terminate him some other way. And he can't be found. We drop his car at the rental lot. Anyone looking for him would trace his credit card charges to the car rental, find out the car was returned, and figure he'd left town." He massages his neck. "Problem solved. I'll call Dr. Benzi." He pulls out his phone as they file out into the dark parking lot.

Donnie opens the door to the rental car. The dome light illuminates the interior. He looks at the passenger and then opens the door to the back seat for a better look.

"Shit! What a stench ... Uh, Nick!" he says. "Don't think we're gonna need the good doctor."

Nick puts his phone away and comes to the car.

Baron is lying in an uncomfortable-looking position. One arm is under and behind him, and his head's hanging off the seat, eyes wide open.

Marcus pushes past Donnie and puts a couple of fingers on Baron's throat. He holds a moment, tries another spot, and then shakes his head.

"Well, that's a stroke of luck," Nick says.

"Yes and no." Marcus chews his lip. "Look." He points to the blood running onto the upholstery and floor carpet, excrement smearing the seat. "We can't turn the car in unless we get it cleaned up. I mean good and proper."

"Well, we sure as hell can't take it somewhere for detailing," Nick says and turns to look at Donnie.

"Well, what're you lookin' at *me* for? I'm sure as fuck not gonna do it!" Donnie exclaims.

"Well then, we gotta make him *and* the car disappear."

"Let's bury everything," Donnie says. "We can borrow your neighbor's backhoe, Nick ..."

"Not on *my* property fer Chrissake!" Nick continues pacing. "Is Ms. Klein still outta town?"

"She ain't expected back for a few days yet." Donnie pulls out a Colt, lights it, and exhales a cloud of aromatic smoke. "At least that's the last report from Max."

"Okay. Put him in the hole. Roll him up in a tarp or something so you don't leave a mess going through the house. We can deal with him permanently once we have her evicted. Meantime, he'll keep."

"And the car? In the lake?" Donnie suggests.

"Not deep enough. It'd be found right away, maybe there'd be evidence left." Marcus scratches his head.

"There's some pretty good ravines out in the badlands," Donnie says. "No one goes there. It'll be years before anyone finds it, if ever. A little bit of a crash to account for the blood, just in case."

"Why not torch it out there?" Marcus suggests. "That'd destroy any evidence and make it look like it was stolen for a joyride."

"Good idea," Nick says. "Donnie, you know a good place?"

"There's that place I went to with Max a couple years ago," Donnie says, "but then why not leave him in the car?"

"The skeleton wouldn't be destroyed, Donnie," Nick tells him, "and if some goddamned antelope hunters stumble on it, with a skeleton inside? It's going to be obvious it's a murder. Okay?"

Donnie frowns.

"Do it," Nick says. "We're going to need this place cleaned up too."

"Are you lookin' at me again?" Donnie asks. "What the fuck? Why me?"

"Because Marcus doesn't have flexible hours of work like you do."

"Okay," Donnie snorts and takes a deep drag on his Colt. "I'll send Diana."

"Seriously? Like we need another witness?"

Donnie takes another deep drag and looks at the ground. "No, I guess not."

"Good." Nick pats his shoulder. "And all of us back here tomorrow night. Seven?"

"I got a council meeting," Marcus says. "We either meet earlier or next day."

"Next day it is then," Nick says, starting toward his Range Rover.

"What do I tell Clarence?" Donnie asks. "He's been callin' every half hour."

"Tell him we need a few days. We don't have that much in cash, need time to get it together. And that we'll call him when it's ready."

"He'll shit bricks when he finds out there's no more money coming," Marcus says.

"It's good for us if he's hungry," Nick opines.

"Sure. But do we trust him not to spill his guts if he gets busted for embezzling?"

"Good point. We'll figure something out. Maybe we forget about

Clarence's house. Concentrate on Ten Front Street." Nick's thoughtful for a moment. "If there really is gold in the house, it's more important than ever. Clarence may be useful to us. 'N' as Donnie says, we don't have to pay him. He can help us with Ms. Klein, or not. Either way, you're right, Marcus. He's a liability. I'm thinking he joins this guy in the hole. You got keys?"

Donnie nods.

Nick slaps both on the shoulders, turns, and goes back to his vehicle. "Good night, boys. Donnie, give me a call tomorrow to confirm everything's buttoned down. We'll set up a meet for Thursday then." Nick slides behind the wheel, starts the engine, and drives away.

Kathy drives her Volkswagen Jetta up the lane behind the house. She backs into the cleared space next to the garage and pops the trunk. Once she's out, she stretches her neck, goes to the back of the car, and pulls out her suitcase and a shopping bag. It'll soon be dark. Tired after her eight-hour drive, she decides to bring in the rest of her things tomorrow.

For now, she'll just have a bath, put the Egyptian cotton sheets she's brought on her mother's bed, and hit the sack. She goes up the steps onto the landing by the back door, unlocks it, pulls everything in, and locks the door again from the inside. Then she turns on the kitchen light and stands for a moment, looking around.

Her stomach clenches. The house feels as ominous as when she left, maybe even more so. There's an unpleasant stench underlying the pungent old-house aroma. *It smells worse than I remembered*, she thinks. *I'm still not used to it.*

She puts the wine in the fridge and rolls the suitcase through the kitchen. As she passes the basement door, she sees it's standing open. *Maybe the smell from the basement is why the house smells worse than ever*, she thinks as she pushes it shut with her foot. Then she lifts the carry-on and climbs the stairs. Once in the front bedroom, she puts the suitcase on the bed, opens it, and pulls out her pajamas before going to start the water in the tub.

While waiting for it to fill, she goes back to finish unpacking. Since discovering the bedroom suite cost $200 in 1930, she has a new appreciation for it. It's handy having a vanity with a big triple-view mirror and a bench. She's already decided that it will be a good place to keep her makeup, perfume, jewelry, and—why not—her undies.

She and Penny packed up the tall boy but didn't get to the vanity, so she'll have to empty it to make room for her own things. She tapes the bottom of another moving box, opens the top vanity drawer, and is struck by the disarray of the contents. She checks the other drawers and finds they're the same. Bras. Panties. Scarves. Girdles, brittle with age. Scanty contents but all in a jumble. Odd. All the things she and Penny had emptied out of the dressers were neatly folded. *My mother is still an enigma*, she thinks, and empties the drawers.

Her phone rings. She pulls it out of her jeans and sees it's Rick.

"Hey, Rick," she says.

"Hi," he says. "Where are you?"

"I'm at home. Well, at the house, if that's home. I decided to drive right through."

"Oh. In that case, can I come over?"

"What's this, a booty call?" She nibbles at a hangnail. "Don't think we're at that point in our relationship yet."

"No. But I like that you say we're not there *yet*." There's a smile in his voice. "I can help you get things outta your car if you want. But I also want to talk to you about some stuff that's happened."

"What stuff? Is the baby okay?"

"Yeah, the baby's doin' great. But Jeanie's another matter. I'd really like to explain in person."

"I was just going to get into the tub."

"You still can. Should I give you half an hour? I won't take up much of your time."

"Okay."

She abandons the job of emptying the vanity and, instead of the leisurely bath she'd planned, has a quick dip, gets out, and towels dry. As she's bending over to dry her feet, she notices a key taped to the underside of the sink. She pokes at it. The tape, yellowed and brittle with age, gives way and the key drops to the floor with a metallic clink. She picks it up and examines it. It's small and doesn't look like it would be for a door. It's more like a padlock key—maybe for the padlock on the attic door? *Well*, she thinks, *too little too late*. It's still puzzling, though.

Why would anyone be so concerned about all the junky old stuff in the attic that the door has to be locked? Not only locked but the key hidden too? She sets it on top of the toilet tank.

When she's toweled dry, she slips into sweatpants and an oversized T-shirt, runs a comb through her hair, and tucks it, slicked-down wet, behind her ears.

The doorbell goes into its ten- or fifteen-note chime.

She trots downstairs, turns on the veranda lights, and opens the door on Rick. He has a six-pack of Corona in one hand and a bottle of wine and plastic grocery bags in the other, and he's wearing a silly grin. *Penny's right*, she thinks. *He is hellish good-looking and has such a disarming grin! It doesn't hurt that he fills out that shirt, those jeans, in a most attractive way as Penny pointed out, either. It's enough to make any woman take notice.*

"I'm a little early," he says, grinning sheepishly.

"Come in," she says. "What's all this?"

"Well, since you've been away for a while, I thought you might not have much in the house."

"I have wine, but it's not cold yet. This one is! Thanks!" She gives him a quick hello kiss.

He follows her through to the kitchen, sets everything on the counter, and unpacks chips and salsa, a lime, a liter of vanilla Silk, a half-liter of Creamo, and a box of Vector cereal.

"See? Dinner *and* breakfast." He smiles and winks. He opens the wine bottle and a Corona. "The convenience store doesn't really have, you know, much in the way of actual groceries. Unless you count Chef Boyardee ravioli, which I know you won't eat. I'm surprised they have the fake milk you like."

"Well, it's very thoughtful. Thank you. Also, thanks for letting the cable guys in. Did you have to wait long?"

"No, they said between nine and eleven, and they came right at nine."

"That's gotta be a first! By the way, did they go downstairs?"

"Don't think so. Why?"

"The basement door was open when I came in." Kathy busies herself opening the tortilla chips and salsa.

"Hmm. I dunno … maybe one of them went downstairs when I was showing the other one where you wanted your Internet thing upstairs. But I'd've thought I'd notice it and close it." He goes to the basement door, tries opening and closing it a few times, without turning the knob. Shakes his head. "I wonder if it just wasn't latched properly? But it doesn't seem to swing open on its own if it's not latched. I guess I just didn't notice they left it open. Sorry."

"Oh, no worries, I was just curious." She leads the way into the living room, sets the chips and dip on the coffee table, and takes the armchair. He sits on the couch next to it, scoops salsa onto a chip, and munches before taking a swig of Corona.

Kathy says, "You said on the phone something's happened?"

"Yeah! You know how you think the Con got this house illegally?"

"Uh-huh."

"Looks like they're trying to scam Jeanie out of her house too."

"What? How?"

"Her scumbag husband's in on it. Tried to get her to, well, basically, sign the property over to them by telling her it was a new mortgage. He's been telling her for years he couldn't give her more than chump change to run the house because he had big mortgage payments to make. But there never was a mortgage," he snorts, "and it's my old buddy Donnie Jeffs who set the whole thing up. He was actually pressuring her into signing the papers without reading them. It was just lucky she twigged to it, took the papers, and left."

"Donnie Jeffs? Your friend from high school? The Prairie Equity guy? You think he's somehow connected to the Con?"

"If he's not one of 'em, he's in their pocket."

"Huh!" Kathy shakes her head. "You know, Penny really has a hate on for the Con. She says we should call them what they are, a cult, and that they're capable of anything. She knows more than she'll talk about. But I believe her. Penny's smart, you know."

Rick nods.

"Growing up in this town …" Kathy shakes her head. "Well, she's put it all behind her and has risen above it."

"I didn't know her that well. I know back in high school she was the brunt of a lot of jokes. I'm ashamed to say I laughed along with the rest."

"Ancient history. Different times." Kathy presses her lips together.

"So, Donnie's not to be trusted either? Do you think he works for the Con, or is it just that they have something on him? You know, their lawyer costs big money. How does a so-called church with a small congregation afford that?"

"Something's rotten." He shakes his head and scratches his jaw.

"So what's Jeanie going to do?"

"She's got a room near the hospital in Saskatoon for as long as the baby's there, which won't be much longer. The boys are at the farm. She's seen a lawyer, and they're getting some legal stuff started to get Clarence out of the house, and her and the boys back home, hopefully before school starts. But she's nervous about a confrontation with him. So for now, he's in the house, and she won't go back until he's gone."

"Poor Jeanie! That's really tough, especially with the kids ... Anything I can do?"

"Just be a friend, I guess. We'll all get together next time Jeanie's here. She was just my annoying little sister when you 'n' I were together back then. Thankfully she's changed. I think you'll like her. Plus, I'd like you to meet Sarah."

"I look forward to it!"

"How was your trip?"

"A lot of driving, but I broke it into three days, so not too onerous."

"Hmm." He takes a swig of beer and more chips. Then he has another swig.

Kathy studies his face, notes he's avoiding eye contact, and wonders if he has more to say, something he's nervous about. The uncomfortable silence goes on for another minute or so before he finally looks at her and says, "I guess you saw your husband."

Oh, that's it, Kathy thinks, and sighs. "Yes." She gets up and goes to the fridge to refill her glass and brings another Corona for Rick when she comes back.

"It's none of my business," Rick says.

"Well, I think it is, Rick." She sits back down in the armchair and leans forward to look him in the eye. "I think you have a right to know my relationship status. It's just ... three years! A record for me." She shakes her head. "I asked him if he'd come here, see what it's like, maybe consider relocating. He might be able to get his company to transfer him. You know, I could sell this house and all the lots and come out with barely enough to buy a condo in Vancouver. He laughed and said something like 'Who would go to Saskatchewan on purpose?' Ha-ha." She sits back. Picks at a hangnail. "That was one of our more civil discussions."

"I'm sorry. It must have been unpleasant." He studies her face. His eyes are dark, intense. "What matters to me ... what I've thought about ... is whether you'll stay if you don't get the house."

"Rick," she says quietly, "I honestly don't know the answer to that." She presses her lips together and frowns, then resumes chewing her hangnail.

He leans toward her, takes her hand away from her mouth, and kisses her fingers. "I hope you'll stay," he says. Her frown dissolves, and they kiss. A couple of gentle kisses.

"Mmm." Kathy sits back in her chair, takes a deep breath, and experiences a pleasant stirring. Nice! No flashback of her mother. Or, more accurately, just a mental image of her mother's face, floating disembodied in the back of her brain. "I don't know what I'm going to do, Rick."

"I know. I don't want to put pressure on you. Just want you to know, well, my feelings about it. So you know before you make a decision. I'm sorry if it makes you nervous."

She nods and takes another deep breath and feels tension slipping away as she sips her wine.

"Do you think he'll change his mind? Your husband? About coming here?"

"No. He's totally a big-city guy. He loves the nightlife. Clubs. Bars. NHL games. Concerts. Blah, blah, blah. I don't even know why I asked him. Just so I could tell myself I wasn't the cause of another failed relationship, I guess. So I can tell myself I gave him a choice, and he chose Vancouver instead of me."

"He's a stupid man," Rick says, "but I'm glad."

She says nothing, just looks at the floor.

"I know what you're thinking," he says quietly and shifts in his seat. "I was the stupid one back then."

When she looks up, she finds he's looking at her, still intense. She looks away and takes another sip of wine.

"Well, I hope I'll have a chance to get to know you better this time."

She studies his face and realizes he's serious. She feels the stirring again and doesn't know how to respond.

After a moment, he gives her hand a squeeze and says, "It's late. You must be tired. I'll let you get to bed." He finishes his beer and stands up.

She gets to her feet and takes a step toward him.

He reaches out and smooths her still-wet hair around her ear. "You smell good," he whispers. "I missed you."

"I … you were … I thought of you a lot too."

He pulls her into his arms, and they kiss. Slowly at first, then more urgently.

He drops his hands to her hips and pulls her tight against him.

She's hit suddenly with a full-blown memory, so vivid it could've happened yesterday: her mother lurking inside the front door. That maniacal fire in her eyes. Waiting to attack. Pushing her back against the wall. *Where have you been? What have you been doing? I can smell him on you! Did you let him stick his filthy man part in you?*

Kathy shudders. "Agghh!" she sobs. *How* could *she do that? I was as big as she was then. Why did I let her do that?*

"What's wrong?" Rick whispers urgently. "What is it?"

Kathy squeezes her eyes shut and takes several deep breaths. When she opens them, she sees Rick's befuddled expression. She closes her eyes again and kisses him with abandon. Sliding her hands down so she's cupping his buttocks, she pulls him hard against her. *Take that, Mother! You're not welcome here!*

After a bit, he pulls back. "Whew!" he exhales and backs away a step. "I don't know what just happened, but I think I better go."

She comes up beside him and takes his hand. Her heart's pounding. She says softly, "Please don't leave."

"Oh God, Kathy," he whispers, his eyes sapphire with desire. "I'm burning for you!"

He strokes her chin, her ear, her throat. Nuzzles her hair.

She trembles as he drops his hands to her waist and draws her close.

Clarence sits across from Donnie in his office at Prairie Equity. The office has been closed for hours, and they're the only two people there. Donnie pulls a bottle of Crown Royal out of his credenza, pours a couple of fingers into two on-the-rocks glasses, and passes one to Clarence.

Clarence stifles his urge to ask when he'll get his next $400,000. *Play it cool*, he tells himself. *It's better to wait.* He thinks how friendly Donnie is, much friendlier than any time in the past. More like they're equals. And meeting here instead of that fucking curling rink! *But if they think they can buy me off, give me a red robe now, they're in for a rude awakening. Too little, too late!*

They talk of nonsense. Last week's football game. How the referees made bad calls that cost the Roughriders the game. How the heat's ripening crops ahead of normal. How Donnie's wife wants to renew their wedding vows.

"Twentieth anniversary," Donnie explains as he lights a Colt and takes a couple of deep draws.

There's a key in the front-door lock. Donnie quickly stubs out his cigarillo and puts it and the ashtray in his desk drawer. They see Nick and Marcus weaving their way through desks in the main office.

As they come into Donnie's cubicle, Nick frowns at the cloud of pungent smoke around Donnie and says, "Hey, Clarence," and extends his hand. Clarence half stands and shakes it. Then he does likewise with Marcus. He can't read their expressions to get a clue about what this meeting is for, other than the money and the red robe.

Then they all sit, the three Illustrious Leaders in their everyday garb across the desk from Clarence. Nick, looking as authoritarian as ever, even in "civvies," is in the center as usual. Donnie pours and delivers drinks to both newcomers.

"So," Nick begins as he accepts the glass from Donnie, "I suppose you're wondering why we wanted this meeting."

"Not really," Clarence says. "I've been fuckin' waiting for my four hundred thousand. Assume I get it now?"

"Well, you know what they say about 'assume.' Makes an ass outta you and me." Donnie chuckles.

Clarence frowns. "What do you mean?"

"Not amused?" Marcus asks. "Haven't you talked to your wife?"

"No. Should I? She's up in Saskatoon. I got my own things going on." He has a brief mental image of Monica screaming at him about some biker coming around, expecting her to sign a rental agreement and demanding a rent payment.

"Oh yeah? How's the bogus loans business going?"

Donnie's question snaps Clarence's attention back. "What the fuck would you know about it?" he snarls and starts to stand.

"Sit the fuck down, douchebag!" Donnie jumps to his feet, launches himself around the desk, and pushes Clarence back down with a thump.

"Now, now, Donnie," Nick says, "lighten up! We're all friends here."

Donnie perches, his ass half on, half off the corner of his desk, and hovers over Clarence, who resists the urge to push his chair away.

Nick says, "Clarence, your wife didn't sign the papers."

Disbelief, rage, and then despair flood through him, but Clarence says nothing.

"So," Marcus says, "where do you think the four hundred thousand is going to come from?"

Clarence takes a deep breath and crumples in his chair, shaking his head.

"You'll be happy to know we've come up with a solution," Nick says. "We're problem solvers."

"Okay, sure, what the hell," Clarence says. "You want another one of my fingers?"

"God no! What a barbaric idea!" Nick says.

"Yeah, barbaric," Clarence snorts. "Okay, what's the big plan this time?"

"Attitude, Clarence!" Donnie says. "Attitude!"

Nick gives Donnie a look before continuing. "Simple, really. We have a problem you can help us with."

"I thought you were the problem solvers."

"Yeah, and here's the solution to your problem, which also solves our problem. Quite elegant, if I do say so," Nick says. "We need Kathy

Klein gone. You need four hundred K. You make the first thing happen. We make the second thing happen."

Clarence jerks to attention and frowns. "You want me to kill her?"

"Oh my, who said that?" Nick chuckles. "You're no killer, Clarence. We know that. All you have to do is get rid of her. It's up to you how you do it. Buy her a ticket to Moscow? Or maybe some ISIS territory? Buy her off? Bribe her husband to come and take her on a lengthy trip? Even take out a hit on her if you want. It's *entirely* up to you. As long as she's never seen around here again."

Clarence considers this and then asks, "Why do you give a shit about that little twat?"

"That's our business," Nick says. "All you need to know is that we want her gone."

"Ahhh!" Clarence brightens. "I get it! She's living in your meetinghouse. Big problem, eh? No tunnel access?" He grins and shakes his head, then leans forward. "Let's renegotiate our deal."

"Not happening, *Brother* Weaver," Donnie says.

"This is a nonnegotiable offer," Nick says. "You accept, or we blow the whistle on your bogus loans scam."

"Then I tell all about your fake church and your shady dealings!"

"We've been a recognized church nearly a hundred years, Brother Weaver." Nick's voice is low and well-modulated. "And what shady dealings? You mean the loan we gave you?"

Clarence's bravado fizzles, and he thrusts his lower lip out. "My brother-in-law's fucking her. Why not get him to deal with her?"

"Clarence, Clarence, Clarence," Donnie says. "Think about it. You answered your own question. He's fucking her. Why would he want her gone? This is your chance to pay him back for dissin' you all these years. I hear how he talks about you. He's an asshole."

Clarence nods, presses his lips together, and squirms in his chair.

"Tick tock, Clarence," Donnie says.

"This is worth four hundred thousand to you?"

"It is."

"Payable now?"

"Well, a hundred K now so you got working capital, the rest on completion." Donnie scratches the mole on his head.

Clarence sits and quietly studies the carpet while his mind races. He stares unseeing at the divots the metal leveling feet of the desk have made. "And you don't care how I do it? Or what I do?"

"No," Nick says. "I don't care as long as there's no blowback on us."

Silence.

Marcus drums his fingers on the desk.

Nick clears his throat.

"Okay," Clarence says, "a hundred thousand now. Three hundred more on completion. When does this have to happen?"

"Well, when you say so. But soon. And you don't get the down payment until you a have a plan," Nick says.

"I see."

"So, when you have a plan, give us a timeline for completion. Then you get the first installment. When you come to us with proof it's done, you get the rest."

"What kind of proof?"

"You figure it out."

"I have a plan," Clarence says after a few moments. "I'll just—"

"Don't need to hear the details, Clarence," Nick cuts him off. "Better if we don't. Plausible deniability 'n' all."

"Just the timeline," Donnie says as he pours fresh drinks for everyone.

"My money now"—Clarence slurps his drink noisily— "and your problem is solved within a week."

"That's my man!" Nick says.

They all clink glasses.

Clarence tosses his whiskey back and says, "You know, this is only the second part of our deal. I need a lot more than six hundred thousand to make my problem at the bank go away."

"We haven't forgotten," Nick says. "You think you're going to get your mother-in-law to join our congregation? Sign over the farm?"

"Absolutely!" Clarence says. "Well, sign over, no. The deal was to get her to join the congregation. She's always taken my side against Jeanie. She knows I'm good for her. And fuckin' jerk-off Rick? She's got a boner for him. Thinks he killed his father, so she won't be holding out to let him inherit the farm. I've talked to Mutti about the Children of Noah lots. She's suckin' it up. It'll be a cakewalk for you guys." Clarence looks over their heads, studying the dusty silk ficus tree in the corner of the room, and says, "She'll join. My wife will too. She just needs a little time. She's just depressed, you know, postpartum depression."

"Good." Donnie pats Clarence's shoulder, stands up, and passes behind Clarence's chair to leave his office.

Clarence tips his glass for the last drop of whiskey as he watches Donnie go to the safe at the back of the main office, open the door, and hunch over in front of it.

When he returns, he sets a satchel on the desk in front of Clarence.

"Go ahead," Nick says, "take a look."

Clarence stands, opens the satchel, pokes through the bundles of bills, and then closes the bag again.

Nick and Marcus get to their feet, and they all shake hands. Nick says, "Looking forward to hearing of your successful completion of this assignment, Clarence. Marcus will see you out."

K athy strips the bed, pulling the sheets into a ball. *I should've washed these sooner*, she thinks. *They've had quite a workout this week!*

A scent, Rick's, wafts up from his pillowcase, and desire, an all-over body blush, stirs in her again. She hugs his pillow for a moment and enjoys the memory of their lovemaking before picking up the bundle and heading down to the basement.

The place still spooks her, even though she keeps telling herself it's childish. Foolish. *Is it my imagination*, she thinks, or *does it smell worse than before? Worse than just the smell of the dampness. It's like something died in here. Maybe there's another dead rat somewhere.*

She stuffs the sheets in the washer, dumps in a cup of detergent, turns on the machine, and holds her breath. After some gurgling, water begins to fill the tub. She heaves a sigh of relief as she does every time the decades-old washer agrees to keep working.

Then she pushes her anxiety aside, plucks up her courage, and searches likely places for a rat trap. Maybe it's behind the workbench. The smell does seem stronger in that part of the basement. But she finds nothing. *It really must be my imagination*, she thinks.

Since it's still cool this early in the morning, she decides to go up to the attic and start going through boxes while she's waiting for the sheets. It's not that anything has to be packed up and disposed of. Everything's fine where it is at least for the time being. She's just curious. So she trots up the three flights.

There's enough daylight coming through the small dormer window to make the attic quite pleasant. *Whoever put all this stuff up here sure wasn't careful about it*, she thinks. *All these clothes not folded, overflowing the boxes, some of the boxes not closed. Just a place to pile a bunch of stuff nobody cared about.* But since there was no shortage of space, there was no need to be organized.

Aside from boxes, there are some things that are very old: a roughly made wooden rocking cradle, for instance, and a finely crafted spinning wheel, both already antiques when the house was built.

Among the discarded or at least stored antiques, there's an art deco floor lamp she judges to be circa 1920 or so. It's beautiful, and it really suits the house. *I should find a spot for it downstairs,* she thinks.

But it's what's in the boxes that interests her most. She starts with the box nearest the stairwell. Interesting stuff, as Rick said. Old photographs of people she isn't able to identify. Some have labels like "Dad's brother Elmer." Writing is a fine, practiced cursive in what looks to be fountain pen ink. But not knowing who Dad is, and never having heard of an Uncle Elmer, the photographs are only that, interesting. She sets a couple of the oldest albums aside to take downstairs, to be gone through purely for entertainment. *Who knows, maybe there's a photo of Great-Granddad and Al Capone! I'll have to check the Internet for pictures of Al, so I'll recognize him.* She chuckles at the thought.

There are so many old clothes, seemingly something from every era. Outdated trousers. Even men's garters. Ladies' suits with padded shoulders, narrow waists, and peplums. Hats. Shoes. Even undergarments with no elastic. World War II?

There are some things she might actually wear, and she keeps those aside. When her stomach growls, she looks at her watch and is surprised at how the hours have flown by. It's past lunchtime. She gathers the albums and clothing items she wants to keep out and takes them down to the spare bedroom, then goes downstairs. She makes herself a sandwich and brings it back up to the smallest bedroom, where her computer and printer sit on the drop-leaf table she and Penny moved up from the living room. With the gateleg leaf up, it makes a serviceable desk.

The Internet's up and operational. She turns on the computer and checks the e-mail from her office. There's been a steady flow, and today is no different. One client wants to add a jewelry floater—price for that, please. Another has bought a fifth horse, taking her over the limit for hobby farm coverage. What can they do about that? Another policy is about to be canceled for nonpayment of premium, and she has to notify the mortgage lienholder. It's surprisingly time-consuming, but at least it's easier on the computer than it was on her tablet.

Her heart's not in it, but she's thankful her employers gave her the option of working remotely, as it's her only income. There's a downside: the work's always there—never a day off, never an escape from it. With the office open seven days a week and the three-hour time difference, she gets e-mail on weekends and well into the evenings. *I just have to turn the thing off outside of regular office hours*, she thinks. *But since I have to be logged in for thirty-five hours a week, it's nice to be flexible about when those hours can be logged. How long will they let me do this, though? I'm getting the figurative paper pushed, but since I'm not physically in the office to help out at the customer service counter when it gets busy, they will want to hire someone else sooner or later. Should I look for a job here?*

Another large question nibbles at her thoughts. She thinks back to Rick's question about her intentions. If she isn't successful in getting the property transfer set aside, if she has no house, will she stay? Will she stay because of Rick? Even if she ends up getting the house, will she stay *with* Rick? Can she trust him? Sure, they were kids before, and she meant it when she told him their history, their breakup, is behind them. But her thoughts jump back to that time often enough to make her wonder if it is, really and truly, behind her. And more important, would a new start with Rick have any better chance of succeeding than any of her other failed relationships? Her mother's face hovers in her mind's eye, and she can almost hear her saying, *"He's a dirty man ..."* She forces the mental image away and thinks, *Oh my God, my mother again! I thought she was gone once and for all! Why can't I quit thinking about her?* Kathy gnaws at a rough edge on a fingernail and nibbles it off.

She isn't able to focus on queries from clients now and turns the computer off. Anyway, it's time to get ready. Rick will be coming by soon. They're going to a Saskatchewan Roughriders game. He's such a fan. Wear green, he said.

Other than the little leather clutch purse and a vintage felt cloche she found in the attic, she has nothing green. She pulls the cloche on. It covers most of her head, leaving only a fringe of dark hair showing around the sides and back. Once downstairs, she transfers some of the contents of her old black shoulder bag into the purse. The purse is barely big enough to hold her wallet and a travel pack of Kleenex. She thinks, *I don't know why I pack around all that other stuff anyway. When was the last time I needed that checkbook? The emergency flashlight? The hand sanitizer?*

She checks her look in the hallstand mirror. *Kind of funky cute*, she thinks, with her skinny jeans, knee-high boots, and a lacy, flowing peasant blouse.

Judging by the look on his face when he comes to the door to pick her up, Rick thinks so too.

Kathy's starting to wake up. Sunbeams squeeze through pinholes and around the edges of the roll-up blinds. She keeps her eyes shut a few moments, thinking about last night. Then opens them and turns to look at Rick. He's already awake, just lying on his side looking at her. She smiles.

He draws her into his arms and kisses her. Then they cuddle, enjoying the contact comfort. Soon the kisses are more intense, desire builds, and they're no longer just snuggling as their hands explore each other's bodies and they press together with urgency. Their joining is thrilling, new, yet familiar. The little sounds they make aren't words, but they express intense pleasure. The age-old dance begins. Slow and luxurious at first, increasing in tempo until they're swept away in the all-over body rush, and they collapse.

After a bit, Kathy whispers, "I'll go make breakfast."

He gives her another kiss and releases her.

As she gets out of bed, she feels his eyes on her, and she's self-conscious because she's naked. She makes a dash for the bathroom, closes the door, and sits on the toilet.

Finished there, she washes her hands and face and runs the brush through her hair, then takes her robe off the hook on the door and slips into it. When she opens the door, Rick's standing there, wearing nothing but a silly grin. It's obvious he's not self-conscious.

"Hmm," he murmurs, "I liked the view better before you put this on." He strokes her robe's lapel and reaches inside to cup her breasts.

Kisses her. Then steps away. "But for now …" He nods in the direction of the toilet.

"I'll be in the kitchen," she says, smiling and letting him pass.

When he comes down, he's in his jeans and T-shirt.

"Make yourself a cup," Kathy tells him, pointing to the Keurig, "and take a seat. How d'you like your eggs?" She's got bacon in the frying pan and bread in the toaster, and she is pouring orange juice.

"Over easy, if you can manage it."

He gets his coffee and sits at the table as directed. But when the toast pops up, he gets to his feet and pulls a plate out of the cupboard and Becel Vegan margarine out of the fridge. He pats her bottom as he passes behind her and butters toast while she watches his eggs.

As she eats her toast with tomato and avocado slices and he has his bacon and eggs, they talk companionably about the game.

"I don't have much I have to do at home," Rick says. "Wanna do something today?"

"Well," Kathy says, "yesterday I started going through some of the things in the attic. Could I interest you in looking at a few things up there?"

"Sure, for a while anyway, I guess," he says as he drains his orange juice. "As soon as you're finished eating we can get into that. It's already nearly eleven. Don't remember the last time I slept this late."

"Slept?"

"Well, more accurately, I don't remember the last time I was in bed this late."

"Are you worn out?" she asks. "Sorry."

"You're not sorry, 'n' I'm not complaining." He stands and kisses the top of her head as he takes his dishes to the dishwasher. "And hey, you got a long way to go before you wear me out. But you keep on tryin', okay?"

She gets up and hands him her dishes to put in the dishwasher while he's got it open, and then they go upstairs.

"I don't need help dressing," she tells him as he follows her into the bedroom.

"I'm not planning on helping you dress," he says. He loosens the belt on her robe and slides his hands up to push the robe off her shoulders before pushing her gently down on the bed. "Just thought I'd prove you haven't worn me out," he whispers as he lies down next to her and draws her close, nuzzling her neck, hair, and ear, while his hands stroke her body. "I can't get enough of you. I can't stop thinking about you."

She feels his erection pressing against his jeans. "If this is farm boys, I'm never going back to city boys," she whispers. "You may not be worn out, but you might give my girl a bit of a rest …"

"Oh? Oh!" He stiffens and sits up. "Sorry, babe." But the big, shit-eating grin on his face doesn't convey regret. He says, "Wait'll I tell my friends you're saddle sore …"

She feels a surge of panic and thinks of the cocky Rick Schoenfeld she knew in high school. All the popular kids orbiting around him, laughing. At her? Her mother's in her head, saying, *They all just want to stick their dirty man part in you … you're nothing but a toilet.* She skitters away, straightens her robe, sits back against the headboard, and grabs a pillow to hug—to use as a shield against him.

When he sees the look of anguish on her face, he says, "Oh! I'm sorry! Did you think … Kathy, I wouldn't brag about you … about us! I wouldn't!" He tries to pull her into his arms, but she's stiff and resists. "Never! I'm sorry! It was supposed to be a joke! I thought I was being funny. Kathy, please believe me! Please?" His brow is furrowed, and he looks so genuinely distressed she can almost believe him.

"I'm sorry, babe," Rick continues, sliding down to kneel on the floor next to her. "What I did before … I'm sorry for that too. Please believe me. I know I was a jerk, an asshole, a total douchebag, and you didn't deserve what I did to you." He takes her hands, holds them awkwardly on either side of the pillow, and fixes her with an intense look. "I know I don't deserve you! You have no reason to trust me, I get that, but I'll do everything I can, anything you want, to earn your trust. Please believe me!"

She doesn't pull her hands away but looks off toward the window.

"Just give me a chance."

She gives a slight nod.

"Okay?" he gets up and sits on the bed next to her, stroking her hair, and says more earnestly, "Okay?"

She says quietly, "Okay."

He kisses her, but her lips are unyielding.

"Do you want me to leave?"

Kathy studies the counterpane, the cove ceiling, the yellowed wallpaper. *Can I believe him?* she wonders. She thinks over how they've been together these past weeks. It doesn't seem phony or like he's just toying with her. *Fools rush in*, she thinks. She sighs and says, "Only until I get dressed."

He draws her into a heartfelt embrace. "Oh, Kathy, babe, I'm sorry. I love you! I won't let you go again!" He scurries out of the bedroom and closes the door behind him.

Once Kathy's dressed, she opens the door to find him across the hall, with the door to the attic staircase open, sitting on the stairs. He gives her a sheepish smile, gets up, and waves her past him and up the stairs.

The attic's hot as before. Rick checks the window in the only dormer, jiggles it a bit, and lifts it. "Huh! It actually opens!" he says. A welcome rush of fresh air stirs the dust motes dancing in the sunbeam. He comes away from the window and starts by pulling out one of the two big steamer trunks. Kathy shoves boxes aside to make room.

"Je-sus!" Rick says. "This fucker's heavy! Must be lead lined. Or maybe there's a body in it?"

"Wanna see?" Kathy asks.

"They're locked," he says, as if he's taken her question seriously.

As she pushes one of the cardboard boxes out of the way, she takes a closer look at the clothes inside. "These don't really look that old," she says, "I mean, not World War II and older like the other boxes."

She pulls out a few shirts. Some Chaps khakis. Ralph Lauren jeans. "More like, what—eighties, nineties? Maybe these are things my dad didn't take when he left!" She starts taking clothes out, hoping to find something she remembers her father wearing.

She pulls out a velour robe. "Oh, Rick, this is nice. Maybe you could use …" Then something slips from it and thumps to the floor.

"What's that?" Rick asks. "A mug?"

Kathy picks it up. Brings it to her nose and breathes deeply.

"English Leather," she says. She pulls a small round brush out of it. The soap, dried and shrunken, is stuck to it.

Her stomach contracts. She can't breathe. Suddenly there's a painful ache in her throat. Tears well in her eyes and run down her cheeks. "It's my father's shaving mug," she sobs. Wipes her eyes on her sleeve.

"Oh. That'll be great to remember him by."

"No! You don't understand, Rick! He wouldn't have gone, you know, run off, without taking his shaving things!"

"I … No, I guess I don't understand. He might've switched to an electric razor?"

"No! Never!" Kathy shakes her head vigorously. "Something happened to him, Rick! He didn't run off! He loved me! My mother told me he didn't, but I never really believed it. He wouldn't leave me. I always knew he wouldn't leave me. Something must've happened to him. Something bad!"

He pulls her into his arms. "Aw, Kathy …"

She lets him hug her with her arms at her sides, the mug in one hand, brush and soap in the other. She desperately tries not to cry while thoughts of her father being murdered flood her brain. Now she has the hiccups.

"You (hiccup) think I'm crazy?" she asks.

"No. I think you may be jumping to conclusions, though. We should see what else might be up here. Clues, I mean. And I think we need to let the cops know …"

"(Hiccup) They've never been any help. Said (hiccup) they don't even have a file."

"Hmm. Well, a shaving mug isn't much to go on." Rick kisses her ear, cups her shoulders, and gives them a rub. "But I'll call Ben Neufeld. I play hockey with him. Old Farts' league. Some call it the beer league. He's stationed here in Pillerton, second in command, their token member of color. He's really the only one of the bunch with any brains, and he's a straight shooter. He won't give us the runaround. Okay?"

She nods. He releases her, pulls his phone out of his pocket, and makes the call. It goes to voice mail. He says who he is and ends with "Call me when you get a chance."

She runs down to the bathroom where she washes her face and blows her nose. After a long drink from the tap to quell her hiccups, she stuffs a handful of Kleenex in her pocket and goes back up into the attic.

In her absence, Rick continued unpacking boxes and has draped shirts, pants, and jackets everywhere for her to see if anything clicks. Although it's a decent eighties wardrobe that may have been her father's, there's nothing else as personal as the shaving mug.

"Well, if your father moved out, either he had a shitload of clothes, or he didn't take much with him," Rick says.

"And my mother apparently kept up the Klein tradition of never getting rid of anything. Except, apparently, my things. Haven't come across any of my old clothes. But this stuff all could've gone to Goodwill. Someone would've made good use of it. It's a shame. I wonder if the theater group could use any of it for costumes."

"Good idea. You should talk to Carl about it," Rick says, checking his watch. "Can we give it a rest for today, babe? Time's marchin' on, and it's fuckin' hot in here. It's cool at Al's 'n' I have a hankerin' for a beer and some nachos. We can watch the BC Lions–Calgary Stampeders game on the big screen there."

Kathy chews her bottom lip as she considers the idea.

"Oh, I know you're not into football."

"It was fun going to the game, though."

"It's fun watching it with the crowd at the pub too. And it'll help get your mind off … well, everything."

She looks at him, cocking her head.

"Okay, I admit I have an ulterior motive," he says, brow furrowed. "I want you to meet everyone. More important, I want everyone to meet you. I want everyone to know we're together."

Next morning, Kathy's starting to stir but rolls over to slow the waking-up process while she mentally reviews everything that happened yesterday. Rick was so solicitous, seemed so genuinely proud to introduce her to all his friends at the pub, although he was noticeably cool toward Donnie and never did introduce her to him. After they came back, he was gentle, sweet, loving. She was the one to initiate another coupling.

When she reviews everything he said during their fight—can she call it their first fight? —she thinks he said he loves her. *Did he really?*

It's too soon, isn't it? It must be something else from her overactive imagination.

She smells coffee, feels a gentle nudge, and opens one eye.

"Good morning, beautiful!" he whispers.

She sits up, pulls the sheets over her nakedness, and smiles.

"Brought you a coffee," he says, indicating the steaming mug on the night table.

"Mmm. My knight in shining armor! Thanks." She picks it up and takes a sip. "You're up and dressed already? Leaving so soon?"

"Yup. Things to do at the farm. Also have to meet the contractor. He needs decisions on a couple of changes I want to make."

"Oh? What changes?"

"Well, bigger ensuite with two sinks in it, for starters."'

"Oh, I didn't think the house was that far along."

"It isn't. I'm just planning ahead." He bends to kiss her. "I'll see you tonight."

"Tonight," she agrees. "Come for dinner. One thing I actually cook, and quite well if I do say so, is spaghetti sauce."

"Sounds great. Even without the spaghetti sauce." He kisses her again and leaves, but turns at the door and says, "Goddamn, I missed Ben's call last night. I was, er, *busy*." He manages to make a leer seem cute. "I'll call him back today." Then he blows a kiss and heads out.

Kathy luxuriates in bed for half an hour or so, sipping her coffee. She's still feeling the warm afterglow of their lovemaking. She's waffling back and forth on whether she can trust him, whether he's being honest or just having fun. She wants to believe, to trust. But for that one careless comment, she would. *It wasn't even really that bad*, she thinks. *Maybe I overreacted. Maybe I'm putting too much weight on it.*

Finally, she gets up and dresses in her work clothes. She'll start the spaghetti sauce, check her e-mail—although nothing's expected until the office opens in three hours or so—and then get back into the attic.

The sauce is simmering on the stove and she's cleaning up the kitchen, when the doorbell rings. She goes to the door and peers out through the clear spot in the leaded glass. It's someone she doesn't recognize. She opens the door on a pudgy man with thinning brown hair and a black mole the size of a dime on his cheek. He's unshaven, and his expensive clothes look as if he's slept in them. Judging by the woebegone look on his face, he's just lost his best friend.

"Yes?" Kathy says.

"Kathy?" he asks.

"Yes?" She frowns.

"I'm Clarence," he says. "Clarence Weaver. Jeanie's husband."

"Oh, sure. We haven't met, but I've heard—"

"Oh, I can imagine what you've heard!" Clarence says and suddenly chokes back a sob. His eyes fill with tears, and he looks away. After a moment, he collects himself. "I just … I know you're with Rick now … I hope you can help me. Please help me! I have nowhere else to turn, and I don't know what to do."

"What can I possibly do?"

"Can we talk?"

Kathy clucks, thinking, *Oh jeez, I don't need this, but can I close the door on a crying man? Well, I was about ready for a coffee break anyway.* She sighs and pulls the door open, beckoning him inside. "Come in, Clarence. Let's have a cup of coffee." She ushers him into the foyer, closes the door behind him, and then leads the way to the kitchen.

"What a fabulous old house!" he says as he follows her through the dining room. "How many rooms?"

"Not as big as it looks from the outside. But four bedrooms." She pulls out a kitchen chair and says, "Have a seat. Cream and sugar?"

"Yes, two sugars please."

"Sugar's on the table."

The Keurig dispenses a cup, and she hands it to him. She gets the Creamo out of the fridge and puts it on the table before getting her own coffee and taking the chair across from him.

"So, you want me to put in a good word for you with Rick?"

"Well," Clarence snuffles as he spoons sugar into his mug and fills it to the brim with cream, "you know Jeanie says she's going to d-divorce me."

"I heard."

"I love her, Kathy! I really do! If only you'll believe me, maybe you can make Rick believe it, and maybe he can get Jeanie to believe it too. You know how close they are." He begins to sob. "I love her! I really love her!" He covers his face with his hands. "Sorry," he sobs, "I promised myself I'd be stronger … that I wouldn't cry. You must think I'm a pansy! But she's my whole world!"

She grabs the box of Kleenex off the counter and puts it on the table in front of him.

After he gets himself under control, she asks, "What about transferring the house to the cult?"

"The cult? You mean, my church? Well, it's not as bad as it sounds. There's a life estate. We would live there until we died. In the meantime, no payments! I tried to explain this to Jeanie. I was going to surprise her. It would be good for our family! My whole paycheck for the household budget and no mortgage payments taken off. A nice retirement nest egg! But she won't listen." He begins sobbing again. "Sh-sh-she's leaving me. I'm only trying to do my best for her. And the kids!" He's crying loudly now. Bubbles of snot billow at one nostril. "Sorry. I just can't lose her. She's my whole life!"

She pushes the box of Kleenex closer to him.

He takes a couple and honks into them.

"I really don't know what I can do," she tells him. She feels a tug of sympathy and then remembers there never were mortgage payments, that he's a liar and a manipulator, and that this is probably an act. But for what possible purpose? Surely he doesn't really think Rick will talk Jeanie out of divorcing him!

"I haven't seen Jeanie since she was a kid. She has to make up her own mind."

"Just talk to Rick? Would you do that?"

He can't maintain eye contact and keeps looking beyond her, over her shoulder. It's unsettling. She quells an urge to turn around to see what it is he's looking at. *What is with this guy?* she thinks. *I'll just agree and get rid of him.* She takes a deep breath. Blows out slowly through her mouth and then nods. "Fine."

"Good!" Clarence brightens and drinks his coffee in one gulp. "Mmm. That's good. Could I get a refill?"

Seeing her hesitation, he rushes on, "Please?" His face contorts. "Talking to you … having someone to talk to really helps. You're so kind! I already feel so much better."

"You know, I have things to do." His inability to maintain eye contact and his mercurial mood changes are making her uneasy. She feels her adrenaline rising and gets to her feet. "I've already said I'll talk to Rick. I can't do more than that. I'd like you to leave now." She takes his cup as she stands.

In a heartbeat, Clarence's face contorts into a mask of rage. He jumps to his feet with astonishing speed. She instinctively takes a couple of steps backward before bumping up against the refrigerator. He grabs a frying pan off a hook above the butcher block and, in one smooth motion, raises it over his head, rushes at her, and smashes it down. She reflexively ducks sideways, but it strikes a glancing blow off the side of her head. Still, with the weight of the cast-iron frying pan and the force of his whole body behind it, the hit knocks her unconscious. She crumples to the floor. The mug bounces out of her hand and skitters under the butcher block.

"There you go, bitch," Clarence sneers. "Now I feel so-o-o much better!" He hadn't realized how nervous he was, concerned that his plan would fail. Now that it's succeeded, he allows himself the luxury of a laugh.

Then, grabbing her under her arms, he drags her to the basement stairs, opens the door, and carefully backs down. Her feet thunk-thunk-thunk on each tread. She's small but surprisingly heavy.

"Dead weight!" he grouses and dumps her on the concrete floor.

He struggles with the cover of the tunnel, but it's wedged in tight. The handles are too far apart to pull both up simultaneously, and lifting one at a time wedges it tighter. It would be a two-person job, likely. He's finally able to work it free, using a pry bar off the workbench, and wrestles it to the side. "Why'd they make the fuckin' cover so much bigger than the hole?" he mutters as he leans over and looks down. It's as black as he remembers but smells far worse.

"Whew! Don't remember it being that bad!" He chuckles. "Enjoy, sweetheart!" He starts to slide her toward the hole and then remembers he needs proof. What should it be?

"They like fingers so much"—he smiles— "they can have another one!"

He pulls his Swiss Army knife out of his pocket, opens it, takes her hand, and saws at her index finger. She moans and starts thrashing. He isn't able to hold her hand down. For a moment he considers slicing her jugular but discards the idea. Too much blood spray! When she's missing, they will check the whole house, basement included. He doesn't want to spend hours on cleanup. And he wants no one to know where he's dumped her.

So instead he punches her face and then shakes his hand. *Damn her! That hurts!* But she's still again. He finishes amputating the finger by disarticulating it at the second joint, humming as he works, and then slips it into his shirt pocket.

There's a surprising amount of blood, and it's run onto the floor. *Damn! Going to have to do some cleanup anyway*, he thinks. *But this is just a small pool. Manageable.*

And then he has another thought. How about a little memento for himself? Holding the lobe of her ear with his left hand, he lays the knife next to her cheek and begins slicing the ear off. The knife slides along the cartilage, and in the blink of an eye, he's holding just the lobe with its little gold hoop earring. He'd wanted the whole ear, but this is really all he needs. Maybe nicer than the whole thing!

The earlobe itself isn't very bloody, but blood gushes from the wound, flows down her neck, and drips to the floor behind her head. Annoying, but also manageable.

He tucks the earlobe into his shirt pocket with the finger, wipes the knife on Kathy's shirt, folds it, and slides it back into his pants pocket. He pulls out his phone, turns her face toward the camera, and takes a picture. When he reviews it, he's satisfied. Her eyes are closed. One ear with its gold hoop earring is intact, the other lobe and earring are gone, and a river of dark blood is staining her neck.

He arranges her damaged hand up by her neck and takes another photograph. Then he thinks, *They don't need to know I have her ear.* He turns her head so only her hand and the good ear shows, and he takes a picture of that. Then he pulls her to the edge of the opening.

But he stops before pushing her in, and thinks, *One little peek, one little feel, no one would know.* He lifts her shirt.

"Ah, nice! Perky!" He decides a picture would be a nice memento to savor when he's on the beach in Belize sipping a cold beverage, so he takes one. Then he pushes up her bra and takes another shot of his fingers pinching her nipple. Not easy with the missing index finger!

Suddenly, he's got an erection. A big one. Maybe his biggest ever. He wonders for a moment if he could just shove it in. *What would it feel like, fucking an unconscious twat? Not much different than fucking my wife,* he thinks, and chuckles. *Only one way to find out, and no one will know.*

He unzips her jeans and works them and her lacy little whore panties down around her ankles, pulls her knees up, and spreads them. He takes a picture, her legs wide and cunt rosy, inviting, wanting to be fucked like the whore she is. Now his erection is throbbing. He unzips, pulls out his penis, and scurries up between her knees. She's dry, but he rams it into her, so hard her body lurches along the floor with every thrust. He thinks, *I feel powerful! I am powerful!* Again. Again. And when he ejaculates, he cries out, "Ahhh! Ahhh! Ahhh!" and groans as waves of ecstasy wash over him.

"Take that, Rick, you bastard! Punch me, will you? Threaten me, will you? I'm fucking your whore!" He bursts into raucous laughter. "Maybe I'll e-mail the photos to you!"

He gets up, straightens his clothing, and drags her over to the hole. Carefully placing one foot on each side, he pulls her across and lets go.

She doesn't fall, though. Her arms, head, and upper torso are on one side, and her feet are on the other. He pushes and prods. Finally, he bends her knees and shoves her feet in. She tips forward as she falls, and her forehead strikes the near side of the opening, but she drops. There's a satisfying thud when she hits bottom.

He wrestles with the ladder. It's an old wooden thing, heavier and more cumbersome than he expected, but he finally manages to drag it out of the hole. He positions it carefully along the front of the workbench and drags the sump pump lid back, wedging it into place.

When he looks around, he sees there's more blood on the floor than he realized, and there's a trail of it leading to the hole. He scuffs at it with his foot, but something more is needed.

He scans the basement. The mattresses leaning against the wall a short distance away will be perfect! He tugs the outermost one, and it flops down flat. He drags it on top of the blood pool. It's big enough to cover the tunnel access hatch too. A dumb place to leave an old mattress, but if anyone pokes around down here, say, when they're looking for the whore, they won't think anything about another stinky old mattress. He decides to put the second mattress on top of the first, for insurance. He's satisfied no one's going to move those, at least not until the Children of Noah want to use the tunnel for some other poor SOB. Won't they be in for a big surprise! He barks a laugh.

Not used to all the heavy lifting, he's sweating profusely. He hadn't expected it to be such hard work and reminds himself it hasn't even been an hour. *Four hundred thousand dollars an hour*, he thinks, *plus I got my rocks off. Nice work no matter how you look at it!*

He climbs back upstairs, careful not to touch anything with his bloody hands. At the kitchen sink, he washes his knife and hands until the water runs clear. He dries them on the dish towel lying by the sink and wipes the sweat off his face while he's at it. Then he uses the towel to wipe the handle of the frying pan before hanging it back on the rack.

He turns off the stove. Don't want the fire department showing up!

He wipes the knob on the stove. The taps at the sink. The table. And for good measure, although he can't remember touching it, the chair. Then, unable to remember where the towel was, he hangs it on the oven door.

He's about to leave when suddenly, he thinks, *Her purse! If she went willingly, she wouldn't leave her purse. Where would it be?* He goes into the hall and spots it hanging on the hallstand. He tucks it under his arm.

He exits the house via the back door, wiping the inside doorknob with his sleeve, and pulling the door shut with his forearm. No prints there! *Thanks to CSI, no one will ever know anything happened here*, he thinks, *or more to the point, that I was ever here!* He gives himself a mental pat on the back for knowing forensic countermeasures.

Usin' the ol' noggin.

He had the presence of mind to park in the lane that morning, behind her car, so no one would see him come or go. He can't do anything about leaving her car behind, but when they realize she's missing, the logical conclusion will be that someone picked her up. *Maybe Rick will get the blame*, he thinks. *Wouldn't that be the icing on the cake!*

He's humming as he drives away down the back alley, dust funneling up behind his car. *Perfect*, he thinks, *it's a perfect, beautiful day.* Clear blue sky. Sun shining. Already hot and going to get hotter. But cold as a grave in the tunnel.

Rick, you fuckin' asshole, think you can beat me up? Threaten to kill me? You won't be such a big man when you find out your little whore's gone, eh? And wait until those high-'n'-mighty assholes realize I've got their six hundred thousand and I'm living free as the breeze in Belize! They not only don't get the farm, but they don't get the house either. So they've paid six hundred K for a three-hundred-thousand-dollar condo. Or, to put a better spin on it, I got six hundred thousand for a three-hundred-thousand-dollar condo. Conned the Children of Noah. He chuckles. *Don't it feel good!*

He's also got the four hundred thousand, give or take, he systematically withdrew from accounts in his various aliases at other banks over the past couple of weeks.

To think that when he married Jeanie, all he expected was that she'd eventually inherit that big, valuable farm. Now he's a millionaire, and he didn't have to wait for years.

And soon, free as the breeze in Belize.

He likes the sound of it. Maybe he'll start writing poetry—under a pseudonym, naturally.

He'll miss those communion rituals but reminds himself he's rich. He can buy all the ass anyone could want for the rest of his life. Boys, if he wants. Young stuff too.

"Free as the breeze in Belize," he sings tunelessly. Then again, louder: "Free as the bree-ee-eze in Bel-ee-ee-eze!"

He drives up the alley behind the Co-op and tosses the purse into the Dumpster's gaping maw before continuing to his house. Once inside, he puts the finger in a zip-lock sandwich bag. He sends the hand/ face photo to his home office printer, puts the print in an envelope, and tapes it to the sandwich bag.

He thinks about printing the other pictures but quickly discards that idea. *Don't get too cocky, my man—plenty of time for that later,* he thinks. *You just pulled off the perfect crime, but you still need to be careful.*

What to do with the earlobe? Don't want that starting to rot. How about pickling it? There's a jar of gherkins in the fridge. He removes the little pickles, replaces them with the earlobe, and closes it up tight. He gives the jar a shake, swirling the contents around, and smiles when he sees that the lobe and its gold hoop earring are easily visible without taking them out. Then he puts some of the gherkins back in the jar, just for a little camouflage. A precaution only, totally unnecessary, of course, but a person can't be too careful. He will replace the pickle juice with formaldehyde when he's further down the road.

Usin' the ol' noggin.

Clarence showers and dresses in Gucci jeans and a Ralph Lauren polo shirt before sticking his feet in his favorite pair of Keens. He takes his bloodied clothes down to the laundry room, throws them in the washer, dumps in detergent, and turns it on. He has no plans to come back, so he won't wait to put them in the dryer. Back upstairs, he takes his trophies and goes out to his car.

He was smart enough to pack his money last night. With the linings cut out of his two biggest suitcases, he laid the bundles of bills inside, creating a nice smooth surface, and hot-glued the linings back in place. He filled both suitcases with as many of his clothes as would fit. He had to leave behind so many of his beautiful shoes and designer clothes, but he just didn't have enough suitcases. He thought about putting them in garbage bags but realized that would be hard to explain to the border gestapo. So he took just what he could get in the suitcases and drove to Estevan. At the Super 8, he paid cash for a room and stashed them there.

Now, when he gets the last payment, all he has to do is head south and make a quick dash to the border from Estevan. It's only fifteen kilometers, and the North Portal border crossing—at night—will be a piece of cake.

He has no illusions he'll see the two-plus million the bastards promised him.

Jeanie is out of his life forever. *Oh well. Just another whore, after all.*

Marriage prostitute, always wanting, wanting, wanting. Needing money for this. Money for that.

And of course, Monica, now there's a whore! He laughs. He would really like to see her face when she realizes her meal ticket's gone, gone, gone!

But maybe best of all, ol' prune face Mutti Schoenfeld will never sit there frowning at him again. She turns every nickel over twice before she spends it. She would never sign her farm over. He's known that from day one. Well, not entirely. Those bastards could've given him the red robe, and then he would've made something happen. If she was stubborn, he'd just give her a nudge and the farm would have been Jeanie's. Well, a nudge for Rick too. And Jeanie—maybe a nudge for her, but only if she didn't start behaving as a wife is supposed to. Questioning him about the mortgage! Not signing the papers he told her to sign! She's getting worse. *She forgets I'm to bear rule in my house. She doesn't give me honor both great and small. It's in the Bible. I am not a monster.*

He feels a rush of pride at how easy it was to do the Klein whore. Sure, he didn't actually snuff her, but smashing the pan down on her head? He hadn't even hesitated. That could have killed her. And that moment when he hunkered over her thinking about slitting her throat? "I would've done it, but it would've made too much of a mess. Would've been stupid. And stupid I am not!" he tells his image in the rearview mirror. "I can get rid of anyone I need to."

She's not dead, but she'll never get out of the tunnel so she's as good as. He feels no remorse. Instead, he's proud. *Reeves underestimated me when he said I'm no killer,* he thinks. *But then, I didn't know it myself! Not such a big deal after all. Just another life skill that might serve me well in the future.*

It's their fault, after all. They didn't give him the money they'd promised, and then they made him get rid of her to get more. And the red robe he's entitled to because of sacrificing his finger? If they kept up their end of the bargain, he could've covered the bogus loans and started sharing in the Children of Noah's wealth. But that ship has sailed. Three hundred thousand dollars for completing the job is the last payment. And he's not only fine with that, but happy about it too.

"Usin' the ol' noggin," he says aloud. "Free as the breeze in Belize!"

He calls Donnie. "Donnie? Clarence. It's done. Get the money ready."

Kathy drifts toward consciousness.

There is a putrid stench that's enough to resurrect the dead.

She draws a quick treble breath and opens her eyes. It's dark. Totally dark.

Her head's pounding. Her ear's throbbing. And there's excruciating pain in her finger. She's lying on something like a lumpy plastic sheet or tarp. When she rolls off, she feels dirt against her bare skin. Am I naked? And my hand … the pain! She moves her thumb and realizes part of her finger's gone. She wails and then slips into unconsciousness again.

When she next comes to, she struggles to remember where she is. She's cold and feels cold earth against her buttocks. Questions flood her mind, but she forces her attention back on her body. Where are her pants? Why are her legs and bum bare? Was she raped? She starts to reach with her right hand, but the stab of pain reminds her of her missing finger. She sobs and then collects herself, reaches with her left instead, and finds her crotch is slimy. *Yes*, she thinks. *Raped.*

"Gaawh! Agggh!" She squirms and shudders violently, but nothing takes away the revulsion. It's momentarily worse than the knowledge that she's lost a finger, and she can't quell the waves of horror, disgust, and nausea coursing through her.

Shivering, she holds the nausea at bay and uses her left hand to tug at her jeans and panties bunched up around her feet. She squirms her pants back up and on, awkwardly using only her left hand. Better, but she's still shivering. She realizes she's in shock.

What happened? How did I hurt my finger? It must have been done to me. It must be related to being raped. But why?

Her bra is cutting into the flesh above her breasts. She sits up and reaches under her shirt to pull it back into position.

Cradling her right hand in her lap, she probes her forehead and the side of her head above her ear. Both have large, tender swellings. Then she tentatively touches her sore ear.

A harsh sob is torn from her throat. *My ear! It's gone too!* She struggles to stay conscious. Gently probing her ear again, she realizes the lobe is gone. At least the bleeding seems to have stopped.

Her mind is whirling. *I've been raped and mutilated! But I'm alive. Keep that in mind*, she tells herself. *You're alive.*

The immediate problem is that she has no idea where she is or how to get out. She tries to remember how she got here, but can't. She was unconscious, and likely for quite a while going by the bumps, mutilation, and rape, but it seems like no time at all. One minute she's answering the door. A man … Jeanie's husband?

The next minute she's here.

Wherever here is.

She thinks, *Clarence! He raped me? Why? And where did he take me while I was out? Anywhere. I could be anywhere.* She's flooded with despair as she realizes she's been dumped there to die. She begins sobbing and then crying lustily. It makes her headache explode.

With supreme force of will, she stops crying, sits still, and tries for a happy thought. Some plan. Something that will save her. Rick's coming for dinner, so he'll be looking for her. Maybe he can make Clarence tell him where to look.

Think. Is there anything that would make him suspect Clarence? Maybe the police will find his fingerprints. But they won't be taking fingerprints, and unless he has a criminal record, they wouldn't know they were Clarence's if they did. What possible motive did Clarence have? They'd never even met.

Oh God, the smell!

And her nose is running. She remembers the tissues she'd stuffed in her jeans the day before. She stretches out enough to get her left hand awkwardly into her right front pocket and pulls out a wad of Kleenex. Is there something stiffer, something cardboard? Whatever it is, it falls out of the Kleenex wad and into the dirt. She pats the ground around where it must've fallen. As her fingers close on it, she realizes it's a matchbook. She remembers taking it from Al's Place so she'd have the Wi-Fi password for Penny. *Thank God I haven't washed these jeans*, she thinks.

She struggles to light a match. It makes a pond of weak light around her, and she realizes she's in a cave. Or a tunnel. Could it be *the* tunnels?

She sees the thing she landed on is a blue tarp, and there's something inside. She doesn't have to check to know it's something dead, and it's about the right size for a body.

The match dies.

She thinks, *This confirms it. I'm in a body dump.* She sits still and quiet to calm herself and rein in her runaway thoughts. She's stopped sobbing but can't stop the shivering. She rubs her arm across her face, knowing she has to keep herself together if she has any hope of getting out.

Plan before lighting another match! How many are in a book, anyway? Don't use them foolishly. Better to light something else. Like a torch! But what?

She tries a Kleenex. She lights a match, holds a Kleenex between the middle and ring fingers of her right hand, and touches the match to it, forcing herself to ignore the pain from her index finger. The Kleenex ignites readily and burns away fast, but not before she sees feet sticking out of the tarp. And cloth, clothing. *I can use the Kleenex to ignite cloth*, she thinks, *even though it means robbing a body.*

She crawls on one hand and knees, finds the tarp, runs her hand over it until she finds the edge, and then pulls the tarp back. *Phew! The smell!* Dead body plus shit.

She lights another match and ignites another Kleenex. She's looking down at the face of the man with the white goatee. He's obviously been dead for a while. His flesh is swollen, discolored, bruised. The skin is sloughing off his face. His eyes are cloudy and sunken, and his lips are pulled back away from his teeth in a rictus. Although she knew it was a body, the decaying face is more terrible than she expected, and she moans in horror.

The Kleenex quickly burns to her fingers, and she drops it. It lands on his face and ignites his goatee and some of the sloughing skin, burning away for a second or two. The scent of burning protein wafts up.

She turns and heaves, then wipes her mouth on her sleeve, telling herself to focus. *This is no time to fall apart. I've lost blood, maybe a lot. My finger still seems to be bleeding.* She uses one Kleenex to wrap it, but it's quickly soaked, and she realizes she needs to conserve the Kleenexes, and find something else to use as a bandage.

Three matches gone. *Make them count*, she tells herself. *His shirt. I can bundle it up. Light it. Maybe make a decent torch.* But how to hold on to it once it's burning? *Maybe I'd be better off putting the shirt on ... warm me up ... I need a torch ... I need a stick. Not likely to find one in here. What if I start the tarp on fire? Would the body burn? Is the tunnel airtight? How long before a fire consumes all the oxygen in the tunnel and I suffocate? Would the smoke poison me?*

Her jumbled thoughts are overwhelming. Her head's pounding. Her ear and finger both throb viciously.

She crawls to the tunnel wall, where she judges the corpse's feet to be, and moves away a few feet. She leans back against the dirt wall. *I'm trapped*, she thinks. *I'm losing too much blood.* She puts her injured hand under her shirt and into her bra, holding it still and upright while providing some compression. The throbbing abates somewhat. She tries to slow her breathing, take fewer, deeper breaths.

The reason I'm so cold is the blood loss.

I'm going to die.

Her chin drops to her chest. She has lost consciousness again.

Clarence pulls his Lexus onto the heaved asphalt of the curling rink's parking lot and drives around to the back of the building where the former emergency exit has become the only entrance. It's after office hours and the Prairie Equity office is closed. They could have met there, and he's suspicious about why they chose this more private venue instead.

Nick's black Range Rover and Donnie's candy-apple-red Escalade are already parked, and he sees the two men standing by the open door into the building. He pulls up beside the Range Rover, turns off the car, and gets out.

"You made me wait long enough," Clarence says by way of a greeting, taking off his sunglasses and hooking them on his shirt pocket as he walks past them and into the darkened interior.

Nick says, "It takes some prep at our end, you know." He and Donnie follow Clarence into the inner room and take seats by the altar, motioning Clarence to take the third chair.

"Thanks. I'll stand."

"So. Your assignment is complete?" Nick asks.

Clarence pulls the folded envelope out of his pants pocket, flattens it so the plastic sandwich bag is on top, and hands it to Nick.

Nick peels the sandwich bag off the envelope. The finger is easily identified without opening the bag. He gives it a glance, opens the envelope, pulls out the print, and examines it for a moment before nodding and handing both to Donnie.

"Where's the body?" Nick asks.

"Hmmpff!" Clarence snorts. "Better you don't know. Plausible deniability and all."

"Well, thing is, Clarence. This wound is survivable. As we all know."

"You think she looks like she survived?"

"It does look like lot of blood, but you know once the heart's stopped pumping, wounds don't keep bleeding."

"Who says it was taken off after her heart stopped?"

Nick leans back in his chair, frowns, and interlaces his fingers on his chest.

Donnie asks, "Did she scream?"

"More of a guffaw. She had my dick in her gob."

"Yer lucky she didn't bite it off," Donnie says, studying the photograph.

"She knew better by then, don't you think?" Clarence grins.

"Looks like she's on cement," Donnie remarks.

"Nothing gets by you, Donnie."

Donnie glares at him but lets the snide comment pass. He scratches his head. "You sure she's not just, you know, faking it?"

"You wanna see for yourself? Go ahead. The body's stashed, but

I'll gladly give you directions if you're giving up that arm's length transaction."

Nick and Donnie exchange looks.

"By the way, where's ol' Max? I miss him hovering over me like a vulture."

Then a big blond man comes in. Clarence doesn't recognize him but knows a biker when he sees one. The three men turn their backs on Clarence and confer in low voices. The biker turns and leaves.

"So, Clarence, where's the rest of the money?" Nick asks as he sets the gherkin jar on the altar with a thump.

Damn, Clarence thinks, I should've stashed that. "Tossed my car, eh?" he says. "You didn't really think it would be there, did you? Every cent so far's gone to fix up irregularities so the auditors don't find them. You know that. Which brings me to the next item on the agenda: when do I get the two point nine million? The rest of my deal?"

"That won't happen until your mother-in-law joins the church. Signs over the farm."

"No, that wasn't the deal. As I said before, the deal was I get her to join. The rest is up to you."

"That's not how I remember it," Nick says, "but set that aside for the time being. When is she going to join?"

"Well, I'm workin' on it. She's going to have to do it PDQ. November's not that far off."

Fart. *Damn it*, Clarence thinks.

Nick and Donnie turn away, have a brief huddle, and turn back.

"Okay. We accept your proof," Nick says, motioning to Donnie.

Donnie pulls a sports bag out from under the altar, gets up, and hands it to Clarence, who thumps it down on the altar. He opens the zipper and rifles through it, picks up the pickle jar, and puts it in with the money before closing the duffel bag and lifting it by the handles.

"I'll talk to Mutti again tomorrow. Maybe bring her by for the afternoon service on Sunday." He heads to the door, turns, and says with a snigger, "Gentlemen, always a pleasure." Then he leaves the room.

Donnie and Nick wait until the outer door bangs shut.

"What the hell was that?" Donnie asks. "All of a sudden he's got a set of balls?"

"Murder must be empowering," Nick says.

"Hmm. Must be. But I wonder … how do you slice someone's finger off while you've got yer dick in her mouth?"

"Pfft! Impossible! That was supposed to impress on us what a tough guy he is. And he's learned how to look you in the eye and lie. And he took a trophy for himself? We've created a monster." Nick shakes his head and clucks. He pulls out his phone. "Yeah, you guys finished going over the house? Anything there?"

He shakes his head. Mouths "nothing" to Donnie. "Okay. Follow him, but very discreetly like we talked about. Don't spook him. He'll head right for the rest of his stash. Don't close in until he's running with all of it." Listens. "Yeah, of course. You guys are in for a big payday. Big! There'll be a nice bonus if the target is eliminated. And you can count on more jobs coming your way. Keep me posted."

Turns to Donnie. "They figure he's bugged out. Not much left in the house but the wife 'n' kids' stuff."

"So you don't think he's gonna bring old lady Schoenfeld to Sunday's service?"

"Donnie. Jeez," Nick says and shakes his head.

Marcus comes in. "Sorry," he says, "last appointment went late."

"Always somethin'," Donnie mutters.

Nick gives Donnie a look and turns to Marcus. "Well, you missed the Clarence Weaver show. Now he's a mover and shaker. But he took her out, anyway." Nick tosses the sandwich bag to him.

Marcus studies the bag, his expression grim.

"Wanna know somethin' else?" Donnie chuckles. "He took a trophy. Sliced off half her ear and has it in a pickle jar!"

Marcus shakes his head. Turns away.

"Whatsamatter?"

"It's nothing to laugh about!" Marcus snaps, turning to glare at Donnie. "She wasn't a soldier. She was just an innocent civilian. A young, beautiful woman with her whole life ahead of her. And I don't like doing women!"

"It was necessary," Nick says, taking the sandwich bag from Marcus.

"I know," Marcus says.

"Good. So, to bring you up to speed, Weaver's on the run."

"But don't worry, *Marcus*," Donnie sneers. "We got him covered. He'll go right for the money. 'N' then he can bend over, put his head between his legs, 'n' kiss his ass goodbye."

16

Rick arrives at Kathy's house about seven. He's surprised to see there are no lights on, but it's a couple of hours before sundown, so maybe she's just enjoying the natural light. He looks to the back lane. Her car's beside the garage, so she must be home. He goes up to the front door and rings the bell.

There's no answer and no footfalls inside to indicate she's coming. He rings again. Still nothing.

Maybe she's in the tub? Or in the basement running the washer? Vacuuming?

He opens the door and steps into the foyer.

"Kathy!" he calls.

She doesn't answer, and there are no sounds of machines or running water. Just silence.

"Kathy!" He goes through to the kitchen and notes the pot of spaghetti sauce on the stove, and all the makings still on the counter. There's a mug, half full of cold coffee, on the table.

Taking the stairs to the second floor two at a time, he shouts, "Kathy!" He opens the door at the bottom of the staircase to the attic. It's dark up there, but he calls anyway, not expecting an answer.

He turns and goes into the front bedroom. The little green purse stands on the vanity. He opens it enough to see her wallet's inside.

"Oh God!" he gasps. "Please! No! Oh God, God, God!"

Don't jump to conclusions, he thinks. *Maybe she went for a walk.*

He goes back downstairs and out onto the back porch, hoping to see her outside, but there's nothing but the buzzing of insects in the late afternoon heat. Back in the kitchen, he looks at the table. What's out of place? Something doesn't belong. Then he realizes it's the Creamo and the spoon by the sugar bowl with a drop of coffee dried in it. She drinks her coffee black, so the coffee in the mug is hers. The Creamo was for him. Someone else was here. Maybe she went somewhere with that person … But she would've at least sent him a text to say something came up, she'd be late, or maybe she couldn't make it tonight after all.

He paces. Even if she went with someone else, would she leave her purse? He goes through to the living room. Rubs his face. Massages his neck.

Then he spots her cell phone on the end table.

"No no no no no!" He collapses to a chair.

A cold ball of dread squeezes his stomach. *Calm down*, he tells himself. *Breathe*. He takes several deep breaths, gets out his phone, and calls Penny.

"Penny! It's Rick. Yeah, hi, how are you? Yeah, you talk to Kathy today? She planning on going anywhere that you know of?"

"No," Penny says. "I talked to her a few days ago. She sounded happy. Said something about exorcising demons. What's up?"

"Well, you'll think I'm being foolish …"

"Okay, cowboy, now you've got me worried. What's going on?"

"It's just … we were supposed to have dinner together. She said she'd make spaghetti. The sauce is on the stove, cold. Her car's here. Her purse's here. Even her cell phone's here! But she's not here." His voice catches. "She was upset yesterday. We found her father's shaving things. She said he wouldn't have gone anywhere without them and thought it meant something bad had happened to him. We talked about you, how you said the Children of Noah might be capable of anything, and she worried they did something to him. But she seemed fine when I left this morning. We were going to search the attic some more tonight to see if there were any other clues. She might just be out for a walk, but I don't see why she would be. She's making dinner. She should be here."

There's a moment of silence. Then Penny says, "Call the police. Don't touch anything, and call the police."

"I thought of that too. I should've called them first … I just wanted to call you in case you had some idea …"

"You know we've stirred up a hornet's nest, going after that cult. And believe me, they are capable of anything. I mean, *anything*. It's not a stretch to think they killed her father back then. And they might have her, Rick."

Fear gnaws at his insides, at his mind. "But she didn't confront them about that! We weren't … there's nothing to indicate they killed him. All we found was his shaving mug."

"Maybe they've just chosen today to settle the lawsuit their way. So call the police. I'm booking a flight right now, and I'll be there tomorrow. In the meantime, Rick, be very careful! Don't trust anyone. I mean *anyone*. But especially not anyone in that scheißen cult."

Rick calls the police as soon as he gets off the phone with Penny and goes out on the veranda to wait.

Ben Neufeld is at his desk. The office is finally quiet now, and he has time to spend on performance appraisal reports, cursing the need for doing them every year when there's so much real work to do. There's a tap at his door.

"Yes?" he says.

Constable Peets opens the door and comes partway in. "We got a call, sir. A guy, Shunfeld, over on Front Street, says someone's missing. He asked for you, but I put him off."

"Who'd you say made the call?" he asks.

She looks down at her notepad. "Rick Shunfeld. Or Showenfelled. Should I call the chief?"

"When he's not on shift? You really are a rookie," Corporal Neufeld says. "Rick's a friend. His name's pronounced *Shanefeld*. We've been trading voice messages for days. For future reference, if someone asks for me, put them through. I not only don't mind, but it's what I want. But what's the address again?"

"Ten Front Street. That spooky old house in the block behind Al's Place. Where we picked up that guy who was trying to break in a couple weeks ago."

"What guy? What break-in?"

"You know. The really white guy with the rain hat or whatever it

187

was. Grogan and I caught him in the act, picking the lock. Grogan brought him in."

"Where's Grogan?"

"He's on days."

"Hmm." Neufeld chews his lip. "I didn't see anything about that arrest in the daily orders. Grab the report for me, would you? And I'll interview Mr. Schoenfeld." He stands and reaches for the hat on the filing cabinet behind him. "Come over to the house when you've got that report. Lights. No siren."

He gets an unmarked car from the motor pool and speeds over to Front Street, red and blue lights swirling on the dash and in the back window. He's familiar with the area and knows there's only one house on the block, so he doesn't have to slow to check for the address. He spots the gap in the overgrown bushes where the gate is. He pulls up to the curb, gets out, and walks up to the veranda where Rick waits. Taking the steps two at a time, he reaches Rick and shakes his hand.

"Hey, Rick. This can't be what we've been trading voice messages about."

"No. Well, it might be connected. I don't know."

"What's going on?"

"It's Kathy. My girlfriend ..."

Corporal Neufeld is distracted by the arrival of a second, marked, car. "Damn!" he mutters under his breath.

Constable Peets gets out and comes up on the veranda. A frowning Neufeld introduces her. "Rick's my right-winger," he tells her. "Okay. Tell us."

"My girlfriend, Kathy Klein, lives here. We were planning on having dinner here tonight. And she's gone. Her purse. Wallet. Car. Even her cell phone's here, but she's gone." He opens the door. "Come in."

They follow him into the foyer and look around. Peets gets her notepad out of her vest pocket.

"Okay. So she's only missing since this afternoon?" Peets asks.

"I don't really know when she went missing. I last saw her about seven this morning. But she was here long enough to make the spaghetti sauce. See?" He leads them into the kitchen, where the two pots, one with meat and one without, stand on the stove. Then he points to the carton of Creamo on the table. "And someone else was here. She's vegan, takes her coffee black. She must've had company or she wouldn't have the cream on the table."

He leads them up to the front bedroom where the little green purse, with her wallet and car keys inside, stands on the vanity. Then down into the living room where her cell phone still lies on the end table.

They head back out onto the veranda.

"I haven't touched anything. Well, I did open her purse, and maybe I touched her mug. I don't know what to do," Rick moans. "Ben, what should I do?"

"Well, for now, stay out of the house. I'm going to call in the Evidence Recovery Team from Regina." He turns to Constable Peets. "Would you put up tape around the whole yard, please?"

"But, you know, she's not even missing a day," Peets points out, "and there's no sign of a struggle. Why do we need ERT? There's nothing to indicate it's a homicide."

"Homicide!" Rick cries.

"Now, Rick, Constable Peets is right. There's no reason to believe it's a homicide. But the Evidence Recovery Team is the best resource for investigating an abduction too. Until we know otherwise, that's what I'm calling this." He nods at Rick.

Then he turns to his subordinate and says, "Constable Peets, join me at the car." He walks to his car, opens the driver's side door, and turns to face his subordinate as she approaches.

"What woman do you know would cook the food and then willingly take off instead of staying home to have dinner with Mr. Schoenfeld?" Neufeld asks. "Without letting him know? And without her purse, wallet, cell phone, or car?" He clicks his tongue and shakes his head. "Get the tape. And stay here until ERT shows up. No one else gets in. Understand?"

She nods.

"Okay. Now, where's that report about the burglar?"

"Uh, I can't find it without a name. Need more time, I guess."

"What did I tell you to do?"

"Well ..."

"Don't go off shift without talking to me," he says sharply. "We'll discuss whether you should second-guess me. And throw out words like *homicide* in front of a distraught man whose loved one is missing. Not to mention what might be a problem with that arrest report."

He radios his request for the ERT and returns to Rick. "Why don't you come back to the station with me, Rick," he says. "There's nothing to be done here. At least for now."

Kathy's dreaming. Horses. The seaside. Some child's birthday piñata. A stray thought invades her dream. *You shouldn't sleep. Concussion. Don't sleep.*

She shakes it off and tries to go back to the warm, sunny day. The happy people. The laughing kids. The birthday piñata. But the thought returns: *Don't sleep.* The realization it's something she should pay attention to pushes through her subconscious, and she shakes herself awake.

Yes. Concussion. I've got a concussion, she thinks. She's coming back to full consciousness when her stomach clenches and she heaves again. Definitely concussion.

Somewhere she heard a person with a concussion shouldn't sleep. Or should be awakened every hour. What exactly is it about concussion and sleep? Then she remembers where she is.

The smell! I'm next to a dead body.

She gags again. Fresh waves of revulsion wash over her as she remembers she was raped. And that's the least of it. She reminds herself she has to be calm. There's a way out of this, there must be, but she needs to stay calm if she's to figure it out.

If she doesn't, she'll die.

She remembers needing something from the body. But what for? Something to make a torch. *That's it! I need a torch. Don't waste a match. Don't look at the body.*

She stretches her left arm over along the wall until her hand comes in contact with the tarp. Then the shoe/feet closer to her. Then a bundle of cloth.

The cloth. What is that? She carefully pulls her right hand out of her bra. As careful as she is, it still sends fiery bolts of pain through her and she utters a cry. She pushes the pain to the back of her mind, gets up on hands and knees, and feels the body's shoes and the bundle of cloth around them. She nearly gags at the stench but forces herself to carry on.

She feels along the edge of the bundle. Her hand touches flesh. Cold, hard, hairy flesh. His shin, she realizes. His pants are down. Was he raped too?

Is this Clarence's work? Is Jeanie's husband a serial killer? Serial rapist?

Keep your mind on the task at hand. So his pants are already nearly off. Don't think about why. Just be glad it makes it easier for you.

She works as best she can in complete darkness, then lights another precious match and another precious Kleenex so she can see what she's doing. The body's boxer shorts are around his ankles with his pants. When flames reach her fingers, she drops the burning Kleenex. It falls into the space between his ankles, next to the boxers. They catch and singe the hair on his legs, but all too soon the little fire goes out. Still, it's enough to give her a plan.

The boxers are a fine, thin, woven material and should be easier to start on fire than the heavier pants. Maybe even easier than the shirt. She works his pants, then his boxers, off his feet. Both reek of urine and are damp. That's not promising.

She finds a foot and takes off the shoe. *I should've done that before I took his pants off,* she thinks. *I'm definitely not thinking straight.*

She spreads the shoe open, and using her thigh as a surface, she folds and rolls his boxers into a tube shape as best she can in the complete darkness and with her mostly useless right hand. The urine smell is strong. She tries to keep the driest part of the boxers on the outside of the roll. When she's satisfied with the tube, she feels for the shoe and guides the boxers into it, snuffling with pain every time her wounded finger bumps something, but she forces herself to continue. Then she lights another match and another Kleenex, and holds it against the tongue of the shoe next to the rolled-up boxers. The shoelaces ignite for a second. The boxers scorch and almost ignite. She feels a surge of hope.

Then it's dark again.

She sits back on her haunches and takes a few deep breaths. She only has one Kleenex left. What are the chances of starting anything on fire with just a match once the Kleenex is gone?

She realizes the pants are not likely to be of help. She'll need the shirt after all. She crawls forward, protecting her right hand, in a sort of hip-hop like a dog on three legs, and finds the edge of the tarp and the man's torso just by feel. She clenches her teeth against the nauseating smell and begins undoing buttons.

How will I get it out from under him? she wonders. *And if I do, will it be so soaked with decaying body fluids that it's impossible to light? I have to rip it.*

But how to start?

She opens the buttons, feels her way down to the shirttail, finds the side seam, and tries to start a tear. No luck. She decides she needs a starting point. If she can burn a hole, even a small one, she should be able to rip it from there, and she can do that without using a precious Kleenex. She feels something warm and wet and realizes the stump of her finger has started bleeding again. She ignores it. Holding the matchbook between her ring and middle fingers, she lights a match and holds it under the shirttail. It burns through quickly, and the flame spreads until the hole is more than an inch in diameter. Then it fizzles and goes out. There's a smell of burning paper overlaying the rotting body smell. She remembers grade twelve sewing class and the tests for identifying the type of fabric. If it continues burning after the match is taken away and smells like paper, it's cotton. *How is it I can remember that and yet have no idea how I got here?* she wonders. She clicks her tongue and forces her attention back to the task at hand. This shirt is a very thin, fine cotton that would be comfortable even in hot weather, which explains how he was able to completely cover himself in the heat of a south Saskatchewan August.

She's now able to rip the shirt, starting at the burn. It rips until something, probably the arm seam, stops it. She feels along the strip and rips it across until she runs into the front placket. Grabbing a firm hold on each side, she puts all her strength into ripping it.

When it gives way, she topples over, landing with something hard bruising her side.

"Agghh!" She collapses back into a sitting position, hugging herself.

Now her ribs can be added to the list of sore body parts. At least for a short time, it made her forget how cold she is.

She attempts to collect her thoughts by some three-part breathing, counting as she does so. She thinks of Kim Li and the ten or twelve yoga sessions she took with her, trying to remember other calming and centering yoga stuff. It comes to her that she should have checked the pants pockets in case there's something there she could use. Maybe he is—was—a smoker and might have a lighter! Why didn't she think of it before? Maybe there is something to that yoga stuff!

She feels her way back to his feet, finds the pants, the belt. There's that strong urine/ammonia reek. She holds her breath and checks all the pockets but finds nothing.

Overcome with disappointment, she allows herself another little cry. *I'm going to die here*, she thinks. *There's so much in my life I should've done differently. So much I still have to do! I think Rick said he loves me. I should have told him I love him too. And now it's too late.*

Stop it, she tells herself. *If you think that way, you are doomed. There's a way out of this. Don't worry about the dark. It's not important. Blind people live their whole lives in the dark and manage to do all sorts of things.*

I should take the belt, she thinks. She pulls it out of the belt loops and awkwardly buckles it around her hips. Then she focuses on the shoe torch. She tears the thin shirt cloth into narrower strips, rerolls the cloth tube to add in the dryer shirt material, and then stuffs it back into the shoe.

When she lights the next match, she counts those remaining. Fifteen. More than she expected but still not enough that she can afford to be careless with them. She touches the match to the edge of the cloth tube, and it ignites. It burns for a few seconds, but then goes out. It's astonishing how dark the tunnel seems after that feeble little light is gone. And how bleak her situation seems.

Is this even going to work, or is it a stupid idea? she wonders. *If it's not a stupid idea, why isn't it working? Maybe it's rolled too tightly.* She pulls it out and rerolls it, then stuffs the more loosely packed cloth roll into the shoe.

In for a penny, in for a pound, she thinks, and pulls out her last

Kleenex. Laying it carefully on the shoe, she pokes it partly into one of the folds to keep it in place, lights it, and holds her breath.

It ignites!

After a few moments, it seems to be burning steadily. The flame is very small and doesn't cast much light, but like the little red light on the GFI in the bathroom that isn't noticeable in daylight but seems to illuminate the whole room at night, it provides enough light for her to examine her surroundings. She sets the shoe on the dirt next to her.

Pushing back against the dizziness and nausea she feels when looking at her damaged hand, she uses a strip of the shirt material to wrap the stump of her index finger and her entire right hand. She works the belt crisscross over her head and shoulder, and uses her left hand to carefully slip her right hand between the belt and her torso like a sling. It feels better.

Then she surveys her surroundings, at least as much as she can see from the small flame. The tunnel ends just a few feet farther on. The entrance must be in the other direction. *It can't be far, surely. No one would pack bodies very far into a tunnel, would they? What if there's a locked door? Worry about that when you get to it.*

Carefully, she stands and picks up the shoe torch, lifting it slowly. Even as carefully as she lifts it, the flame gutters and nearly goes out. She shields it with her hand, holding her breath and keeping still for a few tense seconds.

The flame steadies.

Slowly, she starts down the tunnel.

Clarence transfers the last bundles of cash into various nooks and crannies in the trunk of his car. Once he gets to his motel room in Estevan, he'll hide it like he did the rest. He has one suitcase with no money in it, and he brought his hot-glue gun and box cutter.

There's no limit to the amount of cash that can be taken across the border, but $10,000 and over has to be declared. If he declares the actual amount …! He won't get out of Canada for hours. Days. Maybe not at all.

If he only declares, say, the maximum, the fucking Nazi border-guard bastards might still toss his car. He's probably not the first person to hide something behind suitcase linings. His money is bulkier than he expected, so anyone giving it more than a perfunctory examination would wonder why the lining bulges out like it does, and would find it. They could seize it. He'd be detained, and he would definitely have trouble explaining where he got all the cash. So he'll declare only a reasonable amount, just as much as a tourist would usually carry. If they ask the purpose of his trip, he'll say he unexpectedly got a few days off work and decided it was a good opportunity to take in a passion play in the Black Hills. It's something he's always wanted to do, being the good Christian he is. He'll tell them his wife's in hospital having just given birth, a baby girl, praise the Lord! So she couldn't make the trip with him, but she encouraged him to go. He's traveling so late at night because he was at the hospital until visiting hours were over. That should put a stopper in any other questions.

Once on the road to Estevan, he realizes he's hungry. He hasn't

195

eaten since breakfast, and it's been a long, grueling day, but he's nervous about leaving his car unattended to go into a restaurant.

He stops at the A&W drive-through in Weyburn and gets a couple of Teen Burgers, with fries, onion rings, and a root beer, then sits in his car in the parking lot and wolfs it all down.

A couple of motorcycles roar by on the road. He wonders why he seems to be noticing motorcycles so much lately. Maybe it's because he's thought about getting one himself? A Harley! Maybe he'll get some tattoos too. Once he's settled in Belize.

He tosses his garbage out the window, backs out of the parking space, and drives out of the parking lot, merging into the highway traffic. When he gets to the Super 8 in Estevan, he parks near the back entrance and pops the trunk. Looking around to be sure no one's watching, he pulls the cash from various hiding places and puts it back in the duffel bag before heading into the lobby. He nods an acknowledgment to the cheery "Good evening" from the night clerk at the reception desk and takes the elevator to the second floor and his room.

He debates staying overnight. It's been a long day, after all, and he is physically and emotionally exhausted. His back is already complaining—all that unaccustomed lifting and dragging! He knows it'll be even worse tomorrow. A hot shower, a couple of Oxys, and a good night's sleep would do wonders. The idea is tempting. But he decides against it. He's AWOL from the bank—would they phone Jeanie? He wouldn't want to alert her to the fact he's doing something hinky. He has to stay under the radar. Jeanie's one thing; what could she do about it, anyway? More important, Nick and his henchmen can't get a whiff or who knows what they'd do! He wants to be far away, well into the United States, before those assholes know he's gone.

It takes a bit of time to get the cash hidden under the lining of the last suitcase.

Then it takes two trips to get everything down to his car. This time he uses the back stairwell so the night clerk's curiosity won't be aroused. The clerk saw him come in, and if he doesn't see him go out, he'll assume Clarence is in for the night. He's been careful—signed in under one of his aliases, paid cash, deliberately transposed his car license plate numbers. But if someone is looking for him, somehow traces him this far, and asks about him at the desk, the night clerk will think he's in his room. He's probably being paranoid, but it gives him a rush of pride imagining himself as a spook, or a world-renowned art thief outsmarting all the cops and private dicks who pursue him.

The exit door can't be opened from outside and locks on closing, so he props it partway open with a rock, kicking the rock back into the planter and letting the door slam shut behind him on his last trip out. Somehow, stiffing the Super 8 for the second night's room rental makes him feel good. He thinks, *I'm a millionaire, and millionaires don't have to pay their bills.*

He gets in his car, buckles up, starts the engine, and heads for Highway 39. His iPhone is plugged into the USB port to charge, and seamlessly interfaces with the car stereo. He dials up the playlist that includes "Margaritaville," turns the volume up to ear splitting, and sings along.

In less than half an hour, just after midnight, he'll be in the United States.

He succumbs to a feeling of joy unlike anything he remembers. *Is this what rapture feels like? Who's the man? Outsmarted 'em all! Usin' the ol' noggin! Fucking Rick's whore was the icing on the cake.* His penis swells at the memory.

He's out on the open highway when a couple of motorcycles roar past him. *These aren't the good-citizen type of motorcyclists*, he thinks, *not with those tin-can helmets. Wonder where they're going in such a hurry?* Of course, he's sticking right to the speed limit. The last thing he wants to do is attract attention.

Then he realizes the shitheads have slowed down, and now he's going to have to pass them.

What douchebags. Pass someone and then slow down.

There's not much traffic at this time of night so he easily overtakes them.

It's beyond belief, but he sees them in his rearview mirror, coming fast. They pass him and slow down again. Now there's two more coming up fast behind.

This is ridiculous, he thinks. *I'll put some distance between them and me.*

He pulls out and rockets past them, pressing the accelerator to the floor. The engine hums beautifully, and he's doing a hundred and fifty kilometers per hour in seconds. He's heading into a long downhill. There are no lights behind him now, so he starts slowing back to the speed limit.

Then he sees all four motorcycles coming up behind him.

Before he can blink, they're riding in the oncoming lane right beside him, nearly sideswiping him, squeezing him over. Then there's an oncoming vehicle. They fall back, only to come up beside him again when the traffic clears.

"I'm not going to move over! Go ahead and sideswipe me, asshole," he mutters. "It'll go worse for you than for me!"

He turns his head to give the biker beside him an I-dare-you sneer but sees the man is pointing at him. No, pointing *something* at him. Is that a gun?

Fear!

He spasmodically jerks the steering wheel. The car slews over the shoulder nearly onto the gravel margin. Thanks to steering torque control, it corrects itself, and he's back on the asphalt heading with speed straight ahead. But the road curves left and narrows. There's a bridge abutment looming in front of him. He frantically steers the car toward the center lane to avoid it. It's too much! The STC takes over, but not before the car careens across the oncoming lane. Metal screams as the passenger side scrapes along the concrete abutment. The side curtain airbags blast open.

Then the Lexus is bouncing down the bank, ripping through low bushes, and splashing to a jarring halt in the river.

Clarence is momentarily stunned but collects himself. The driver's airbag didn't deploy when it went into the water. *Not enough of a front impact*, he thinks. *It's just as well. People get injured by the airbag. I'm shaken up but okay.*

The car's filling with water but seems to have settled on the bottom. The river isn't deep here or the car hasn't gone in far, so although it's at an awkward angle with the front end considerably lower than the back, he'll easily be able to get out and get to shore. Thankfully the lights are still on, even though the engine has gurgled and stalled.

He works at the seat belt. It's stuck, owing perhaps to his weight leaning against it, and doesn't release. The water's up over the dash now, and it's surprisingly cold, but it seems to be level with the water flowing around the car, so he's not in danger of drowning.

He braces his legs against the floor to push his weight off the seat belt, and gets it undone. Then he struggles to open the door. Once he's out, he wobbles and steadies himself by holding onto the door. The current is strong, but he's mostly protected from its pull by the car. The bottom's muddy, though, weedy and steeply sloped too. His feet tangle and slip, but the back end of the car is still up on shore so he'll be able to hang onto it and pull himself to safety. The car can go in. The important thing is to get to shore.

Lights push the darkness away. He looks up and sees, not rescuers, but four motorcycles. And they're aimed his way! Off the road, following the scar his trip down the bank tore through the low bushes and grass.

Clarence's panic returns. Of course they would come back. *They must be after my money. How could they know about it? Goddamn Children of Noah! I should have known those bastards couldn't be trusted! They won't find the money on their own, but they could hurt me, make me tell them. I need to get away. Swim downstream and hide in the weeds. Call for help. My phone! It's still in the car!*

He dives back in. The dash lights glow eerily but give some light. He keeps his head up and feels along the dash to the console where he'd set the phone. He has a moment of panic when he fears it might not still be there, and if it is, it's wet and might not work. Then he hears voices and realizes someone else is in the water, splashing up behind him.

His hand's just closing on the phone when he's given a hard shove, propelling him farther into the car. He flails frantically and manages to get his head above water, gasping to fill his lungs.

He can outwait them. It's cold but not *that* cold. Hypothermia isn't a concern at this time of year. Even if the car sinks, he'll swim to shore and recover his suitcases when the car's pulled out tomorrow. Then he hears the trunk pop open and the bikers' excited voices. He realizes they're taking his luggage. And in minutes, they're hooting and yelling. They've found his money.

Worse, the car is starting to move forward, farther into the river, and he realizes they're pushing it in. Now it's partly floating and sinking fast. He scrambles to get out, but the current's stronger now. Water is pressing against the door, and he can't push it open. He flips over onto his back to push on it with both feet, but his left foot slides between the seat and the seat belt. Still, he's able to get it open, but when he tries to slide out, his left leg goes farther through the seat belt. The seat belt's now right up in his crotch, painfully cutting into his testicles; however, he notices that only as a footnote. The door's closing on his legs as the car goes deeper.

He's pulled under with the car. He tries to free himself from the seat belt, but it's futile. He's desperate for air. His lungs burn. The last of his remaining air bubbles go out through his nose, and then he can't stop his body from gasping for air but finds only water. He flails frantically.

Then darkness.

Kathy discovers a skeleton.

After the decomposing body, the nice, clean skeleton is only momentarily shocking. She's hopeful this body will have a lighter or maybe more matches, something useful anyway, and she pulls at the gauzy rags clinging to it when she realizes it's not real. *Who would plant a fake skeleton here?* she wonders. Then she feels a bloom of optimism. *This must mean the tunnel is used for something. Could it be part of the Al Capone tunnel tour?*

One of the leg "bones" has been broken away, with the shoe still attached. *Would this make a better torch?* There's no sock or anything in the shoe, and she decides the shoe she has is better, unless she can figure out a way to attach the cloth roll to the "bone". She attempts different means of attachment but needs to be so careful not to wreck what she already has. With no success, she decides against continuing. Still, the bone/stick might come in handy at some point, so she keeps it.

The gauze burns better than the boxers and the shirt material. She bolsters the cloth tube with it, careful not to bind it too tightly and extinguish the flame. She's already had to relight it twice and worries about running out of matches. Once she's got the roll burning steadily again, she clamps the bone/stick into her armpit, picks up the shoe torch, and moves on.

Soon she's in an area of the tunnel that's been widened and deepened considerably, with a table of sorts in the center, and she makes her way to it. *Is that wax? It is!* Different colors of wax in thick gobs on the top. Candle wax, she realizes, from many different candles. Maybe many years' accumulation. There are dark stains too, and the top's badly scarred, even worse than the butcher block in her kitchen. Well, she corrects herself, what may be her kitchen. The table is solid and heavy. *Why would anyone drag it in here? What is this place?*

She peels up one of the wax blobs and sets it on her torch near the sputtering flame. It starts to melt and soaks into the gauze. And for a moment, the flame burns higher. Brighter. She scrapes up as much wax off the rough surface as she can, ignoring the slivers, and pokes it in among the folds of cloth. Confident now her torch is going to keep on burning, she continues across the cavern and into an opening, the continuation of the narrow tunnel.

She hasn't gone far when she sees what looks like the end of the tunnel just ahead. It doesn't make sense. Where is the access to this place? She hasn't missed a turn, has she? Maybe that's where the door is. She goes forward, realizing as she nears it that it's blocked off, all right. But it's not dirt. It's brickwork. And there's no door.

No! There has to be a way into this tunnel! There are no other side tunnels. Would Clarence have had the time, or even the ability, to build a brick wall after he dumped her?

Impossible. She feels the bricks. The mortar. It's solid.

Her head's pounding. Her body aches everywhere. She's exhausted. Hungry. Thirsty. Cold. Shivering. Her teeth chatter. Despair slumps her shoulders and wobbles her knees. She collapses to the floor.

Penny pulls her rental car up to the curb next to Al's Place. Front Street teems with RCMP vehicles and is cordoned off. There's an officer lounging next to the cruiser, and he snaps to attention as she walks toward him. "Good evening, officer," she says.

"Good evening, ma'am. Sorry, no one's allowed past this point."

"I'm a friend, a close friend, of the missing woman. I'd like … I *need* to be there."

"I'll check. What's your name?"

She tells him, then waits while he speaks into the transceiver on his shoulder, listens, and after a moment, lifts the yellow tape. "Okay, go ahead up there, and see the officer at the gate."

She hurries up to the gate, passes the officer waving her through, and approaches Rick, who's coming down the steps. He sweeps her into a hug.

"She was fine yesterday morning, Penny! Everything was fine. And now ..." He's shaking with emotion.

Penny's been barely holding it together since her phone conversation with Rick the day before, and now she breaks down, welcoming the shelter of his hug. They stand like that for minutes. Rick collects himself and holds Penny until she takes a deep breath and breaks away. Then he leads her up onto the veranda.

A woman on the porch swing gets up as they approach, and Rick says, "Penny, this is my sister, Jeanie. You probably don't remember her. She was four or five years behind me in school."

"Hello," Penny says. "I vaguely remember you, Jeanie, or at least I remember Rick had a sibling in school. How's your baby?"

"She's doing great, thanks, well enough to be transferred back to Regina. So I came to be with Rick." She loops her arms around his waist and hugs him tightly.

His lips are pressed together, and his chin quivers. Watching him, Penny can't stop her eyes from filling with tears again. *He's hardly keeping himself in check,* she thinks. *A lot must have changed between him and Kathy these past few weeks.* She brushes her eyes with a hand, sniffs, and then says, "It's been over twenty-four hours. There must be something ... Is there anything yet?"

Rick shakes his head.

"Well, there is *something,*" Jeanie says. "Nothing good, though. They've found a second coffee mug under the island in the kitchen, and there's blood and semen on the basement floor. At least they now believe Rick—that there was someone else here and that something, er, a struggle happened. There's a mattress down there with a massive amount of blood on it, but it's very old so it's not Kathy's. They're still busy all over the house."

Penny's knees suddenly don't feel able to hold her. She leans back against the rail.

"Someone organized a search." Rick's voice trembles. "They're searching the town. Fields around town. Anywhere she might have gotten to on foot. Doesn't seem likely. Well, at least it's something. I have to think they're looking for an injured person, not a body!"

"They'd tell us if they were looking for a body, wouldn't they, Penny?" Jeanie asks.

"Yes, absolutely!" Penny says in what she hopes is a convincing tone, although she's not really convinced herself.

"The cops want me here. I can't do anything but wait, and they don't tell me much," Rick says. "Maybe they think I did something to her!"

"I'm sure that's not true," Jeanie says.

"Think about it, muffin! How likely is it that this is random? They always look at the husband or boyfriend first."

"Sounds to me like they've told you quite a lot, Rick," Penny says, pushing away her own dread and trying to be a steadying influence. "If they're not telling you more, it's because they don't know much. This is just evidence recovery at this point, remember, in hopes of finding something that tells them where to look. I don't think you're a suspect, but if you are, they'll get DNA from the semen and prove it wasn't you. And what about the guy who's been poking around, the guy you chased off that time? You told them about that, didn't you?"

"Yeah. Maybe. I think so."

"Well, remind them. Also, I'll tell them about the lawsuit. Maybe it's a motive." Penny rubs her face with both hands, her calm evaporating. "Oh God," she moans, "did I cause this? By getting her to issue that writ?"

Another police cruiser pulls up to the barricade. It's waved through and joins the others parked helter-skelter in front of the house. The constable gets out and speaks to the officer at the front gate, who points to the group on the veranda and lets him pass.

They all get to their feet as he approaches.

"Good evening, folks," he says. "I'm looking for Jeanette Weaver."

Penny notices Rick's shoulders relax and she heaves a sigh of relief, but it's a momentary reprieve as she wonders if it could be bad news about the baby.

Jeanie steps forward. "I'm Jeanie … Jeanette," she says.

"Mrs. Weaver, can we talk for a moment?"

"Yes. Why? This is my brother. And a friend. We can talk in front of them. What's it about?"

"Is there a place you can sit down?"

"No. Well …"

"I've got her, Officer," Rick says, looping an arm around her waist. "What is it?"

"Your husband is Clarence Weaver?"

Jeanie nods.

"Ma'am, it's my sad duty to tell you your husband's car went off the road and into the Souris River last night. I'm sorry to inform you he drowned."

Jeanie's silent for a moment and then says, "No." She shakes her head. "Souris River? He couldn't be at the Souris River. Moose Jaw River, maybe. But no, he couldn't drown. He can swim."

"No, ma'am. This was south of Estevan. Almost at the US border."

"Estevan? It's a mistake. It can't be Clarence. He wasn't going to Estevan. He has to go to work tomorrow at the bank in town here. Even if you mean the Moose Jaw River, he can swim. He's a good swimmer. He couldn't drown. It must be a mistake."

"His wallet was with him. He's been identified from his driver's license. But we'd like you to come and give a positive ID when you're up to it."

Jeanie's knees buckle, and Rick lets her sink to the porch swing. "It can't be him … Doesn't make sense."

"Where's his body now?" Rick asks.

"At the morgue in Weyburn. I can get someone to take her there when she's ready if she's not up to driving." He pulls a card out of his vest pocket and hands it to Rick. "Just give me a call. Or if I can do anything. If you need anything. Sorry for your loss, ma'am." He tips his hat, turns, and leaves.

Rick slides onto the seat beside his sister. Penny sits on the railing.

They're quiet as the stunning news sinks in.

Finally, Rick says, "What next?"

The throbbing of her amputated finger breaks through her dream, and Kathy awakens with a start. She's disoriented again but soon flooded with the realization this is really happening.

She hadn't meant to fall asleep. She was just so tired! *Blood loss*, she thinks, *and the concussion*. Still, she shouldn't have let herself fall asleep. Now she has to light her torch again, and she has only a few precious matches remaining.

She gropes around in the dark, picks up the torch, and steadies it between her knees. She pulls the matchbook out of her pocket and strikes one. It doesn't light. The booklet is soft and feels damp. She strikes it along the rough strip until the head's worn off, but it stubbornly refuses to light.

She takes several deep breaths and closes her eyes, although that seems redundant since the tunnel is completely without light and she might as well be blind. She sobs.

"Stop it! If you're going to get out of this place, you have to be strong! You can be strong! You are strong! And you need to be strong now." She realizes she is talking to herself but doesn't stop. It's a comfort to hear her own voice in the deathly quiet tunnel, as if it confirms she's still alive. "But I've lost a lot of blood … I'm so cold … I'm too tired … I need to rest.

"No! If you rest now, you die! There is a way out of this place. You just have to find it."

Then she thinks she hears music. What? She holds her breath to listen.

A piano? Very faint piano music?

It can't be coming through the dirt. It must be from the other side of the brick wall. There must be people there.

She clumsily strikes another match. This one ignites, and when she holds it against the scorched cloth on her torch, it ignites again too. It seems dimmer than before, and she worries the dry cloth and the wax have been used up. If so, before long it won't be of any use.

Don't think about that. At least for now you have light. Not much, but light.

How long until it fizzles out?

Cold. I'm so cold.

What can she do to let the people on the other side of the brick wall know she's here? That is, if there really are people there and she's not still dreaming

She yells. Yells again. Pounds on the wall with her good hand. She kicks it, but her slip-on canvas Keds don't make a sound any louder than her hand does, and she can't kick very hard without hurting her foot, so it's more from frustration than any hope it will alert someone on the other side.

She keeps screaming until she's exhausted and her voice is ruined, and then sinks back down to the ground. At least the physical activity has warmed her somewhat. Once her breathing is back to normal, she holds her breath and listens again.

The piano music stopped but seems to have started up again. If there are people there, they didn't hear her. It's hopeless.

"I can't knock on the wall … I need something …" She spots a softball-sized rock embedded in the dirt near the brickwork. She digs at it, but it's in deeper than she expected, and the dirt around it is hard. She manages to free a smaller rock and uses that to scrape the dirt away until the big rock is loose enough to pull out. It fits quite nicely in her hands, and she sets to work pounding on the bricks. She pounds away, using both hands, ignoring the jolts of pain from her right hand every time the rock impacts the wall. Her amputation is bleeding freely again, soaking the cloth wrapped around it and splattering drops of blood on her face. She's smashed the rest of her fingers bloody too. *My mother would need a bigger bottle of Tabasco sauce*, she thinks, and holds up for a moment. *Am I crazy? Can a brick wall even be broken by a rock?*

Maybe. If the wall's old enough … if the mortar's crappy enough … if the bricks are crumbly enough. What choice do I have? Where's the weakest point? In the middle. At the top.

She pounds as high up the wall as she can reach, which is at least a foot below what she judges to be the weakest point. Not for the first time, she curses the fact she's only five foot three.

Chips of mortar break away, flying around, falling on her head. One stings her face just below her eye. *I should have protective eyewear*, she thinks. *Lost an ear. Don't want to lose an eye. Can't afford to lose any more body parts!* She giggles, then sobs, and tells herself, "You have well and truly lost your mind!"

Maybe it's hopeless. The music's stopped, or at least she can't hear it anymore. Undeterred, she fiendishly pounds on the wall, trying to hit the same spot repeatedly. If she can just weaken it enough! If she can't break it, at least if there *are* people on the other side they might hear her!

After a time she stops, exhausted, and sinks to the ground to rest and catch her breath. *I just can't get enough power behind it*, she thinks. *If only I had a hammer, one of those big ones.* "You're just not doin' it," she says to the rock in her hand and drops it.

The bone stick from the skeleton is just plastic, so it's useless.

Or is it? She picks it up and lays it next to the rock. If she can attach it somehow …

She pulls her arms out of her T-shirt. By now the pain from her amputated finger is constant so she can almost ignore it, but pulling her right hand out of her sleeve momentarily takes the pain to the next level. She winces and cries out but carries on, removing her bra and then pulling her shirt back in place. The rock is too big to fit neatly into one of the cups, but the bra, with its stretchy back and sides, is better than just a strip of cloth would be. In minutes she has the rock attached to the end of the bone stick. *I won't be able to pound it like you could with a hammer*, she thinks, *because that would break it right away. But I should be able to get some force behind it just by swinging it.*

Ignoring the pain, she takes the improvised sledgehammer in both hands, hefts it a couple of times, and then swings. With a satisfying crunch, it strikes the wall much closer to the top than she could reach before.

Again.

Again.

Suddenly, bricks and mortar shatter. She hears screams from the other side of the wall. Another good whack and light pours in through the hole.

"Help! Help!" she calls.

From what must be a room on the other side of the wall, there are more screams and scuffling sounds as if furniture is being scraped across the floor. Then the light's blocked as if something's covering the hole.

"Help!" she yells again.

"Get a flashlight!" a voice says. "Who is it? Is someone there?"

"Yes! Yes! I'm trapped in here!"

In minutes, a flashlight beam shines in. The beam of light sweeps her face.

"Kathy? Is that you?"

"Carl?"

"Kathy! Everyone's looking for you!"

"He tried to kill me!" she wails.

"What? Bloody hell! Get away from the wall! We'll break it down."

She steps back a couple of feet and collapses.

Rick's beside the gurney as paramedics ready Kathy for transport. They hug and cry together. She wails about her missing finger, her mutilated ear, and although she doesn't remember it, the rape. He's helpless to do anything other than assure her she's still beautiful and the rape makes no difference to him, but he'll do whatever she needs him to do to help her get over it. He's so glad to see her that he wouldn't care if she had no fingers and no ears. She laughs. He laughs too. It's emotionally cathartic. Then they're both sobbing again, and he's got a death grip on her left hand. He asks what happened. She can only tell him about Clarence coming to the door and how she got out of the tunnel.

Corporal Neufeld is introduced to Kathy. He requests her permission to record their conversation, and she agrees. He turns on his recorder, and she begins talking, slowly at first and then in a rush. She tells him all she knows: Clarence introducing himself at the door, waking up in total darkness to find her terrible injuries, realizing her pants were down around her feet, that she'd been raped and discarded in the tunnel to die.

And belatedly, she remembers there was a body in there too. The man who'd been skulking around her house.

Kathy's not able to explain how she got in the tunnel, though. And she wonders why she would be piled on top of the dead person.

She's wrapped in warmed flannelette sheets but can't stop shivering, and her teeth are still chattering. A mask is placed over her mouth and nose, and she's told to breathe deeply.

"What is it?" Rick asks.

"Nitrous oxide and oxygen," the paramedic says.

"Laughing gas?" Penny asks.

"It helps with the pain and will calm her."

It seems to be working, as Kathy's eyes are closed.

"Okay," Corporal Neufeld says, "go ahead." He nods to paramedics. He says to Kathy, "I'll see you at the hospital."

She pulls the mask off her face. "Officer! Please! I didn't mean to desecrate that body! I just needed the cloth … His pants were already down around his feet …" Her voice catches.

He squeezes her shoulder. "It's okay. It's okay. Keep the mask on. You did what you had to do to stay alive. You did good."

"Thank you, Ben," Rick says, "thanks for believing me. Believing she wasn't just, you know, that I wasn't just being …"

"It's okay, buddy," he says. "You go take care of your lady." He steps away.

"Ready to roll," one of the paramedics says with a nod to Rick. "One of you want to ride with her?"

"You go, Rick. I'll come in the car," Penny tells him. "See you there!"

"Thanks," Rick says and climbs into the ambulance.

They shut the back doors, and the ambulance goes off.

Nick's behind the bar in the billiard room, too keyed up to sit. He's pacing back and forth in the confined space and smoking one cigarette after another.

"Thought you quit," Marcus says. He's on a barstool facing Nick. He empties his glass and pours himself another Chivas from the bottle Nick pushes toward him.

"Yeah, I thought I did too. Picked a helluva poor time to do it, though." He stubs his cigarette out in the overflowing ashtray and fills his own glass with Chivas.

Donnie's on the stool at the opposite end of the bar from Marcus and lights up another Colt. "Well," he says, exhaling a cloud of the aromatic smoke, "I think it's about fuckin' time we can smoke in here."

The TV above the bar is tuned to the twenty-four-hour news channel. There's a "breaking news" banner scrolling across the screen. Nick grabs the remote and runs up the volume. The late-night news anchor, a well-spoken, pretty blonde, introduces the item. "The man who drowned when his car went into the Souris River south of Estevan yesterday has been identified." The screen switches to video of a body bag on a stretcher being loaded into an ambulance and a wrecker pulling the car out of the water onto the bank. She continues, "Clarence Weaver, age thirty-three, was the only occupant of the car. It appears he lost control of the vehicle and hit the bridge abutment before plummeting down the bank into the water. The cause of the crash is being investigated, but speed is thought to have been a factor. He leaves behind a wife and four children." The screen switches back to the anchor, who pauses for a moment and then says, "The polls have closed in the much-watched by-election in Indian Head ..."

Nick clicks the TV off. "Son of a bitch! Son of a fuckin' bitch!" He thumps the bar with his fist. "Did the cash go down with him? Where's the fuckin' car now? And what the hell good was Arnie's crew?"

"Arnie hasn't checked in?" Donnie asks.

"No, he fuckin' hasn't. He's not answering my calls either."

"You don't think ..."

"Those fuckers got the cash 'n' then put him in the river?" Nick asks. "Yeah, it crossed my mind."

"There was a helluva lot of commotion going on around Ten Front Street when I drove by on my way here too," Donnie says. "They even had

Main Street in front of Al's blocked off. Something must've happened at the pub, and I guess she's—"

"Maybe they found, you know, *him*," Marcus interrupts. "Might've been a mistake dumping him there."

"Shut the fuck up, Marcus." Donnie slams his glass down. "Yer always so goddamned smart after the fact. No fuckin' way they found him. How would they fuckin' find him? They ain't looking for him. The bitch's been reported missing. That's why they're there. Why the fuck would they look for her in the sump pump? That's the only way he could be found. And it has to be something else, something connected to the pub, or else why would they block that off? Think about it. Use yer fuckin' brain before you run yer mouth, why doncha?"

"Donnie …" Nick begins.

"You know, Donnie," Marcus says mildly, "I think I've about had enough of your temper and your nasty attitude."

"Oh, you have? What're you gonna do about it?"

"I think you need to get some anger management counseling."

"Fuck you! *I* think *you* ought to get some respect! 'N' if you can't do that, maybe you'd like to resign? Better think long 'n' hard on that!"

"Nobody resigns," Nick says. "Donnie, lighten up. We got a problem. A big one. We don't need to be fighting among ourselves."

"Oh yeah, Nick!" Donnie snarls. "Take his side again, why doncha? I've been in this a helluva lot longer than he has! Maybe it's time you reminded him I got seniority! You should back me, not him! Just 'cause he was runnin' a crew out at the coast, guns 'n' drugs or whatever, you think he's big time and the sun shines outta his asshole? You gotta kiss his ass all the time? Why didn't he stay there, huh? Why'd they squeeze him out? Ask yerself that! He's not a good fit here 'n' you know it. He hasn't got the balls."

"But he's got brains."

"Meaning I don't?"

"Donnie," Nick says quietly, "come on."

"Yeah, yeah, yeah. Donnie, come on. Easy, Donnie. Donnie, lighten up. I don't *fuckin'* believe it!" Donnie stands abruptly, knocking over his barstool. "Can't stand to hear the truth? Why don't you two fuckin' smart-asses solve this then." He strides across the floor, through to the family room, and out, slamming the patio doors behind him.

"Well," Marcus says in the silence Donnie left in his wake. He clears his throat.

"Don't worry. He'll be okay once he cools down." Nick coughs. "Loose cannon. And a hothead. He's not the sharpest tool in the shed. It's always amazed me that he's so good with numbers."

"He *is* that."

Nick comes around from behind the bar, rights the stool Donnie knocked over, and sits on it. "He's not someone who should ever be Imperial Leader," he says conspiratorially, locking eyes with Marcus. "I've known that for quite a while. At first I thought he might, well, *mature* into the job. I never thought of sending him to anger management counseling. That would be a good idea, except there's no way he'd go. So now he's just another problem, and I'm really getting tired of it. Or maybe just tired. When I said nobody retires, that wasn't quite true. Between you 'n' me, I'm about ready to pass the torch. How's your Latin?"

Rick's been watching the monitors next to Kathy's bed since he and Penny returned to the hospital after a quick lunch. They sit in chairs in the narrow space between the hospital bed and the window, and now that Kathy's awake again, he's holding her left hand.

Dr. Nevens raps on the doorframe before coming into the room. "Just me again!" she says with a smile. She leans over Kathy, shining a light first in one eye, then in the other; she straightens and clips the penlight back into the breast pocket of her scrubs. "Well, Kathy, I think you're good to go. This morning's CT scan shows no brain bleed. I'll give you a prescription for the headaches, but you won't likely need more than over-the-counter analgesics after a few days. The headaches typically resolve within a few weeks."

She looks at Rick and Penny. "Will either of you be able to stay with her for a couple of days? Just to make sure she continues to improve?"

Both nod. Rick says, "For sure. But don't you think it might be too soon? I mean, why can't she remember what happened? Doesn't that mean something's still not, you know, right?"

"It's not unusual. Think of it like a computer that get's unplugged when you're working on a document. The trauma interrupts the flow of information to short-term memory, and then of course the document never gets moved to long-term memory, which is like saving it to a file, when the computer's plugged back in again. So it's just, well, gone. That's why often patients can remember everything after an accident but have no recollection of a period of time before it. The gap can be a few seconds or even several hours. In your case, Kathy, you've suffered a grade three concussion. You were unconscious for quite a while. I'm not at all surprised your amnesia is—what? Fifteen minutes? Long enough for your attacker to drink his coffee and … well. It's not a sign of anything more seriously wrong. We're always concerned about a brain bleed, but yesterday's images were clean, and like I said, this morning's are good too. So you just need to rest. The best place for you to do that is at home, as long as you can take it easy." She pats Kathy's arm. "Your body's pretty banged up, and you've been through a lot emotionally too. I know you talked to the counselor yesterday. She and I both recommend continued counseling. Try to avoid stress, and definitely keep your physical activity to a minimum for a few days. Okay?"

"I don't feel like dancing," Kathy murmurs.

"Lethargy's common, and so is fatigue and depression. You might experience dizziness, and that's fine. It should pass. The headaches too. But if you start throwing up again, or have blood or fluid discharge from your nose or ears, or if you have any thoughts of suicide, your friends need to bring you back in right away."

"We'll keep watch on her, Dr. Nevens," Penny says.

"Okay. I'll discharge her then."

They say their thank-yous, and Dr. Nevens leaves.

Penny stands and pulls up the plastic bag containing clothes she brought for Kathy. She gives Kathy's arm a squeeze. "I'll help you get dressed." Her voice breaks. She tears up. "You've been through a hellish ordeal. You're such a trooper! I'm so proud of you!"

Rick gets to his feet and moves to the foot of the bed, giving Penny's shoulder a rub as he passes behind her.

There's a tap on the door, and Corporal Neufeld pokes his head in. "Good afternoon, folks! All right to chat a bit?"

Kathy nods and says, "Come in."

He closes the door behind him and comes to stand next to Rick. When he looks at Kathy's bruised and swollen face, her bandaged ear and hands, he shakes his head and clicks his tongue. "How's the head today?"

"Okay, thanks. But I think I'm going to ache all over once the painkillers wear off." Kathy squirms into a more upright position and grimaces.

"Yeah, I bet." He furrows his brow. "Any of you got thoughts on why Clarence would do this?"

"No," Rick says. "I've been wracking my brain. It doesn't make sense. Why would he go and beat up Kathy, leave her for dead, and then head for the border? It just doesn't make sense."

"It looks like he was robbed," Corporal Neufeld says. "His suitcases were on the riverbank, torn apart. There were clothes dumped everywhere. Guys who accidentally go off the road into the river usually don't toss their suitcases out first. Traffic's passed it over to Criminal Intelligence, and they're treating it as a homicide. They'll want to talk to Kathy at some point to try to determine the connection."

"I don't know about Clarence," Penny says, pushing up her glasses, "but Kathy has a lawsuit against the Children of Noah for fraudulent transfer of real estate, namely that house and all the other lots on the block. We know Clarence is, er, *was* a member of that cult. Would they kill her because of the lawsuit? Could they have somehow convinced him to do it?"

"Maybe it *is* all about money," Rick says. "Clarence tried to get my sister to sign their house over to them. They were going to pay him four hundred thousand dollars. 'N' my old buddy Donnie Jeffs at Prairie Equity was in on it. My sister didn't sign the papers, though, so Clarence didn't get the money. Could this have been another way for him to get it? And why would he need it badly enough to kill for it? No normal person would even consider it, no matter how much they needed money."

Corporal Neufeld puts a hand over his eyes and massages his

temples. "This gets stranger by the minute," he says. "The other thing. The body in the tunnel? His prints are on RAFIAS. He's got a rap sheet, warrants, in the States. A detective with the organized crime task force in Chicago called, delighted to hear we have his guy and not at all sorry he turned up dead. He was a made guy in a syndicate they've been watching for years. Any idea why he'd be sniffing around your house?"

They all shake their heads.

Penny says, "He's from Chicago? He sure came a long way to break into a house that's got nothing in it! We wondered about him, why he kept showing up, and it makes even less sense now."

"Any idea how he got dumped in the tunnel? Or why there's tunnel access from that house in the first place?" Corporal Neufeld asks.

They all shake their heads again.

"We're not much help. Sorry," Rick says.

"He couldn't've gotten in there any other way, could he?" Kathy shivers. "Someone brought him through the house when I was in Vancouver."

"We're getting the locks changed and putting in a security system." Rick squeezes her shoulder. "And the tunnel access is going to be permanently closed off."

"Good. I hope Criminal Intelligence can figure all this out," Corporal Neufeld says. "Oh, one other thing. The blood-stained mattress? DNA's degraded, but they can still get something called autosomal DNA. Maybe determine some family connections."

"It's from a murder?" Penny asks.

"No one could lose that much blood and survive, they tell me. It could be an accident, but they found human remains, badly decomposed, inside the old furnace. So that's definitely suspicious, whether or not it's the person who lost all the blood."

"My father?" Kathy's face, already pale under the bruises, turns a shade whiter.

"Well, they'll want a DNA sample from you to see if it's a match, both to the blood on the mattress and to, er, the remains. My guess would be that it probably is your father, Kathy. Sorry," Neufeld says. After a moment, he heads to the door. "If you think of anything, call?"

"For sure," Rick says. He follows him out to the hall and shakes his hand. "Thanks, Ben."

"There's a lot I can't tell you, Rick," Ben says quietly. "But there'll be changes in personnel at the station. The DOA in the tunnel was picked up trying to break into Kathy's house. Where he got to from there, no one knows, or at least no one's telling. No arrest report was filed. And I didn't want to say anything in front of Kathy because it looks like she's still shaky, but if Clarence wasn't in it alone, and it seems unlikely he was, she's still in danger. We'll have a marked car posted outside short term, but she should stay elsewhere for a while at least. I'll leave it to you to explain that to her when she's stronger."

"Understood."

Nick leaves his house at three in the afternoon. He plans to see Tina for a haircut before stopping by Prairie Equity. He's set up a meeting for the Triumvirate but wants time alone with Donnie ahead of that so he can smooth his ruffled feathers before Marcus gets there.

It still pisses him off he has to placate Donnie yet again. *I should never have let Tommy name him to the Triumvirate, make him one of the Illustrious Leaders*, Nick thinks. *He's nothing but an ill-tempered thug.*

He gets into his Range Rover, clicks the button to open the overhead door, and backs out of the garage, stopping to light a cigarette, and cough. Then he sends the door back down and buckles his seat belt before heading out to the gravel road that fronts his acreage. Thinking of how many times he's had to sweet-talk Donnie to get him back in line angers him. He stomps the accelerator harder than he planned and sends the truck rocketing onto the road, narrowly missing the gatepost. Clouds of dust follow, and even with the cabin air filter, he can smell it. The dried grass in the ditch as well as a wide swath of the wheat fields on either side of the road are grayish brown with dust. Is it the dust or the cigarette that's making his chest raspy? He goes into another, more intense coughing spasm. *Gotta give up these coffin nails once and for all*, he thinks. *I will as soon as we get this Klein problem solved. In a few months, maybe in January, I can leave Marcus in charge and Marlene and I can go someplace warm for a few weeks. Cuba, maybe.*

Arnie still hasn't returned his calls. By now it's obvious the bikers have the cash and don't plan to return it. If they didn't, Arnie would've checked in and said Weaver's car went into the river before they got to him. Money? What money? Nothing to see here, folks. That would have been the end of story. But Arnie is too stupid to do that.

Stupid, yes, but not someone we can fuck with, Nick thinks, *especially without Max. Even with Max, one guy against Arnie's army? Plus, they seem to be friends. So forget about Max. He's unlikely to come back anyway. So how can we get the money back?*

If that wasn't bad enough, Johannsen called that morning with the news Kathy Klein had been found alive. Johannsen didn't know where or how because he and half his crew were put on administrative leave and are officially out of the loop. What a scandal: the NCO-in-charge and half his staff out of the department with no indication when or if they'll be back! The scandal's one thing, but the loss of the friendly cops is of more concern long term.

Nick was on the verge of asking him if the body was found but stopped himself. They couldn't have found it; they would have had to find the tunnel access first, and how could they? They wouldn't look in a three-foot-by-three-foot, six-inch-high raised floor section marked "sump pump" in their search for Klein. Besides, Johannsen would have said something. And Nick couldn't let on he knew about the body. Some things even a greedy police chief might not be able to turn a blind eye to.

No news is good news, Nick thinks. Whatever Clarence did to Kathy, there is no way they can trace anything back to the Children of Noah. It's not really such a huge problem, the loss of the money aside, but they can't have infighting. They're back to square one in a sense. They just need to get rid of Klein and quash that annoying challenge to the transfer of title to Ten Front Street. The loss of the money stings but doesn't cut them off at the knees. And if there is truth to what Baron said about the Al Capone gold, it will go a long way toward making up for the loss of the cash.

They still need Klein gone so they can search for the gold. It's possible the gold is in something like a desk or a secret drawer in a dresser, so unfortunately for Ms. Klein, unless she agrees to leave all the contents, that's her death warrant. There's some valuable antiques there. Why would she agree to leave them? So she'd take the contents and the gold with them. Nick wonders if it might be stuck somewhere else, like behind a wall or under the floorboards, but they can't take that chance; once they tore everything apart and didn't find it, Kathy and the antiques would be out of reach. Maybe they could buy the house and all its contents. But it's starting to look like a lot of money.

He's also antsy about the body in the tunnel. How long before someone stumbles on the tunnel access, and then the body? It's widely known the house is the meeting place for the Children of Noah. They might be able to deny knowledge of the tunnel access, but who knows what evidence is with the body? Fingerprints? DNA? Maybe only Marcus's and Donnie's. Did he touch Baron? Could he possibly have left his DNA on him? Even if he didn't, he'd have a hard time convincing anyone he didn't know about it, and he can't trust Donnie not to rat him out. He's not sure if he can trust Marcus, either. Retirement is looking more and more appealing, but less and less possible.

He's a couple of kilometers from his house when he checks his rearview mirror and sees a vehicle raising dust on the gravel road behind him, closing fast. It pulls up beside him but doesn't pass; instead it matches his speed, and when Nick turns to look, he sees the passenger window is rolled down and there's a gun pointing at him. He feels a jolt of adrenaline and reacts in a heartbeat, tromping the accelerator to the floor. The Range Rover with its supercharged V8 engine leaps ahead; for a few moments, the other vehicle keeps pace and then drops back. *He probably doesn't like being in the dust,* Nick thinks, *probably can't see anything. I need to get to the highway ... I've got nearly five hundred and fifty horses. I can outrun him ...* He ignores the stop sign at the correction line intersection, hitting the brakes just long enough to negotiate the left turn, and floors it again.

The SUV comes boiling up behind him again, and he realizes too late there's a crosswind and the plume of dust he's raising is being blown off the road instead of back in their faces. His pursuers have him clearly in their sights. He shouldn't have turned! He could have gone straight ahead. Asselstine's farm was just a couple of kilometers farther along. He could have pulled in there. How far to the next farm?

The tailgate glass shatters, and bullets spray the interior of the Range Rover, crashing through the dash, blasting out the big touch screen. Nick steers in a zigzag pattern, but the SV Autobiography isn't a sports car and doesn't handle like one. The traction control is fighting him. He can feel the automatic brakes pulsating. He's betting heavily the other SUV isn't as good as the Range Rover, though, and that the driver isn't used to gravel roads. But when he zigs left, it rockets up beside him, blocking him from going back to the right. Then it slews over and sideswipes him. The tires on the Range Rover's driver's side plow into the ridge of gravel at the margin of the ditch, and Nick has to fight the steering wheel to keep it on the road. He has no choice but to slow. It's enough that he's dropped behind the other vehicle now.

Should he stop and turn back? Could he be back at the correction line road before they notice and get turned around to follow? Not likely. He decides against it. He'd be a sitting duck, a big target, while he was turning. He'll stay behind them and take the next crossroad as soon as those bastards go past it.

But the other vehicle slows and moves to the middle of the road, blocking him from passing on either side without taking the ditch, and forcing him to slow too. He realizes he'll have to go into the ditch and is weighing his chances of doing that without crashing when the shooter turns in his seat and sprays the Range Rover with bullets, shattering the windshield. Nick's face is stung with shrapnel, and then he feels something heavy impact his shoulder. He realizes he's been hit. His shoulder looks as if it exploded, and his right arm refuses to move. He isn't able to stop the Range Rover from slewing into the ditch. It tears through the tall dusty grass, rips through the waist-high wheat and rolls, coming to rest on its roof.

Nick's stunned. His shoulder's bad but he's not critically injured. The engine has died, but he can hear the wheels spinning. Airbags have deployed and deflated. He knows the automatic distress call will have already been sent. He just needs to get out of the seat belt. Will they think he's dead? Who the hell are they anyway? He struggles to release the seat belt. The blood rushing to his head has given him an instant, pounding headache, and he's seeing spots, fighting to remain conscious.

And then legs appear in the bruised vegetation at the window beside him, and a big man slowly crouches and looks inside. His wide, flat face is emotionless as he says, "This is for Alfie," and brings the pistol up.

Donnie's at Al's Place, slouched on a stool at the end of the bar. He's more than a little tipsy but not ready to leave yet. He was already pissed off when he came in, and then, when he ordered another pint of draft—maybe just his third, fourth at the most—goddamned Carl gave him the third degree. Asked for his keys, even offered to call his wife to come and pick him up.

"Leave my fuckin' wife outta it," he told Carl. "I'm not drivin', I'm walkin'. Stayin' inna office. You ain't my wife. I don' need you bitchin' at me too."

Carl frowned and shook his head, all holier than thou, like he's never had a few too many, Donnie thought. But he gave up his keys and proceeded to get good and blotto.

He feels a bolus of hot rage burning in his gut when he thinks about goddamned Nick. First the "Now, now, Donnie" crap he laid on him yesterday. Took fuckin' Marcus's side. No loyalty whatsoever! And then today, calls a meet at Donnie's office, likely to suck up. But doesn't show. He waited two hours. No call. No answer when Donnie called him.

Fuckin' Marcus showed up, though. Sat in stony silence, his caterpillar eyebrows raising practically to his hairline every time Donnie tried to start a conversation, as if everything Donnie said was so-o-o shocking. And a look on his face, like he had a mouthful of shit. Well, that's not new, just his usual expression. But he wouldn't even drink with him. One shot, that's all. Asshole.

Finally, Donnie hustled him out the door, walked over to Al's, and sat at the bar. He called Schoenfeld to see if he'd come and have a drink with him, but fuckin' Schoenfeld didn't pick up. Didn't respond to his voice mail either, and even ignored his text. And this after snubbing him every time he runs into him?

So now he's drinking alone. Well, except for Carl, who's hanging over the bar, yammering in that fake Limey accent, acting like he's having a good time running drinks out. No Entertainment Room tonight, it's still sealed off. Donnie asked about it, but Carl put him off. Too fuckin' busy to talk to an old friend.

Donnie knows pretty well everyone in town, so when he spots a couple of strangers, both sitting with their backs against the wall and looking like they're engrossed in ESPN running without sound on the TV above the bar, he's curious. He gets up, takes his drink, and goes over to their table. *Mutt 'n' Jeff*, he thinks. The scrawny, little rat-faced bastard with slicked-back dark hair and bobbing Adam's apple in his immaculate pinstriped suit, and the big, stupid-looking motherfucker in a cheap suit two sizes too small that looks like he slept in it. The two of them stick out like sore thumbs in the crowd of blue jeans and T-shirts.

"Hey, guys," he says, "new in town er juss passin' through?"

"Fuck off," the big man says.

"Fuck you, then!" Donnie hisses and flips them the bird. He stumbles back to his seat at the bar.

The next time Carl's behind the bar and not busy with anything other than wiping up what he's spilled, Donnie nods in their direction and asks, "Who's them guys?"

"Don't know." Carl takes Donnie's empty glass and continues wiping the bar. "Said they're businessmen, interested in real estate. That's all I could get out of them. Not real big talkers. Why?"

"Saw 'em out in fronta my office."

"Oh yeah? So?"

"So? It's fuckin' weird. Don' like strangers hangin' aroun'. Plus, they're assholes."

"It's a free country, mate," Carl says. Then he sings out in his melodious baritone, "Last call ladies and gents! Last call!"

Donnie looks at him as if he has two heads. *Actually singing that? It's not a fuckin' line in a musical, dickhead*, he thinks. But at least he pulls Donnie a fresh pint and sets it on the bar in front of him before scurrying off to get everyone else's final drink orders of the night.

When he returns, he says, "Hey, you were askin' about the Entertainment Room being closed ... your mate Schoenfeld. His girlfriend was missing? You knew that?"

"Think I live in a cave?" Donnie snorts. "What about her?"

"Yeah, well," Carl continues, "she battered down the brick wall in the Entertainment Room. *Some* surprising, really scared the shit outta me 'n' everyone else, believe it. I always thought that brick wall was just decoration, you know, to make it look more like an old Prohibition speakeasy, and all this time there's been another branch of the tunnels behind it."

What? Donnie thinks. But he just says, "Huh!" and tries to keep shock from registering on his face. His gut cramps, and his sphincter tightens. *Klein's alive. That's bad. And if they've found the tunnel, they've found Baron! But they can't connect that body to me*, he thinks. *Say something!* "How'd she get in there?"

"I heard she doesn't know. Coppers 're being all secretive about it, but I saw them haul a body out too. Shut the Entertainment Room down, crime scene. Just blew me off when I asked who's gonna pay for the lost revenue. Don't give a shit about the little guy."

Little guy, my white ass, Donnie thinks. *You got your fingers in lots of pies, and you know I know it.* He has a fleeting thought Carl may be one of the potential new members Nick alluded to; he does have the means to buy his way into the True Believers, maybe even start earning right away.

But right now he has more serious things to worry about.

Goddamn Nick, he thinks. *Would've been better to bury the albino on his acreage, car and all, as I suggested. Never find him there. 'Course Nick always has to have the last word. He's so fuckin' smart. Knows fuckin' everything. Now what am I going to do? They'll have my fingerprints on the body ... that arrest back in Portage La Prairie ... would my prints still be on file? Naw ... I was a kid then ... Record's likely sealed. Even if they have something on me, I'm okay ... I didn't kill him ... I'll make a deal.*

Donnie quaffs his pint and slams the empty mug down on the bar. He gets unsteadily to his feet, digs a couple of twenties out of his pocket, and slaps them down next to his empty glass. Then he weaves his way through tables and out the door into the warm south Saskatchewan night.

The two strangers get up as he's leaving and stumble out close behind him. He gives them a back-the-hell-off glare. The little one wobbles, and the big one loops an arm around him to keep him upright. They begin singing in loud, slurred voices.

He shakes his head in disgust and says deliberately loud enough for them to hear, "Fuckin' Yankees." He tries to walk faster to put some space between him and them, but he's got a wobble himself. He decides to let them pass him, so he stops and lights a Colt.

Curiously, the two strangers quit singing and are no longer stumbling. Then they're on each side of him, bump into him, and nearly knock him off his feet.

"Fer Chrissake, you fuckin' assholes!" Donnie hisses. "Get the fuck off me or ..."

The little one grabs his arms and pins them to his sides. The Colt drops from his lips, and he feels a big hand clamping onto the back of his neck; then another hand, nearly large enough to cover his face, is over his mouth, and he's propelled into the darkness of the alley. When they reach the farthest corner, they turn his back to the building and push him up hard against the sandstone. The instant the hand is away from his mouth, the big man punches him in the gut. He doubles over, gasping, and then he's forced upright against the wall again.

"We thought you might enjoy some of the same treatment you gave our friend," the little guy tells him, "but we don't have that much time."

"Your friend?" Donnie gasps. A fist impacts his nose with a meaty crunch. His John Deere ball cap is knocked off. He tries to call for help, but the big hand is on his mouth again. He struggles, squirms to get away, but he's held firm.

"Yeah, our friend. You remember Alfie, don't you?" The little guy exchanges a look with his partner. "He doesn't remember Alfie."

"Alfie?" Donnie's alcohol-muddled mind races, trying to decide on how to play this, how to talk his way out of it. "Don't know any Alfie," he says.

"Well, me 'n' my partner, we might believe that, except Alfie told us all about you. Your fuckin' goofy church. The scams you run. He even watched one of your meetings. Didn't know he was upstairs while that thing was going on, did you? What was it?" He turns to the big guy again. "Did he say they cut some guy's finger off 'n' then fed it to him?"

"Yeah." The big guy chuckles and nods.

"That's some crazy church. Takin' that whole 'body of Christ, blood of Christ' thing to a new level."

"Well, everyone ... well, we don't ..."

"Pretty good view from the top of the stairs, Alfie said. Very entertaining. Ring a bell now?" The small man's forelock has fallen forward over his face, and he smooths it back. "But to our situation here. Alfie wasn't sure how far you'd go to protect the gold, so he told us all about you, photos even, in case something happened to him."

"Gold?"

"Yeah, he believed that story, his great-grandfather's gold 'n' all that. He spent a lot of time in this little shit-hole town lookin' for it. The house ain't that big. How many places are there to hide it? No one else ever believed that crap, nothin' but a fairy tale, but Alfie believed it 'n' you killed him for it."

"N-no! Not me!"

"Oh? Now you remember?"

"I just didn't think … Alfie … I only knew his last name.'N' I didn't do nuthin' to him! It was the other guys!"

"The other guys?"

"Yeah, the other guys. I told them it was a bad idea, but they wouldn't stop! I can help you! I'll tell you who they are! Where to find them!"

"He's gonna help us," the big guy says.

"Oh, you'll help us?"

Donnie feels a surge of hope and nods his head vigorously.

"Maybe you'd like to join us? Be part of our organization?"

"I would! You guys could take over—"

"Here's the thing. We already know who the other guys are. We not only don't need you, we don't *want* you. You can't whack one of our guys, for starters, 'n' now we know you're okay with bein' a rat."

At a nod from the small man, Donnie's spun around so his back is against the big man, and something slips around his neck, cutting off his air as it tightens. He clutches frantically at the wire that's cutting into his throat. He manages to get the fingers of his left hand under it but can't pull it away as the wire bites into them, and he's still unable to scream or even breathe as he's lifted off the pavement. His feet flail and he loses his bowels, but he's held tight …

Marcus is enjoying a late breakfast on the deck. His wife's gone in to get more coffee.

She comes back with the carafe. "You won't believe what I just heard on the news," she says. Her hands are trembling as she tops up both cups.

"Oh? What?"

"Two bodies were found in town last night! Well, one in town, right on the main drag. The other west of town somewhere."

"Really?" Marcus puts down his fork. "Have they said who they are?"

"No. But imagine!" She sits. Picks up her cup and sets it down again. "And so soon after they found that other body!"

"The other body?"

"Oh, you didn't hear? Yes, a body. Right in town. So this makes three. Besides that, the missing woman. She was kidnapped, but thankfully they've got her back and she's all right. You said Pillerton was a safe place to live!" she wails. "It's not worth leaving our friends, and it's not worth enduring such cold winters, even for the big house, if a person's afraid of being kidnapped or murdered! We should've stayed in Surrey!"

"You know we couldn't stay in Surrey, dear." Marcus feels his gut churn. He squirms and tells her, "There's nothing for you to worry about. Pillerton hasn't had anything worse than kids spray-painting swear words on abandoned buildings in fifty years. This is just an aberration." He pats her hand. "Oh, about going to Regina this morning, I just remembered I have to run into the office for a bit. Okay if I come back and pick you up in a couple of hours?"

"Not again!"

He stands and kisses the top of her head. "Go have a shower. Get prettied up. I'll be back before you miss me."

She shakes her head, scowling.

She's pissed at me again, he thinks. *Probably means I'll be sleeping in the guest room for another week.* But he hurries away, grabbing his cell phone and car keys on the way through the house.

Once he's on the road, he calls Donnie. There's no answer on his cell and no listing for a landline. He calls Prairie Equity, but Diana says he hasn't come in yet.

He calls Nick and gets no answer on his cell phone either, but he does have a home phone number in his Contacts, so he touches that.

He's about to end that call, too, when a woman answers.

"Hello?"

"Hello. Is Nick there?"

"No."

"No? Is this Marlene?"

"No. Marlene's my mother."

"Could I speak to her?"

"She's … What's this about?"

"Well, I'm wondering where Nick is."

"Who's this?"

"It's Marcus. I'm a friend, a business acquaintance of Nick's. He didn't show up for a meeting last night."

Silence.

Then she says, "Dad's dead," and breaks into sobs.

Marcus hits End.

Kathy Klein found alive? Three bodies, one of them Nick? Donnie MIA and possibly one of the other bodies?

His wife may have nothing to worry about, but he does.

He'd better get to the bank and clean out that safety deposit box.

Corporal Neufeld is at his desk, dwarfed by the mountains of paperwork that have landed on him since half the staff was placed on administrative leave. He yawns. The long hours are starting to catch up with him, and when he does get rack time, he sleeps badly. They haven't given him a timeline for replacements, so he has no idea how long they're going to have to run short-staffed. Maybe permanently if they consolidate some of the departments. And his thoughts are haunted by the ordeal Rick's girlfriend went through and the murder of the gangster right under their noses. Now two more murders.

He goes to the lunchroom for another cup of coffee. When he returns to his office, he finds Chief Malone, Criminal Intelligence Services Saskatchewan, is in one of the chairs, and there's a pack of TimBits on the desk. He stands when Ben comes in, and they shake hands. "The receptionist let me in, said you were expecting me," Chief Malone says. "Thanks for seeing me on short notice, Ben."

"I'm glad you could come. Could I get you a coffee?"

"No thanks, I went through the Timmie's drive-through before I left Regina." He nods toward the TimBits.

"Great! Thanks," Ben says, opening the carton and helping himself. "I'll hold off taking these back to the lunchroom for a bit!" He grins and goes to his chair behind the desk.

"So I hear you've been having some fun around here lately," Chief Malone says, settling back into his chair.

"Fun we could do without. We don't have a lot of murders. Make that no murders. And as you know, we're a little short-staffed at the moment. I'm not a detective, so I'm glad for any help I can get, but I'm a little surprised CISS is interested."

"Well, we might not have been if it wasn't for a made guy, the body in the tunnel, being one of the victims."

"I know, crazy isn't it? How does a gangster from Chicago wind up dead in Pillerton?"

"Chicago PD is hoping some of his associates can shed some light on that, but it's really unlikely any of them will talk. And then there's Weaver. What possible motive did he have to attack the woman? Then he puts her in the same body dump with the gangster. How did he know about it, about that hatch leading down into the tunnel? And guys who do stuff like that, they usually stick around, don't try to run unless they become suspects, but he ran even before Klein was found. Why? Then he accidentally puts his car in the river but tosses out his suitcases first? And there's Hell's Angels. A witness saw a car just before the bridge surrounded by bikers, and there were motorcycle tracks down the bank to the river. Then the garroting of Jeffs." He leafs through his notebook. "Donald Jeffs. Classic mob hit. And the grand pooh-bah of the Children of Noah murdered. So we have the Mob. A cult. And possibly HA. It's a lot to put together. They've lifted prints off the tarp the body was in. Also the house. There's a lot of prints as you can imagine, and it'll take time to process everything." He takes a deep breath, his cheeks puffing out as he exhales through his mouth. "Your missing person, Klein, you said she used to be in the Children of Noah cult. She knew Reeves was an elder. What about Jeffs? Weaver?"

"Klein left home as a teenager to get away from it and says she hasn't been involved since. You know how these cults are: if you're lucky enough to get out, you're dead to them. So she doesn't know if Jeffs was in the cult. But we've confirmed he was instrumental in a shady deal cooked up through Prairie Equity so the Children of Noah could get Weaver's house. Actually, the money was payable to Weaver, so he was willing, although his wife didn't know about it."

"Tsk." Chief Malone shakes his head and looks out the window while he thinks for a minute. "So now possibly an investment company's involved too? A shady investment company and three, possibly four, bodies with connections to the Children of Noah. That can't be a coincidence. There must be someone around who's currently in the cult and can tell us something."

"We've done a house-to-house. Pillerton isn't that big. You'd think it'd turn up something. Everyone admits knowing the Children of Noah exist, but nobody's talking."

There's a tap on the door. Constable Peets sticks her head in. "Excuse me, sirs. Sorry to interrupt."

"What is it, Peets?"

"They just found another body in the alley behind the bank. Looks like he was garroted."

"ID'd?"

"Not yet."

"Thanks, Peets," Corporal Neufeld says. "We'll go have a look." He turns to Chief Malone. "Don't imagine there'd be two unrelated garrotings in two days, eh?"

"And you say you're not a detective."

Rick's attended to a few errands and is returning from the grocery store. He's got four bags, two in each hand. He nods to the occupant of the marked police car as he trots past it and up the steps onto the veranda.

Penny steps out onto the veranda and pulls the door closed behind her.

"Something wrong?" he asks.

"No, not really. Well, maybe. I wanted to give you a heads-up." Penny bites her lip. "Her husband showed up."

Rick looks puzzled and puts the bags down on the swing. He paces back and forth, hands on his hips. "Should I leave?"

"Well, it's up to you. I just didn't want you to come in and be surprised."

"Well I *am* surprised. I didn't think she would call him."

"She didn't call him, the cops did."

Rick throws up his hands. He marches over to the corner of the veranda, turns, and faces her. "Why would they do that unless she asked them to, like to notify next of kin? Would she really want him notified?"

"Rick, she didn't tell them to call him. You said it yourself. They always look at the husband or boyfriend first."

"But surely they don't think he had anything to do with it, being thousands of kilometers away."

"You can ask Ben, but I imagine they'd want to know where he was when she went missing, just to make sure he was actually in Vancouver.

He would've asked the Vancouver Police Department to interview Brent. He says he was 'interrogated' by VPD."

Rick's shoulders relax a bit. "Just routine I suppose," he says.

"No one expected him to show up here. He didn't give us any advance warning, even." Penny crosses the deck to stand next to him, puts a hand on his arm, and looks him full in the eye. "You know she's been through a lot. She needs counseling, Rick, not just for this but for things … what went on when she was a kid." She lowers her voice. "She had a horrific childhood. Mine was bad enough, thanks to my parents being in that scheißen cult, but my mother was a gem compared to hers, that psycho *Hündin* from hell. I know she has repressed memories. She's starting to remember now because of being back here, I guess. But it's taken a toll. Has she said anything to you about her, er, *rocky* romantic history?"

He nods. "Three exes?"

"Well, three's just the ones she lived with. There were others, all the same: intense, a hundred and ten percent in from day one, then a traumatic breakup when she discovers he's not as invested in the relationship as she is. But she bounces right into another, equally bad. Talk about low self-esteem! I'm not saying she's totally without sin. She has some issues, and at times, like when she goes into a funk, she wouldn't be fun to live with. Brent's not good for her. He just adds to the problem. But she has to come to that realization herself. And since he's here, I'm hoping they resolve things one way or the other and get out of limbo so they can both move forward." She shrugs apologetically. "That's my counselor speaking."

Rick looks away, shaking his head slowly.

"She has to make the decision," Penny continues, "and because I don't want to see you get hurt, she needs to make it before you're in too deep."

Too late, he thinks. He stands arms akimbo and gazes unseeing at the ragged caragana.

"For what it's worth, I know she has feelings for you. But it's different. I think she's holding back a little with you, and that's actually a good thing." She pauses. Then, after a moment, she says, "So if you're up for it, be the bigger man. Come in with me, and I'll introduce you."

Rick considers it for a moment and then nods.

They go back to the door. Penny picks up a couple of the bags, Rick takes the other two, and they go inside.

"Look who's here!" Penny calls, leading Rick down the hall to the kitchen. They put the grocery bags on the table and double back through the dining room into the living room.

Kathy's recumbent on the couch, but sits up when they come in.

Brent's in the wing chair near her head, a scowl on his face.

"Brent," Penny says, "this is Rick."

Rick takes a couple of steps toward him and says, "How d'ya do," as he sticks out his hand.

Brent gets to his feet, still looking murderous, but he gives Rick's hand a quick shake before sitting back down. He reaches across and takes Kathy's bandaged hand, pinning it to his knee.

"Kathy's lucky to be alive," Rick says. "She's had a terrible ordeal."

Brent nods. "Yup, she's a survivor all right."

"You here for long?"

"Haven't decided yet."

"Going for a walk," Penny says. "See you guys later." She turns and goes through the kitchen and out the back, closing the door with a bang.

"Well." Rick stands awkwardly for a moment and then turns to Kathy. "I just dropped off a few groceries I thought you might need, Kathy. I gotta run." He heads out the door, letting the screen door slam behind him.

Kathy pulls her hand out of Brent's grasp and looks out the window to see Rick hurrying across the veranda, then slouches back until she's lying almost flat again.

"So," Brent says, "that's the real reason you're so determined to stay here."

"No. At least not the only reason." Kathy closes her eyes and rubs her temples. "We agreed on a trial separation, remember? I told you about him."

"You didn't say you were fucking him."

"That's crude! And I wasn't. Not then."

"So. What's up?"

"I … what do you mean?" Kathy leans up on an elbow and searches Brent's face.

"You and him. Together?"

She frowns. "We're not exactly together."

He snorts.

"We're not exactly together."

"Yeah, you just said that," he snorts. "Do you think he'd be hanging around if you had nothing? Like you were when I met you?"

"I doubt he would care. But anyway, I still don't have anything."

"Oh? What about this house? It's worth *something*. And all the rest of the lots in this block?"

"I don't have the house or the lots yet, and I may never have them. Penny told you that."

"Kathy, you know I love you. That farmer could never love you as much as I do, no one could. You don't really think he'll stick around if you don't get this house, do you?" He moves over next to her on the couch, draws her into his arms, and kisses her. "I'm sorry about last week … I just lost control. I want you to come back. Say you will. I'm really sorry. I love you so much! I don't know what you can do about your finger, but it mostly doesn't show anyway, and you can get plastic surgery to fix your ear. We'll sell this place, buy something nice, maybe in North Van, and you go back to your job, our lives. Our life together will be like it was, and Pillerton will just be a bad memory."

Kathy's quiet for a moment or two, studying him, cocking her head to the side. Then she says, "You know, when I was down in that tunnel, when I thought I'd probably die—"

"I know," he interrupts, "it was a hellish ordeal, to quote Penny. You need to move on. Put it behind you."

He gives her another kiss. She's stiff, unyielding, but he pulls her into an embrace, careful of her ear and hand. "I love you," he murmurs. "I'm sorry I lost control when you were home last week. It's just because I love you so much. You know I love you. No one else could ever love you as much as I do."

Then after a bit, once the tension leaves her body, he says, "There *is* something I've been wondering about, though."

"Oh?"

"Well, how did that guy get in?"

"What do you mean?"

"He didn't break in. You must've let him in."

"I ... I guess I must have."

"Why would you invite that man in?"

"I don't know."

"Come on! You must know." He abruptly takes away his arm from behind her. "You said you never met him before. Why would you invite a complete stranger in when you were here alone?"

Kathy tears up, shakes her head, and says softly, "I don't know. I just don't know. He was Jeanie's husband ..."

"You hadn't even met Jeanie, though, had you?"

She shakes her head.

"Yeah, well, decisions have consequences." He leans back and expels a big breath. "Sometimes bad ones! But it's over. Obsessing about it does no good. You have to stop thinking about it."

"I can't," she whispers.

"Well, you have to. It's over, Kathy."

She stands and goes to the foot of the stairs, then stops and closes her eyes. After a moment, she turns back and says, "Maybe for you." She goes up to her room and shuts the door.

Kathy's still in bed. The blinds are closed and the draperies drawn although it's after noon, so the room is gloomy.

Penny comes in with two mugs of tea in one hand and a plate of peanut butter toast in the other. She sets it all down on the night table. "Open your eyes, Kathy," she says. "I know you're awake."

Kathy takes a deep breath. "How'd you know?" she asks, opening her eyes.

"I didn't know. I was guessing."

Kathy reluctantly squirms to a sitting position and picks up the tea. "Thanks," she says.

"Are you planning on staying in bed all day again today?"

Kathy sinks back against the headboard, puts the mug back down, rubs her face with her left hand, and massages her temples. The bandages on her right hand are smaller now but still make that hand clumsy.

"Still got that headache?"

She nods.

"Want a pill?"

"Tempting," Kathy says, shaking her head. "But I don't want to get hooked on those things."

Penny sits on the bed next to her and rubs her forearm. "Are you depressed about agreeing to make the separation legal?"

"No. It was my idea." She shakes her head, picks up her mug again, takes a sip, and studies the bump in the covers that's her feet. "Why did I let him in?" she asks quietly.

"What?"

"Why did I let him in? Clarence, I mean. Brent's right. Why would I let a strange man in the house when I was here alone?"

That fucking Arschlöch, Penny thinks. "You should know better than to listen to Brent," she says, rather more sharply than she intended. "This isn't the Lower East Side of Vancouver. It's Pillerton, for Pete's sake. People here don't even lock their doors. You knew he was Jeanie's husband. He must've told you something, talked his way in. End of story."

"But I—"

"No, Kathy, end of story. I mean it. This was *not* your fault. That's victim blaming, and I can't believe that *Scheißekopf* tried to lay that on you, and I *won't* let you believe it! Okay?"

Kathy's still staring at her feet

Penny leans over so her face is right in front of Kathy and she can't avoid looking at her. "Okay?"

Kathy takes a deep breath and nods. "Okay."

"So. About Rick. He's been by every day. Want to see him?"

"I don't know."

Penny takes a sip of her own tea and says, "Look, honey, it's good you're resting, but three days in this stuffy room? You should get up. I'm not saying you should hippity-hop around the neighborhood, but you should do a little something. Here's what I was thinking: We could maybe do a little weeding, just the easy bits you've already started to clean out. Or, if you're up to going through things in the attic, we could get back to that. Maybe we'll find some other keepsakes of your father's. Or clues about relatives. Or maybe just get into those funky old clothes you were talking about and play dress up like when we were kids."

Kathy takes a deep breath. "I wouldn't want to be a kid again," she says quietly.

There's a roar of motorcycles in the street below. They seem to be stopped, idling, in front of the house. Penny goes to the window, opens the drapes, and teases the blind up.

"What is it?" Kathy asks.

"Looks like a bunch of bikers."

Kathy gets up and goes to stand beside Penny. Half a dozen motorcyclists have congregated next to the curb just in front of the marked police car. They appear to be conferring among themselves, looking up at the house. After a few minutes, they all get back on their motorcycles and roar away.

"Well, that was odd," Penny says.

"Oh my God, Penny!" Kathy says. "It's like the gangster! Like when I saw the gangster!"

"Well, they're gone. If they were up to no good, they wouldn't've stopped with the cop sitting right there." She unlocks the window and raises it. "That's better. It's so stuffy in here. Now come on. Get dressed. We'll go look through those boxes. Maybe start with the steamer trunks you and Rick didn't get to last time." She pulls Kathy away from the window.

Kathy goes to the bathroom before returning and pulling off her pajamas. She digs a pair of yoga pants and an oversized T-shirt out of the dresser and puts them on, and they climb the narrow staircase to the attic. Penny finds an ottoman among the disused furniture and sits Kathy on it to finish her tea.

"I *love* this lamp!" she says, pulling out a brass and stained glass floor lamp. "Vintage art deco, isn't it?" She jiggles the glass shade.

"I think so."

"Wonder why it's up here. It's nicer than the ones in the living room. Don't you want it downstairs?"

"I haven't thought about it."

Penny pushes up her glasses. "Well, you know that bedroom you said I could call mine? That I can stay in as often and as long as I want? Could I put it in there until you want it somewhere else?"

"Mmm-hmm. Sure."

"You got light bulbs?"

"Somewhere. Linen closet maybe."

"I'll find 'em." Penny grins. She wraps the cord around the base to stop it dragging behind her and disappears down the stairs.

"It looks terrific!" she says when she's back. "It'll be perfect for reading in bed."

Then she goes to the steamer trunk and jiggles the top. "Locked," she says.

"There's lots of boxes. We don't need to look in that thing."

"True, but aren't you curious? Why is this locked? I want to see what's so valuable."

"Well, then, go get a hammer or something and pry it open. There's tools in the basement."

Penny cocks her head, considering that idea. "Well, that would probably work, but I'm not sure it's the right thing to do. It would damage the trunk, and it might be quite valuable. Worth hundreds, maybe. We can get a locksmith."

"Oh," Kathy says, "I wonder if that could be what the key is for."

"There's a key?"

"Yes, I found it taped to the underside of the bathroom sink. Thought it might be for the padlock that was on the door, but it isn't. I just put it back in the bathroom, on the back of the toilet."

"I did see a key there," Penny says. She trots down the stairs and is back with the key in a minute. At first it doesn't appear to fit, but with a little jiggling, she gets it in. One quarter turn to the right and the lock releases. "Ta-dah!" she exclaims, and opens the lid.

There's a shallow tray covered with paper that matches the paper lining on the inner walls of the trunk, but it's mostly empty except for a few unidentified photos, some playbills, a chocolate box full of buttons, and odds and ends of ribbons and lace.

Penny lifts the tray out and sets it aside, exposing the carefully folded clothes underneath. "Wow, girlfriend! Look at this!" She holds up a dress. "Gorgeous! Vintage!"

Kathy shrugs. "Clothes? They're really so valuable the trunk had to be locked?"

Penny pulls out more dresses. There are shoes to match. And shawls. "Someone had some bucks, that's for sure! Bias cut silk. You wouldn't get *this* from a Sears Roebuck catalog. Whoever wore these was a *babe*!"

Kathy puts her tea down on the floor, gets to her feet, and comes up beside Penny to have a closer look. "They *are* beautiful," she agrees, stroking the seafoam-green flapper dress Penny's holding up. "It would be beautiful on you. Your color for sure."

"Yeah, and as soon as I start wanting to wear fancy dresses, I'll shrink ten sizes and buy it from you!" Penny chuckles and is gratified to see the shadow of a smile on Kathy's face in return.

They pull all the dresses out and lay them carefully aside. The last item in the trunk is a thick layer of newspaper. "Even this is amazing," Penny says. She pulls the papers out and shuffles through them. "*Regina Leader Post*. Oh, and look! *Chicago Tribune*! They're old, all right. September 1927, the year this house was built. Hey, I wonder if there's one about the Wall Street crash!" She carefully pulls all the newspapers out and piles them on the floor next to the ottoman. Then she sits, picks up the first one, folds it along its original fold line, and begins reading.

Kathy's still standing, looking at the clothes draped over the edge of the trunk. "Penny," she says.

"What?" Penny answers without looking up.

"Penny!"

"What?" She looks at her friend.

"Look at this."

Penny comes to stand next to the trunk and looks down to see what Kathy's pointing to. "What?" she asks again.

"Don't you see? The bottom doesn't match the sides."

"Oh, you're right. So?"

"So, it's not likely original to this trunk. Why?" Kathy bends into the trunk and taps on the bottom. "I think it's a false bottom. Why would someone put a false bottom—"

"Only to hide something!" Penny says. She tries to work her fingers

in around the edge. "I need something small enough to slip in there …"
She runs down two flights into the kitchen and comes back with a knife
and fork. The knife fits in, but there's still no way to lift the bottom. She
slides the fork in, letting the tines curve under the cardboard. She's able
to lift it enough to get her fingers under it. It's tightly fitted but comes
out easily enough once it's away from one end.

When it's removed, Penny and Kathy are looking down at gold
coins. The bottom of the trunk is covered with them.

After a moment of stunned silence, Kathy says, "Wow!"

"Oh my God, Kathy! You're rich! You're rich, rich, *rich*!" Penny
grabs Kathy by the shoulders and dances her around in a circle. "My
friend's as rich as Oprah! She's as rich as Oprah!" She laughs.

"Woo-hoo!" Kathy yells and picks up a handful of the coins. "I
wonder if the second trunk's the same. And if there are any other
trunks!"

Together they heave the second steamer trunk out from under
the eaves. The same key opens it. Now careless of the clothes, they
dig through and are mildly disappointed to find no mismatched,
wallpapered cardboard bottom, and that the bottom is firmly attached.
Then they shuffle the other boxes around enough to confirm there are
no other trunks.

"My God," Kathy says, "we've uncovered a small fortune, and now
I'm bummed because there isn't more! How did I turn into a greedy
rich person so quickly?" She giggles and then turns serious. "I just had
a thought. Do you think this could be what the gangster guy was after?
Maybe the bikers know about it too?"

"Huh? How would any of them know about this?" Penny asks. She
goes to kneel beside the trunk and drink in the sight of the glimmering
gold coins. "How would anyone know about them? Did your mother
know?"

"Until I came back, I never really wondered why the attic door was
locked, and I just accepted the fact I wasn't allowed to come up here.
Maybe she knew, and that's why … But why would she have lived like
a pauper?"

"Well, she could've sold the vacant lots and lived well, and she didn't. Likely, she just didn't want anyone finding your father's clothes, or they'd know he didn't run off."

"Why not just get rid of them, burn them? We had a burning barrel out back, everyone did. Or donate the clothes to a thrift shop? Also, if she knew about these coins and for some reason didn't want to do anything with them herself, wouldn't she at least have told someone when she knew she was dying? Maybe give them to the Con?"

"You'd think so." Penny runs her hand through the coins as if she's stirring bathwater. "But now that you're an adult, I'm sure you realize your mother had one or two loose screws. Although I think you're right, she'd have given them to the scheißen Con, since she seemed to love them so much."

"Uh-huh. I know she was crazy. The things I've started to remember now that I'm back in this house …" Kathy heaves a sigh.

Penny gives her friend's shoulder a rub. "I know. It's tough. You're doing great." Then she brightens. "So, the coins. Maybe your mother knew about them. But that doesn't explain where they came from. Wasn't she just a farm girl from out in the Badlands? She couldn't have gotten them herself. They must have come from someone else. Who? Could they have been your father's?"

"Where would he get them? I remember him leaving the house every day to go to work, but I have no idea what he did for a living. And I think if they were his, he'd've spent them."

"I wonder." Penny takes a handful of the coins and sits on the ottoman to examine them more closely. "Do you think they could've belonged to your great-grandfather? Maybe that's what he was murdered for?"

"Hmm. That's really the only thing that makes sense."

"They would've still been fairly common back then. Worth a great deal, but still commonly available. Maybe he got whacked before he could tell anyone, like your grandfather for instance, about them."

"Maybe. I guess we'll never know. And now what do we do with them?"

Penny shakes her head, finger-combs her hair, and pushes up her glasses. "Well, we can't take 'em to the Mercedes Benz dealership and start spending them, that's for sure!"

"Should we put them somewhere else?"

"You know, they've been here so long, safe here for so long, I say we put the bottom back in, fold the clothes nicely, and put everything away until we figure out what to do."

Kathy chews her lip. "That makes sense. But it can't hurt to keep a few out."

It's ten o'clock and Penny has gone up to her room to read for a while before bed.

Kathy lays out the coins on the dining room table. "So," she tells Rick, "there's a whole bunch more of these. I just grabbed a handful, and then we packed everything back the way it was. It's really nerve-wracking, having something so valuable in the house, now that I know about it!"

Rick slides his chair close to hers and takes her hands. "I'll call Ben first thing tomorrow and tell him about these," he says, "and also about the motorcycle gang. He won't think them showing up is just coincidence, I bet. You know cops. They don't believe in coincidence. I'll stay here with you tonight, and tomorrow you girls come back to the farm with me. There's plenty of room. Or maybe Jeanie'd like some company."

"Oh!" Kathy says. "She has room?"

"There's a spare room downstairs. You'd rather go to Jeanie's?"

"I don't know if I could take on your whole family right now. And in your house, in separate beds?"

"No, no more of that!"

"You know your mother would have a conniption if we slept together."

"She'll get used to it."

"Well, it's such a temporary thing … I'd rather not give her more reason …"

"I guess you're right, babe. And I think Jeanie will welcome the company right now. You can help with the baby." He rubs the back of her hand with his thumb, careful of her amputation. "I missed you so much these past few days, babe. I was so worried, you know, when you didn't want to see me."

"I'm sorry. It wasn't just you. I didn't want to see anyone, not even Penny. I was even short with her. I don't know why. I was just in a funk. It was stupid. I feel better with you here." She squeezes his fingers.

"I can't tell you how happy that makes me." He brings her hand to his lips. "I wanted to ask you ... about my house. I'd like you to help me pick out stuff. Like siding. Doors. Shingles. Flooring. Paint colors. Bathroom fixtures. Light fixtures. You know, all the stuff you have to choose."

"Oh. Sure. But you don't want to do it?"

"I'm no good at that kind of thing." His face is solemn, intense, as he says earnestly, "Kathy, I know it's early in our relationship, but really, we've known each other all our lives. Over the years I often thought of you, imagining what it would be like if we were together. I didn't want, I mean, I didn't want for us to break up back in high school. I was falling for you then. If I hadn't been such a bastard, I would've quit seeing Tina when you and I started going together. And then ... well. You don't know how many times I've kicked myself for being so shallow. I never thought I'd get a second chance. And here you are. Here we are. I feel so good when we're together. I want it to be your house too."

"Phew!" Kathy takes a deep breath and breathes out through her mouth. Then she pulls her hand out of his, stands, and paces out into the living room and back, hugging herself.

He gets up and gathers her into his arms for a deep, heartfelt kiss. He whispers, "When I look at you, my heart melts. I want you in my life for the rest of my life. I love you."

Kathy pulls away enough to look into his eyes.

Rick's shoulders slump. He says quietly, "I didn't think it was too soon, what with you going ahead with your separation 'n' all. How we've been when we're together ... I thought you ... well, that you felt the same way."

"I'm ... it's ..." Another big exhale. "I'm afraid."

"Afraid of me?"

"No. Afraid of *me*."

"I don't understand."

"There's things we have to talk about, Rick. We're just beginning to know each other. I'm not the same naïve seventeen-year-old you remember. Please, sit back down."

He reluctantly moves away and pulls the chair under him as he sits.

She takes a chair across the table from him. "There's a lot you don't know about me, things that might make you change your mind. Think back to grade twelve. When you and I split up."

"Okay."

She stands again, takes a step back. Paces around, gathering her thoughts, her courage. "Remember I didn't graduate?"

Rick frowns. "No. I don't remember. I seem to think you missed a lot of school, all the time."

"But I didn't graduate. And I didn't go away to university. That was a lie. Somehow someone came to that conclusion, and I just went along with it. The fact is"—she cups her shoulders, her crossed arms press against her breasts, and her lower lip quivers. "I ran away from home. Hitched to Vancouver. I was a street kid."

Rick gets up. Comes and gently takes her hands away from her shoulders. Pulls her into a hug. "That was awful … must've been awful for you."

"I did things. Not nice things." She burrows her face into the crook of his neck, trying not to cry, unable to say more until she collects herself. Then she continues in a rush. "I did *bad* things. Penny saved me. She was living downtown and saw me one day as she was walking home from work."

Rick's quiet. He kisses her temple and then just holds her.

"So, you see," she says, "you don't know me."

"That's it? That's your deep dark secret?" He pulls away enough that they can look into each other's eyes. "I've got things in my past I'm not proud of either. You need me now, and I want to be there for you."

"I guess that's my point. I'm too needy. I don't like me."

"Well, I guess that's important. But I like you. I love you, but I like you too."

"I need to like myself too."

Rick chews his lower lip. His brow's furrowed. He takes a step away from her and asks quietly, "Are we breaking up?"

"No, please believe me, when I'm with you, I have to pinch myself to make sure I'm not dreaming. Is it love? It feels like it is. But when I was in the tunnel, I promised myself if I got out, I would stop trying to use someone else to complete me. Penny's right. I need to be okay on my own before I can be okay with someone else."

He thinks about what she's said for a moment or two and then asks, "Do you know what it'll take? For you to be okay on your own, I mean? When you'll know you're okay on your own?"

"I guess it'll just be a feeling. I have moments when I feel strong. You wouldn't know it, being as I've been such a basket case, but the tunnel, that I got myself out of that tunnel, makes me feel strong, empowered, and I feel good about myself."

"You should! Lots of people wouldn't have been able to do what you did."

"Well, I don't know about that, but it's a start. If it wasn't for the strength I got from that one thing, I might not have been able to send Brent away. And for us, the two of us … I don't want to screw this up. I don't want another failed relationship. I want both of us to be sure it's right and not just a carryover from what we had back in high school. I'm different. You're different. Think of everyone who got married right out of high school. How many of those marriages lasted? Maybe ours would've been the same as yours and Tina's."

"Oh, I doubt that," he says. He thinks for a minute. "Maybe it's different in the big city, but lots of couples around here are still together. I'm the only one of my friends who's divorced."

"Is it because their marriages are good? Do they both value the marriage, take care of it? Is it a matter of finding the right person to start with, or are they just lucky?"

"Lucky, all around," he admits, furrowing his brow and shaking his head. "It's sure not because my buddies are model husbands." Then a sheepish grin tugs at the corners of his mouth. "I wasn't one myself. But I'll do better."

He strokes her cheek. Kisses his fingertips and touches them light as butterflies to her healing ear. "So, meanwhile … we're still a couple?"

"We're still a couple."

Kathy holds Rick's hand under the table and looks across at Jeanie. "Have the kids asked about their dad … do they ask about him very much?" she asks.

"Not much," Jeanie says. "Not too surprising since he was never very involved in parenting, other than to yell at them." Hearing sounds of battle from the backyard, she gets up, goes to the patio doors, and yells at the boys. "Put those sticks down! Don't swing them around! You've been told about …" Then she sighs, turns, and says, "Oh jeez, now I'm yelling. And why do I bother? We survived our childhood. I imagine they'll survive theirs! More coffee, anyone?"

"Not for me, thanks," Penny says.

"I'm sorry you have to go so soon, Penny," Jeanie says, "just when we're all getting to know you."

"Well, thanks. I've enjoyed being here with you guys too. And I may be back more often than you'd expect."

"She's made at least one other friend in the short time she's been here," Kathy tells them. "I'm pretty sure that's the real reason she wants to spend more time here."

"Oh, don't sell yourself short," Penny says. But a tinge of red creeps up her neck.

"I hope things are more settled around here soon so we'll be back in my house. I'll get a plumber and have a shower put in. And you can stay without fearing for your life."

"What's that?" Jeanie asks. "I thought you said the fingerprints on the tarp that body was in are from two of the dead guys. And the murders were mob hits. And the bad guys have gone back to the States."

"Doesn't mean they'll stay there," Rick says. "They might still be after what the gangster was after. I'm convinced he knew about the coins. All those double eagles! American coins were never *that* common in Canada, and everyone else around here was dirt poor. Think of an American who might have had that much money and who was here back when Kathy's house was built—Al Capone! And it was common knowledge Henry Klein was involved with him. The tunnels connected the hotel where Capone lived and Klein's house, so both of them had an escape route if they needed it. I think Henry got the coins somehow."

"He may have stolen them," Penny speculates, "and that's why he was murdered."

"Yeah, that makes sense. Any idea how the gangster would know, or why Donnie and that other guy, the councilor, would kill him, though?"

"Well, those two had to be connected to the Con, but how would any of them know about the tunnel access? The Con had their meetings in the house, but surely they wouldn't be poking around in the basement," Kathy says.

"And," Rick continues, "why would the they want him dead? Clarence's murder is unsolved too, and there's still no motive for that or for what he did to Kathy. My theory is somehow those two guys, likely acting for the Con, got suspicious of the gangster for some reason and beat him until he told them about the money. Kathy's mother must have known about the tunnel access and told the Con, who knows why. When they had a body on their hands, they just figured it was a safe place to dump it. Then the Con paid Clarence to dump Kathy down there too and leave her to die, so they'd have no opposition to the title transfer and therefore the coins. Or maybe he was supposed to kill her and thought she was dead." He realizes the enormity of that, and can't go on. He gives Kathy's hand a squeeze and gasps, "My God!"

"But how could he do that, even for money?" Jeanie cries. "I don't know how I could have lived with a monster capable of that!"

"Psychopaths can be very manipulative," Penny tells her and pats her forearm. "Look at Ted Bundy. He was so charming, all those women he killed went with him willingly."

"But why did Clarence head south? He left before Kathy was found, so no one knew he'd done anything." Rick blows out a sharp breath. "And how are the Hells Angels involved? They were at the river when Clarence drowned, and now they've showed up at Kathy's house. That can't be a coincidence. So even with the cops sitting outside, it's best if Kathy isn't in the house. They took the gangster into custody and then somehow mislaid him, after all. I wouldn't trust those yahoos to guard my lunch."

"I know you have to go home, Penny, but, Kathy, you can stay forever!" Jeanie says. "Well, not forever, but a long time. I'm glad for the company."

"I guess I'll be here for a while. I can't thank you enough." Kathy smiles at Jeanie and then turns to Rick. "I'm not sure I really want to go back. That place gave me the heebie-jeebies before, and now … thinking about my father being murdered there and his body in the furnace all those years! And my … my … what Clarence … what he did to me … But has Ben said when it might be safe for me to go back?"

"He doesn't know about the gold coins yet," Rick says, "or the bikers coming to your house. He's been so busy. I called him last night and left a message, but he hasn't gotten back to me yet. We'll see what he thinks about alerting the news media to your find. After we move the coins to a safety deposit box, that is."

"Once those've been moved and it's public knowledge, nobody should want to get into the house anymore," Kathy says. "Seems like the right idea. Did you see them, Jeanie? They're really quite beautiful." She digs in her purse, pulls out the little cloth with the coins tied up in it, and hands it to Jeanie.

Jeanie pours them onto the table. "Oh, wow," she says, "they are really … I can't believe it, like tiny sculptures."

"The most beautiful coins ever minted, according to Wikipedia. They'll have to be cataloged." Penny scratches her neck. "They're worth way more than the value of the gold. I did a quick Internet search. Depending on the vintage and condition, they're each valued at anywhere from fifteen hundred dollars all the way up to the low six figures, and there's hundreds of them. I can't even imagine the value of the lot."

"At the moment, I'm not thinking about that. I'd just like to put this all behind me," Kathy says, carefully scratching her healing ear. "I wonder if that's the end of the Con. I don't know for sure, but the three mob hits? The Con's always had three elders. We know Nick Reeves was one. We know Donnie Jeffs was connected to the Con. It's not a stretch to think he was an elder. Just guessing about the other guy, the councilor. But Clarence?"

"Well, Clarence *was* talking about becoming a lay preacher," Jeanie says.

"Hmm, could he have been an elder? Maybe they changed their setup and had four elders? Or one of the other two guys is connected in some other way? In any case, the head's been cut off the snake. That's probably the end of them." Penny chuckles, takes off her glasses, and polishes the lenses on her shirttail. "That scheißen cult's been a blight on Pillerton for—well, for at least since I was a kid. Bad as their deaths were, it really couldn't happen to a nicer bunch. Sorry, Rick—I know Jeffs was your friend."

"I don't think he ever really was," Rick says and clicks his tongue. "Funny how you reevaluate things, a lot of things, in time."

"Time and trauma!" Penny says.

"What a hornet's nest I got you into, Penny," Kathy says, biting her lip.

"Don't even start feeling guilty! You're the one who's been through hell. For the rest of us, it was terrifying, but we were never facing death. And of course, I got some good out of it. I never would've met Reese otherwise." Penny pushes away from the table and stands. "Well, guys, I've got a flight to catch, and I need to turn in my rental car. I'll keep you posted on the lawsuit, Kathy, but I'm sure the death certificate and, of course, the title transfer will be set aside now that we know your father was murdered all those years ago and your mother is implicated."

"I guess we'll never know for sure she did it," Kathy says.

"Does it matter?"

"I suppose not." Kathy shrugs. "You know how everyone's always talking about closure? I think I understand it now. I can finally stop thinking my father will come looking for me someday, and there's comfort in knowing he didn't abandon me."

Rick loops an arm around her shoulders and gives her a squeeze.

They all get to their feet to accompany Penny out the door and to the car. They share hugs all around.

As they're standing watching her drive away, they hear sirens and see a pillar of black smoke.

"Oh, a fire," Kathy says.

"Looks like it's all the way on the other side of town," Jeanie says. "Could it be on Front Street?"

Rick frowns. "Well, it's in that direction, anyway."

His phone rings. He answers and mouths, "Ben." Then he says, "Oh no."

Epilogue

There have been many changes in Pillerton.

One of the most well-known landmarks in town, the infamous old house at Ten Front Street, is gone. As is common with such a complete burn, the cause of the fire was never determined with certainty. Any evidence that might have survived the fire was blown to bits when the fuel oil tank in the basement exploded, rattling windows all over Pillerton and leaving behind a massive crater. The passerby who called 911 to report the fire said she saw flames in a second-story bedroom window. Kathy was able to confirm that the only electrical device in that room was a 1920's art deco lamp. The fire commissioner filed the official report as "accidental fire of undetermined origin, believed electrical."

A developer was interested in buying the entire block of lots on Front Street, having it rezoned commercial, and putting in a strip mall, but discussions stalled owing to the "no excavating" bylaw. The town won't issue building permits for replacement of the house and not even for demolition. They put a chain-link fence around it and added the cost to the taxes. Penny and Reese are working on a challenge, but it's a slow process.

Kathy got a job at Province-Wide Insurance Agency. She's taking insurance courses with a view to moving up to office manager someday. She bought a small rancher walking distance (everything in Pillerton is walking distance) from work. The down payment came from the sale of the gold coins she'd kept out of the trunk. The house at Ten Front Street was uninsured, so she had to take a mortgage, but the payments are manageable. She sees a counselor twice a month. Her dark hair is streaked with white. Rick says he likes it.

Rick has moved into his new house, but spends most of his time at Kathy's.

When Max heard of the murders, he came back to town. He and Jeanie had a few dates but quickly realized they would never be anything more than friends. He found a good situation in northern British Columbia, and when his house sold, he went back there, promising to stay in touch.

Evan Briggs, fired from the bank, is the new manager at Prairie Equity.

Chief Johannsen retired from the RCMP amid persistent rumors of corruption. Despite those rumors, he easily won the by-election for councilor and has already announced he'll run for mayor in the fall.

Carl Dowdle promoted Marge to manager of Big Al's, and he now manages just the Entertainment Room in the tunnels. He's still active in the local dinner theater, which has changed venues. New home: The Entertainment Room. It's undergone an expansion. Carl had no trouble getting a permit. It's busier than ever now, thanks to the notoriety of the murders, but it's always closed Sundays. Behind the new brick wall, there's an alcove with a hidden door.

About the Author

Gayle Siebert has always been crazy about horses, reading and writing. She grew up in Saskatchewan and Alberta, and now lives on a small horse farm on Vancouver Island, British Columbia.

Of the dozens (and dozens) of short stores and novellas Gayle's written, one had characters that continued to emerge. The Pillerton Secret, Gayle's first novel, is the result.